TOMO

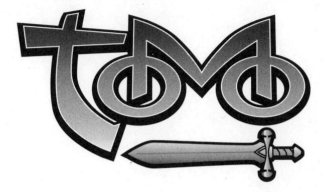

Secret Alliance

ZONDERVAN®

Secret Alliance
Copyright © 2008 by Funnypages Productions, LLC

Requests for information should be addressed to:
Zondervan, Grand Rapids, Michigan 49530

CIP applied for
ISBN: 978-0-310-71304-3

This book published in conjunction with Funnypages Productions, LLC, 106 Mission
Court, Suite 704, Franklin, TN 37067

Series Editor: Bud Rogers
Managing Art Director: Merit Alderink

Printed in the United States of America
08 09 10 11 • 5 4 3 2 1

GRAPHIC NOVELS

tom

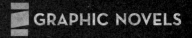

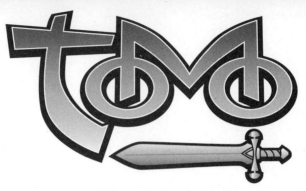

Secret Alliance

SERIES EDITOR
BUD ROGERS

STORY BY
JIM KRUEGER

ART BY
ARIEL PADILLA

CREATED BY
TOM BANCROFT AND ROB CORLEY

funnypages PRODUCTIONS

ZONDERVAN®

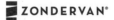

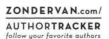

ZONDERVAN.com/
AUTHORTRACKER
follow your favorite authors

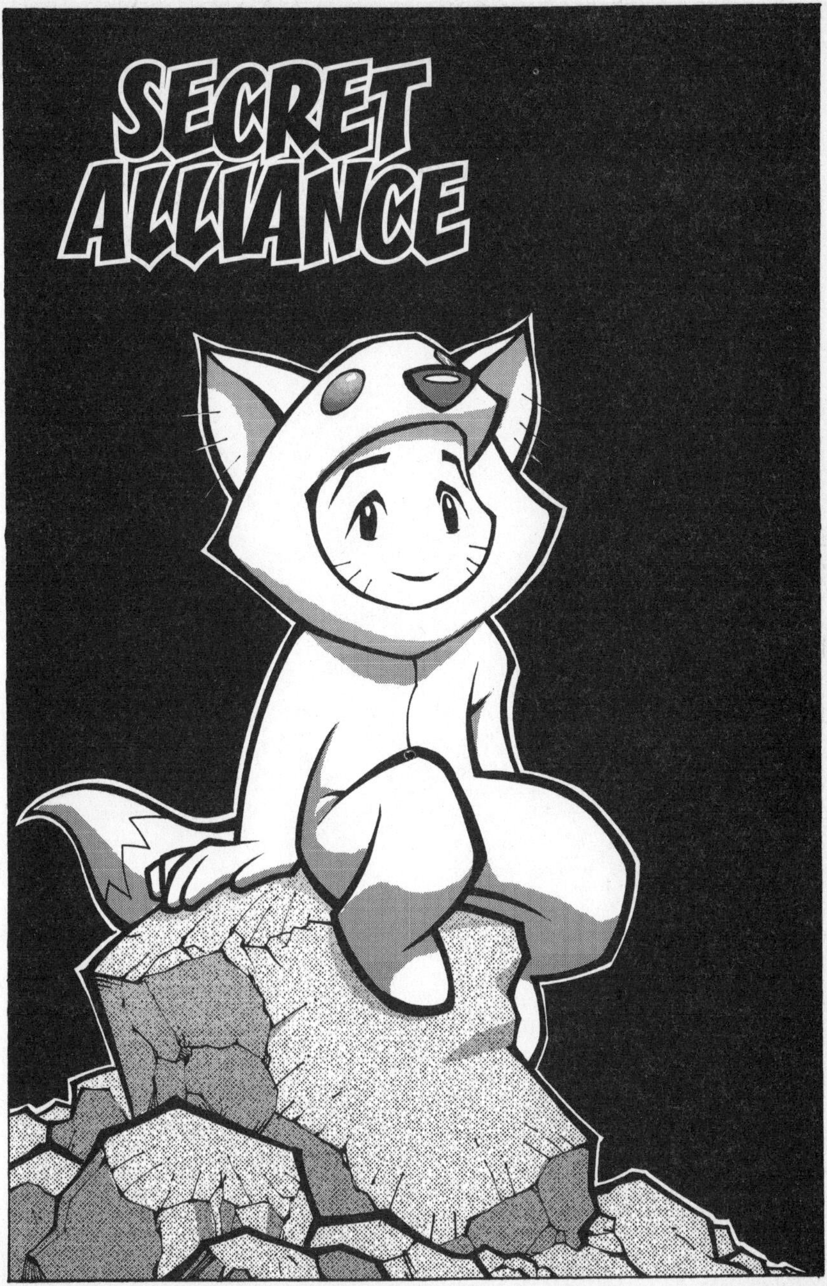
SECRET
ALLIANCE

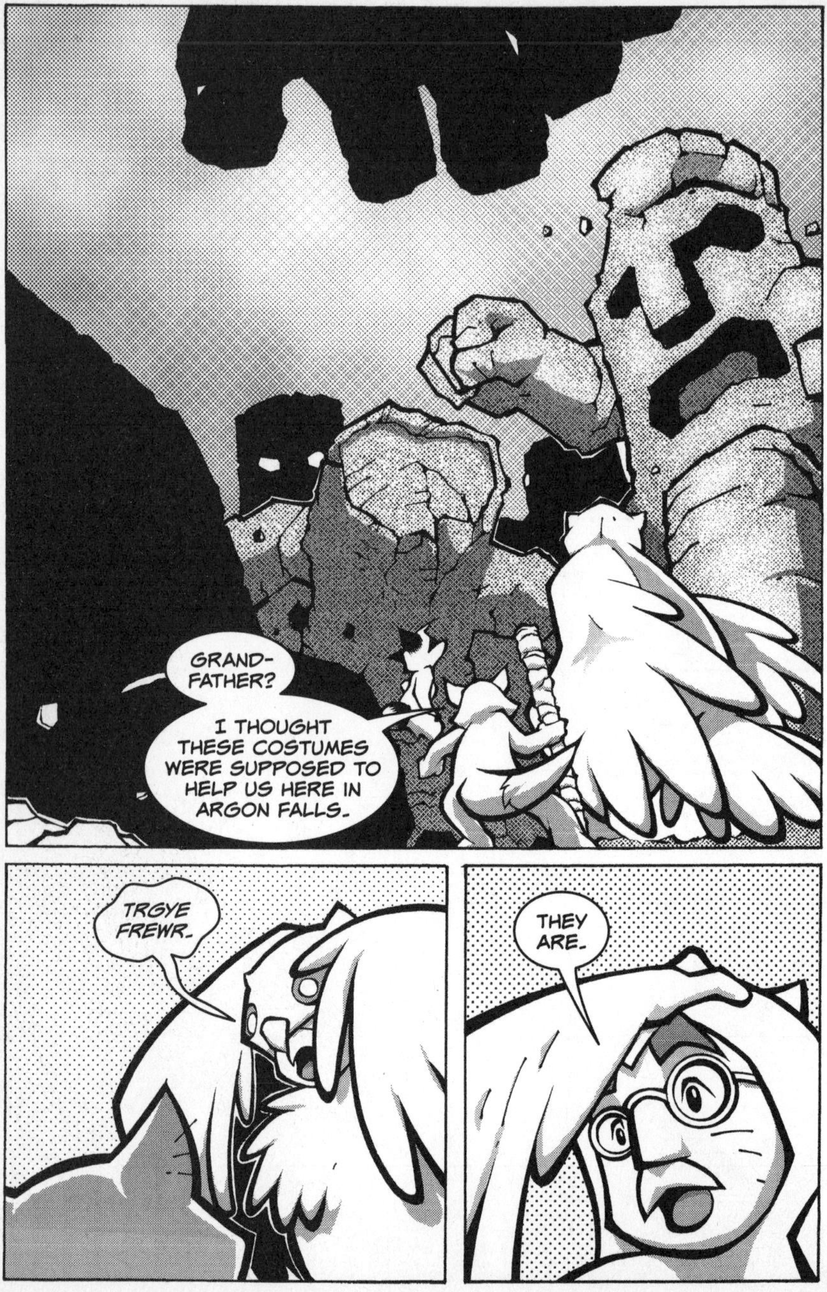
GRAND-FATHER?
I THOUGHT THESE COSTUMES WERE SUPPOSED TO HELP US HERE IN ARGON FALLS.
TRGYE FREWR.
THEY ARE.

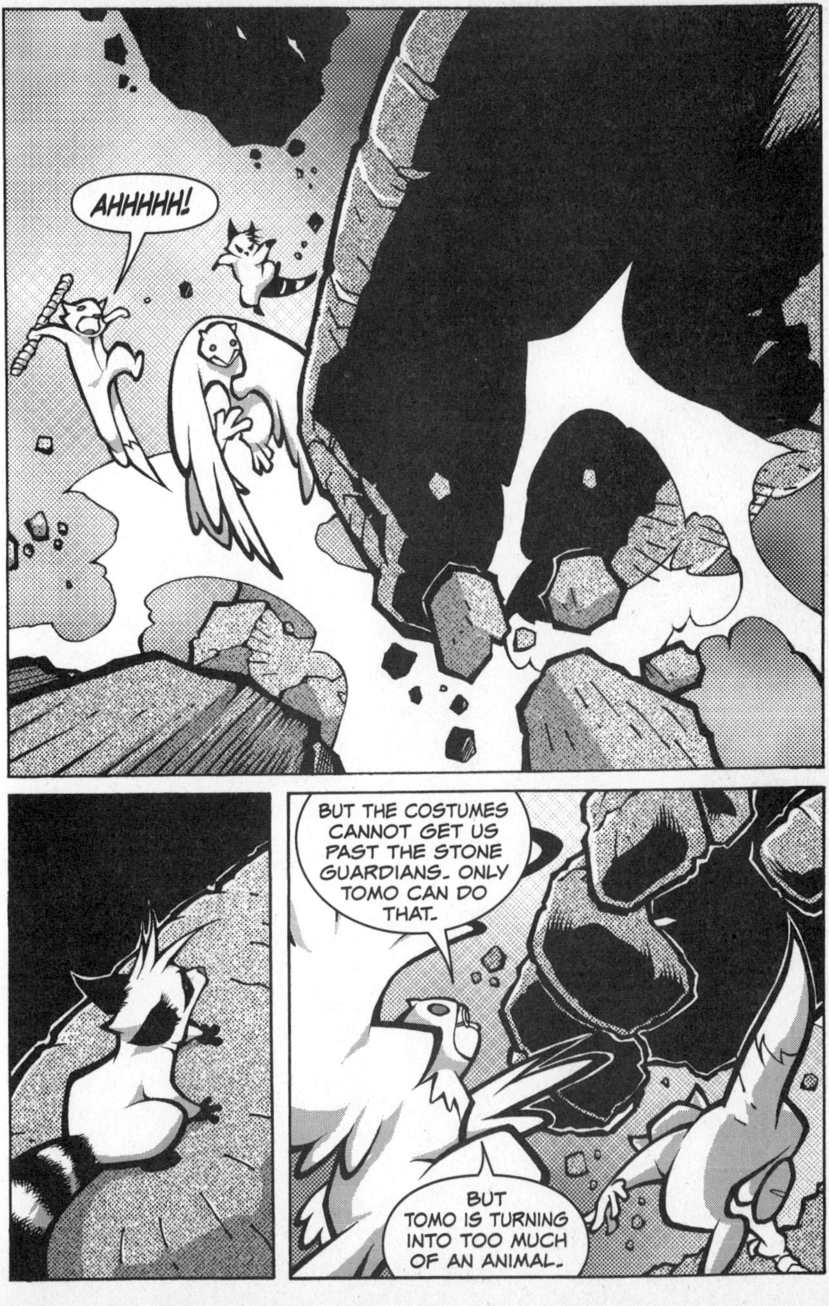
AHHHHH!
BUT THE COSTUMES CANNOT GET US PAST THE STONE GUARDIANS. ONLY TOMO CAN DO THAT.
BUT TOMO IS TURNING INTO TOO MUCH OF AN ANIMAL.

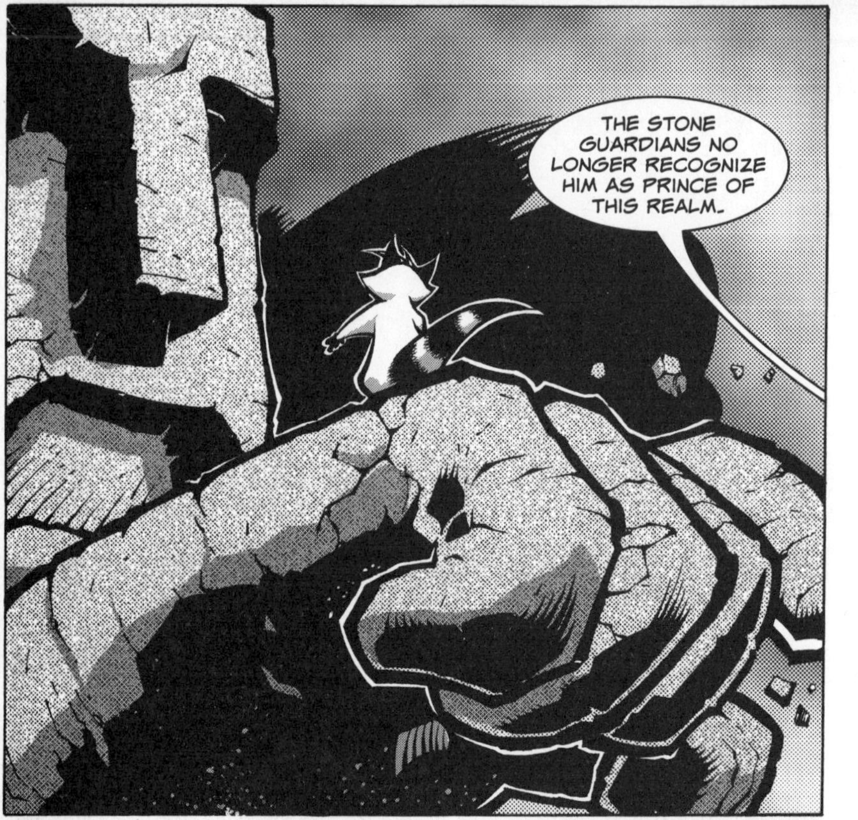
THE STONE GUARDIANS NO LONGER RECOGNIZE HIM AS PRINCE OF THIS REALM_

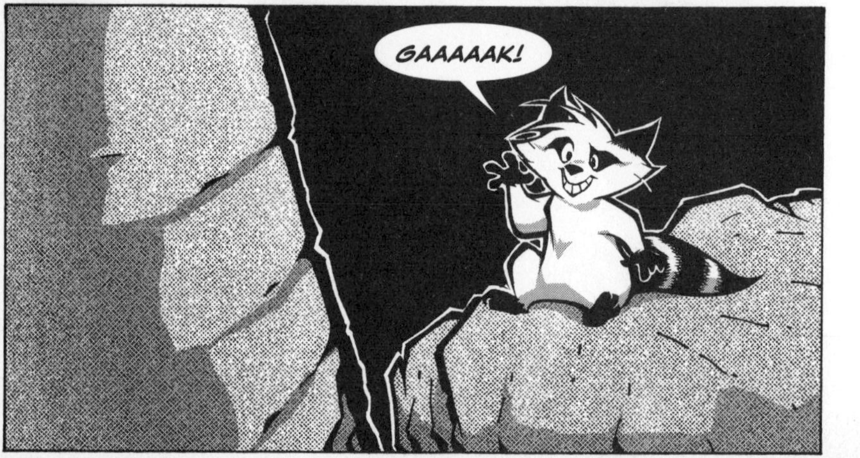
GAAAAAK!

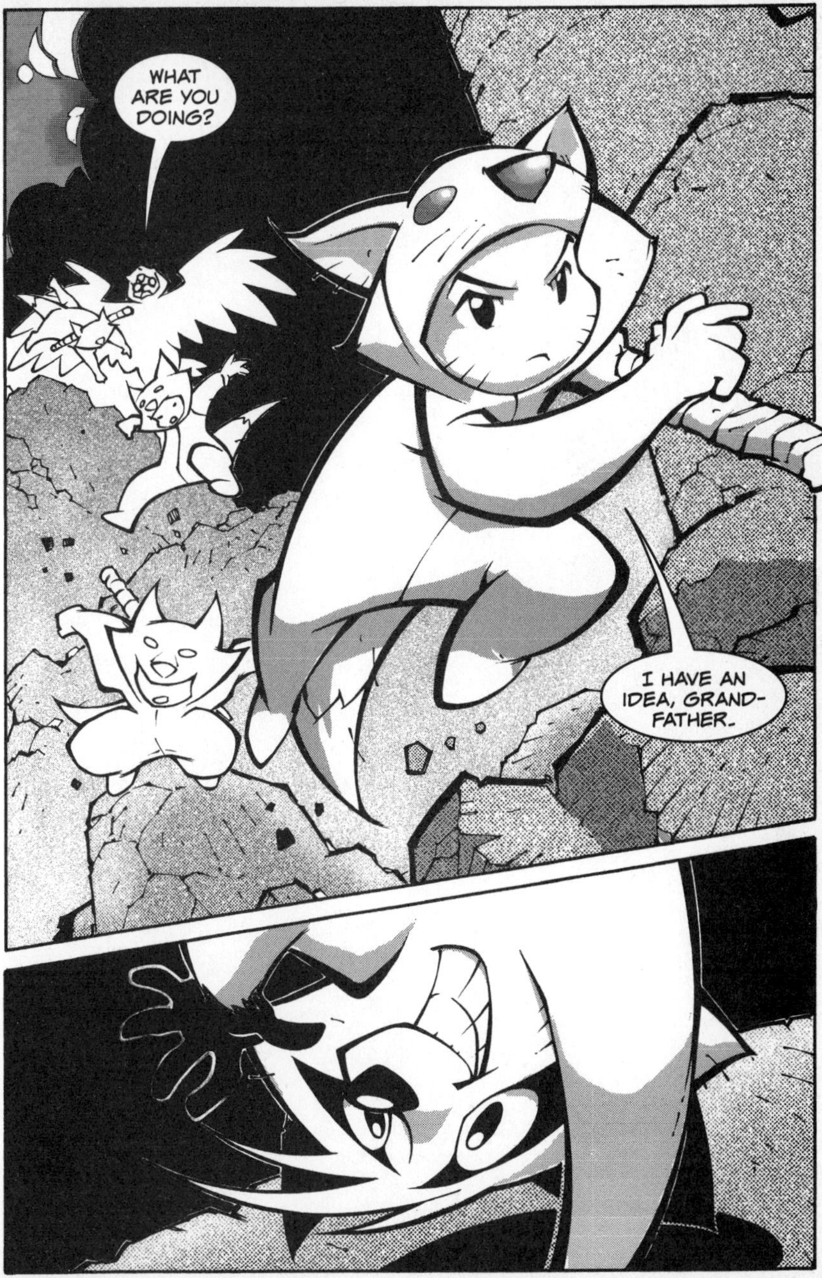
WHAT ARE YOU DOING?
I HAVE AN IDEA, GRAND-FATHER.

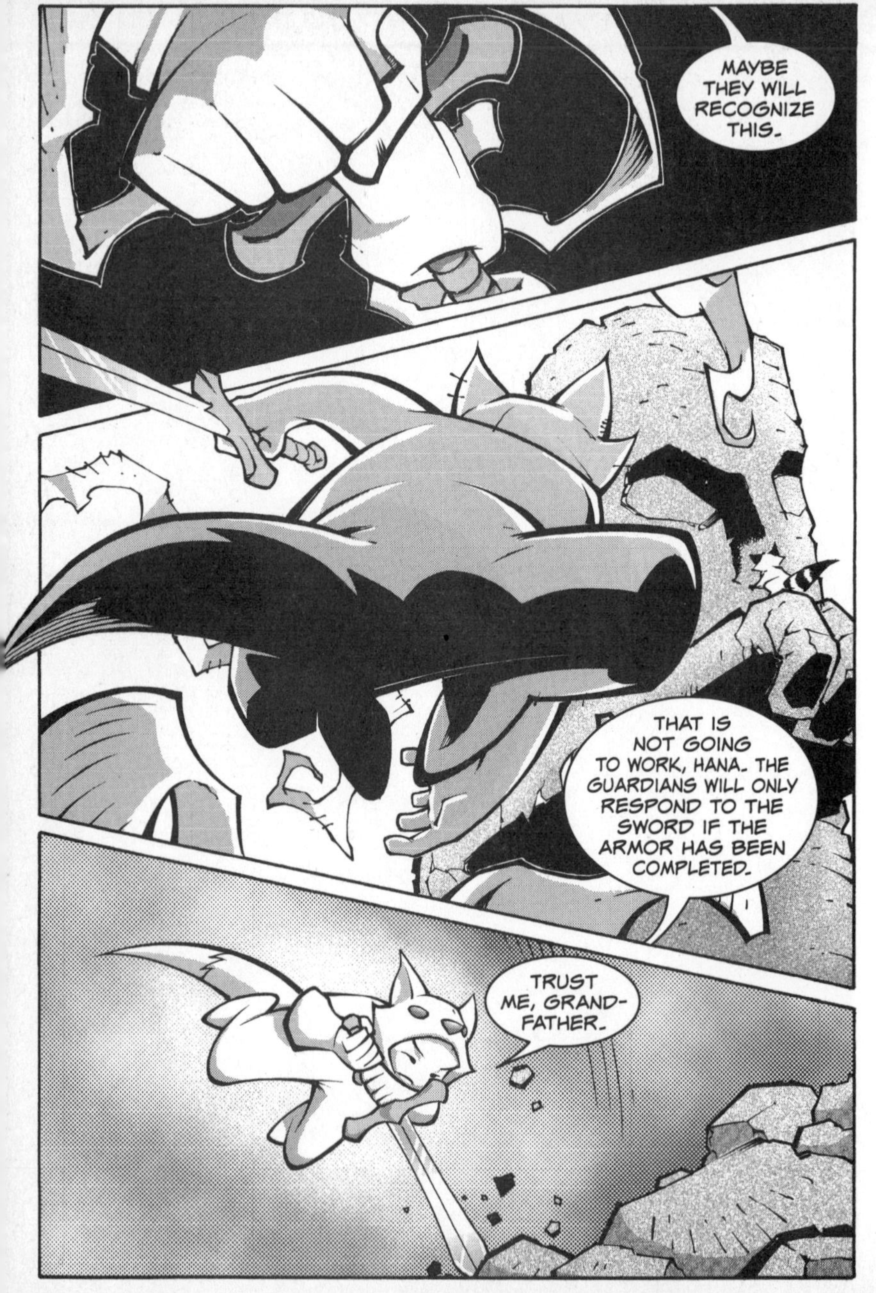
MAYBE THEY WILL RECOGNIZE THIS.
THAT IS NOT GOING TO WORK, HANA. THE GUARDIANS WILL ONLY RESPOND TO THE SWORD IF THE ARMOR HAS BEEN COMPLETED.
TRUST ME, GRAND-FATHER.

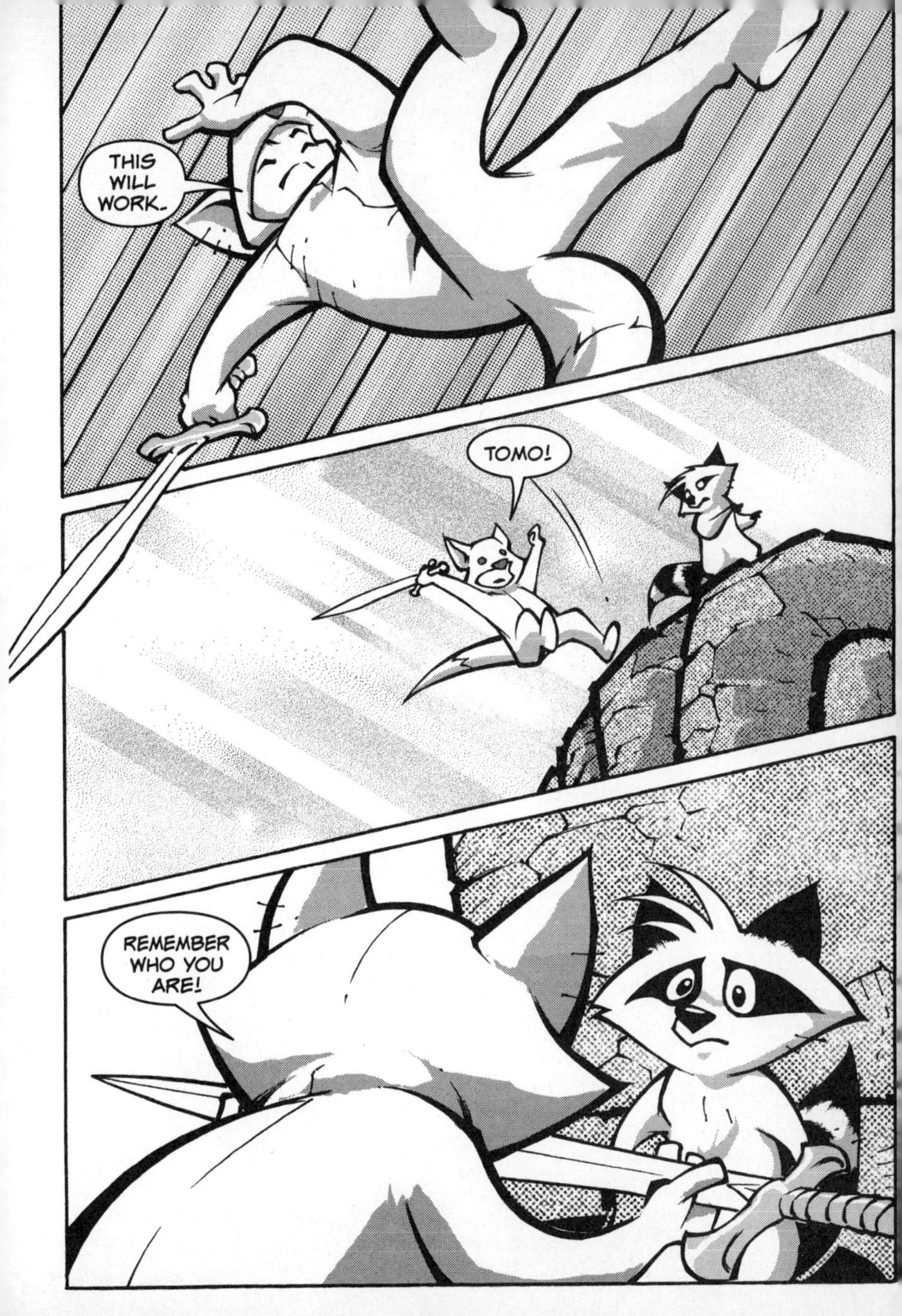
THIS WILL WORK...
TOMO!
REMEMBER WHO YOU ARE!

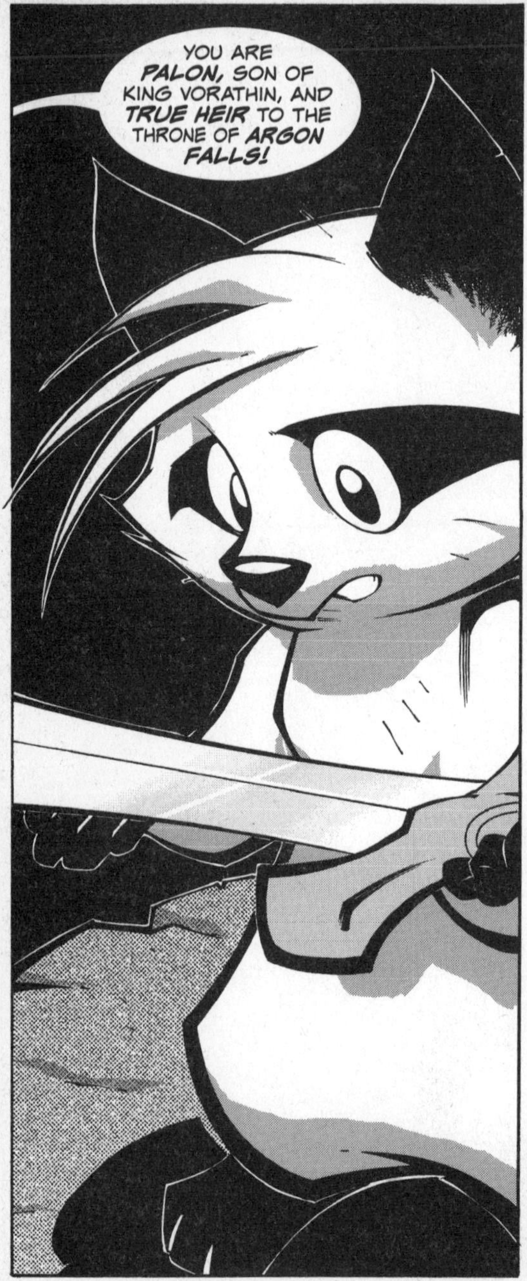
YOU ARE PALON, SON OF KING VORATHIN, AND TRUE HEIR TO THE THRONE OF ARGON FALLS!
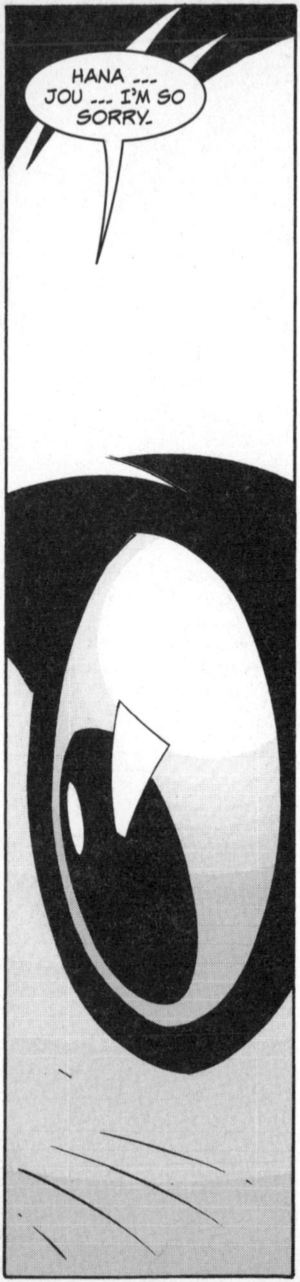
HANA ... JOU ... I'M SO SORRY.

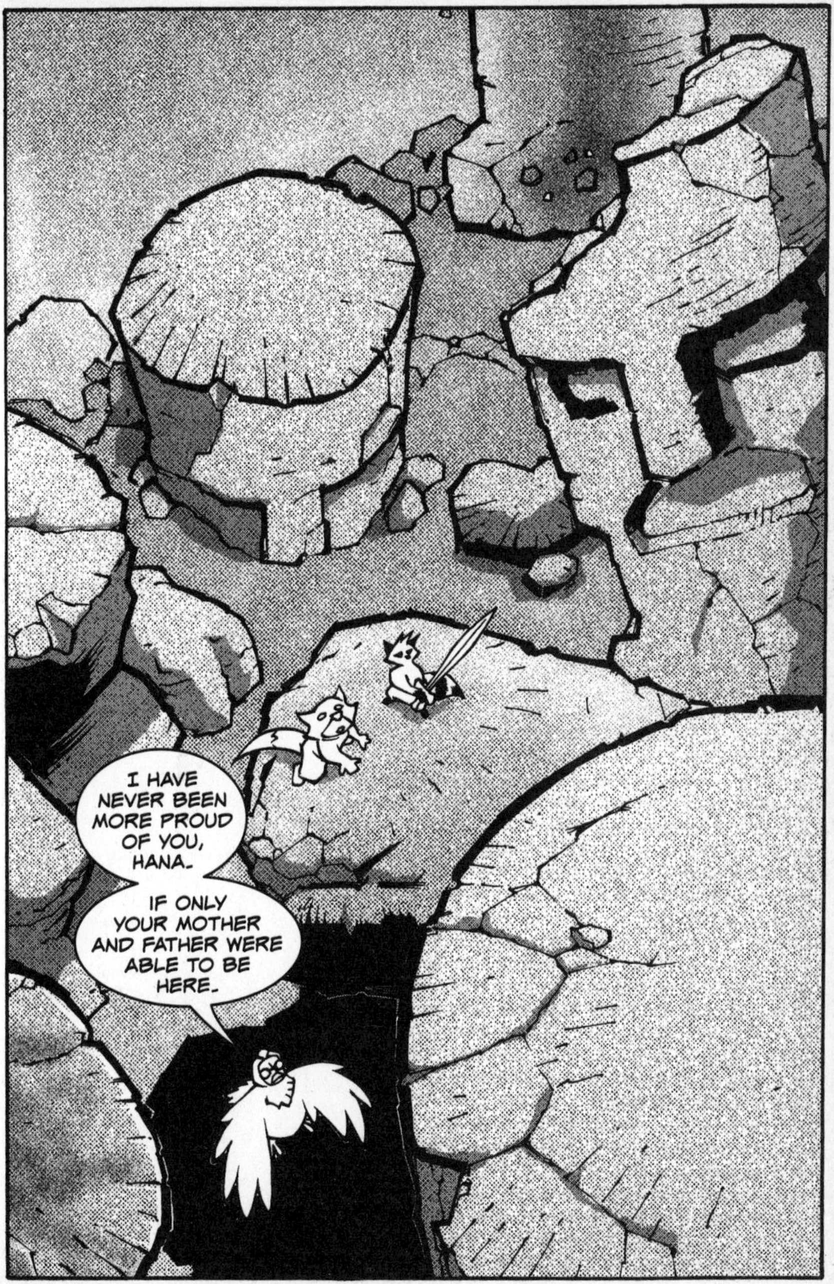
I HAVE NEVER BEEN MORE PROUD OF YOU, HANA.
IF ONLY YOUR MOTHER AND FATHER WERE ABLE TO BE HERE.

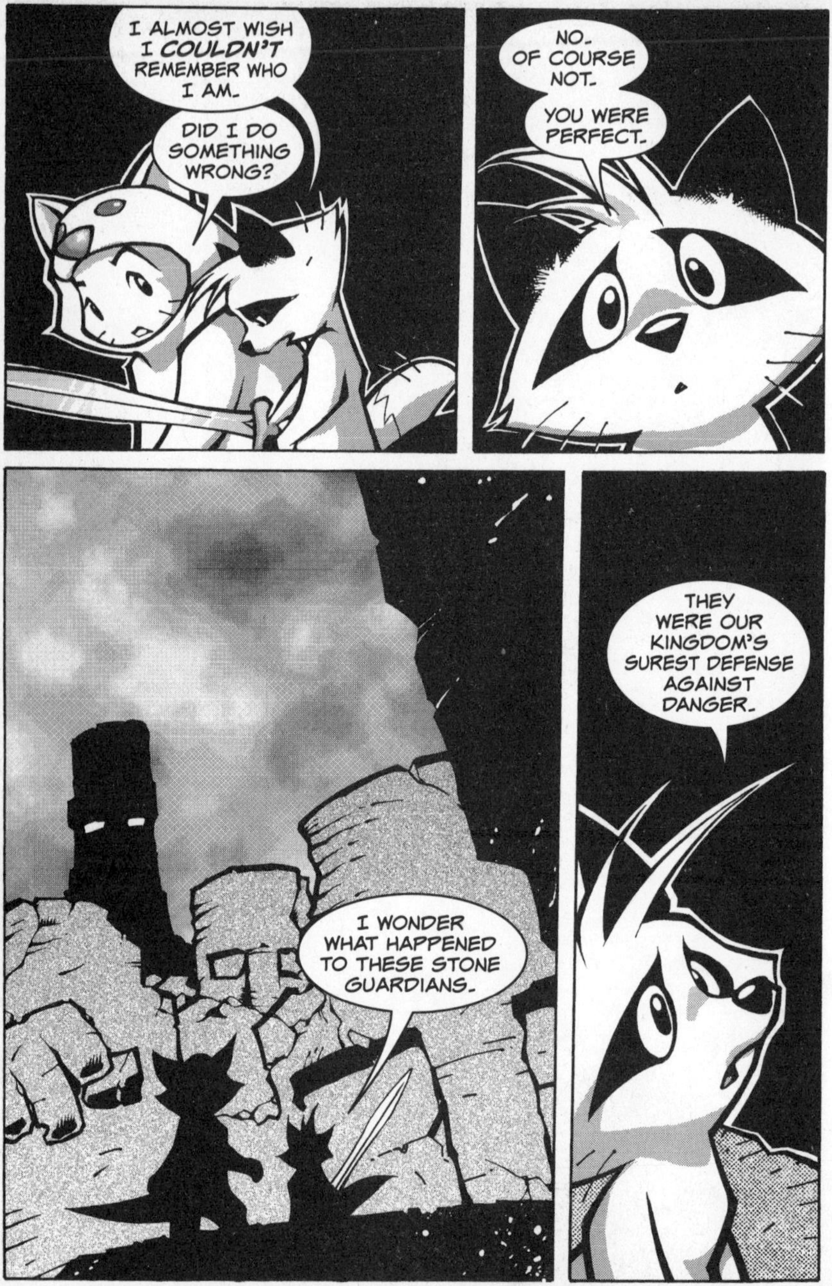
I ALMOST WISH I COULDN'T REMEMBER WHO I AM.
DID I DO SOMETHING WRONG?
NO. OF COURSE NOT.
YOU WERE PERFECT.
I WONDER WHAT HAPPENED TO THESE STONE GUARDIANS.
THEY WERE OUR KINGDOM'S SUREST DEFENSE AGAINST DANGER.

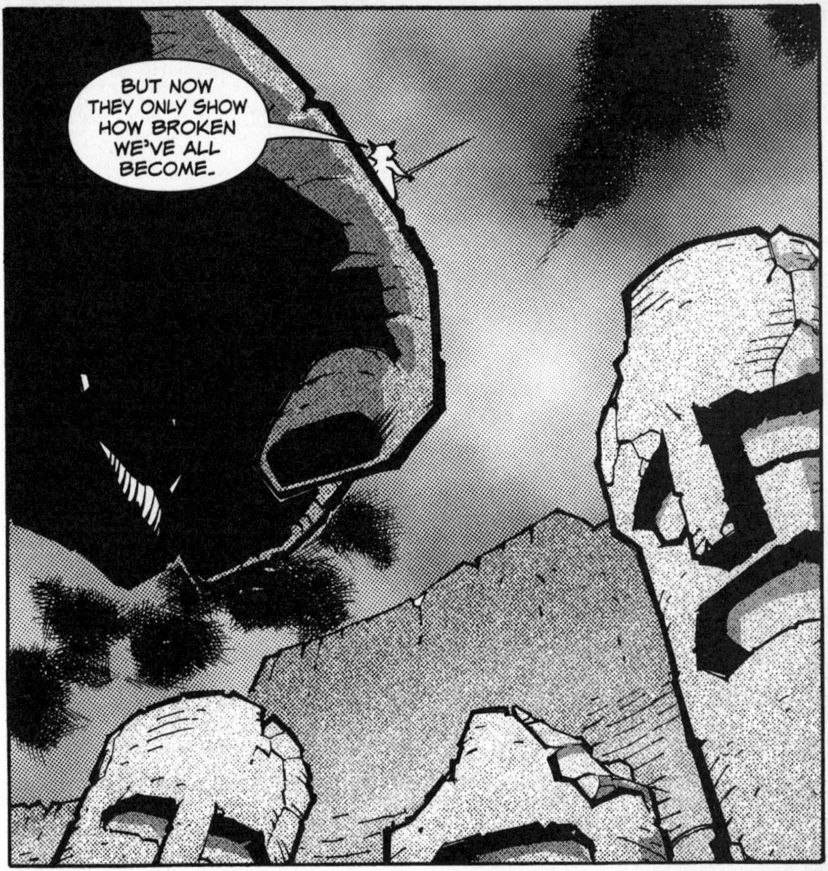
BUT NOW THEY ONLY SHOW HOW BROKEN WE'VE ALL BECOME.
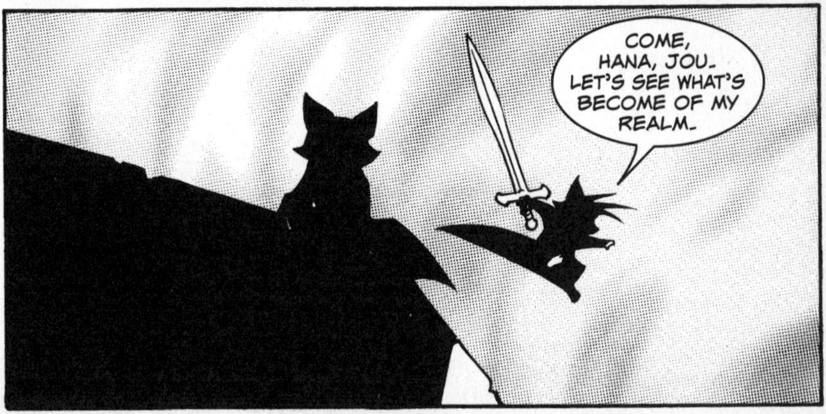
COME, HANA, JOU. LET'S SEE WHAT'S BECOME OF MY REALM.

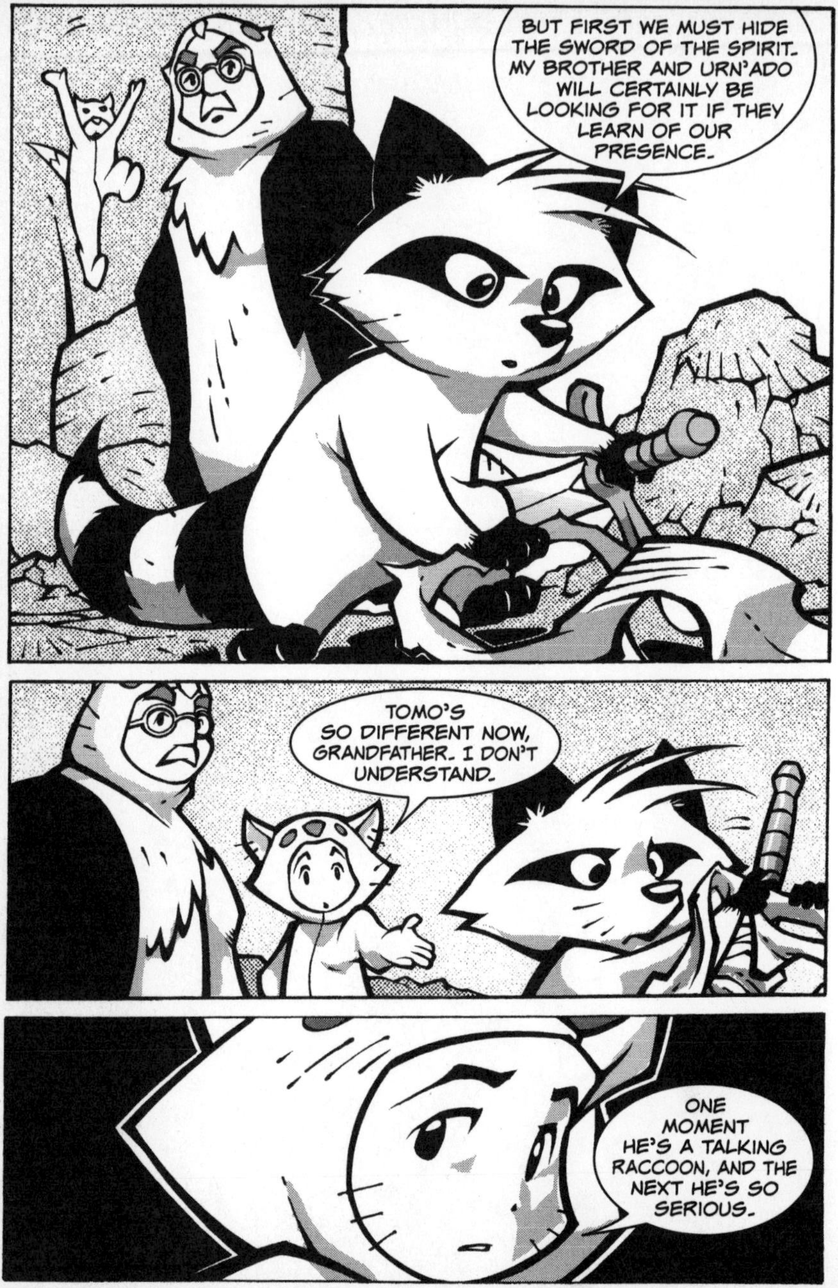
BUT FIRST WE MUST HIDE THE SWORD OF THE SPIRIT. MY BROTHER AND URN'ADO WILL CERTAINLY BE LOOKING FOR IT IF THEY LEARN OF OUR PRESENCE.
TOMO'S SO DIFFERENT NOW, GRANDFATHER. I DON'T UNDERSTAND.
ONE MOMENT HE'S A TALKING RACCOON, AND THE NEXT HE'S SO SERIOUS.

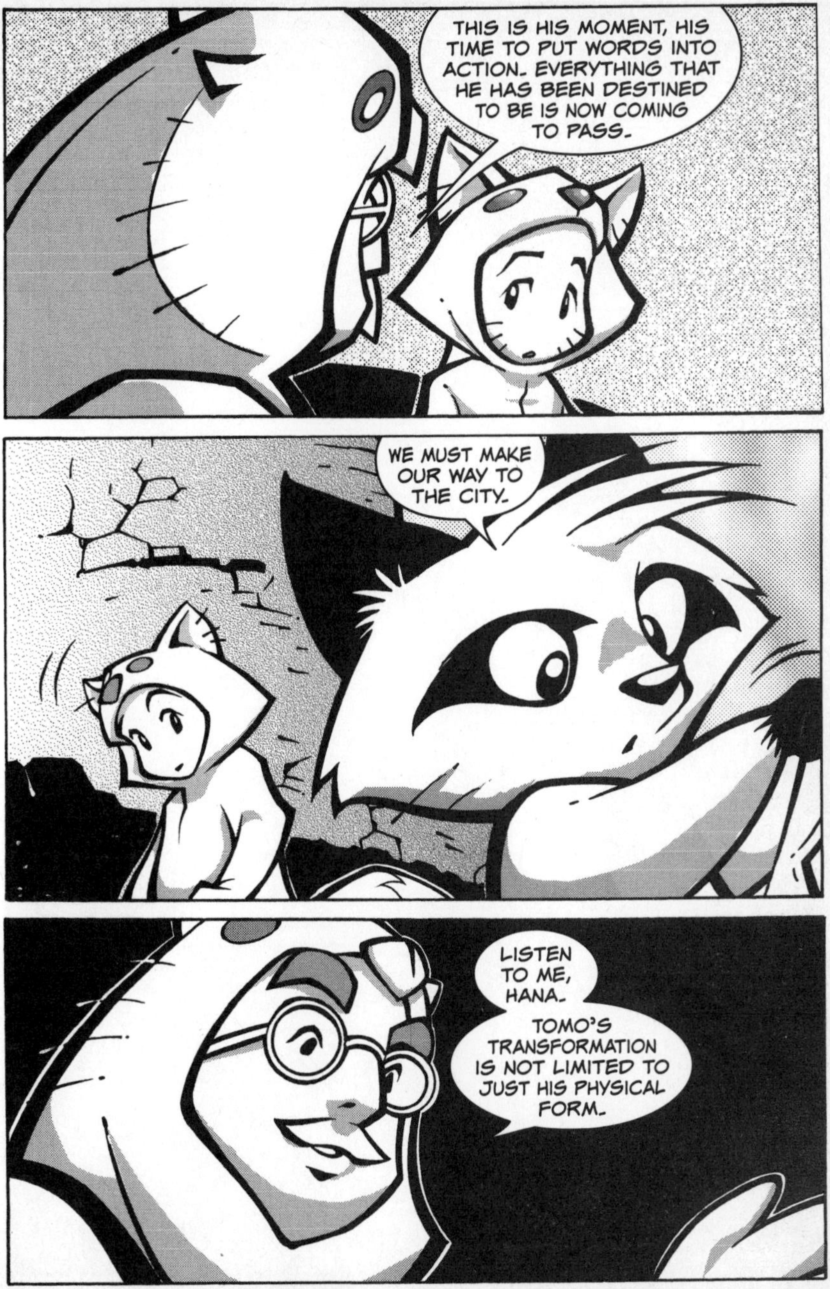
THIS IS HIS MOMENT, HIS TIME TO PUT WORDS INTO ACTION. EVERYTHING THAT HE HAS BEEN DESTINED TO BE IS NOW COMING TO PASS.
WE MUST MAKE OUR WAY TO THE CITY.
LISTEN TO ME, HANA.
TOMO'S TRANSFORMATION IS NOT LIMITED TO JUST HIS PHYSICAL FORM.

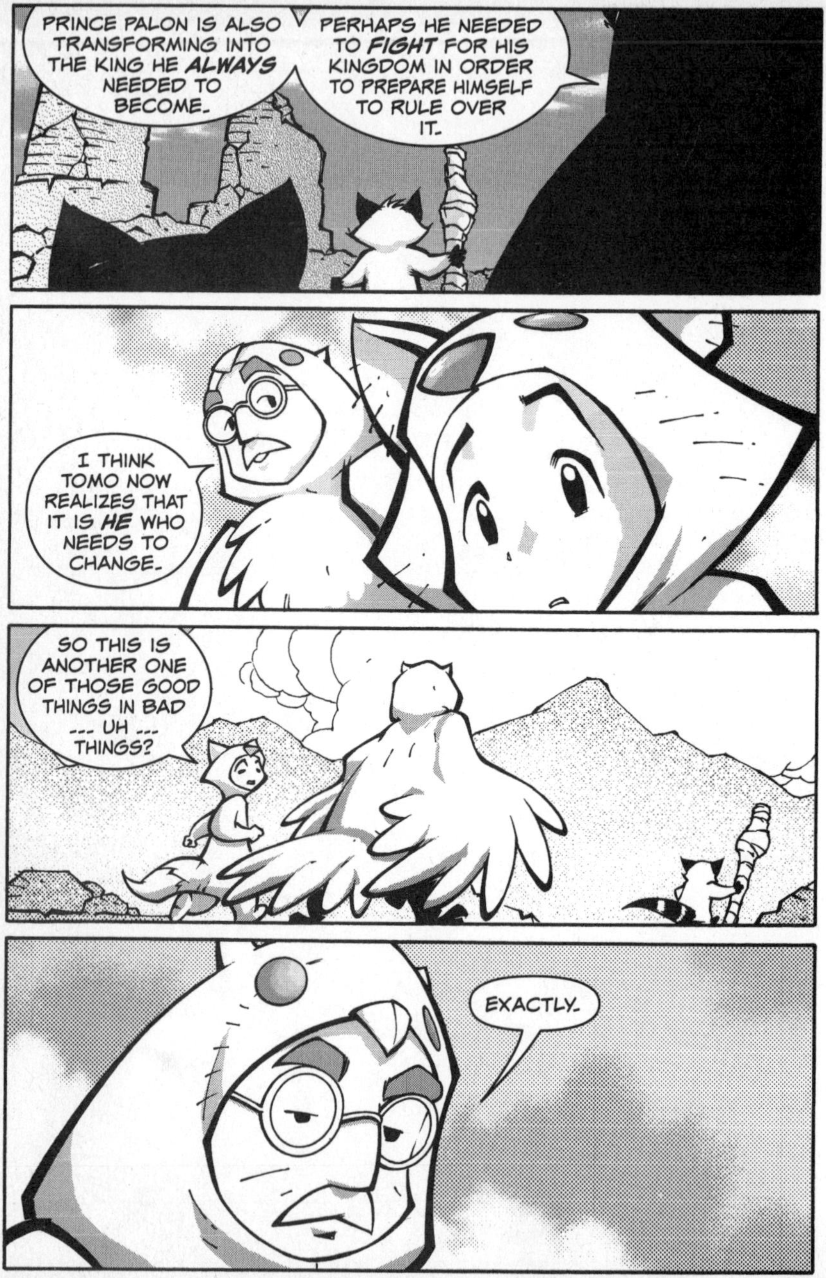
PRINCE PALON IS ALSO TRANSFORMING INTO THE KING HE ALWAYS NEEDED TO BECOME.
PERHAPS HE NEEDED TO FIGHT FOR HIS KINGDOM IN ORDER TO PREPARE HIMSELF TO RULE OVER IT.
I THINK TOMO NOW REALIZES THAT IT IS HE WHO NEEDS TO CHANGE.
SO THIS IS ANOTHER ONE OF THOSE GOOD THINGS IN BAD --- UH --- THINGS?
EXACTLY.

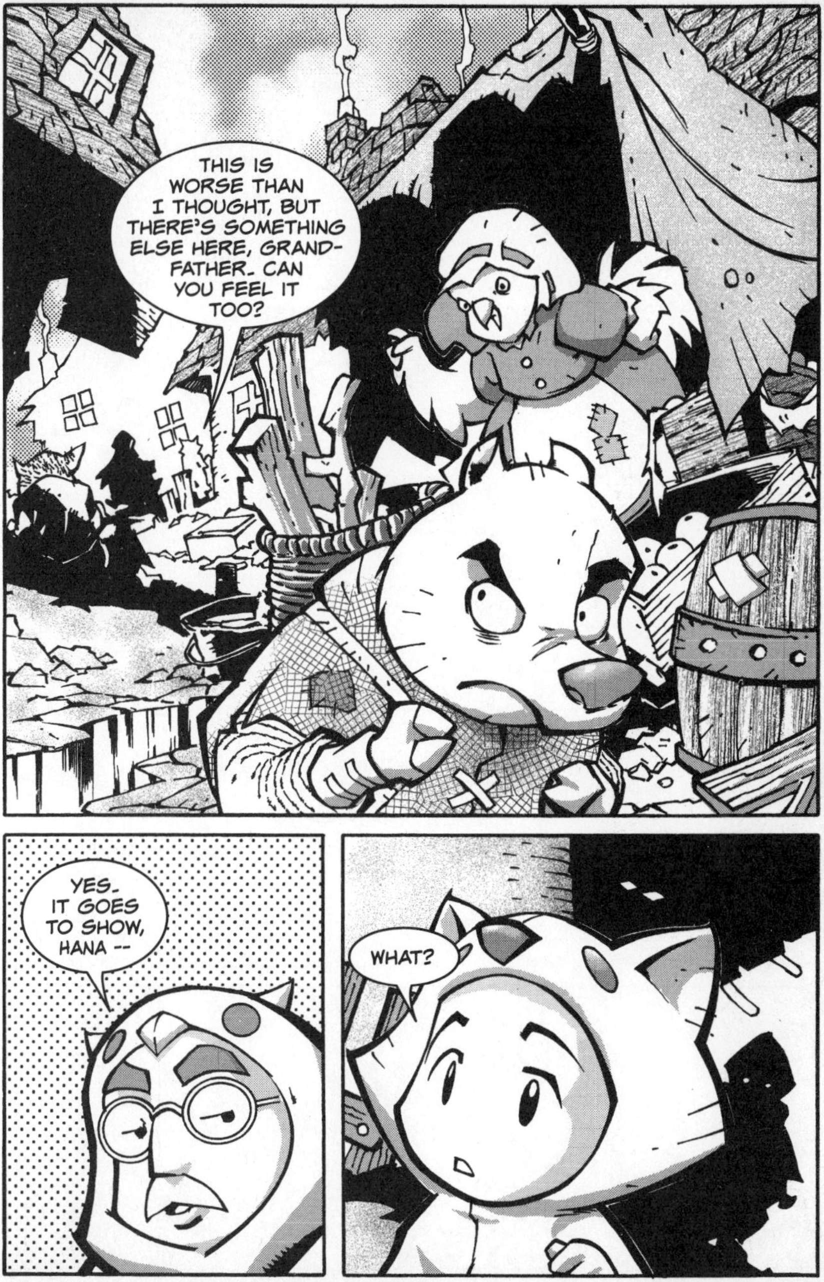
THIS IS WORSE THAN I THOUGHT, BUT THERE'S SOMETHING ELSE HERE, GRAND-FATHER. CAN YOU FEEL IT TOO?
YES. IT GOES TO SHOW, HANA --
WHAT?

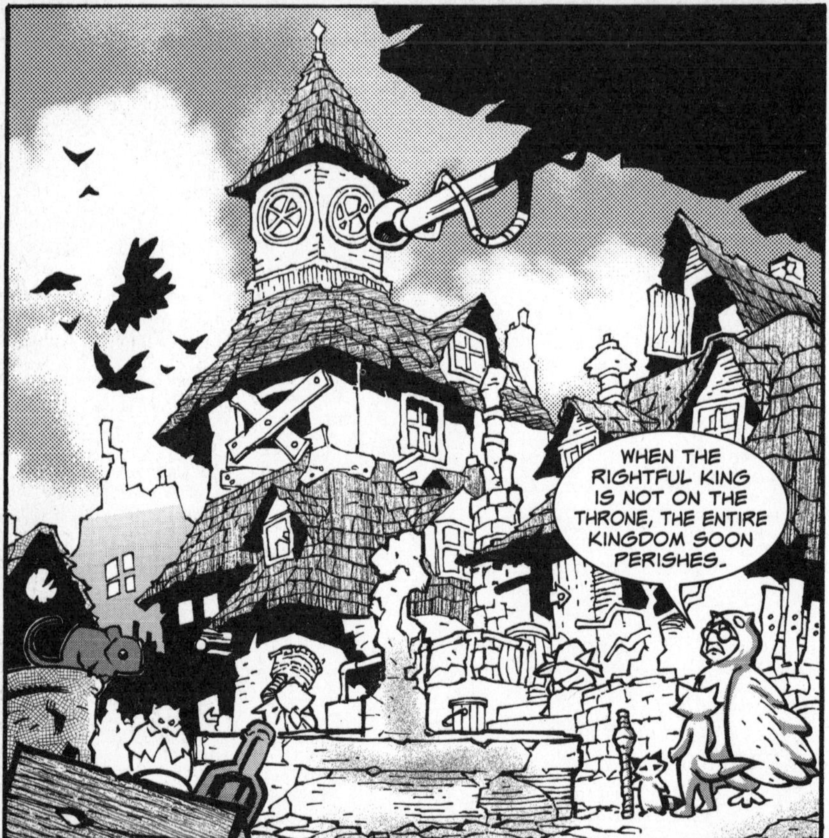
WHEN THE RIGHTFUL KING IS NOT ON THE THRONE, THE ENTIRE KINGDOM SOON PERISHES_
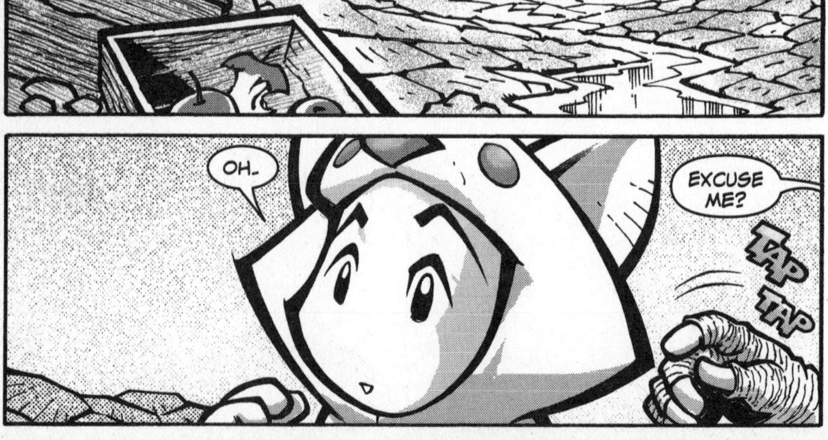
OH_
EXCUSE ME?
TAP TAP

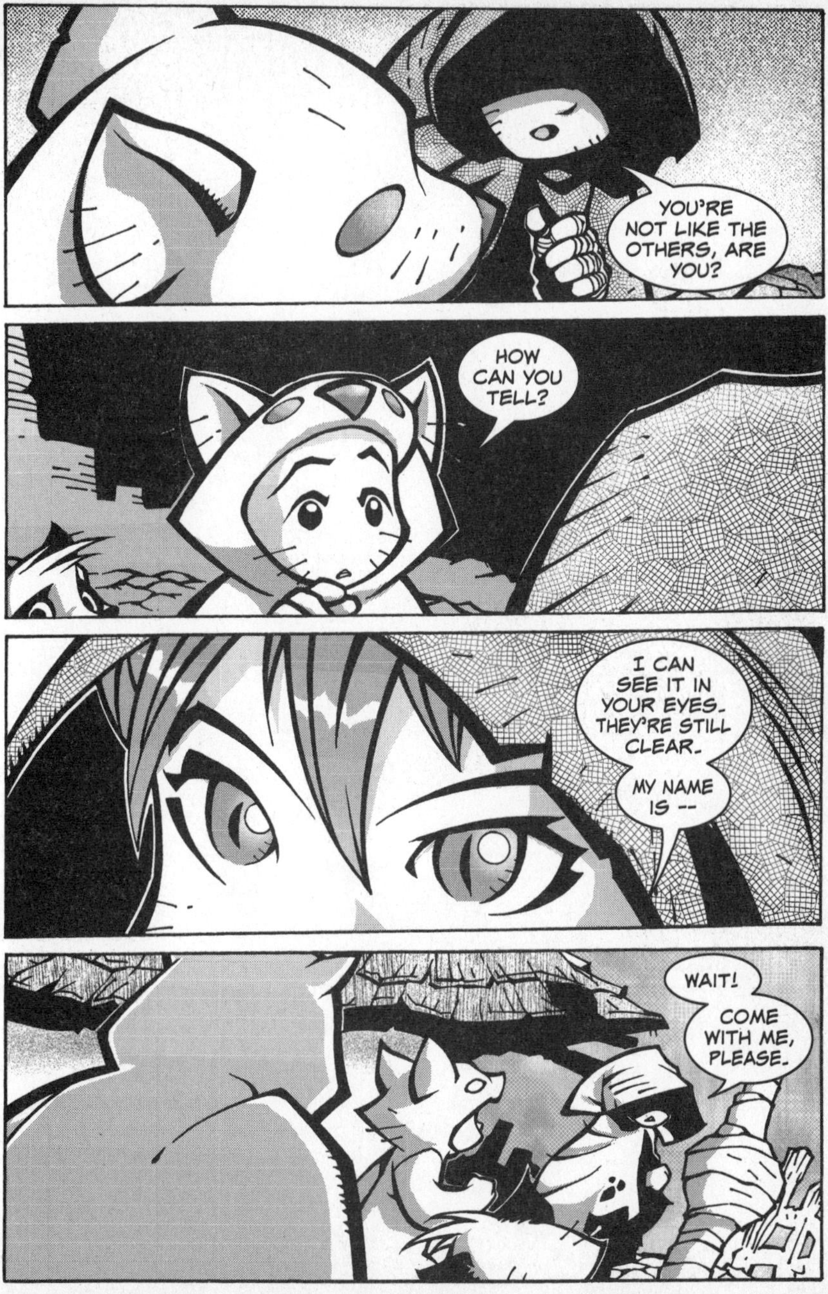
YOU'RE NOT LIKE THE OTHERS, ARE YOU?
HOW CAN YOU TELL?
I CAN SEE IT IN YOUR EYES. THEY'RE STILL CLEAR.
MY NAME IS --
WAIT!
COME WITH ME, PLEASE.

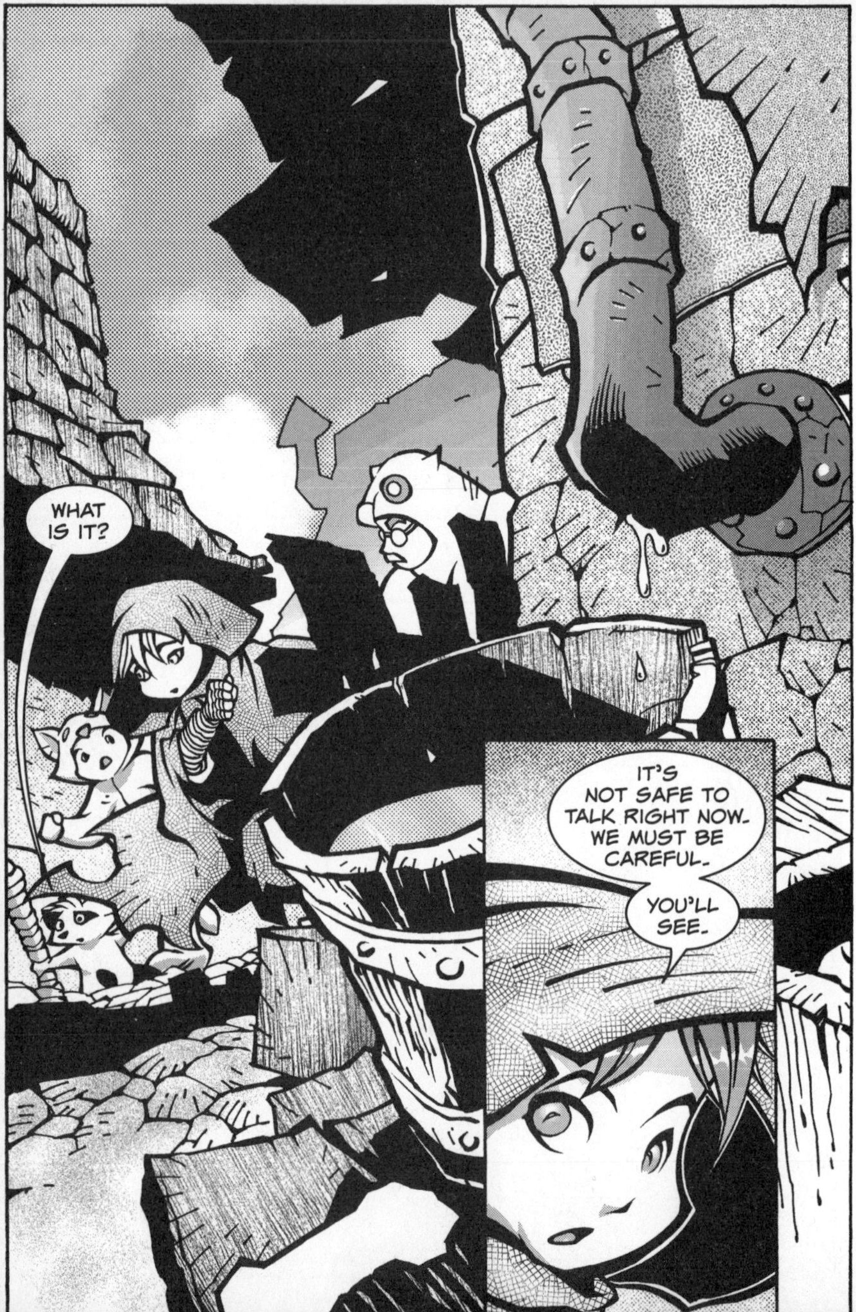
WHAT IS IT?
IT'S NOT SAFE TO TALK RIGHT NOW. WE MUST BE CAREFUL.
YOU'LL SEE.

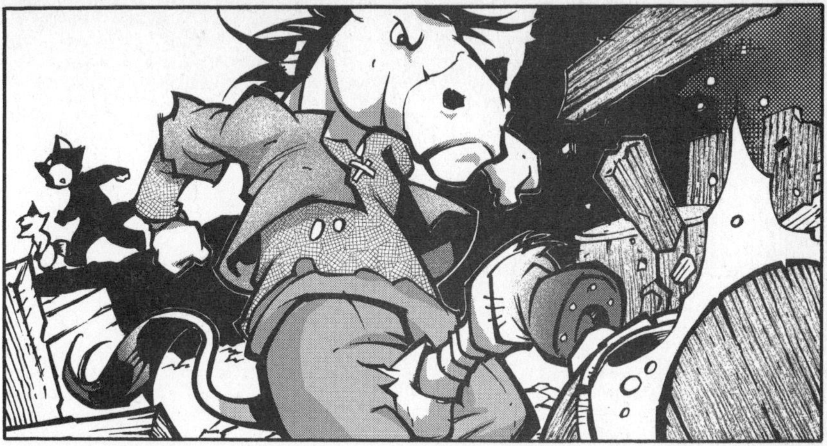

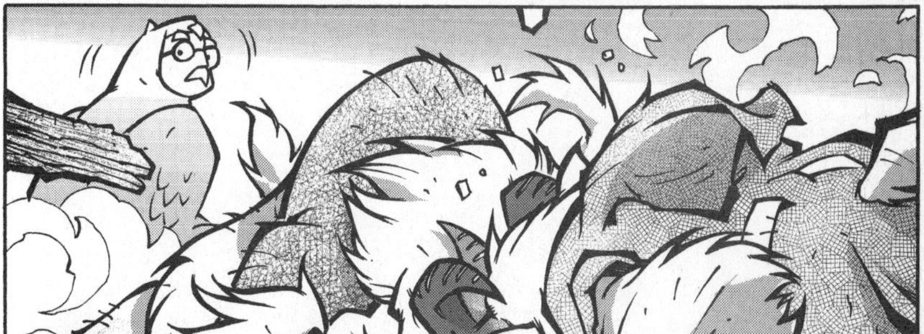

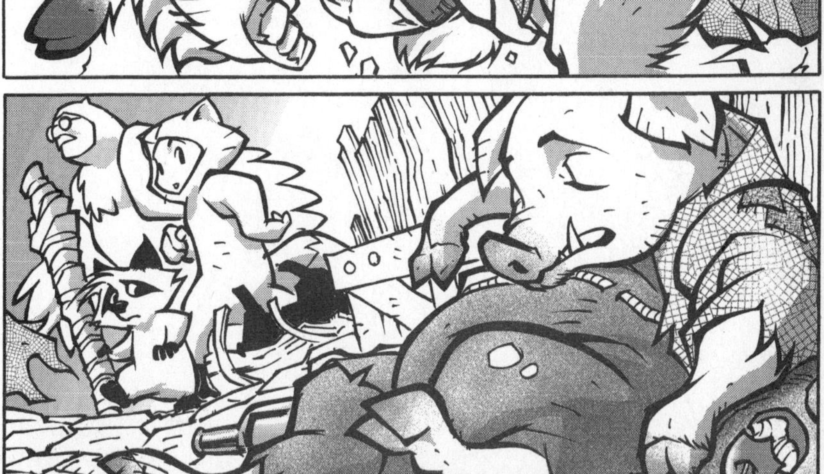

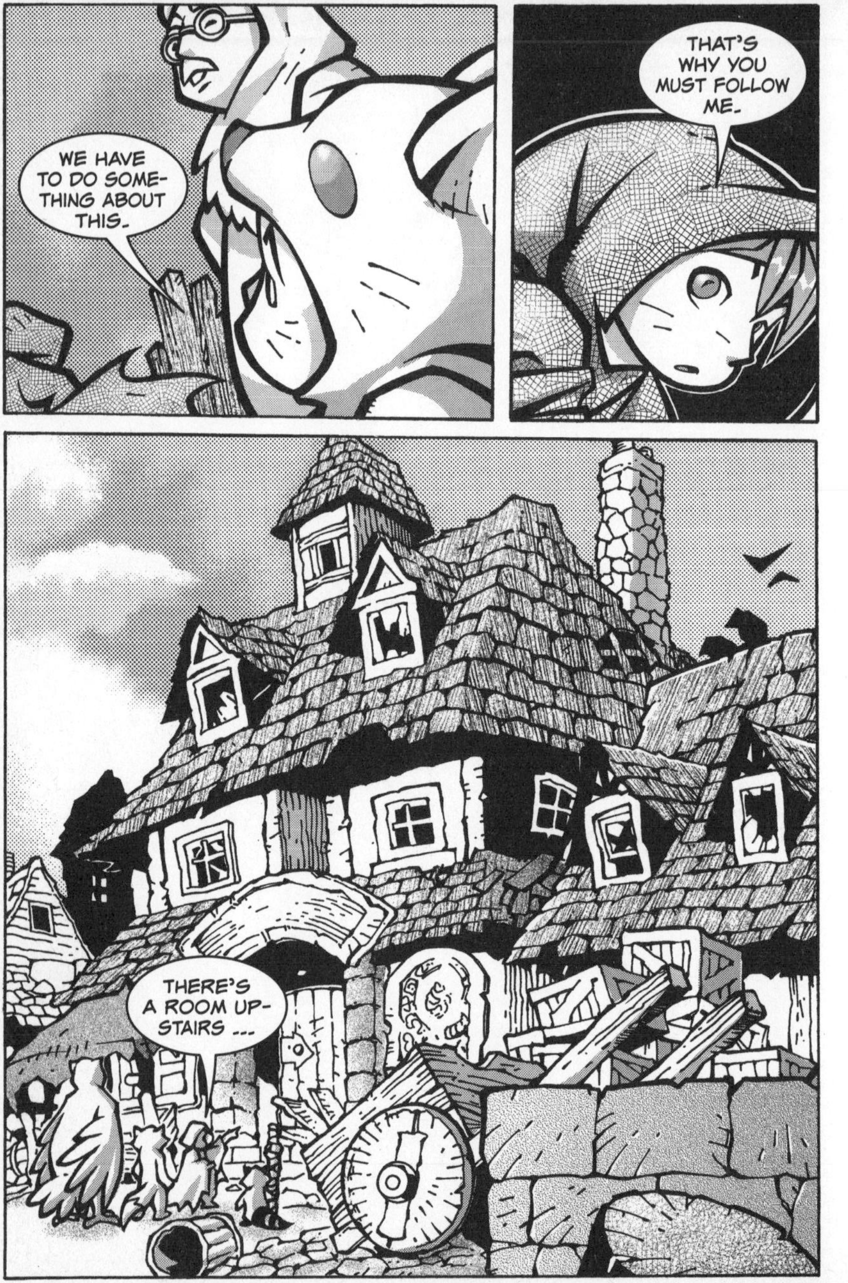
WE HAVE TO DO SOME-THING ABOUT THIS.
THAT'S WHY YOU MUST FOLLOW ME.
THERE'S A ROOM UP-STAIRS ...

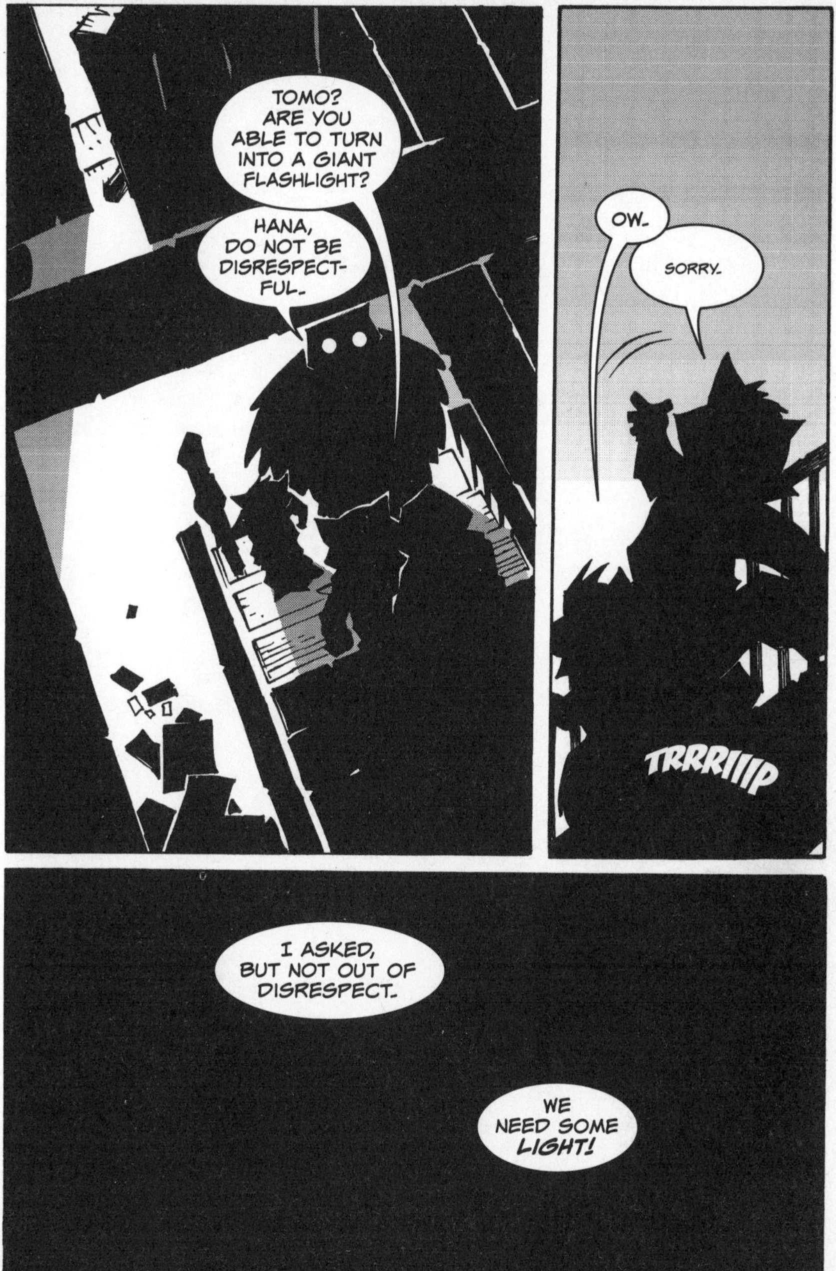
TOMO? ARE YOU ABLE TO TURN INTO A GIANT FLASHLIGHT?
HANA, DO NOT BE DISRESPECT-FUL.
OW.
SORRY.
TRRRIIIP
I ASKED, BUT NOT OUT OF DISRESPECT.
WE NEED SOME LIGHT!

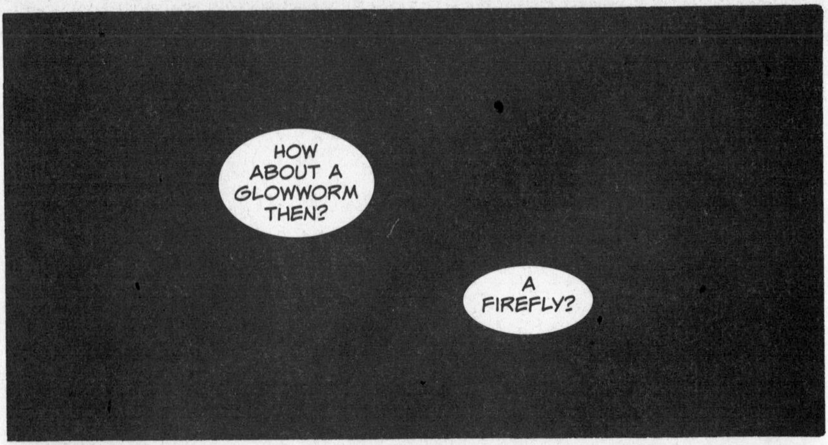
HOW ABOUT A GLOWWORM THEN?
A FIREFLY?
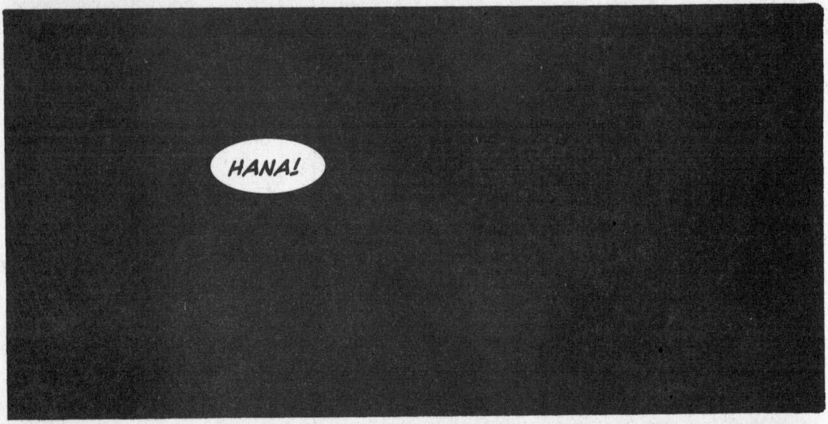
HANA!
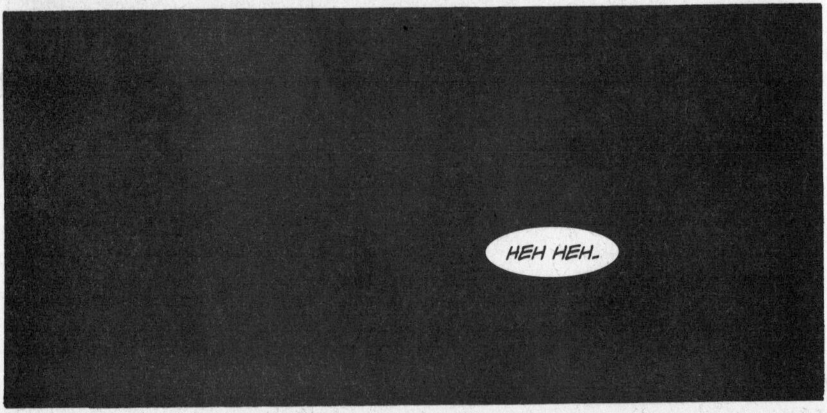
HEH HEH.

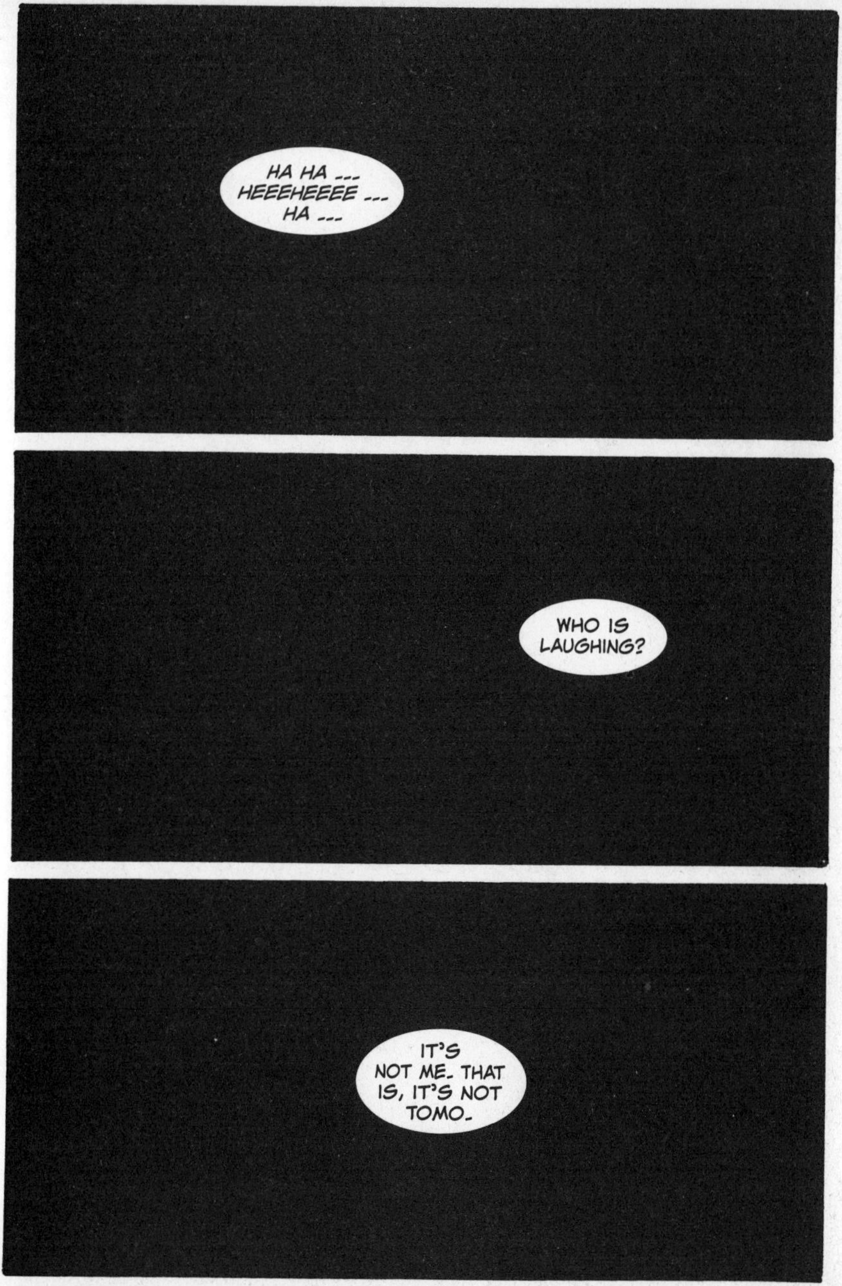
HA HA ... HEEEHEEEE ... HA ...
WHO IS LAUGHING?
IT'S NOT ME. THAT IS, IT'S NOT TOMO.

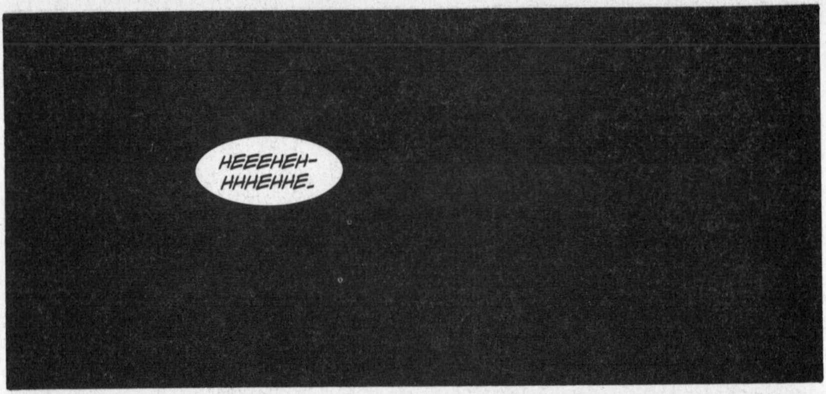
HEEEHEH-
HHHEHHE.

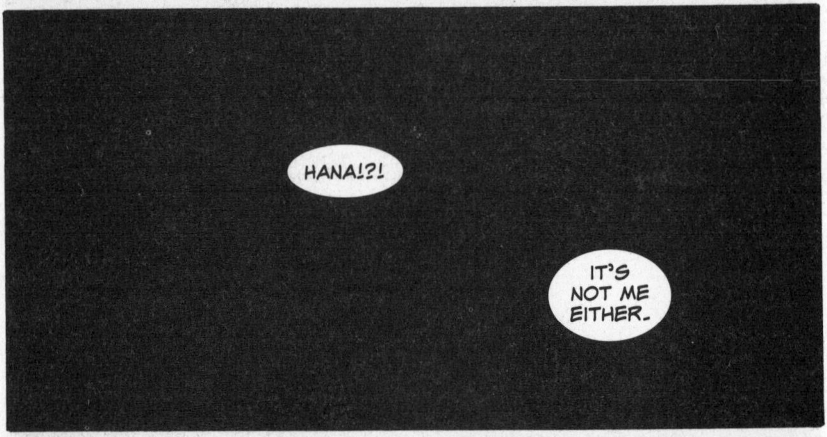
HANA!?!
IT'S NOT ME EITHER.

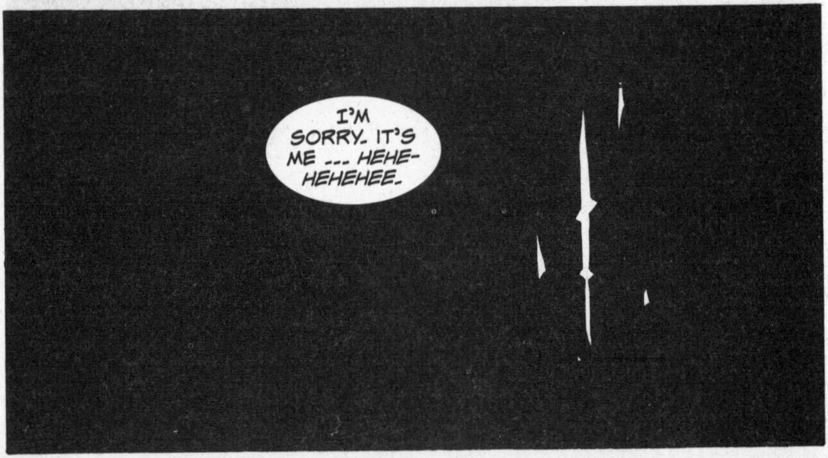
I'M SORRY. IT'S ME ... HEHE-HEHEHEE.

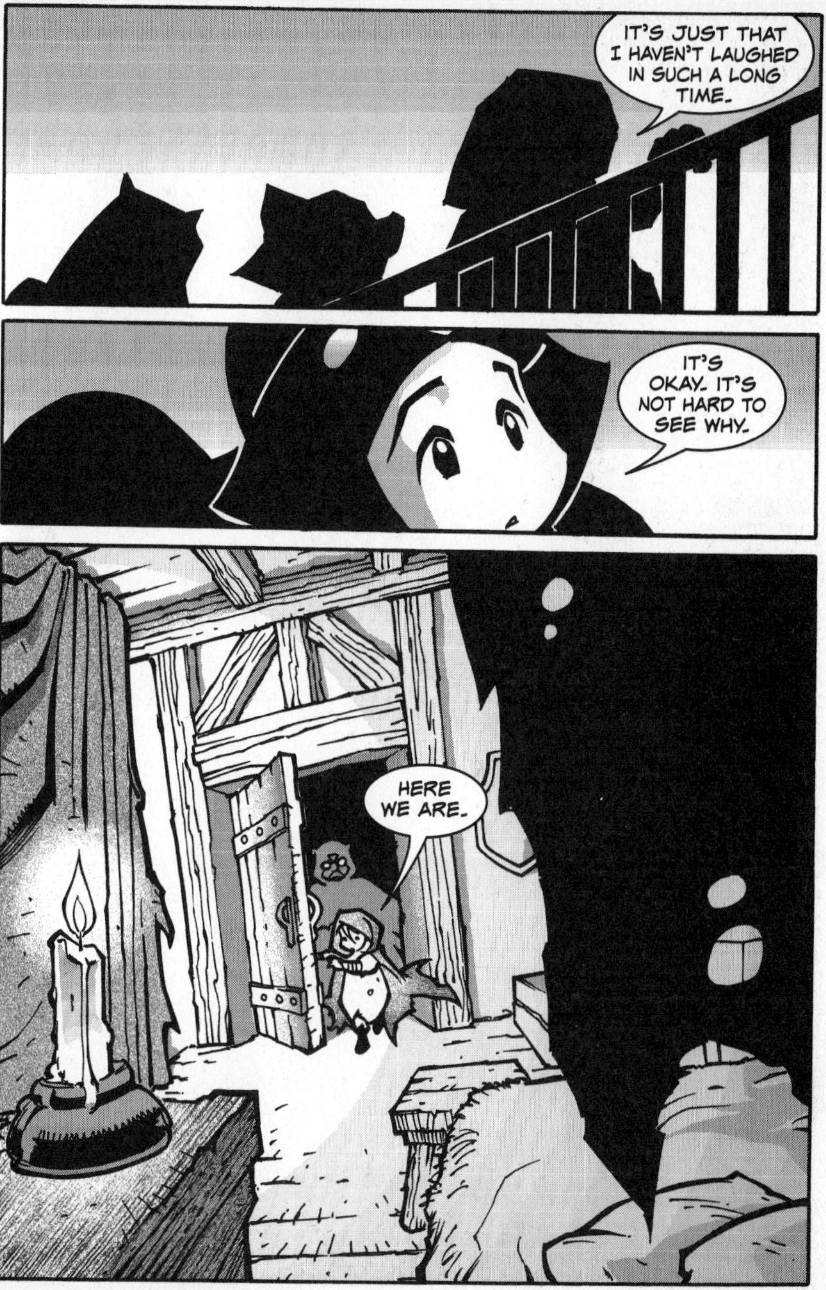
IT'S JUST THAT I HAVEN'T LAUGHED IN SUCH A LONG TIME.
IT'S OKAY. IT'S NOT HARD TO SEE WHY.
HERE WE ARE.

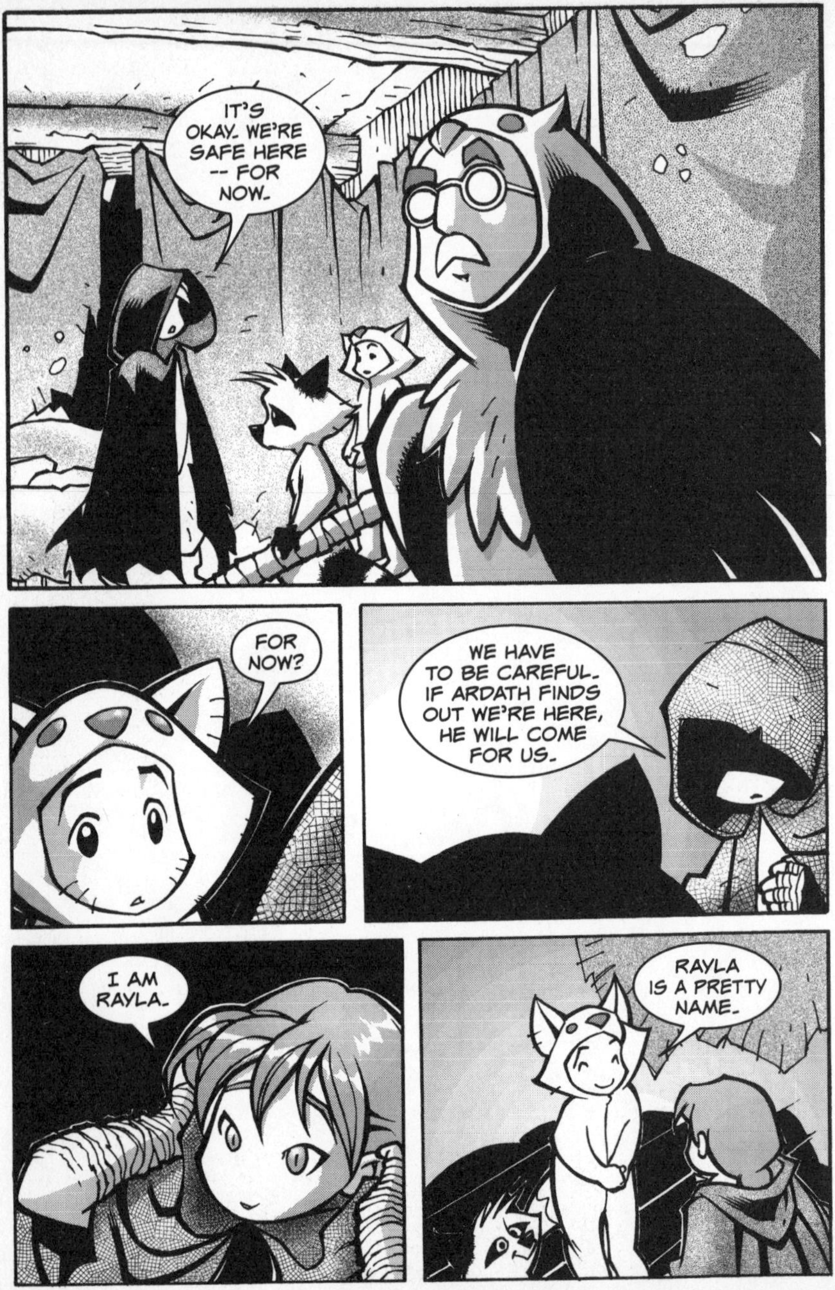
IT'S OKAY. WE'RE SAFE HERE -- FOR NOW.
FOR NOW?
WE HAVE TO BE CAREFUL. IF ARDATH FINDS OUT WE'RE HERE, HE WILL COME FOR US.
I AM RAYLA.
RAYLA IS A PRETTY NAME.

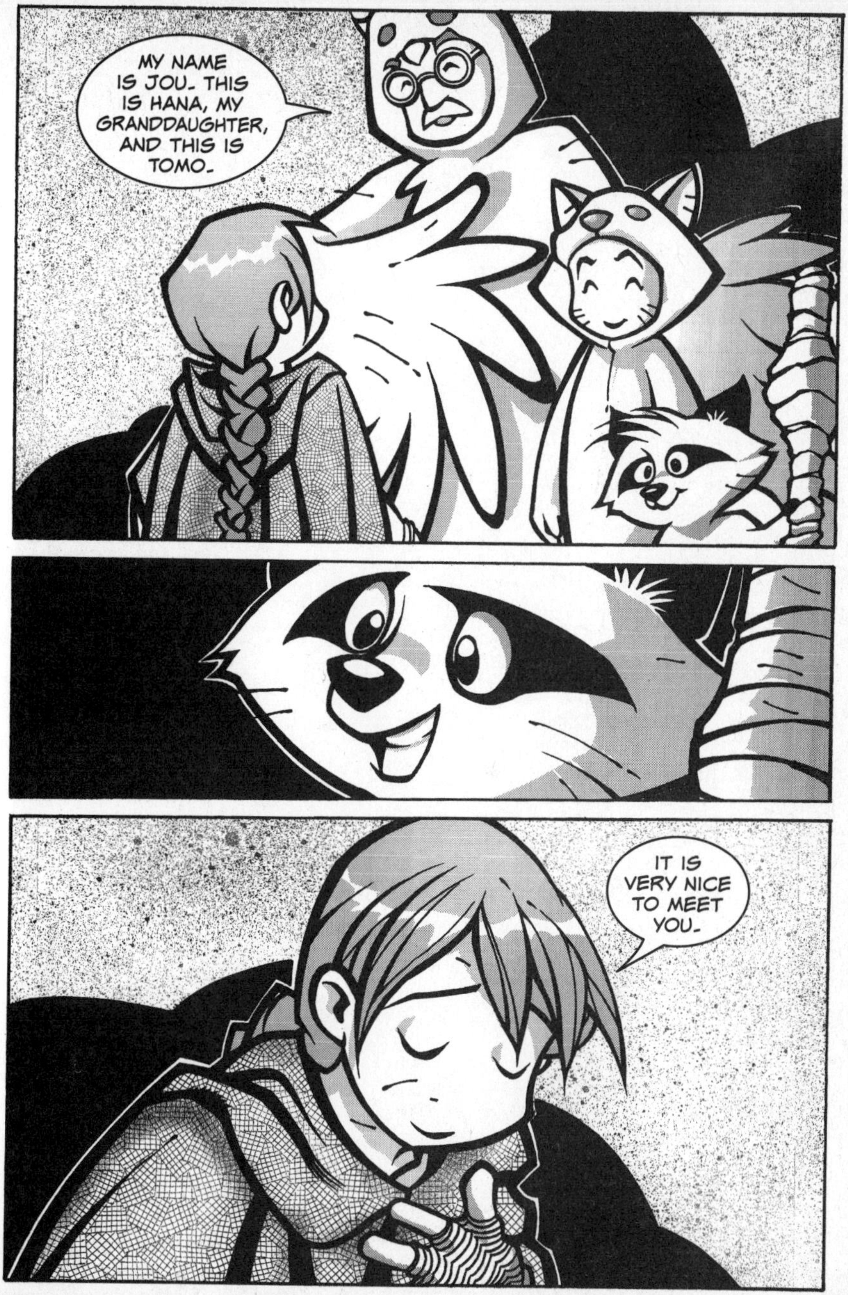
MY NAME IS JOU. THIS IS HANA, MY GRANDDAUGHTER, AND THIS IS TOMO.
IT IS VERY NICE TO MEET YOU.

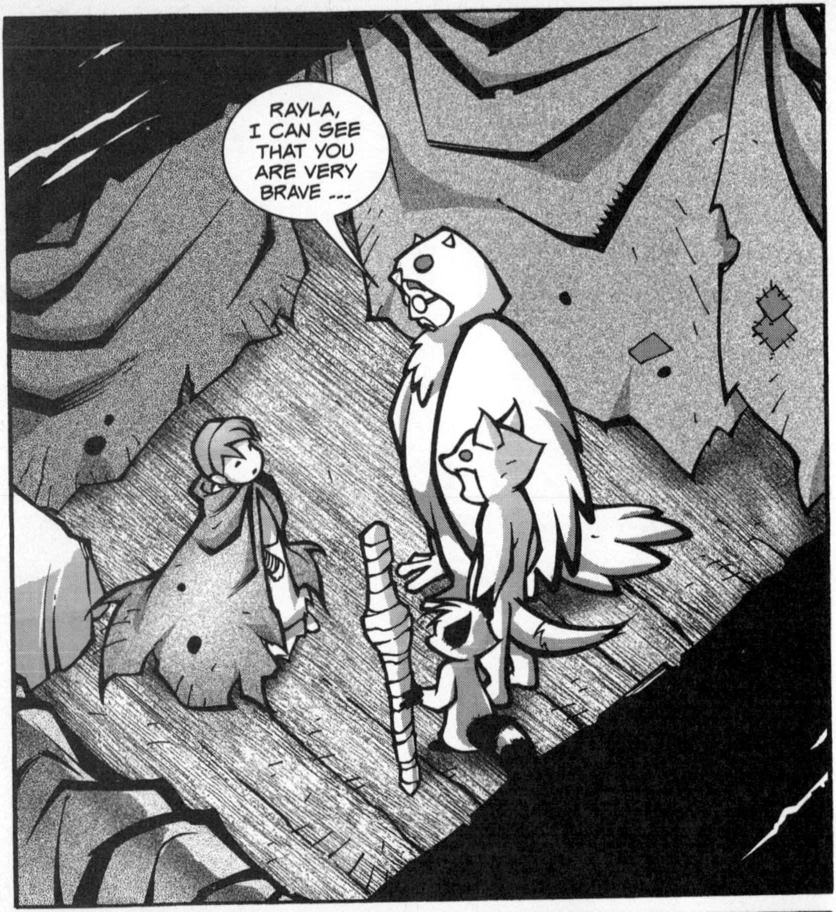
RAYLA, I CAN SEE THAT YOU ARE VERY BRAVE ...
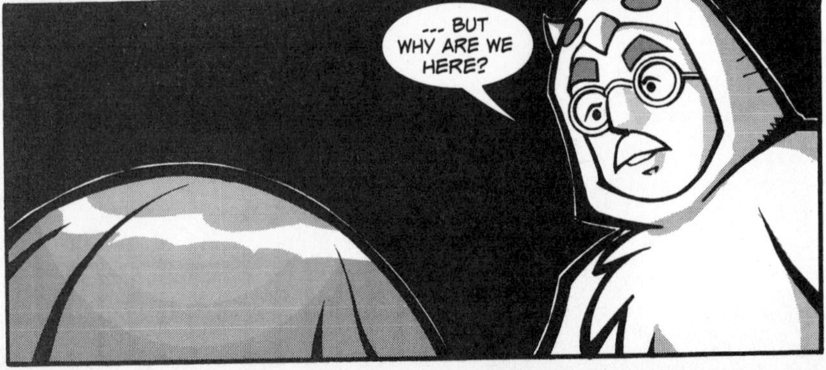
... BUT WHY ARE WE HERE?

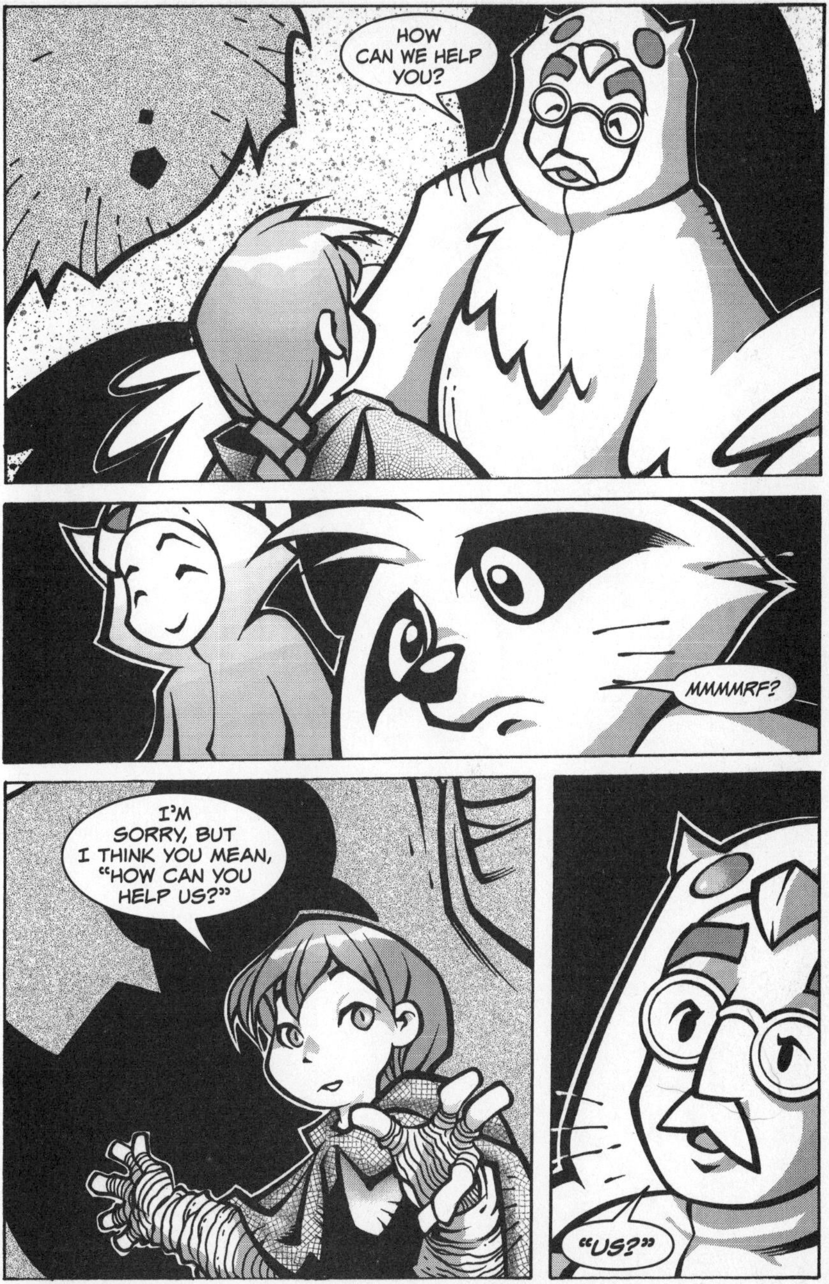
HOW CAN WE HELP YOU?
MMMMRF?
I'M SORRY, BUT I THINK YOU MEAN, "HOW CAN YOU HELP US?"
"US?"

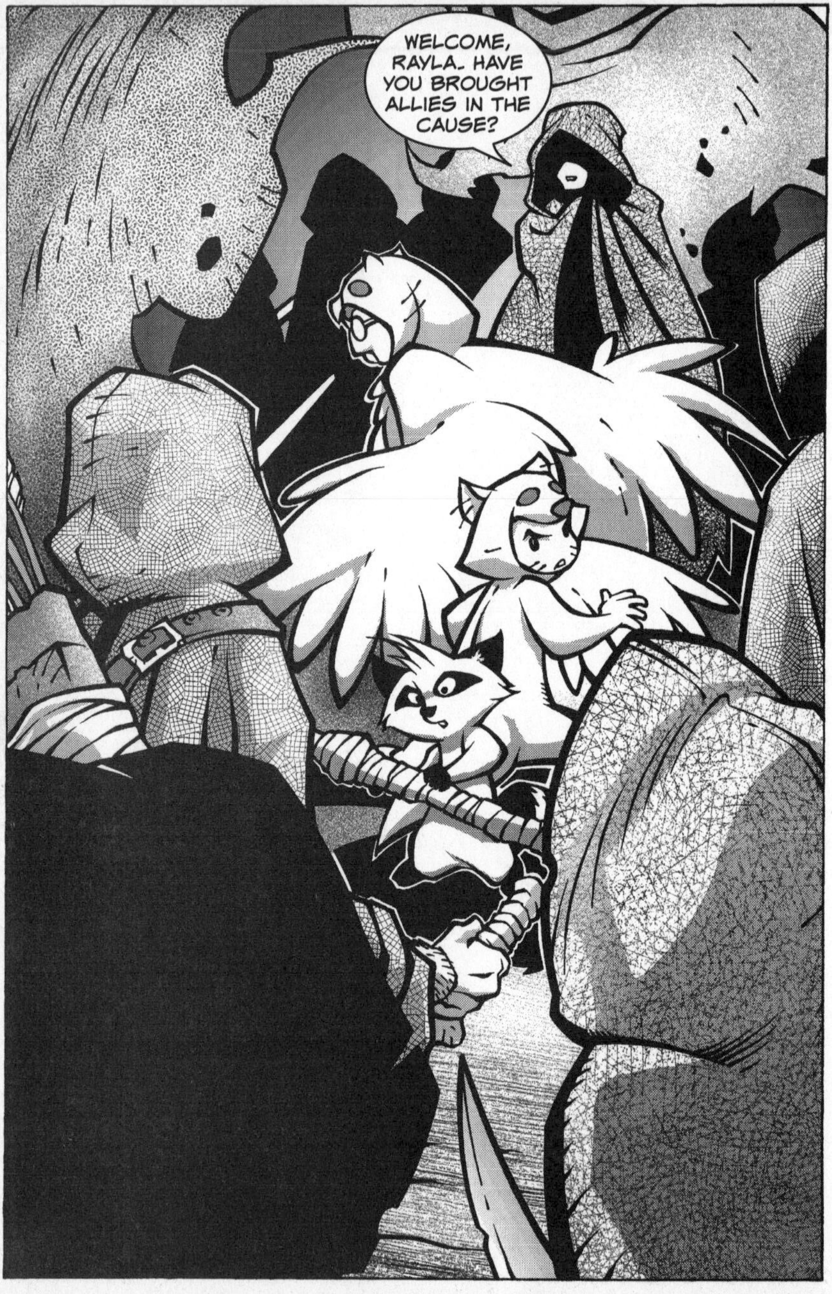
WELCOME, RAYLA. HAVE YOU BROUGHT ALLIES IN THE CAUSE?

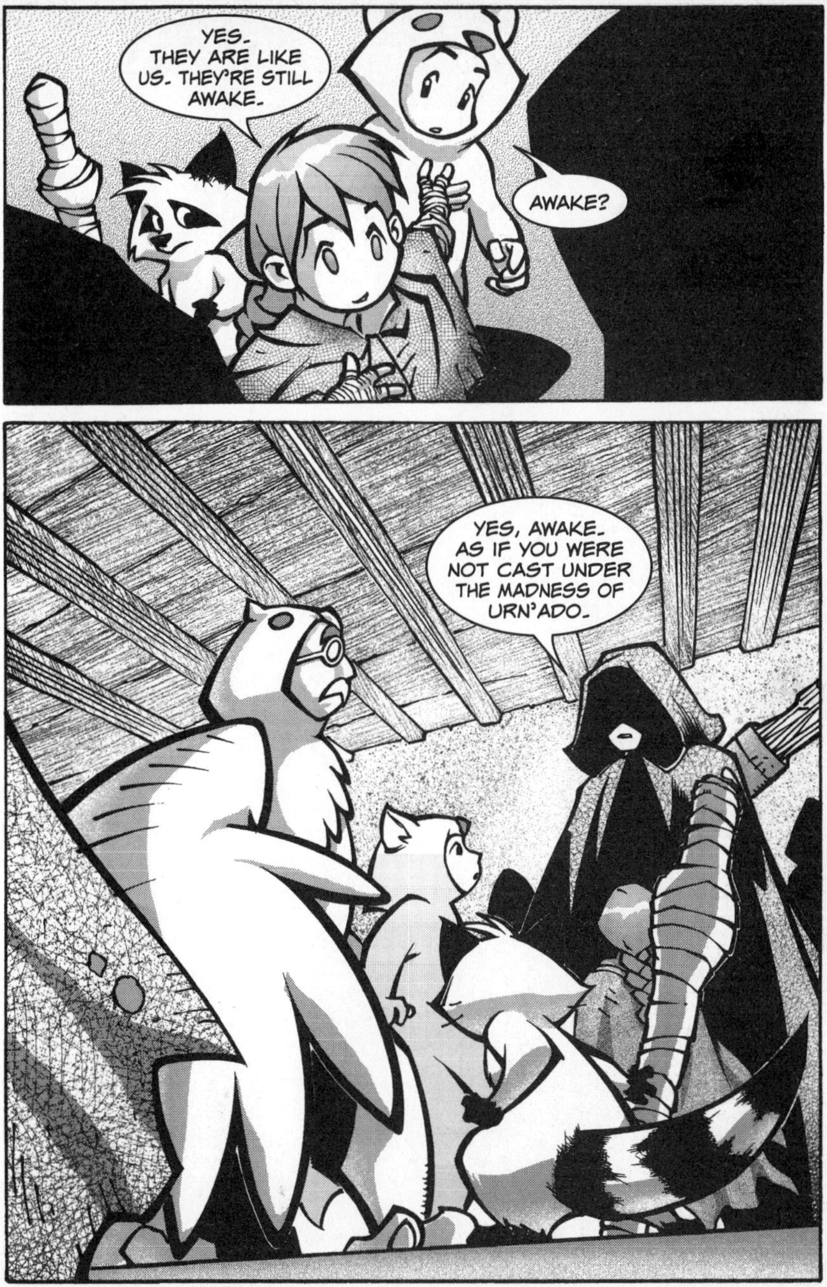
YES. THEY ARE LIKE US. THEY'RE STILL AWAKE.
AWAKE?
YES, AWAKE. AS IF YOU WERE NOT CAST UNDER THE MADNESS OF URN'ADO.

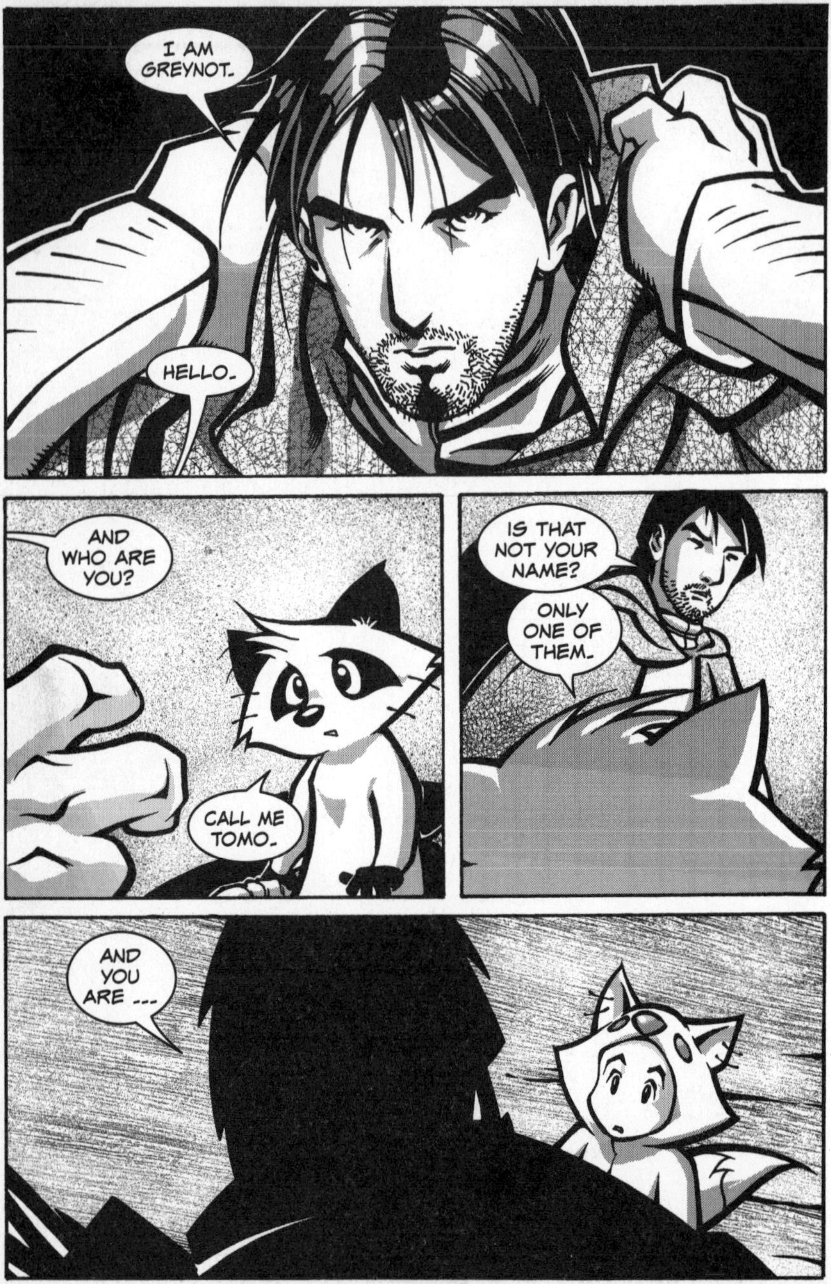
I AM GREYNOT.
HELLO.
AND WHO ARE YOU?
CALL ME TOMO.
IS THAT NOT YOUR NAME?
ONLY ONE OF THEM.
AND YOU ARE ...

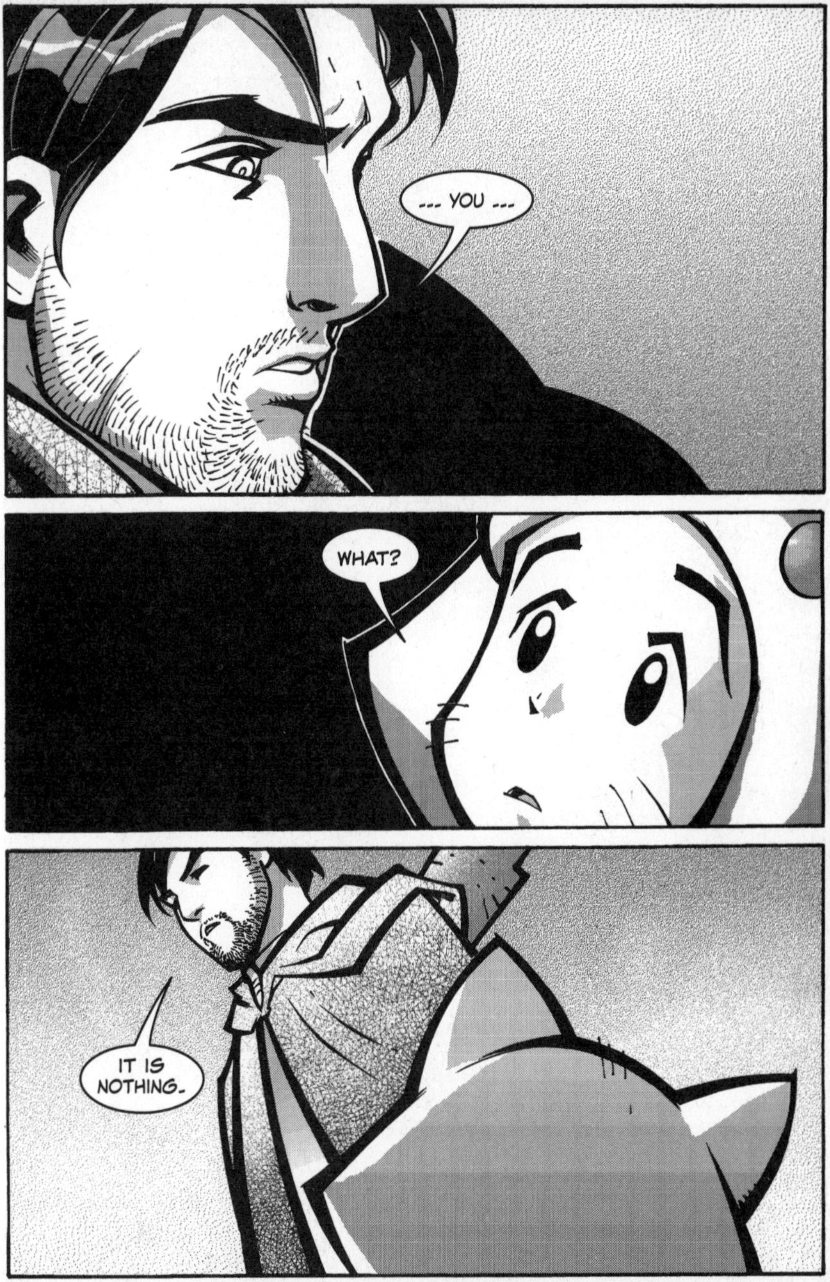
--- YOU ---
WHAT?
IT IS NOTHING.

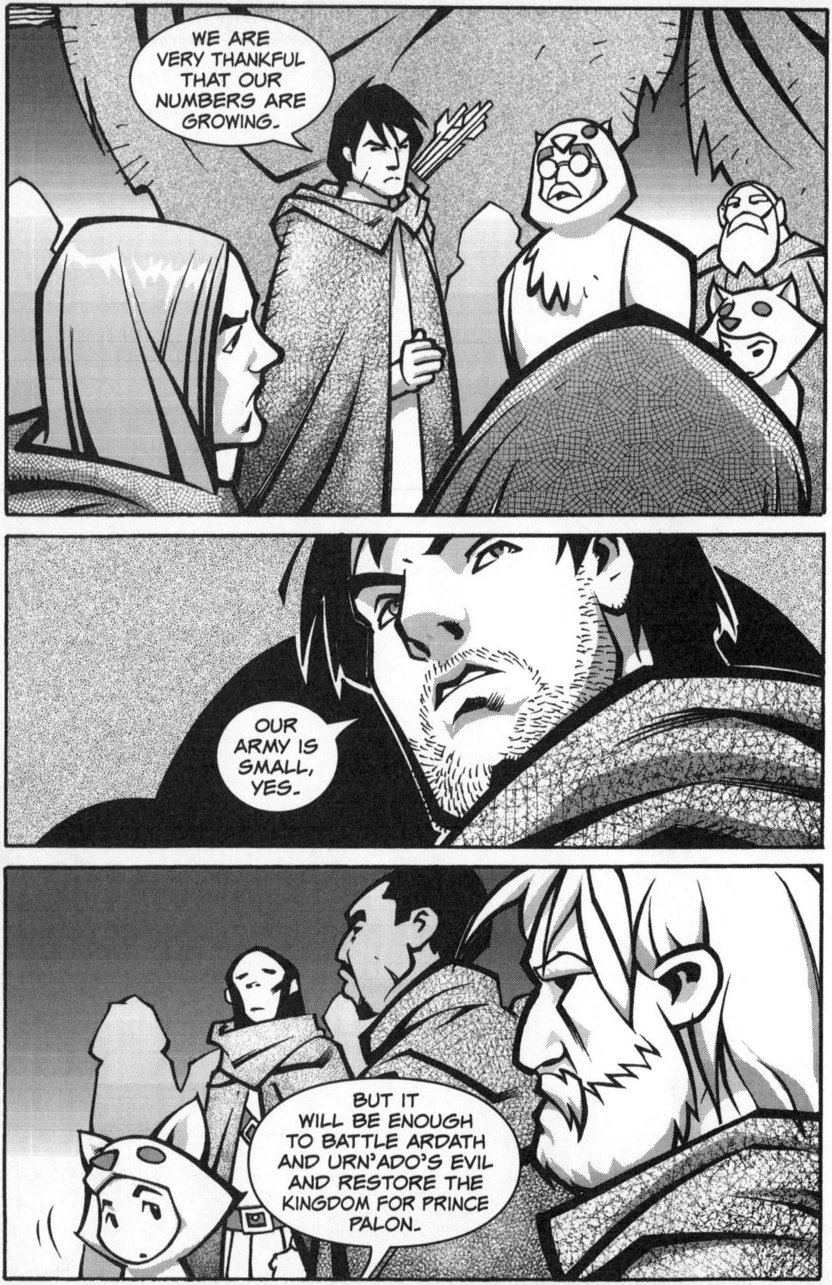
WE ARE VERY THANKFUL THAT OUR NUMBERS ARE GROWING.
OUR ARMY IS SMALL, YES.
BUT IT WILL BE ENOUGH TO BATTLE ARDATH AND URN'ADO'S EVIL AND RESTORE THE KINGDOM FOR PRINCE PALON.

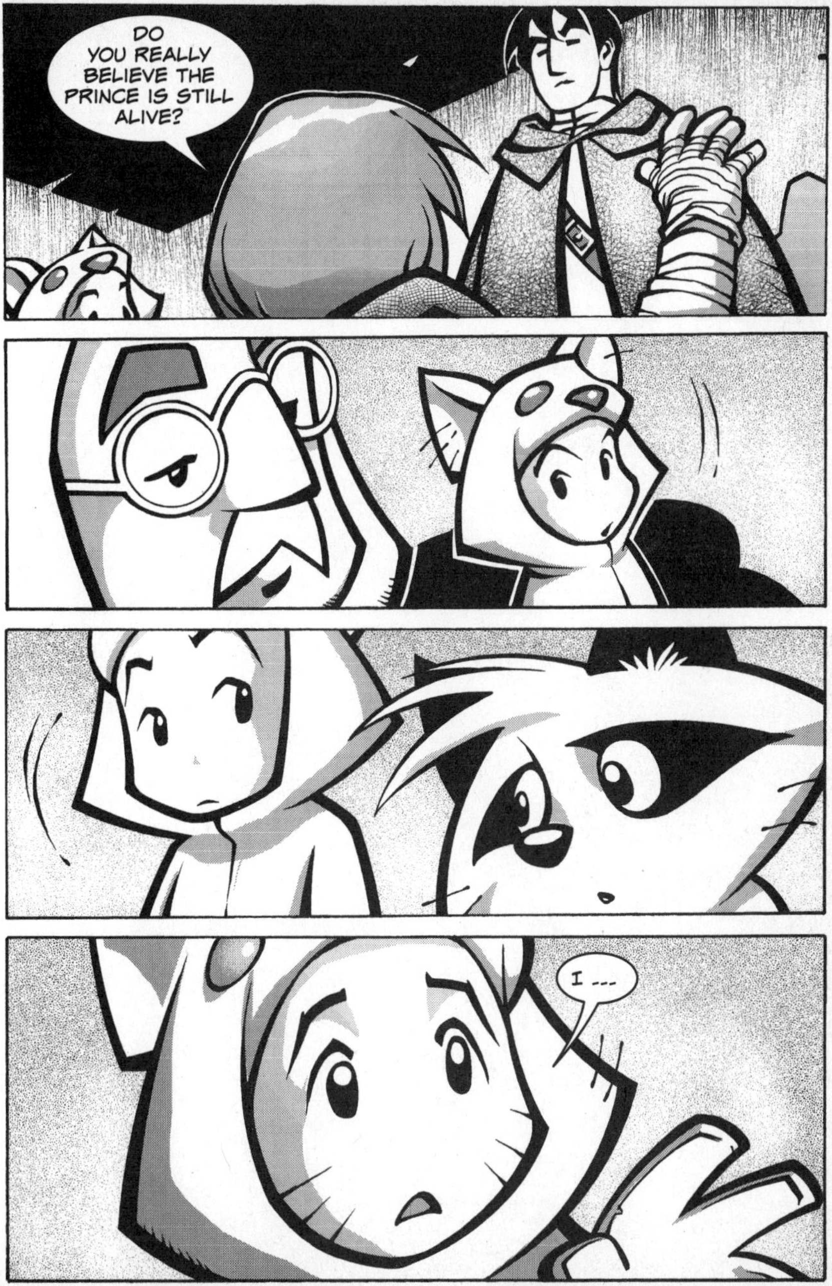
DO YOU REALLY BELIEVE THE PRINCE IS STILL ALIVE?
I ---

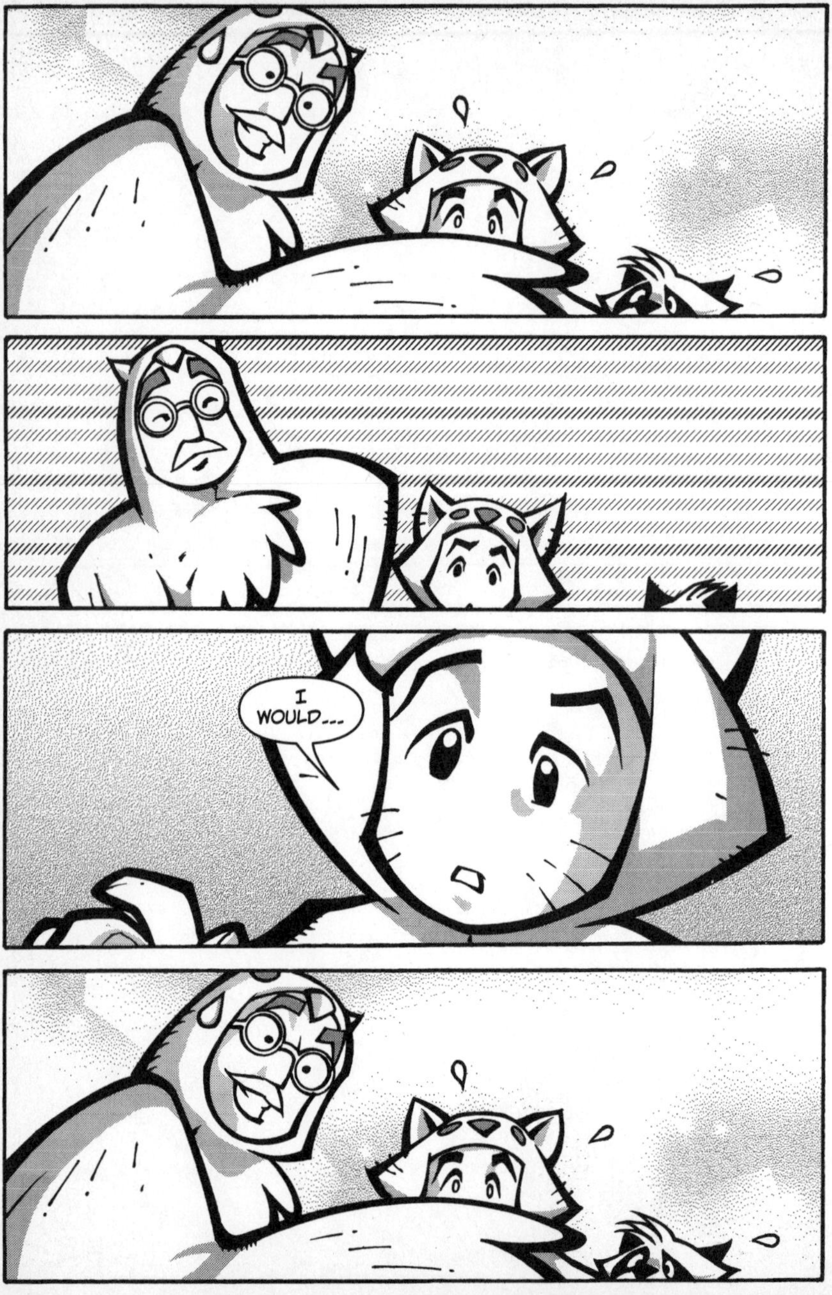
I WOULD...

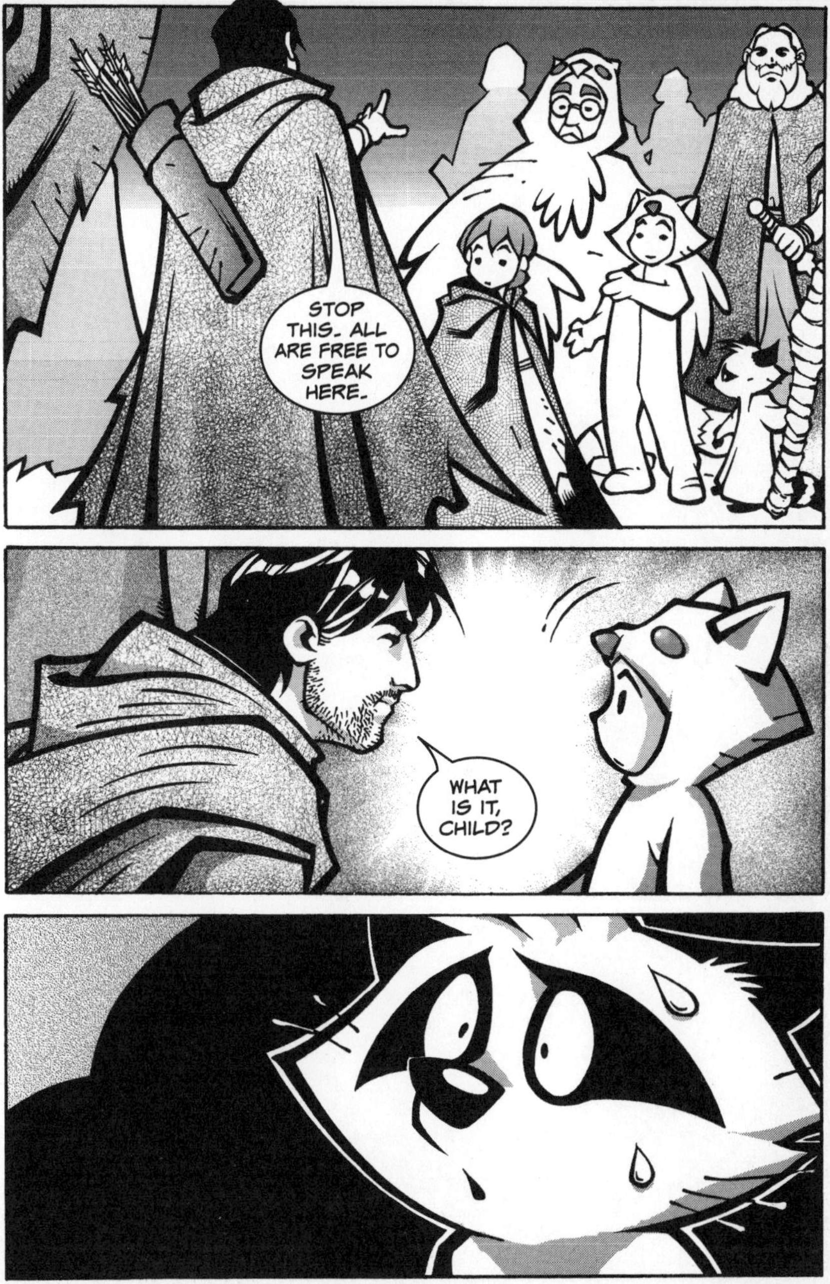
STOP THIS. ALL ARE FREE TO SPEAK HERE.
WHAT IS IT, CHILD?

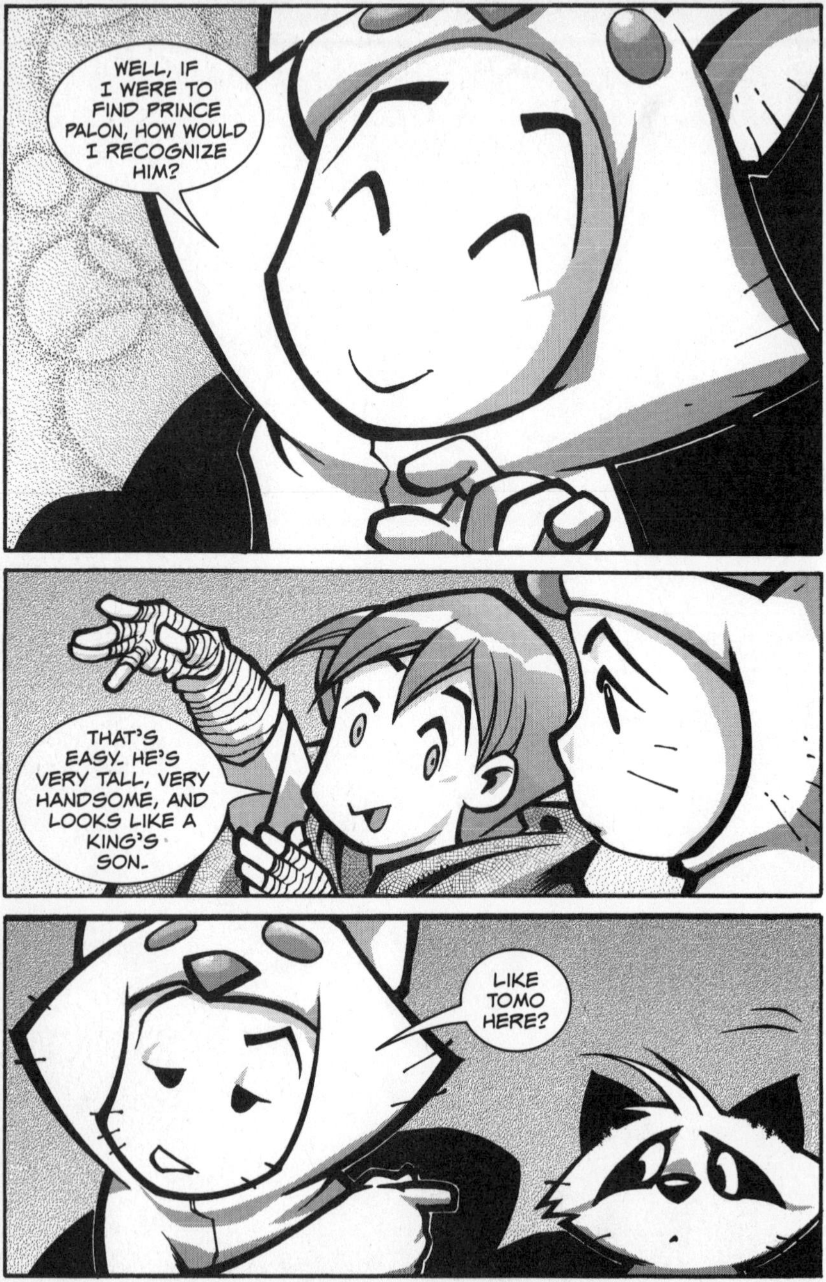
WELL, IF I WERE TO FIND PRINCE PALON, HOW WOULD I RECOGNIZE HIM?
THAT'S EASY. HE'S VERY TALL, VERY HANDSOME, AND LOOKS LIKE A KING'S SON.
LIKE TOMO HERE?

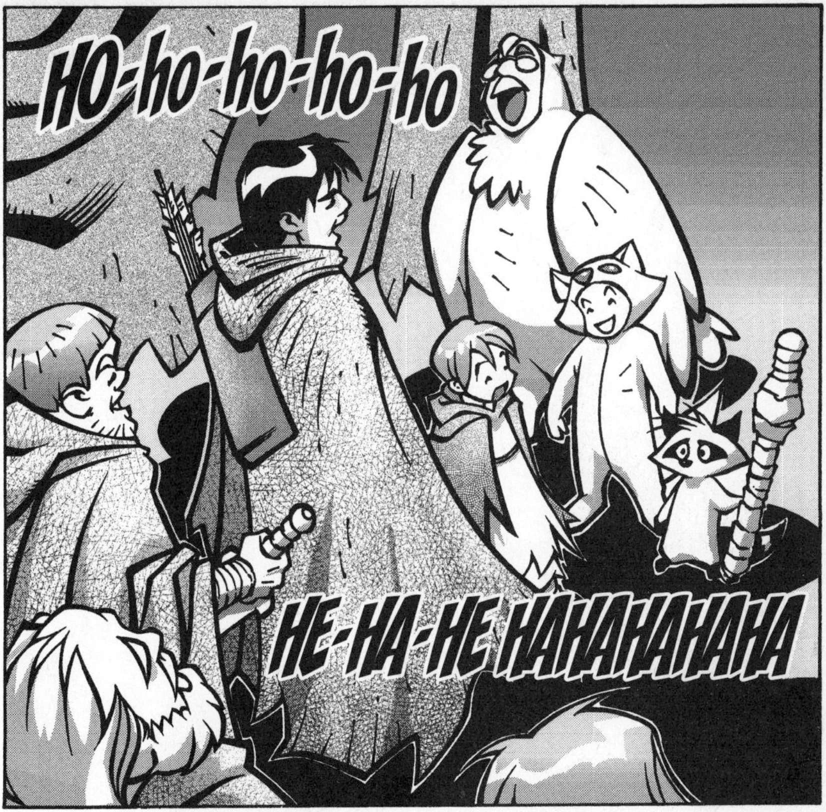
HO-ho-ho-ho-ho
HE-HA-HE HAHAHAHAHA

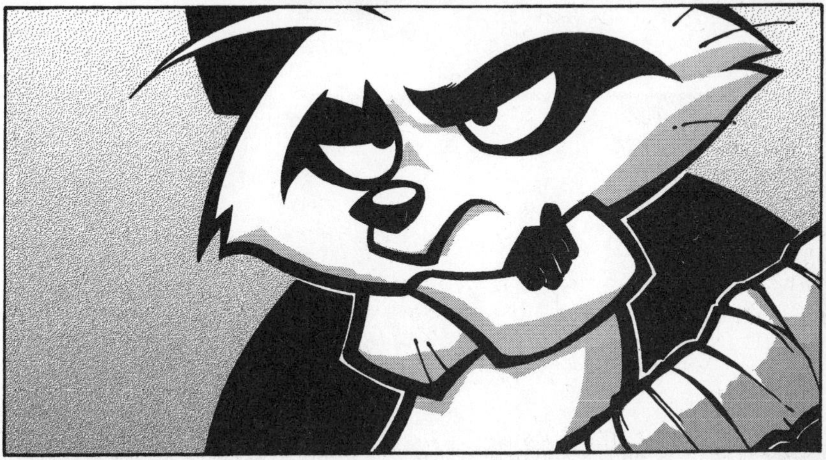

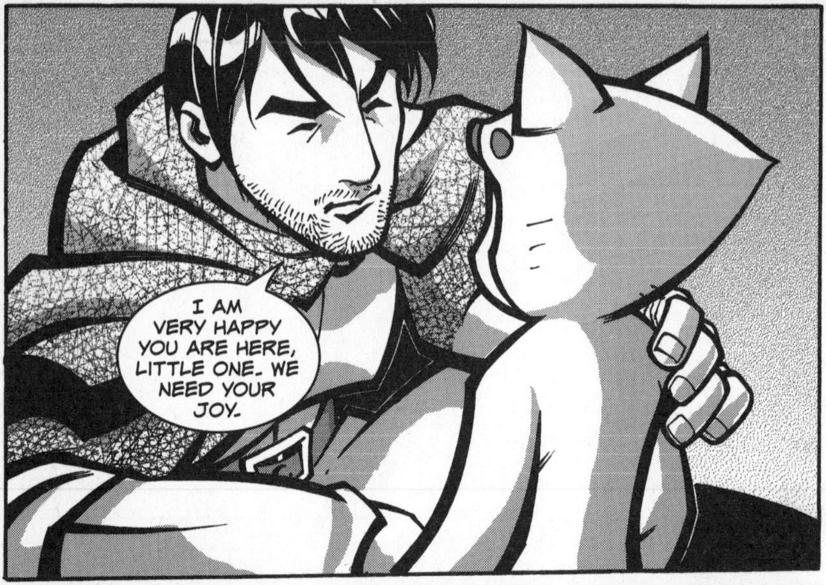
I AM VERY HAPPY YOU ARE HERE, LITTLE ONE. WE NEED YOUR JOY.
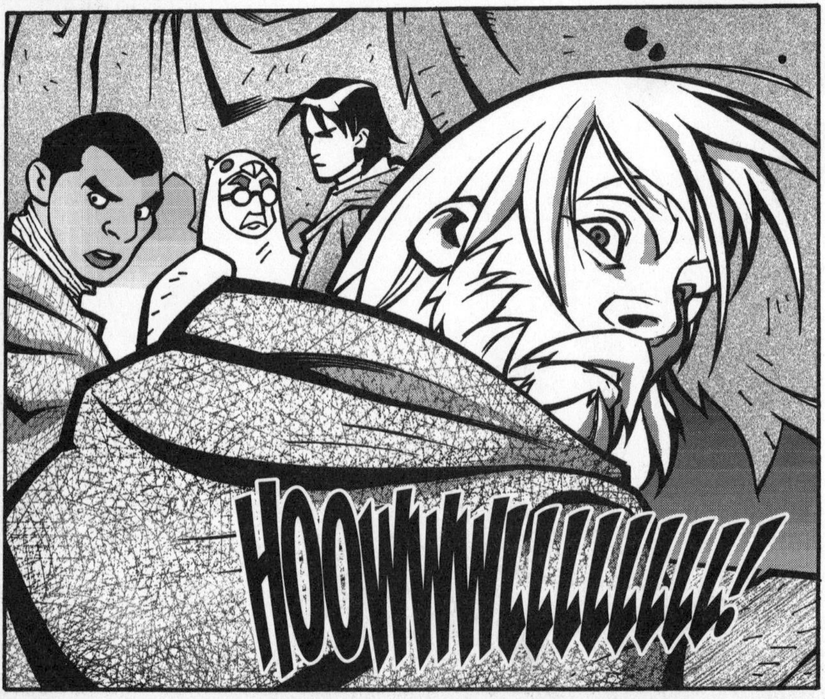
HOOWWWLLLLLLLLL!

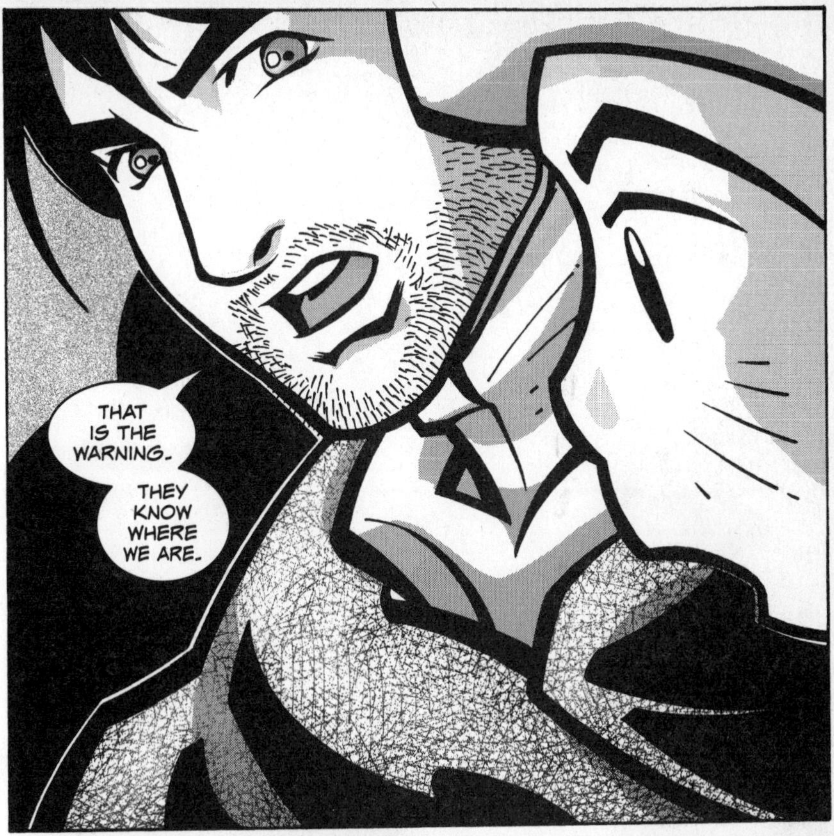
THAT IS THE WARNING.
THEY KNOW WHERE WE ARE.

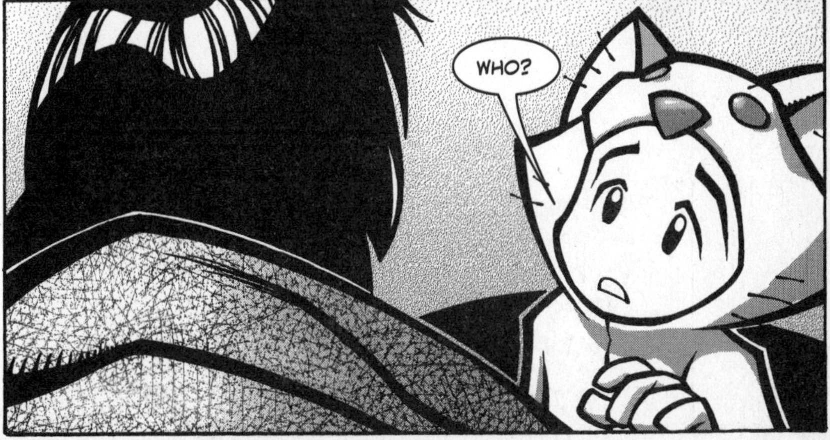
WHO?

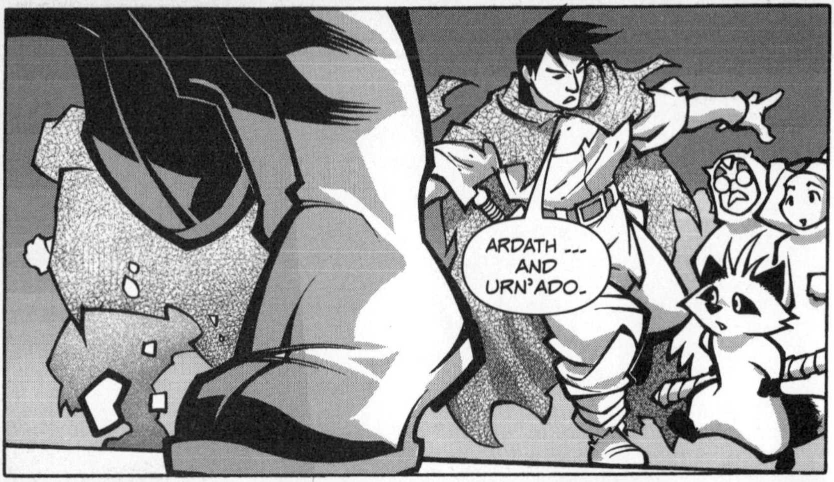
ARDATH ---
AND
URN'ADO.

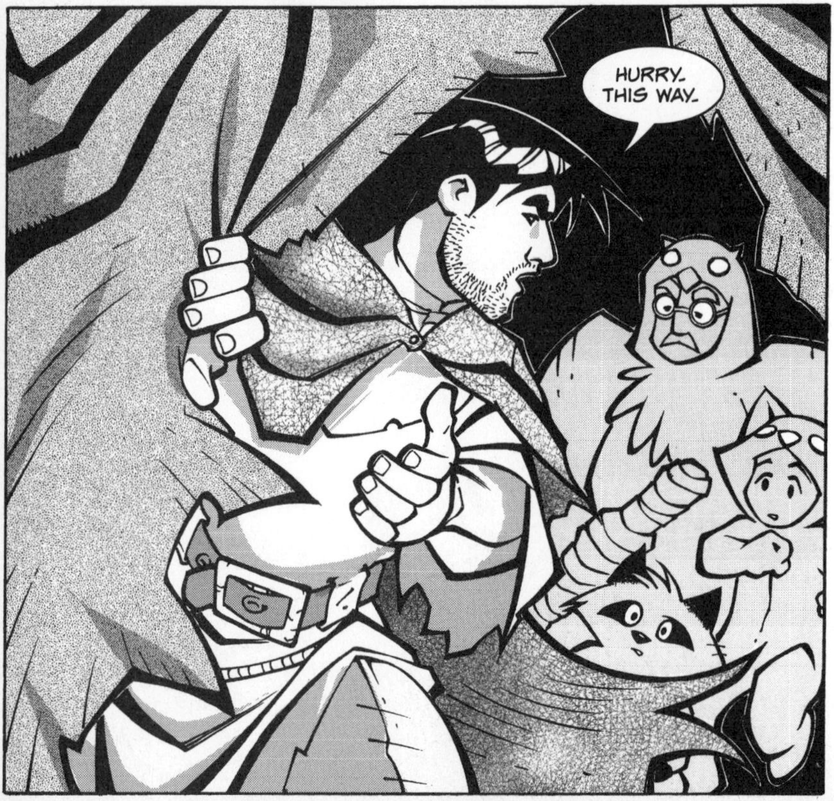
HURRY.
THIS WAY.

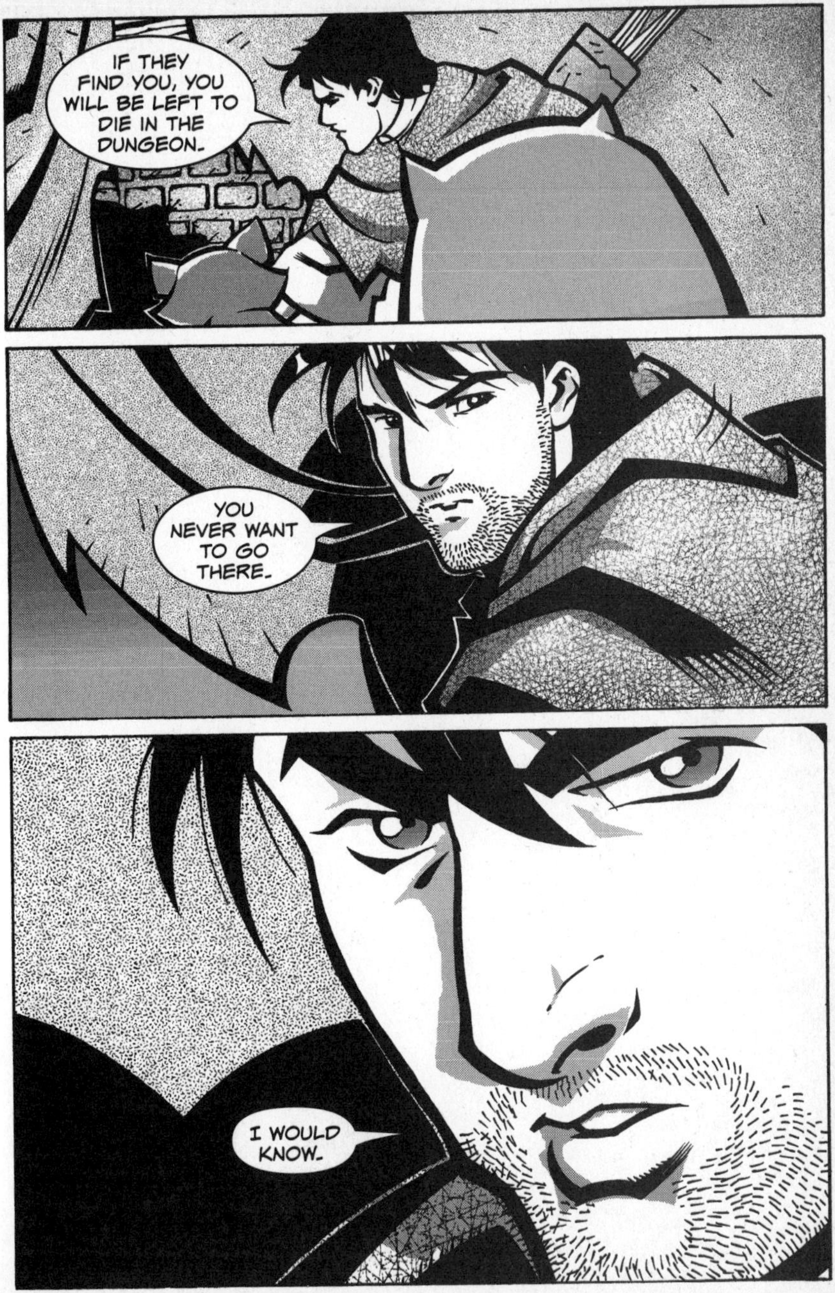
IF THEY FIND YOU, YOU WILL BE LEFT TO DIE IN THE DUNGEON.
YOU NEVER WANT TO GO THERE.
I WOULD KNOW.

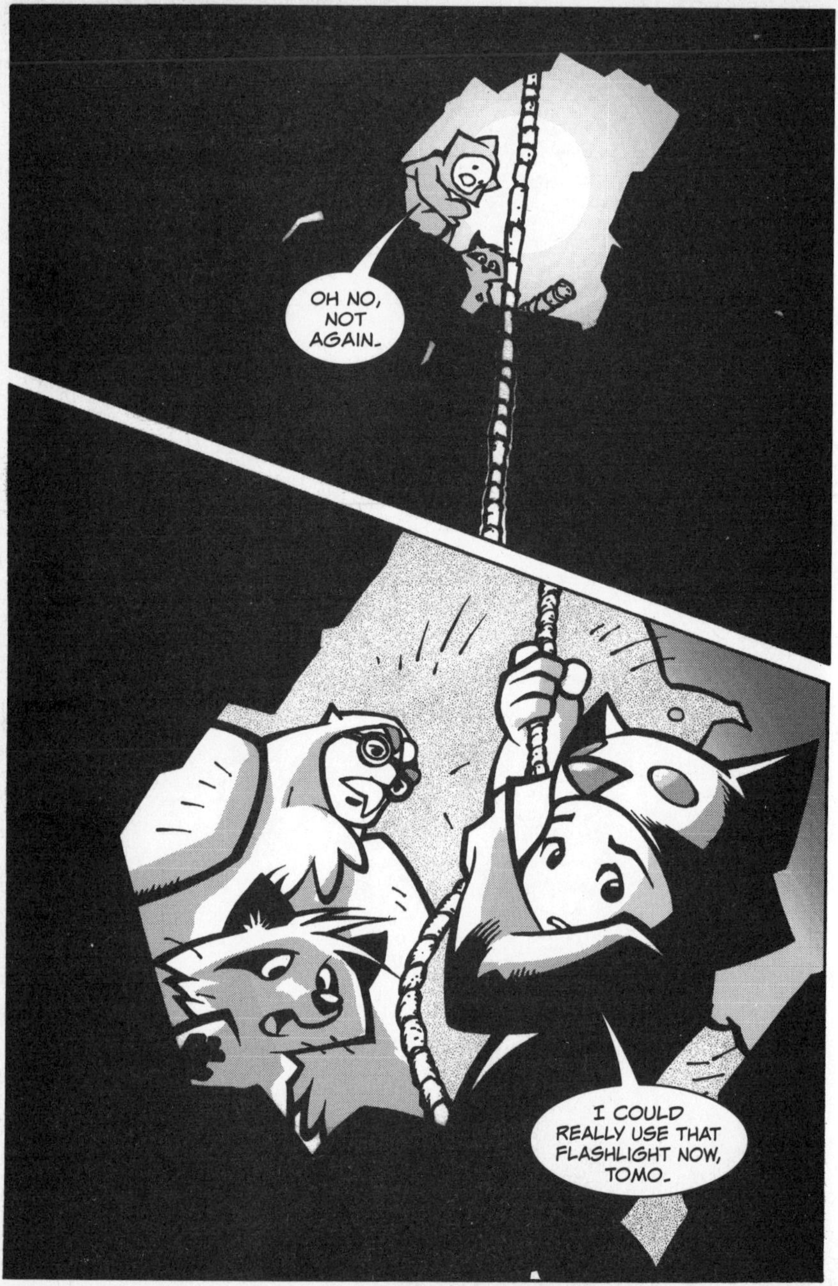
OH NO, NOT AGAIN.
I COULD REALLY USE THAT FLASHLIGHT NOW, TOMO.

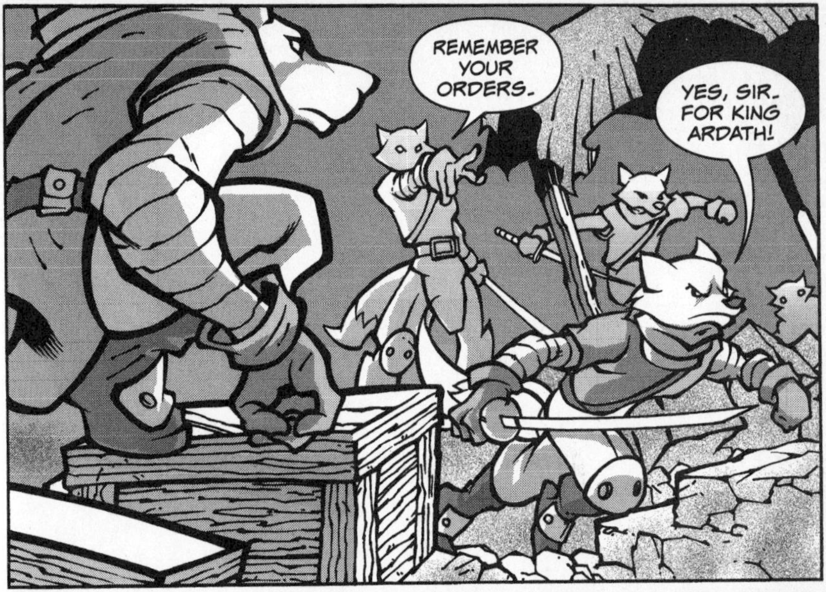
REMEMBER YOUR ORDERS.
YES, SIR. FOR KING ARDATH!
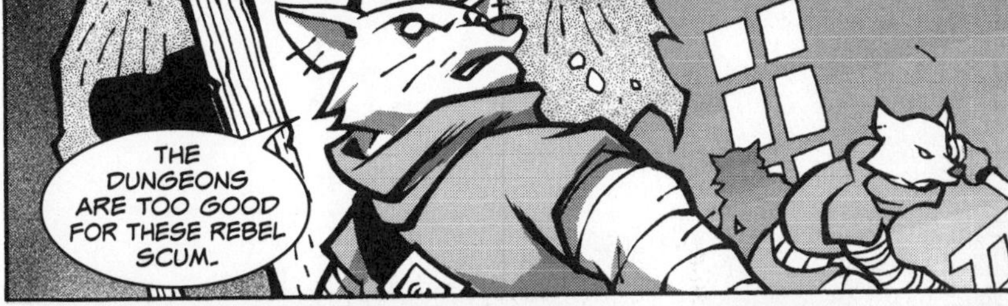
THE DUNGEONS ARE TOO GOOD FOR THESE REBEL SCUM.
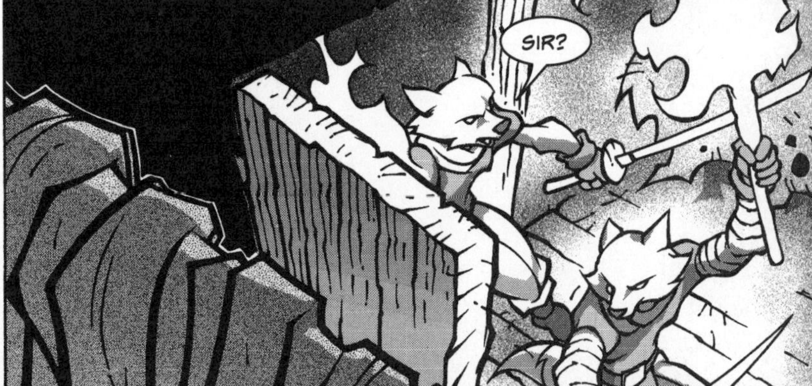
SIR?

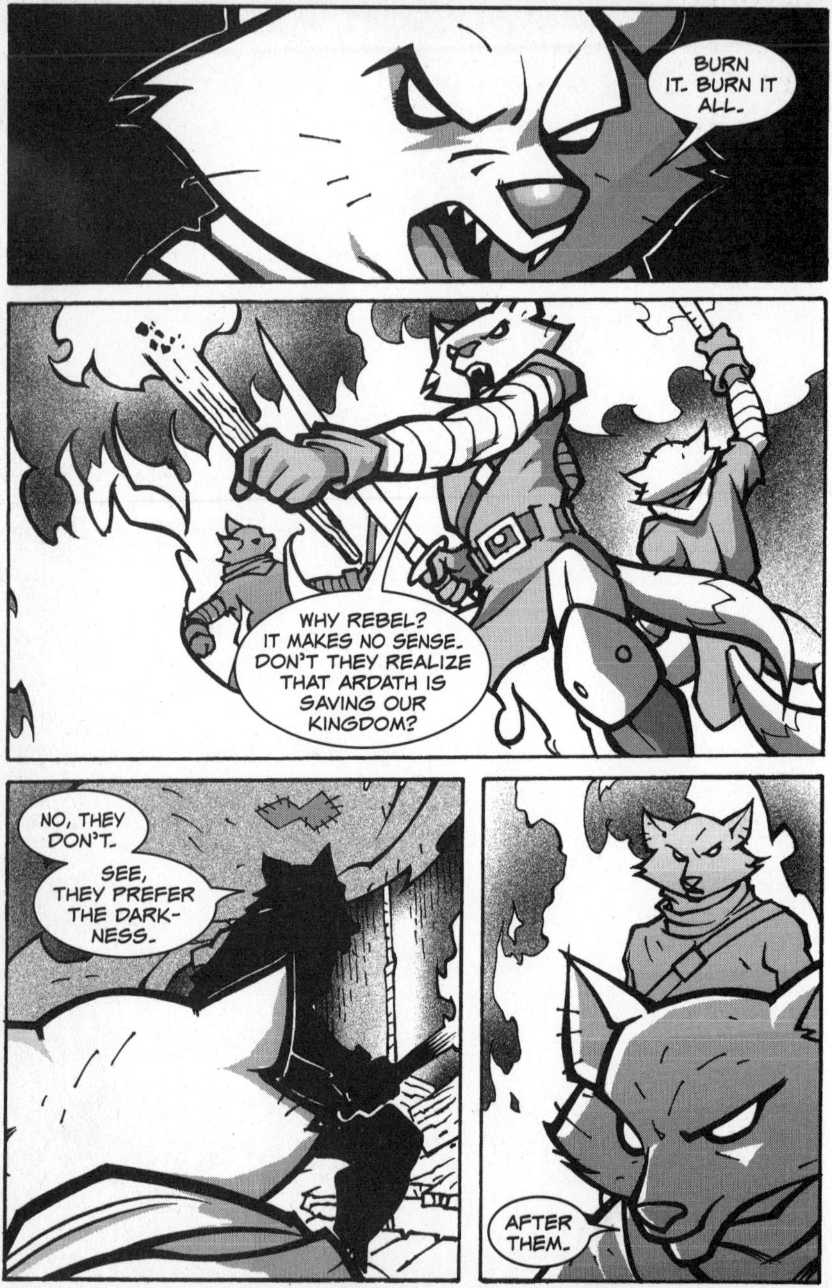
BURN IT. BURN IT ALL.
WHY REBEL? IT MAKES NO SENSE. DON'T THEY REALIZE THAT ARDATH IS SAVING OUR KINGDOM?
NO, THEY DON'T.
SEE, THEY PREFER THE DARK-NESS.
AFTER THEM.

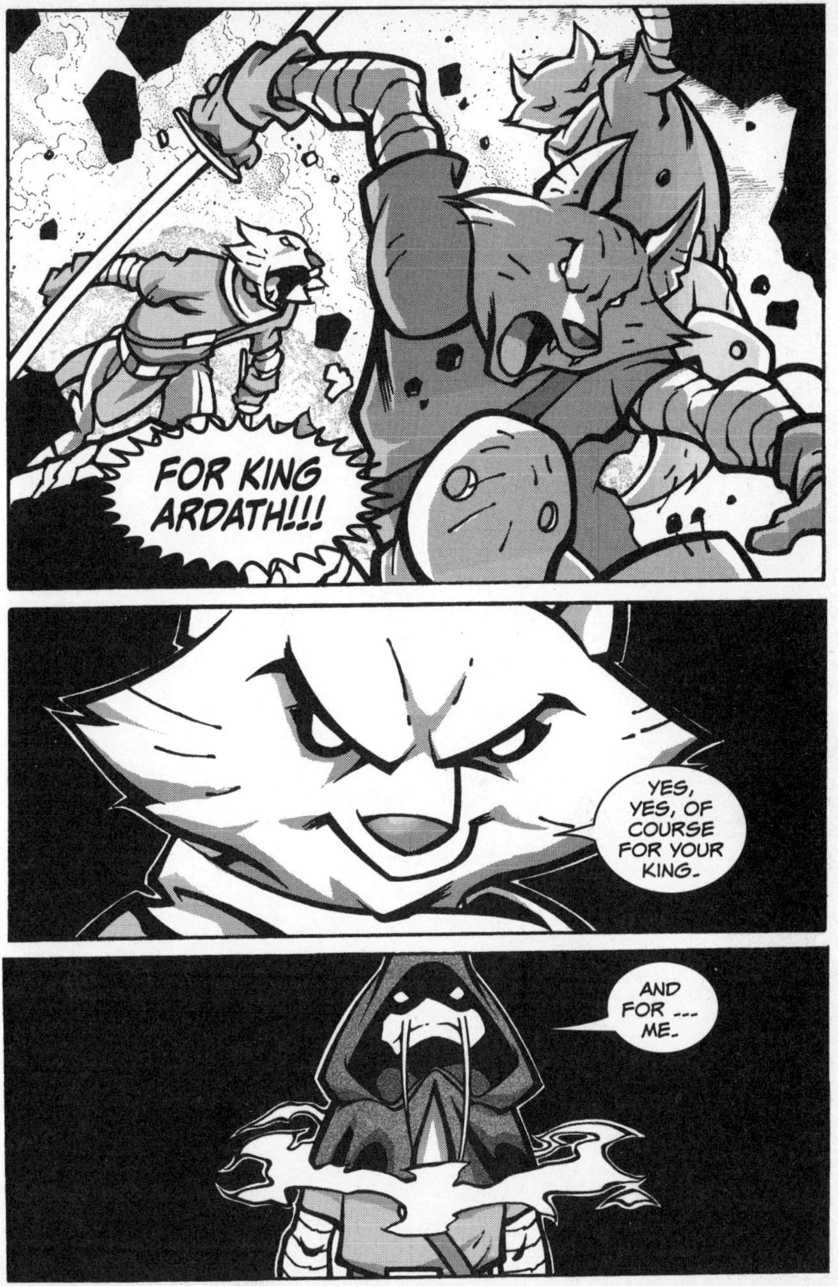
FOR KING ARDATH!!!
YES, YES, OF COURSE FOR YOUR KING.
AND FOR --- ME.

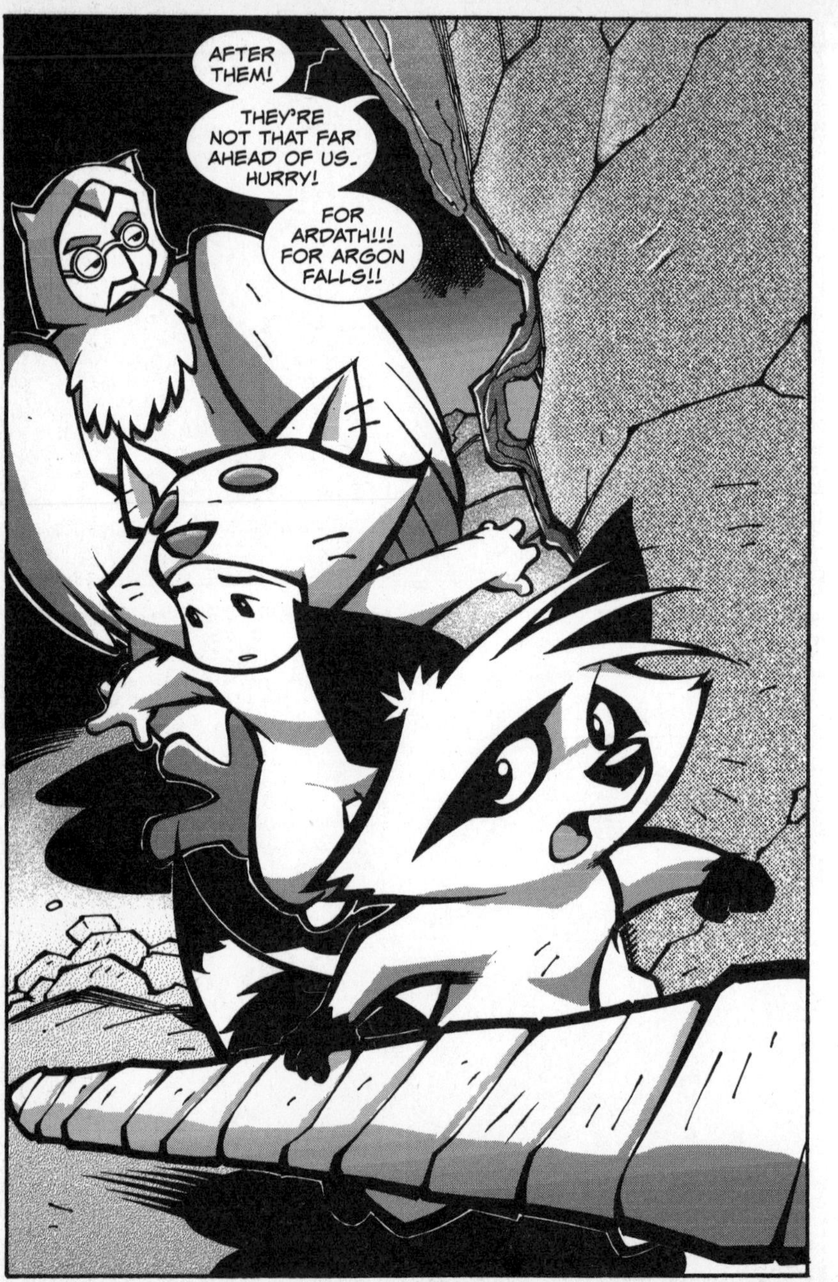
AFTER THEM!
THEY'RE NOT THAT FAR AHEAD OF US. HURRY!
FOR ARDATH!!! FOR ARGON FALLS!!

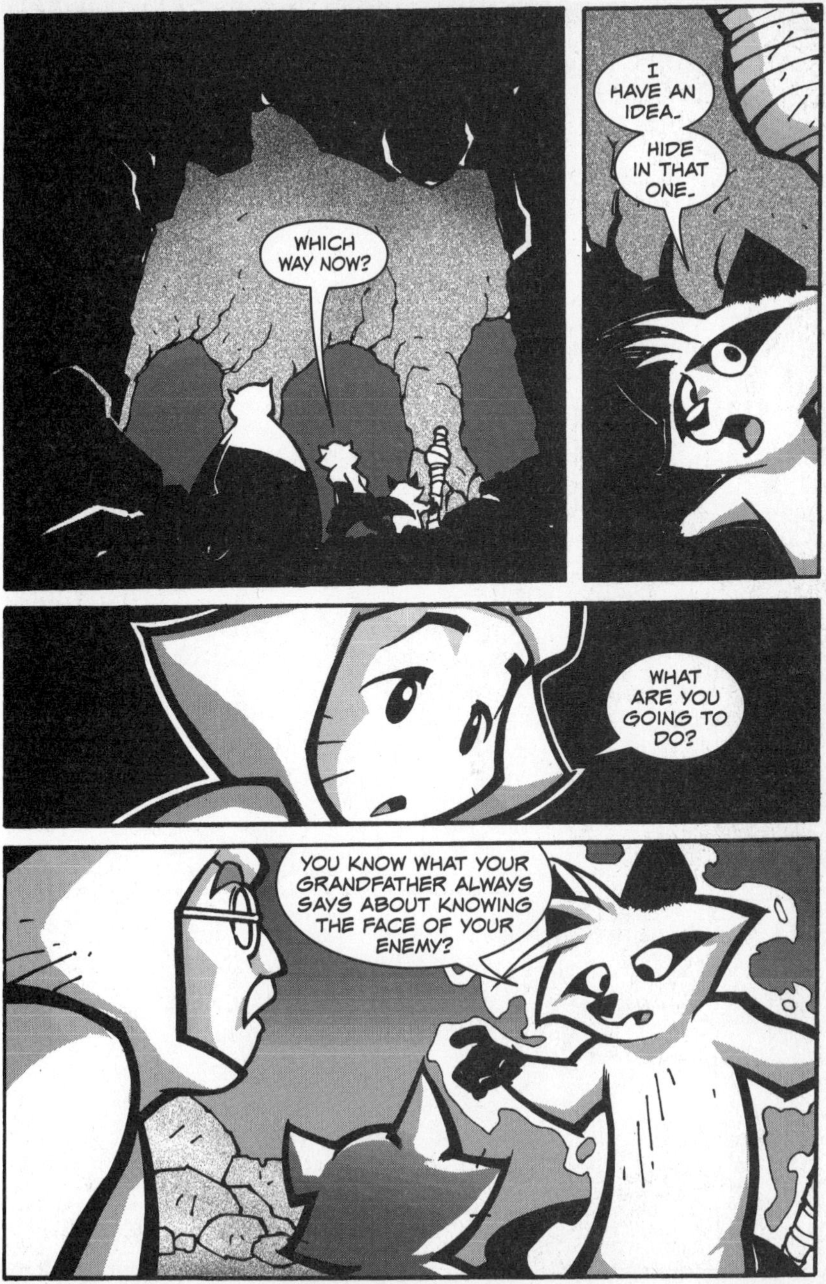
WHICH WAY NOW?
I HAVE AN IDEA.
HIDE IN THAT ONE.
WHAT ARE YOU GOING TO DO?
YOU KNOW WHAT YOUR GRANDFATHER ALWAYS SAYS ABOUT KNOWING THE FACE OF YOUR ENEMY?

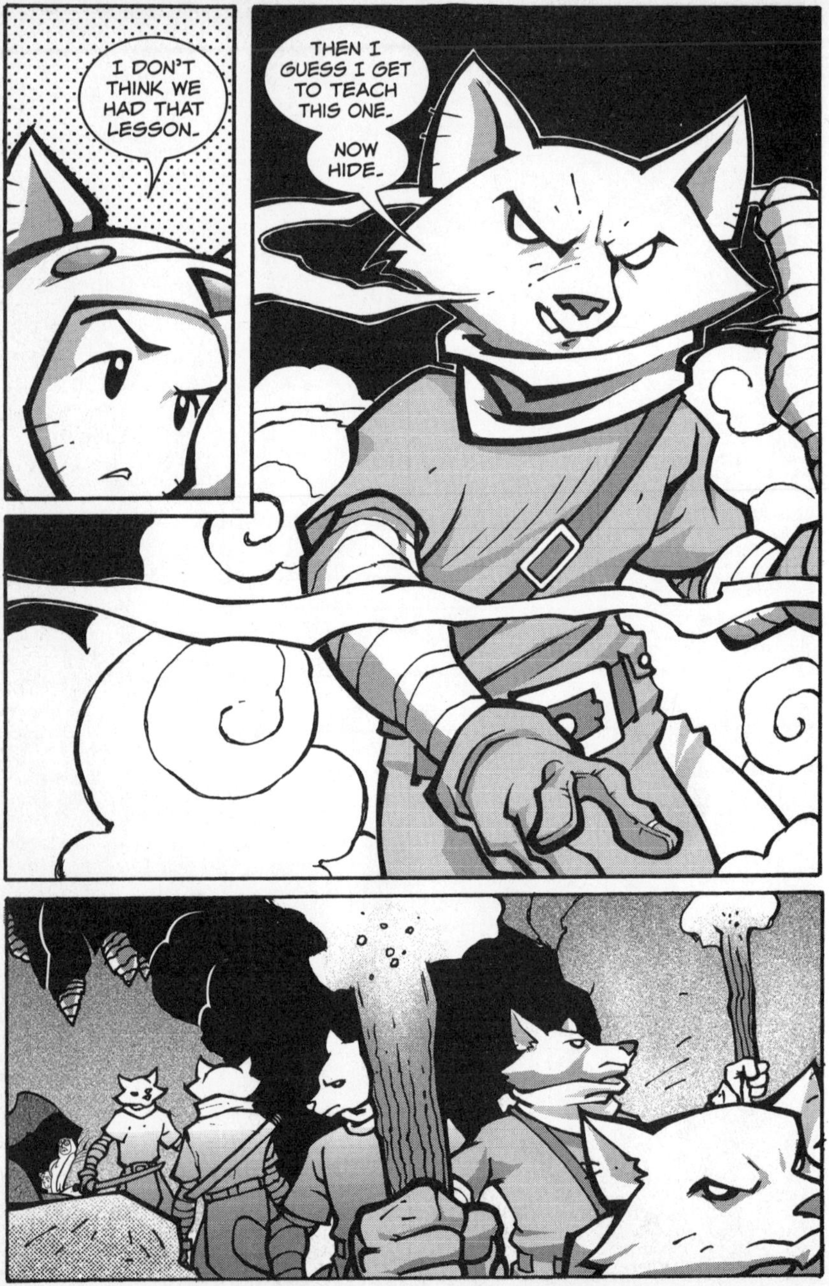
I DON'T THINK WE HAD THAT LESSON.
THEN I GUESS I GET TO TEACH THIS ONE.
NOW HIDE.

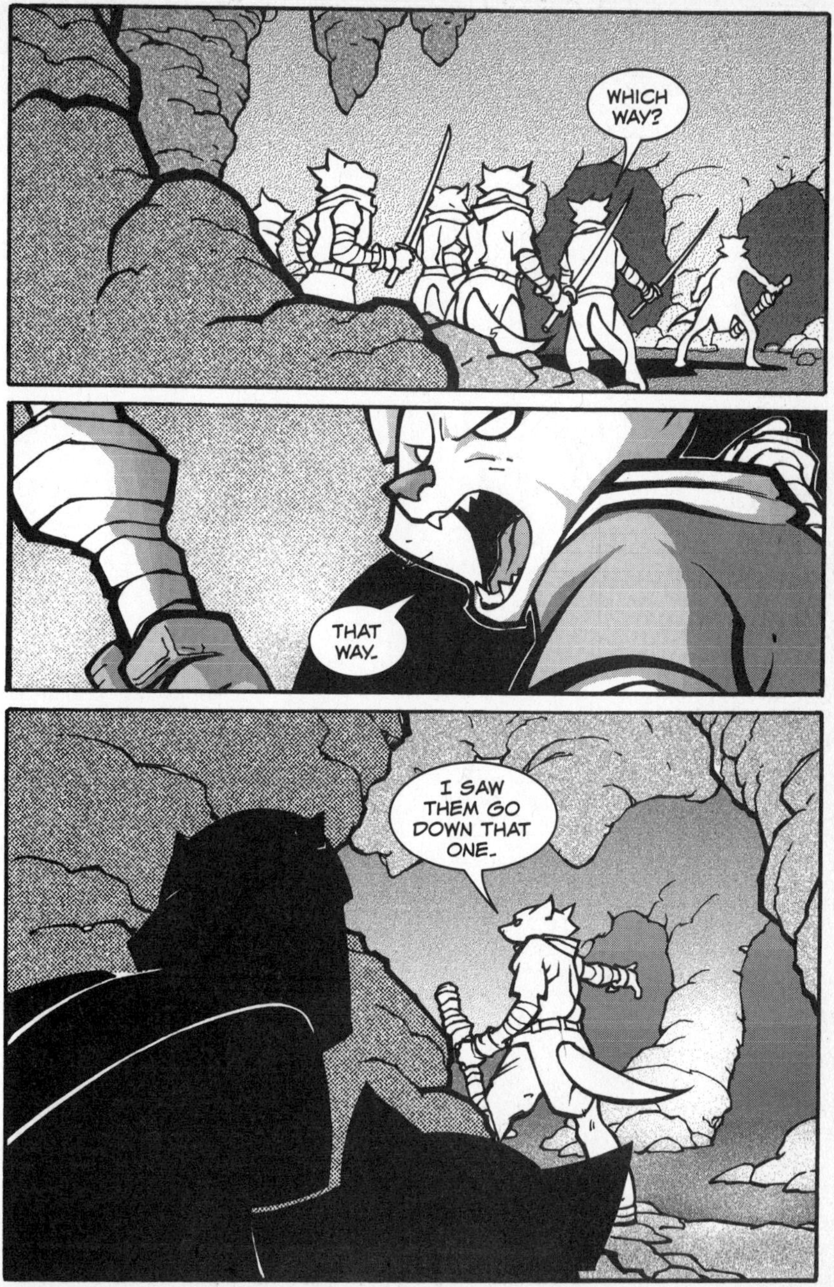
WHICH WAY?
THAT WAY.
I SAW THEM GO DOWN THAT ONE.

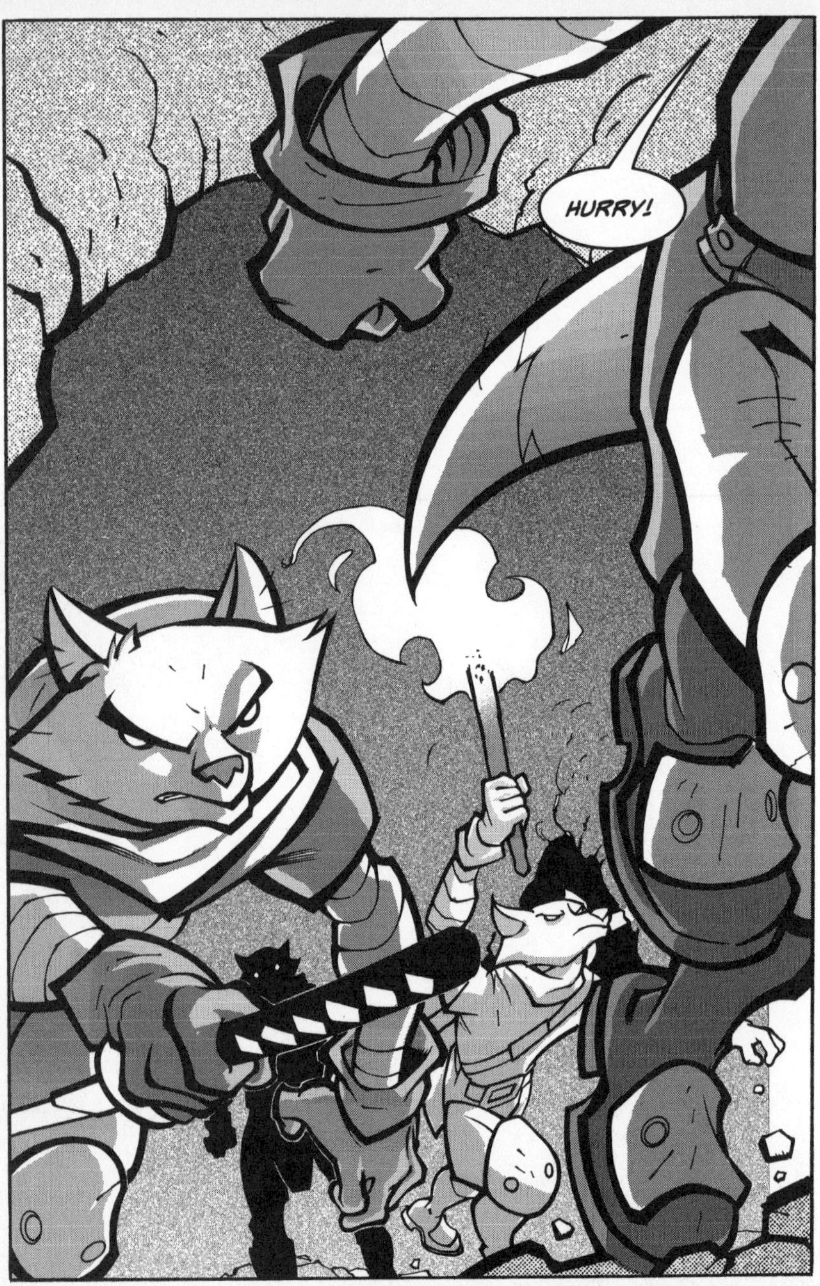
HURRY!

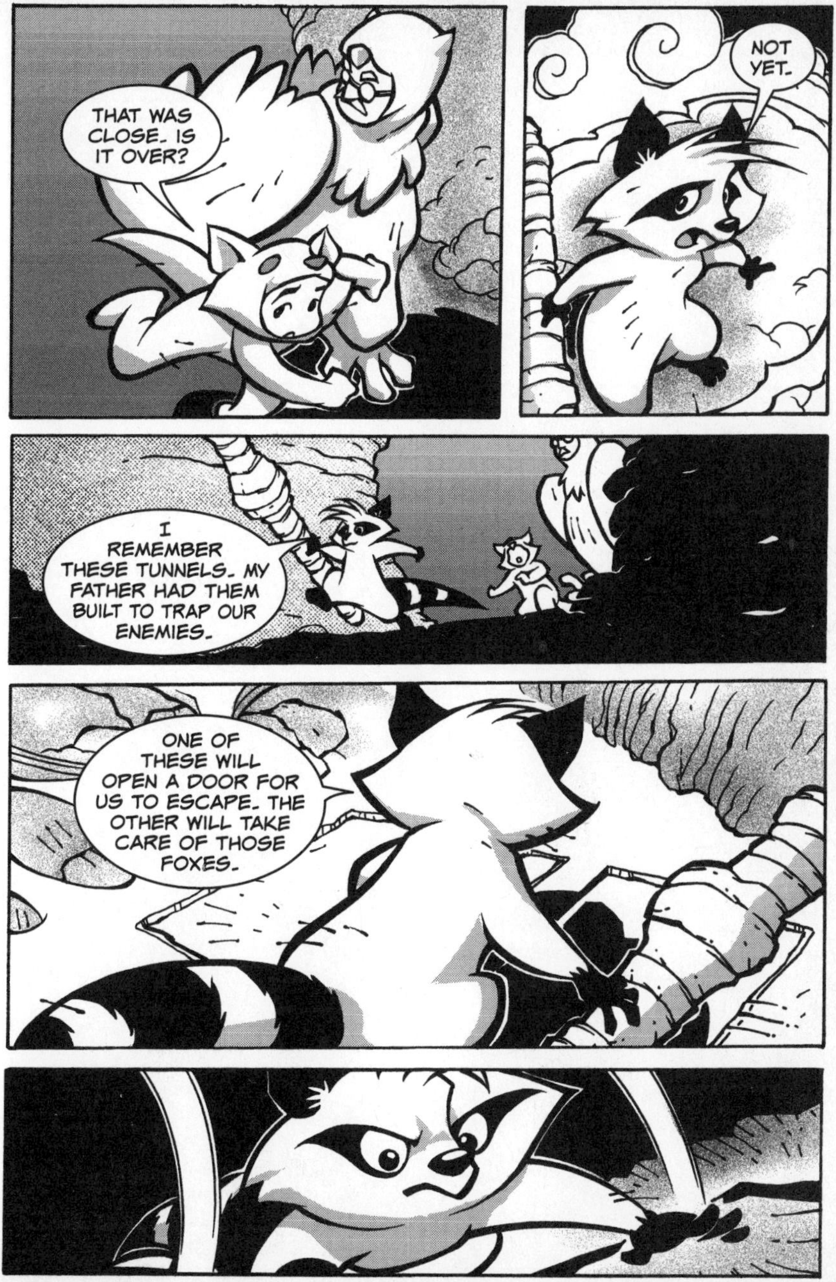
THAT WAS CLOSE. IS IT OVER?
NOT YET.
I REMEMBER THESE TUNNELS. MY FATHER HAD THEM BUILT TO TRAP OUR ENEMIES.
ONE OF THESE WILL OPEN A DOOR FOR US TO ESCAPE. THE OTHER WILL TAKE CARE OF THOSE FOXES.

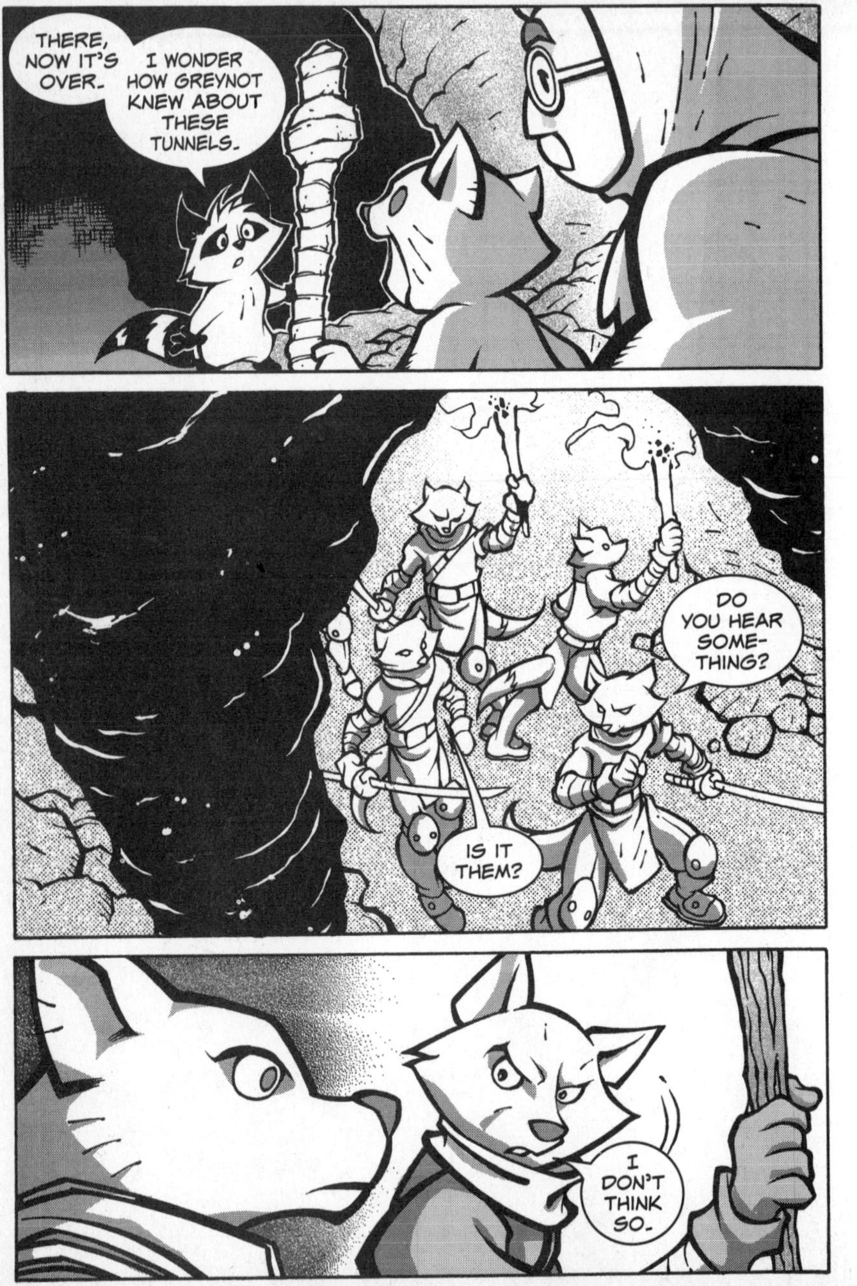
THERE, NOW IT'S OVER.
I WONDER HOW GREYNOT KNEW ABOUT THESE TUNNELS.
DO YOU HEAR SOME-THING?
IS IT THEM?
I DON'T THINK SO.

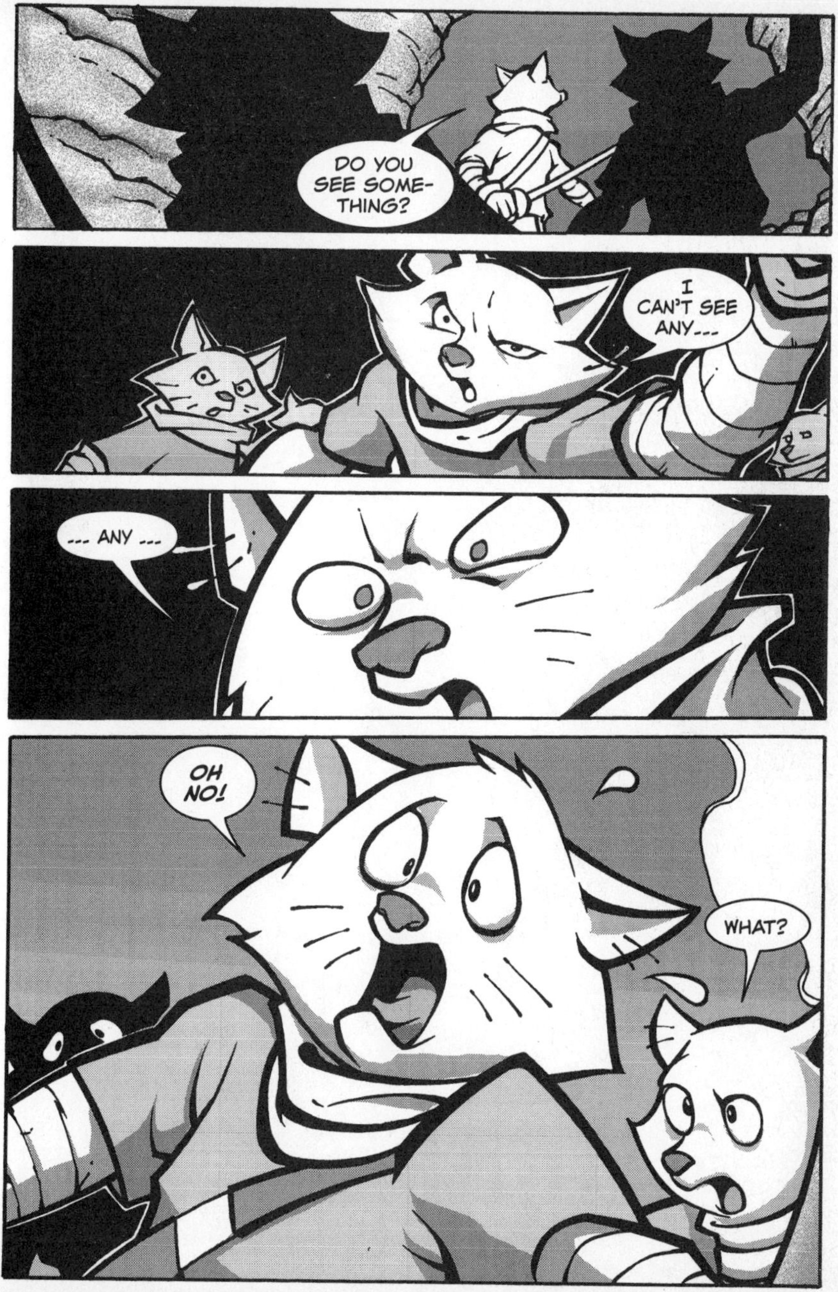
DO YOU SEE SOME-THING?
I CAN'T SEE ANY---
--- ANY ---
OH NO!
WHAT?

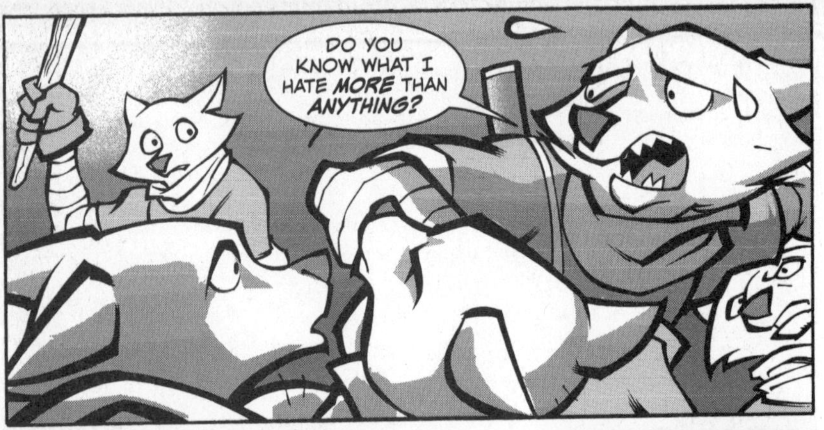
DO YOU KNOW WHAT I HATE MORE THAN ANYTHING?
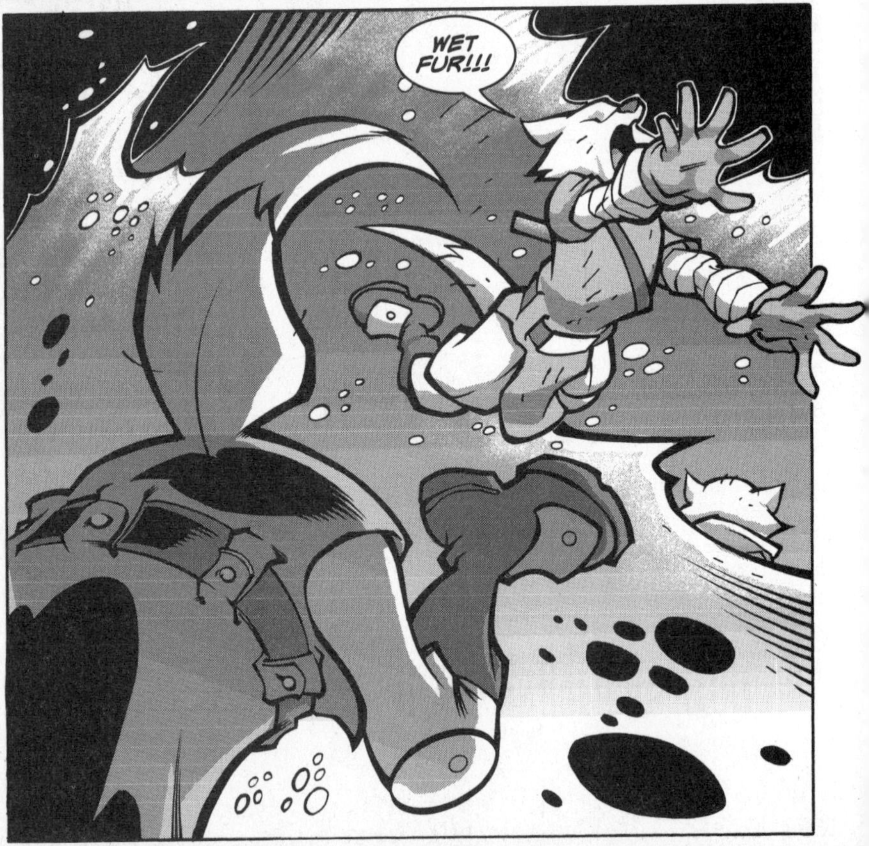
WET FUR!!!

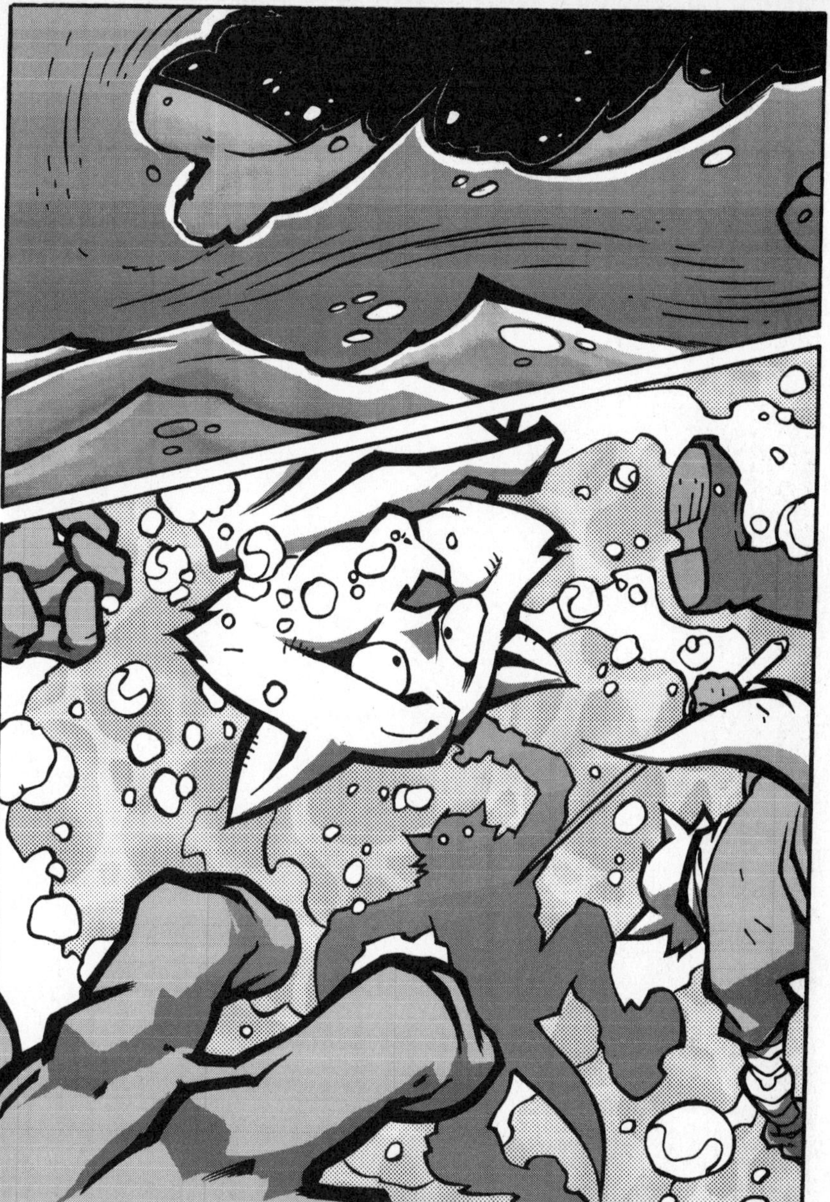

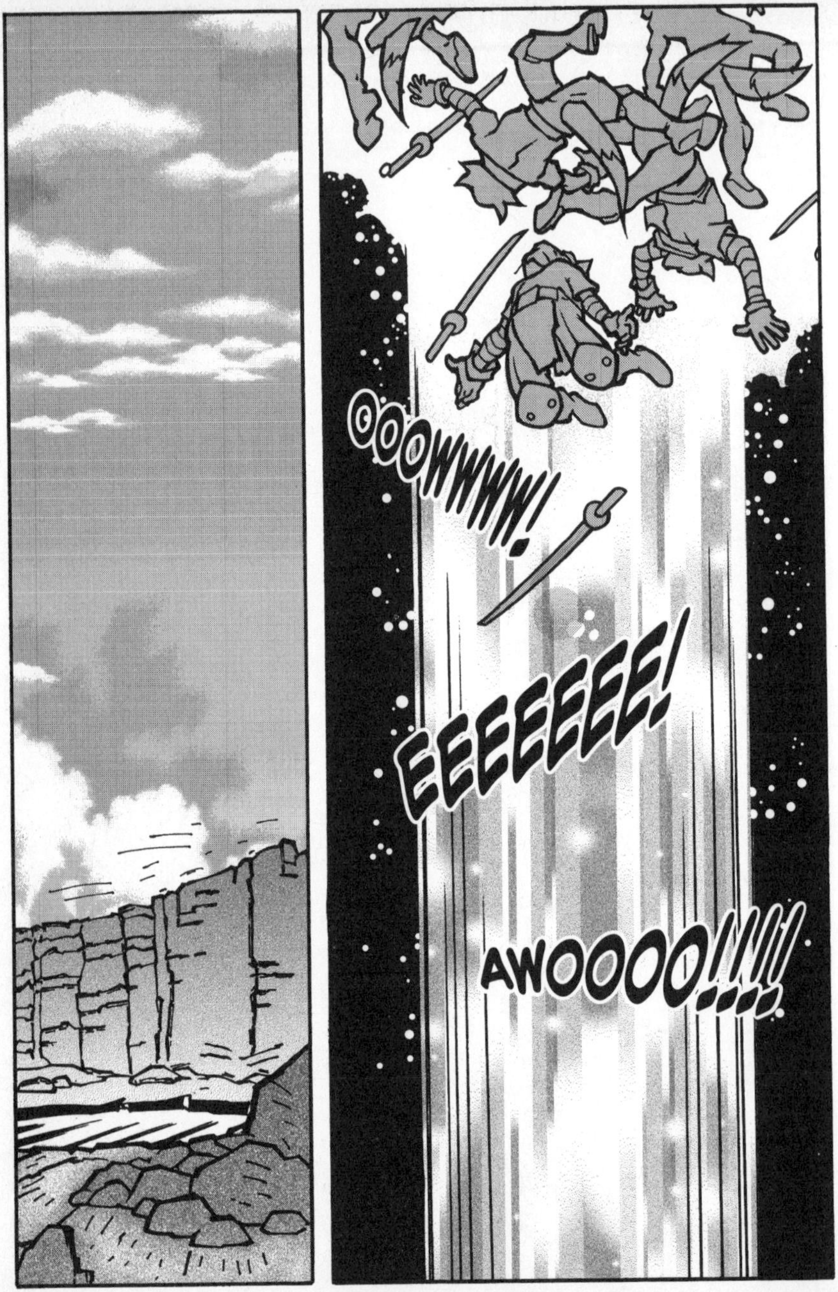
OOOWWWWW!
EEEEEEE!
AWOOOO!!!!

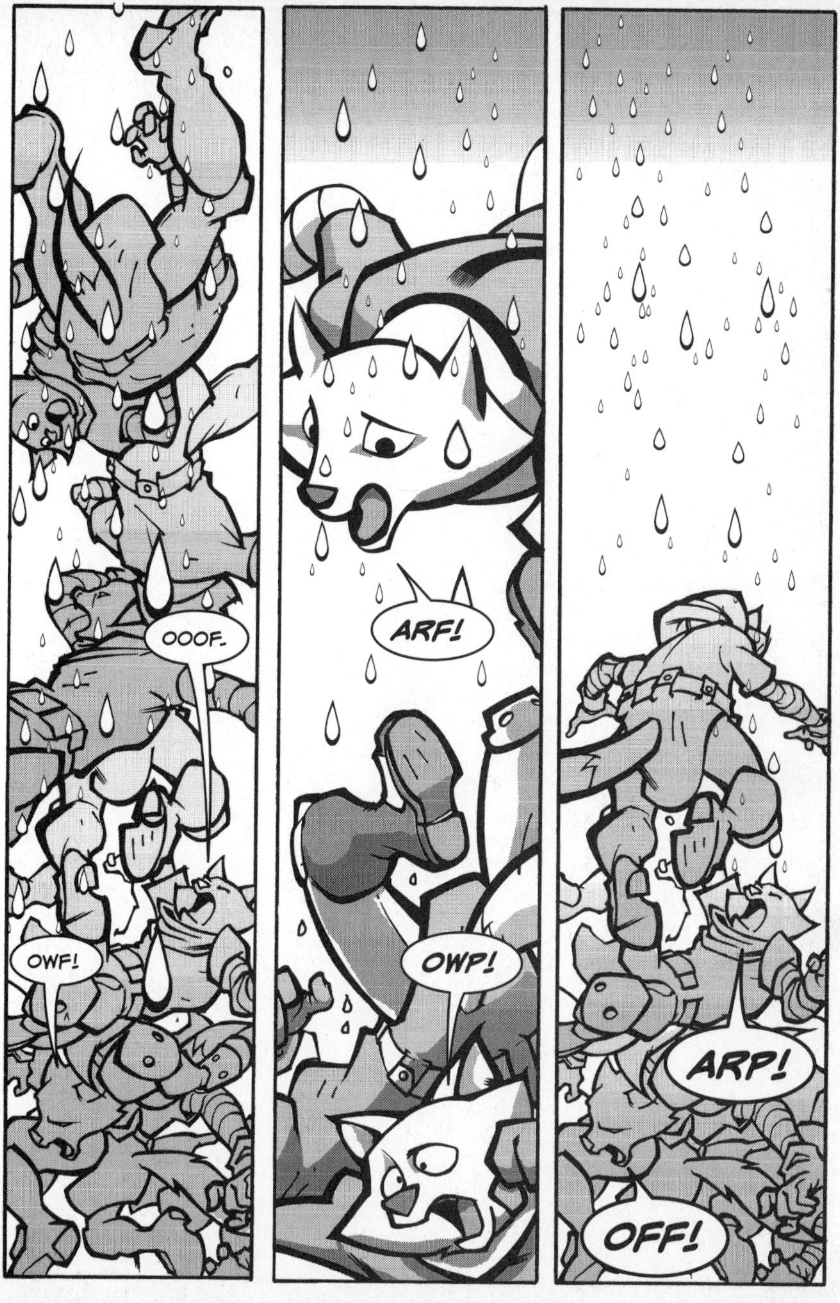
OOOF.
OWF!
ARF!
OWP!
ARP!
OFF!

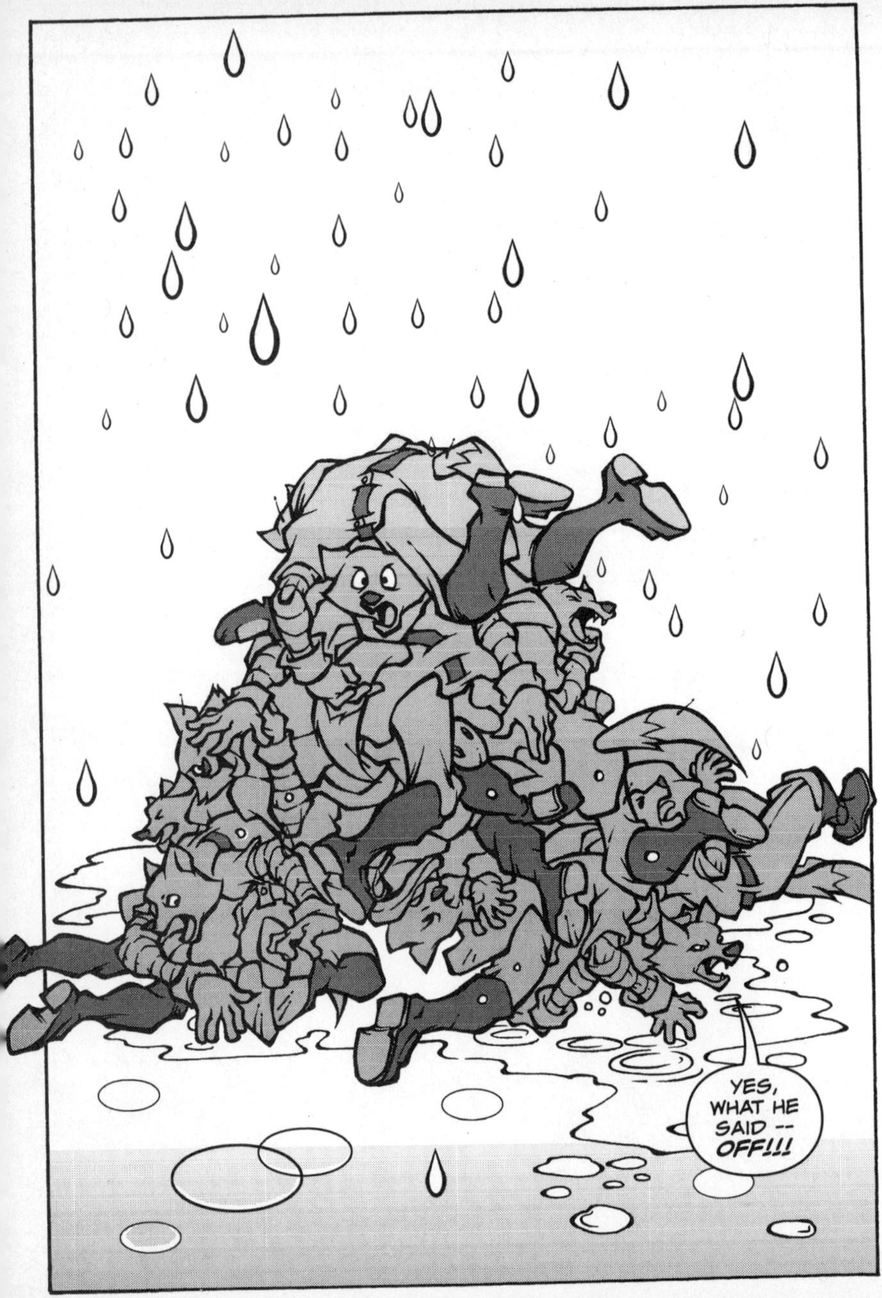
YES, WHAT HE SAID -- OFF!!!

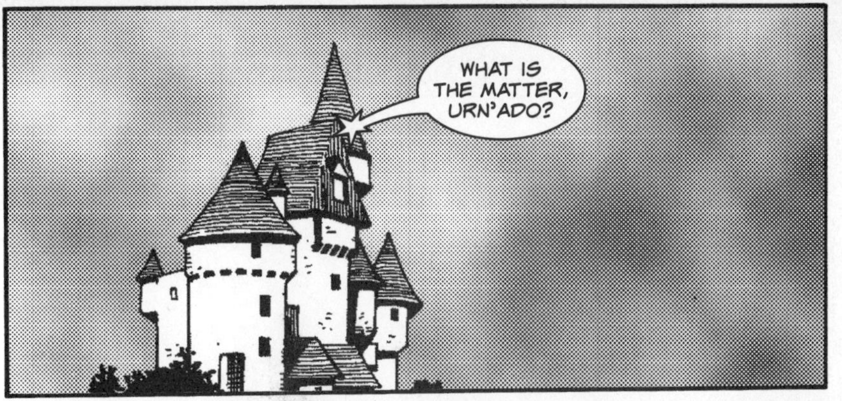
WHAT IS THE MATTER, URN'ADO?

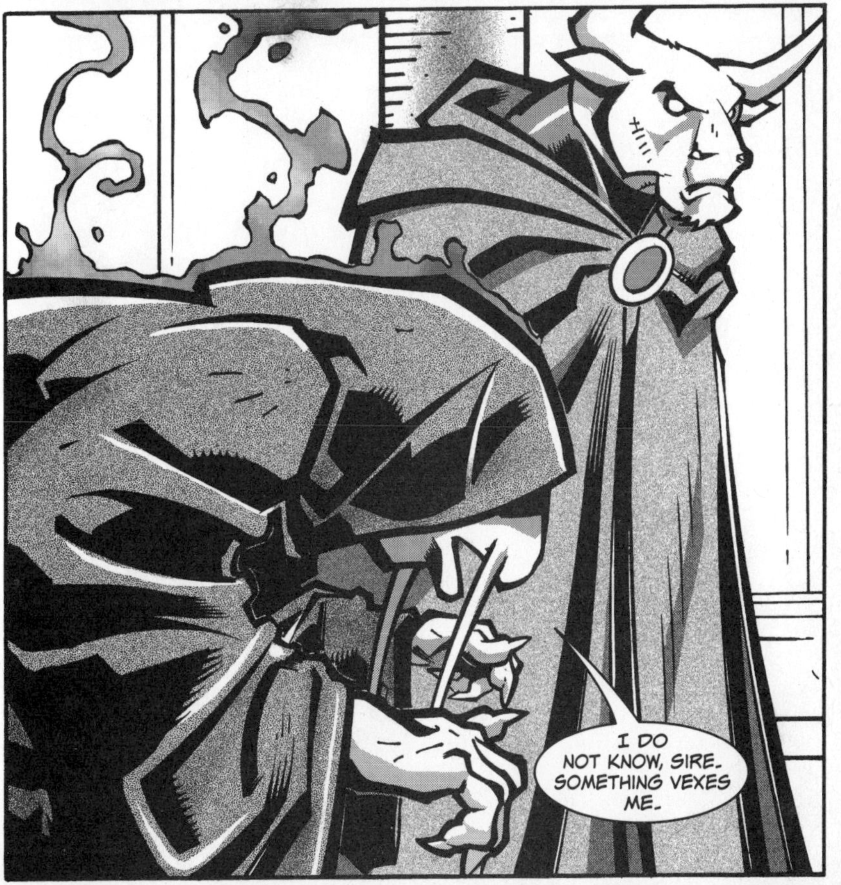
I DO NOT KNOW, SIRE. SOMETHING VEXES ME.

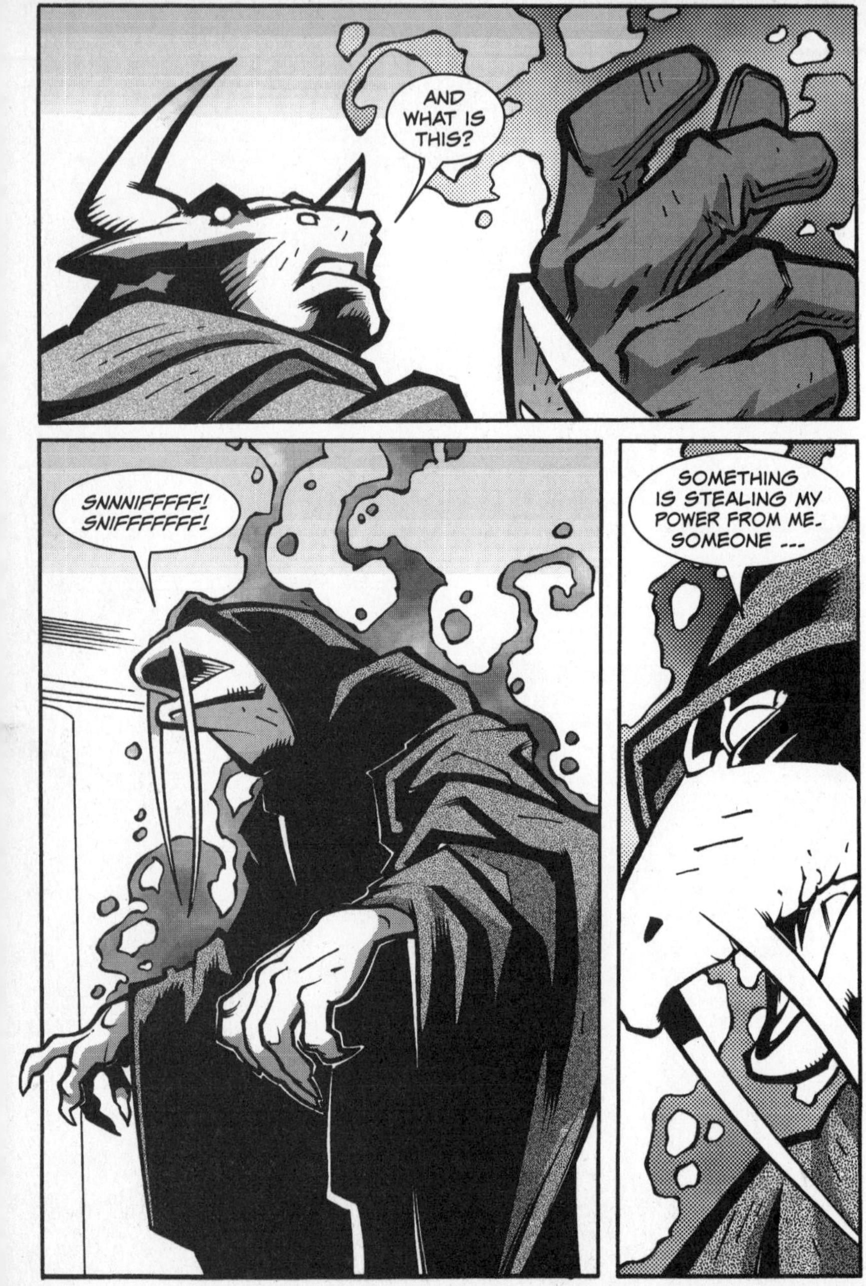
AND WHAT IS THIS?
SNNIFFFFF! SNIFFFFFFF!
SOMETHING IS STEALING MY POWER FROM ME. SOMEONE ---

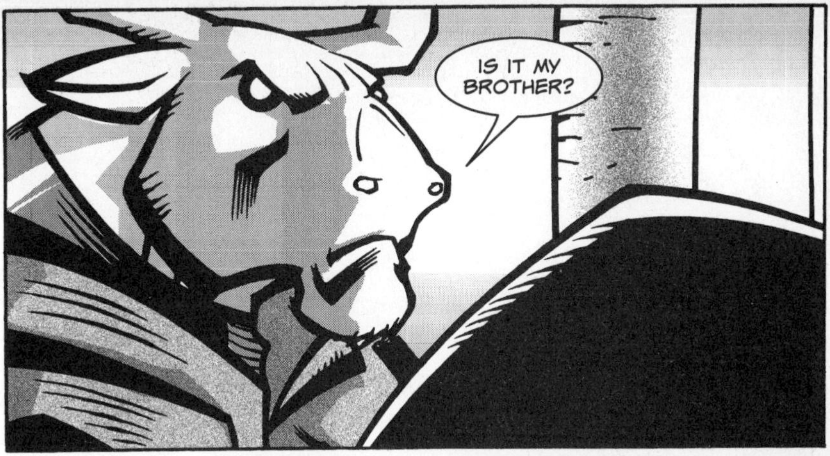
IS IT MY BROTHER?
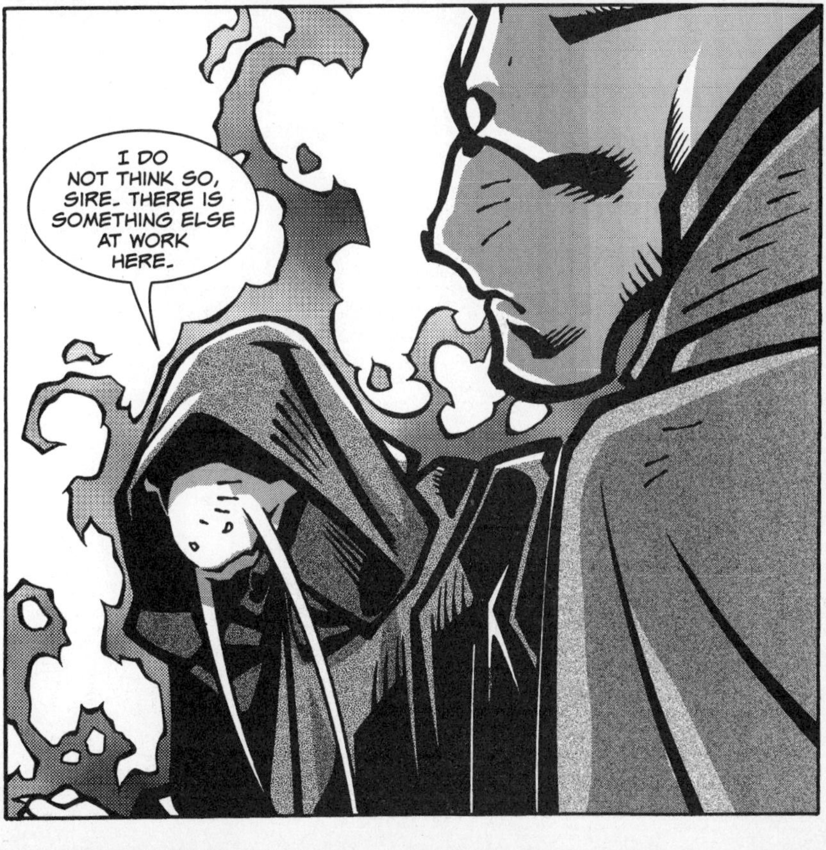
I DO NOT THINK SO, SIRE. THERE IS SOMETHING ELSE AT WORK HERE.

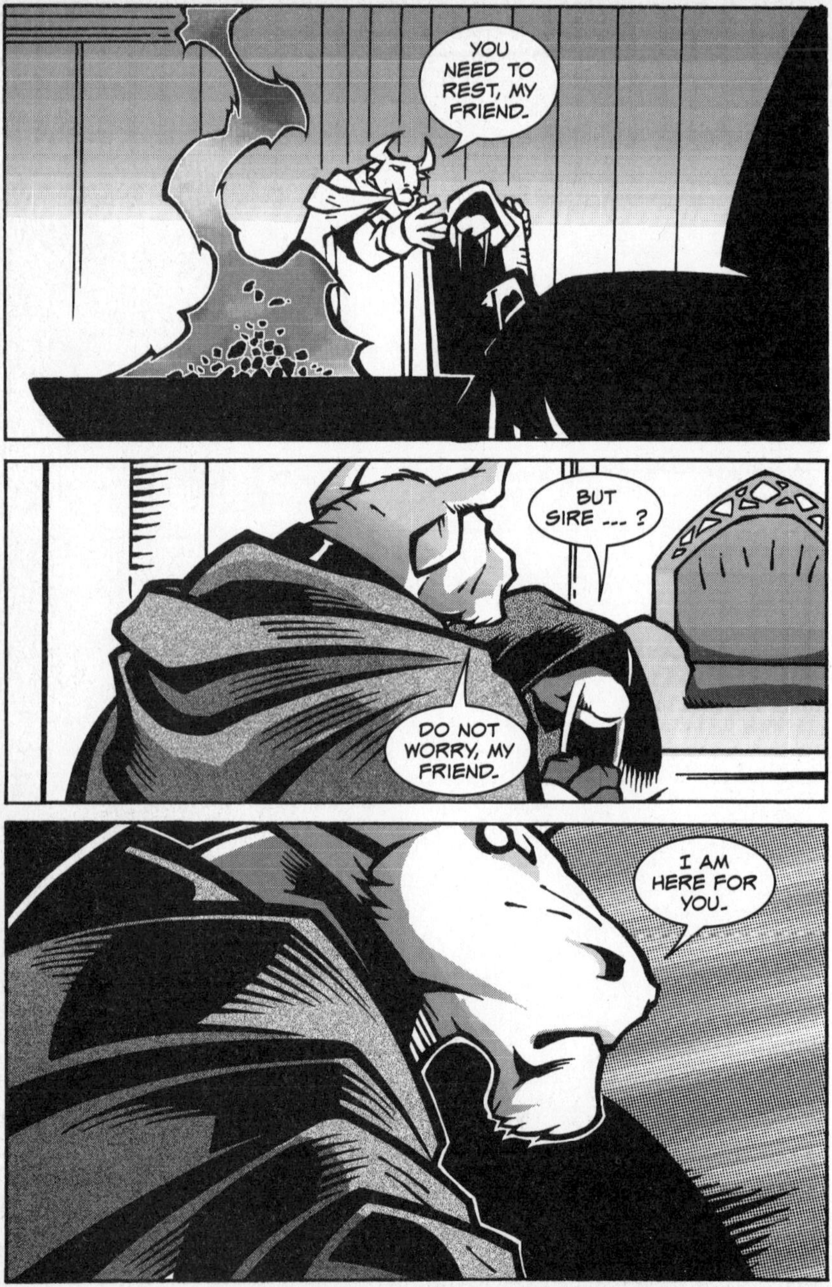
YOU NEED TO REST, MY FRIEND.
BUT SIRE --- ?
DO NOT WORRY, MY FRIEND.
I AM HERE FOR YOU.

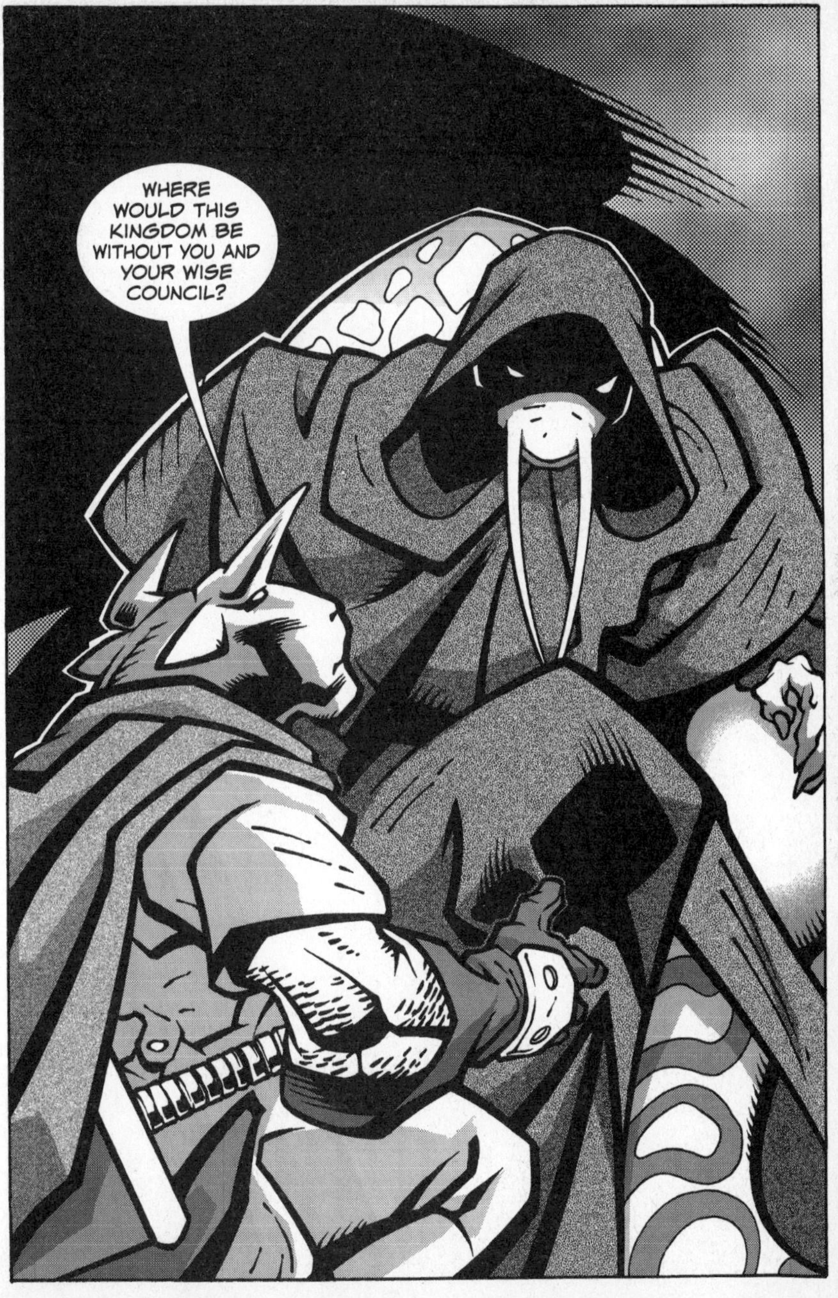
WHERE WOULD THIS KINGDOM BE WITHOUT YOU AND YOUR WISE COUNCIL?

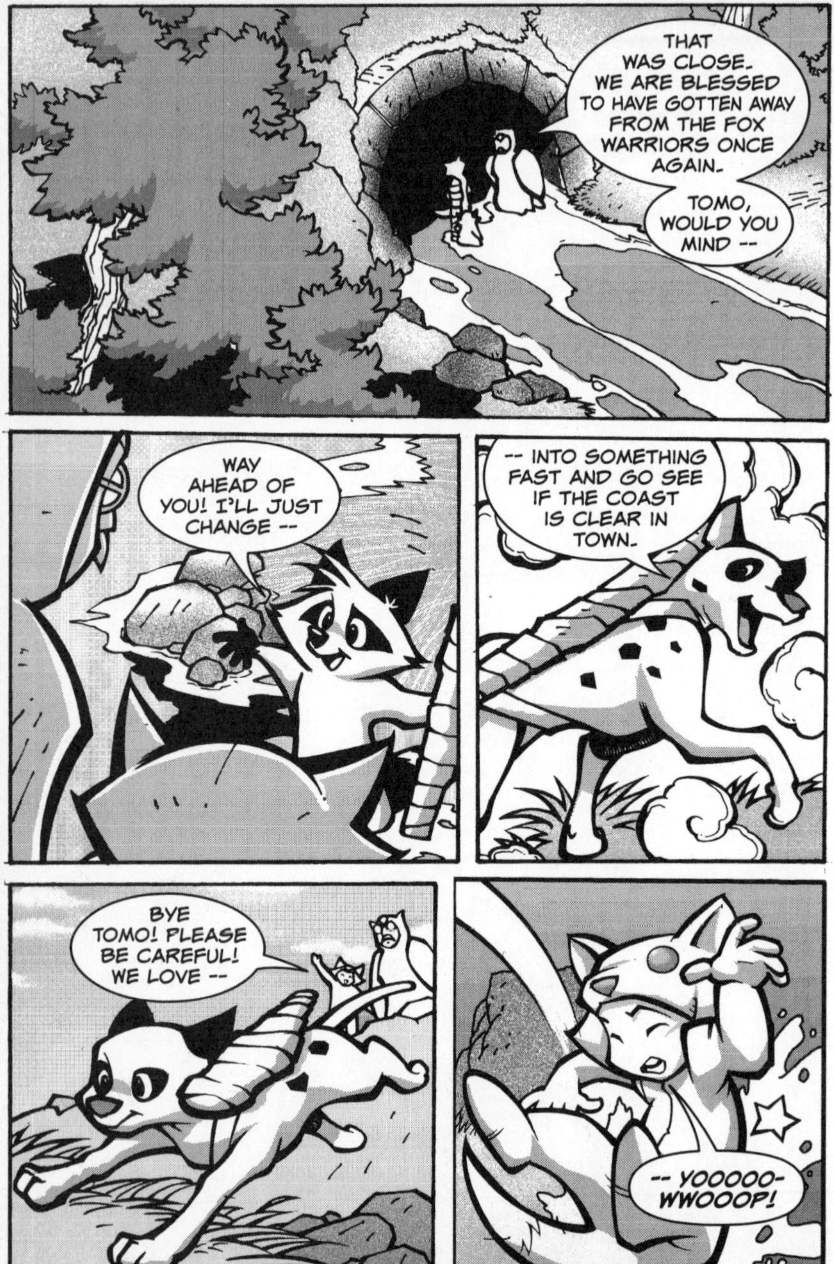
THAT WAS CLOSE. WE ARE BLESSED TO HAVE GOTTEN AWAY FROM THE FOX WARRIORS ONCE AGAIN.
TOMO, WOULD YOU MIND --
WAY AHEAD OF YOU! I'LL JUST CHANGE --
-- INTO SOMETHING FAST AND GO SEE IF THE COAST IS CLEAR IN TOWN.
BYE TOMO! PLEASE BE CAREFUL! WE LOVE --
-- YOOOOO-WWOOOP!

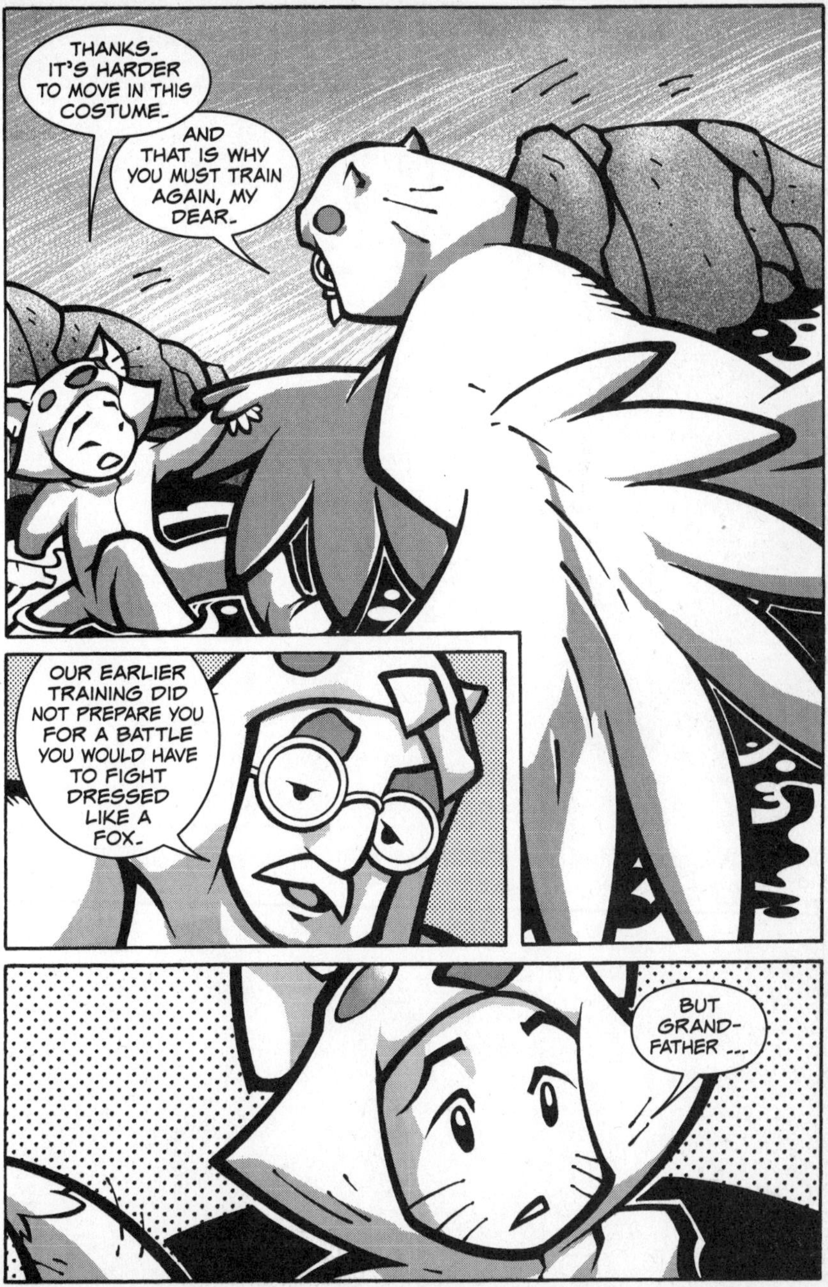
THANKS. IT'S HARDER TO MOVE IN THIS COSTUME.
AND THAT IS WHY YOU MUST TRAIN AGAIN, MY DEAR.
OUR EARLIER TRAINING DID NOT PREPARE YOU FOR A BATTLE YOU WOULD HAVE TO FIGHT DRESSED LIKE A FOX.
BUT GRAND-FATHER ...

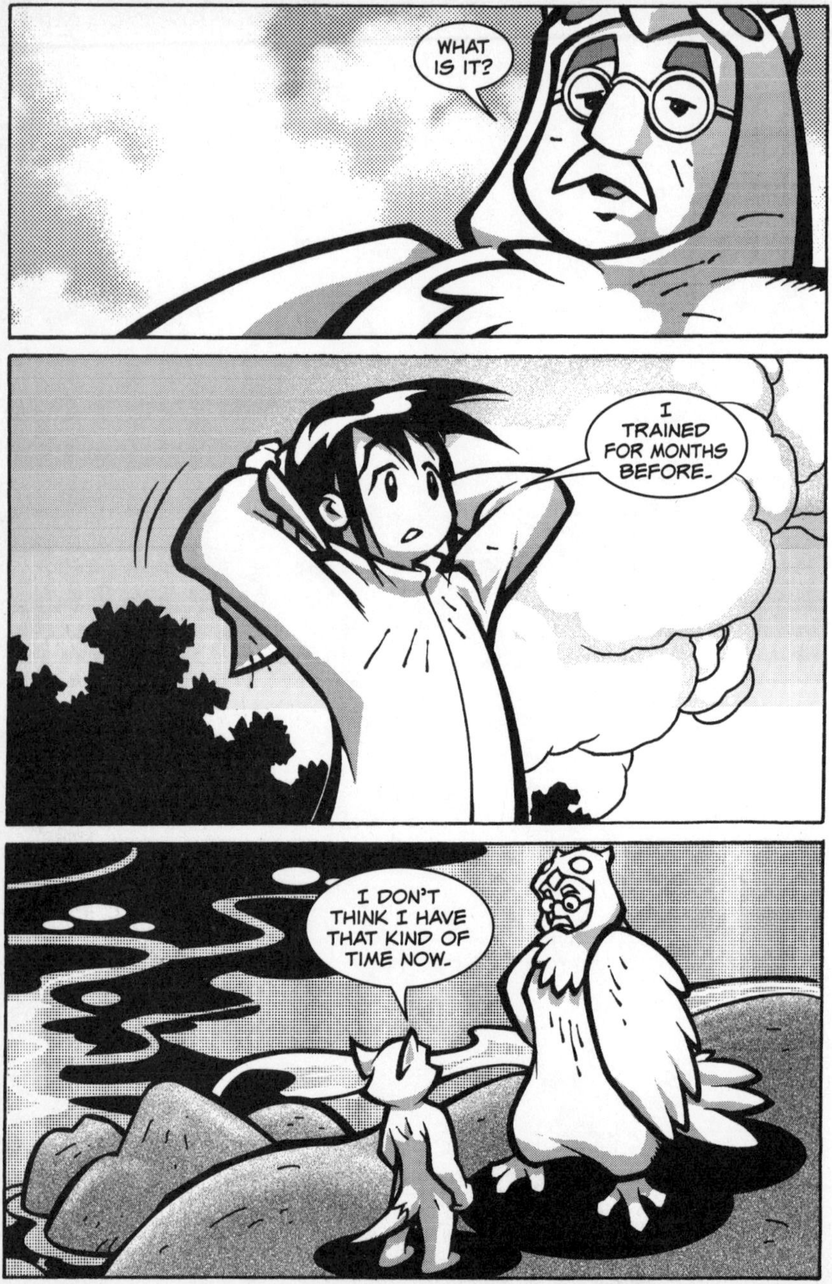

WHAT IS IT?
I TRAINED FOR MONTHS BEFORE...
I DON'T THINK I HAVE THAT KIND OF TIME NOW...

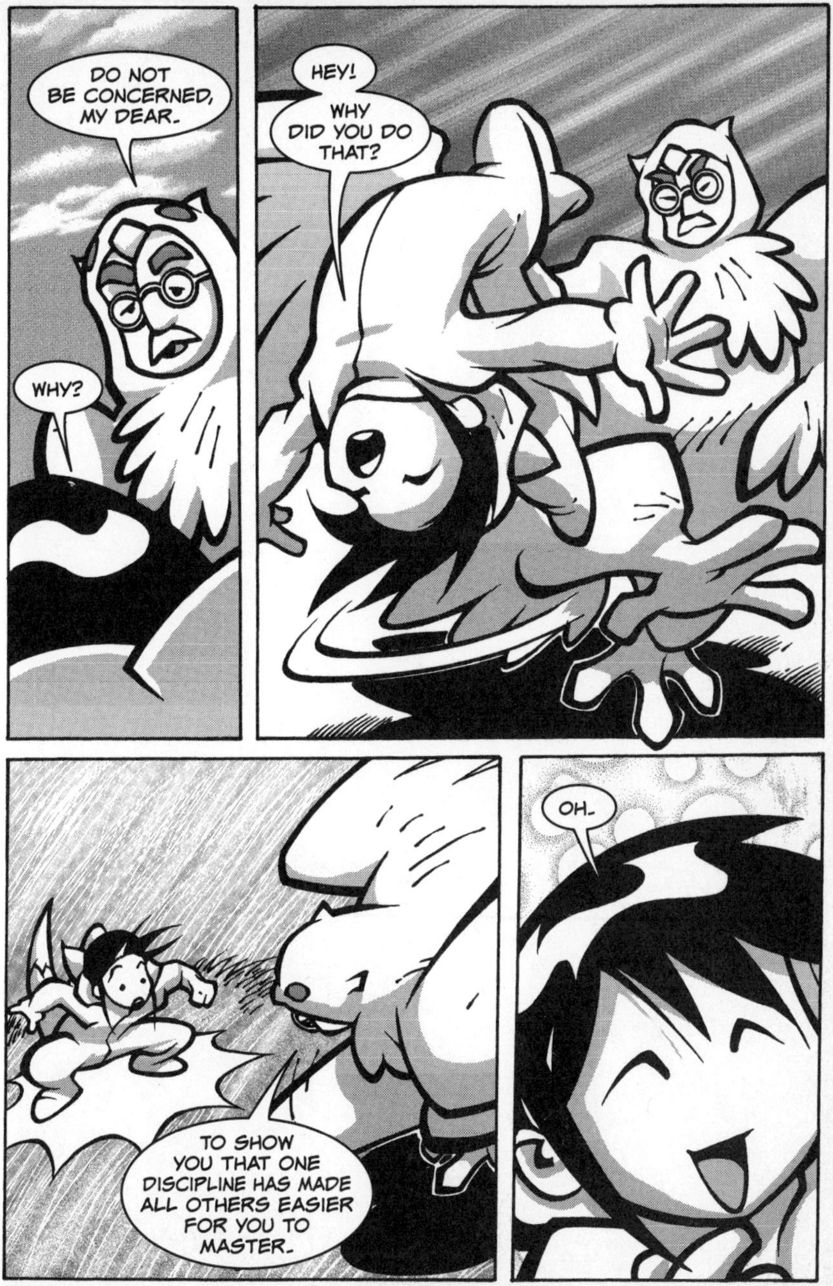
DO NOT BE CONCERNED, MY DEAR.
WHY?
HEY!
WHY DID YOU DO THAT?
TO SHOW YOU THAT ONE DISCIPLINE HAS MADE ALL OTHERS EASIER FOR YOU TO MASTER.
OH.

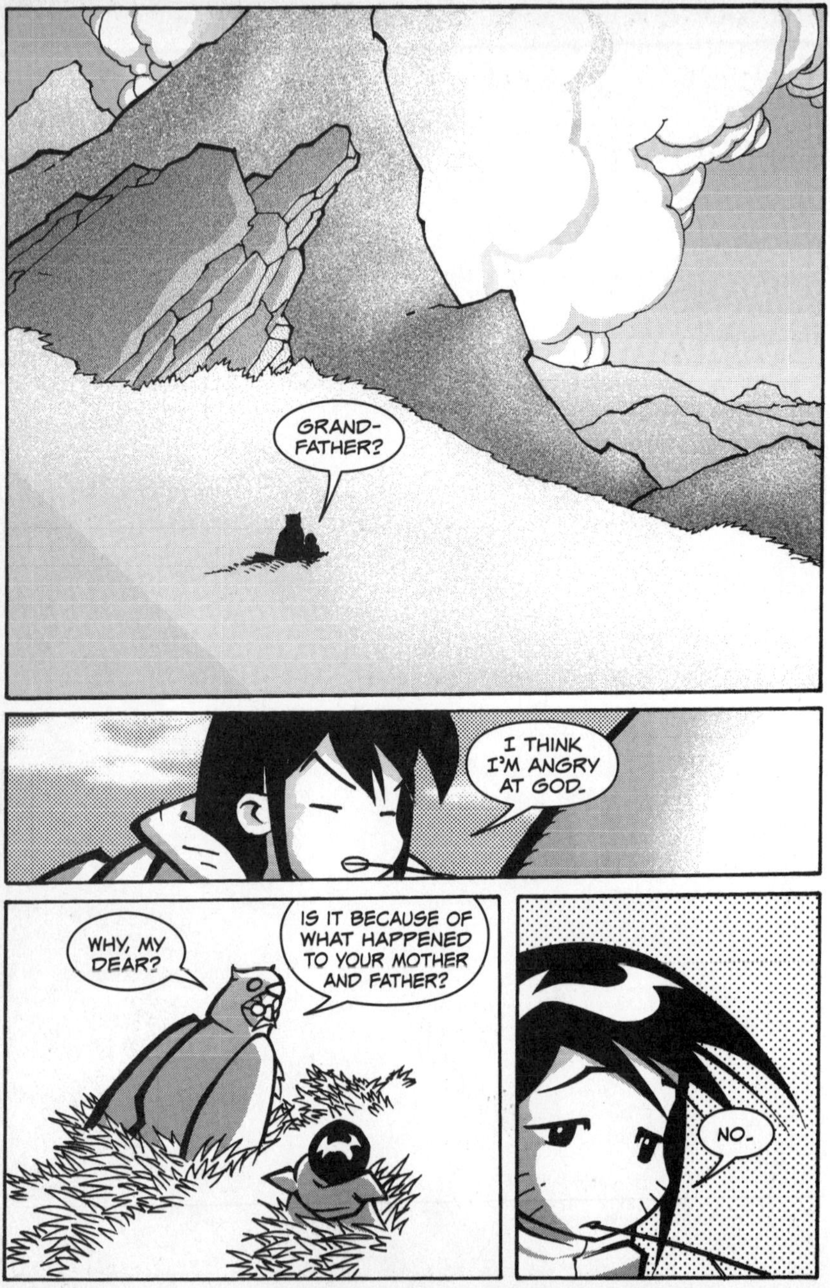
GRAND-FATHER?
I THINK I'M ANGRY AT GOD.
WHY, MY DEAR?
IS IT BECAUSE OF WHAT HAPPENED TO YOUR MOTHER AND FATHER?
NO.

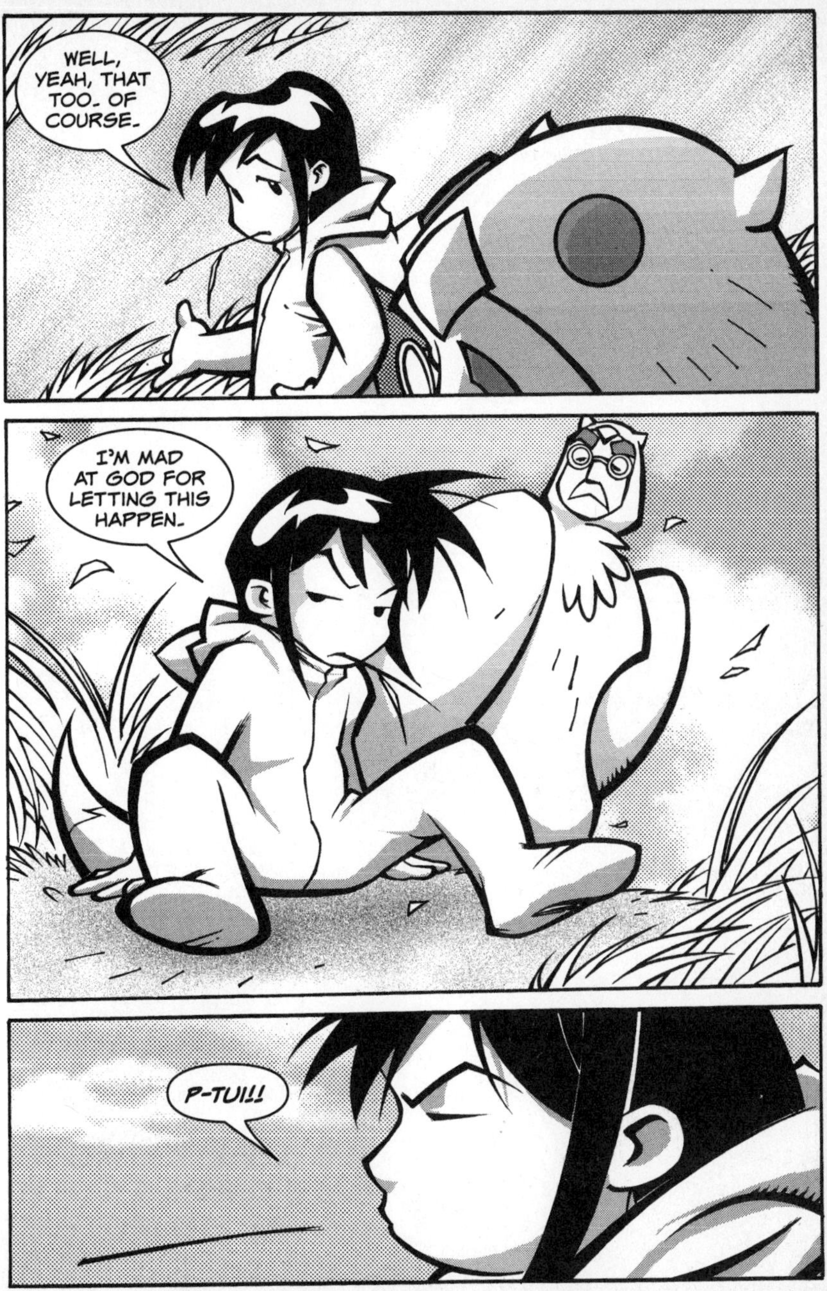
WELL, YEAH, THAT TOO. OF COURSE.
I'M MAD AT GOD FOR LETTING THIS HAPPEN.
P-TUI!!

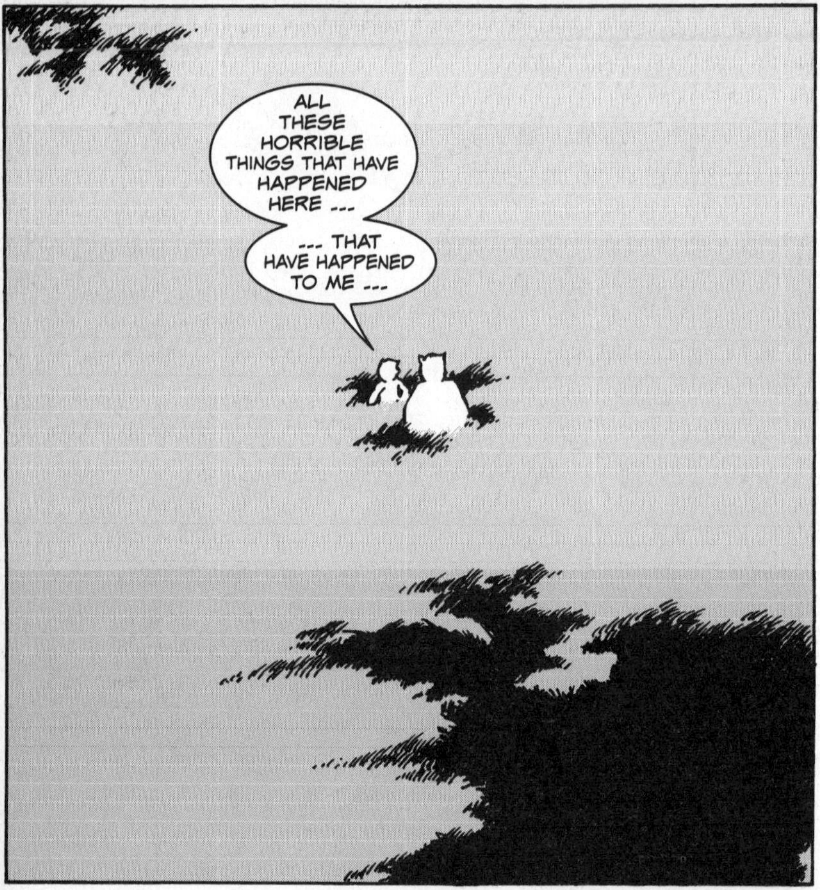
ALL THESE HORRIBLE THINGS THAT HAVE HAPPENED HERE ---
--- THAT HAVE HAPPENED TO ME ---

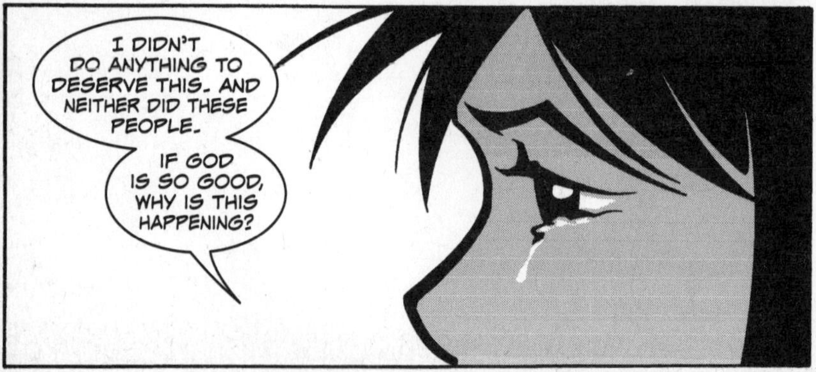
I DIDN'T DO ANYTHING TO DESERVE THIS. AND NEITHER DID THESE PEOPLE.
IF GOD IS SO GOOD, WHY IS THIS HAPPENING?

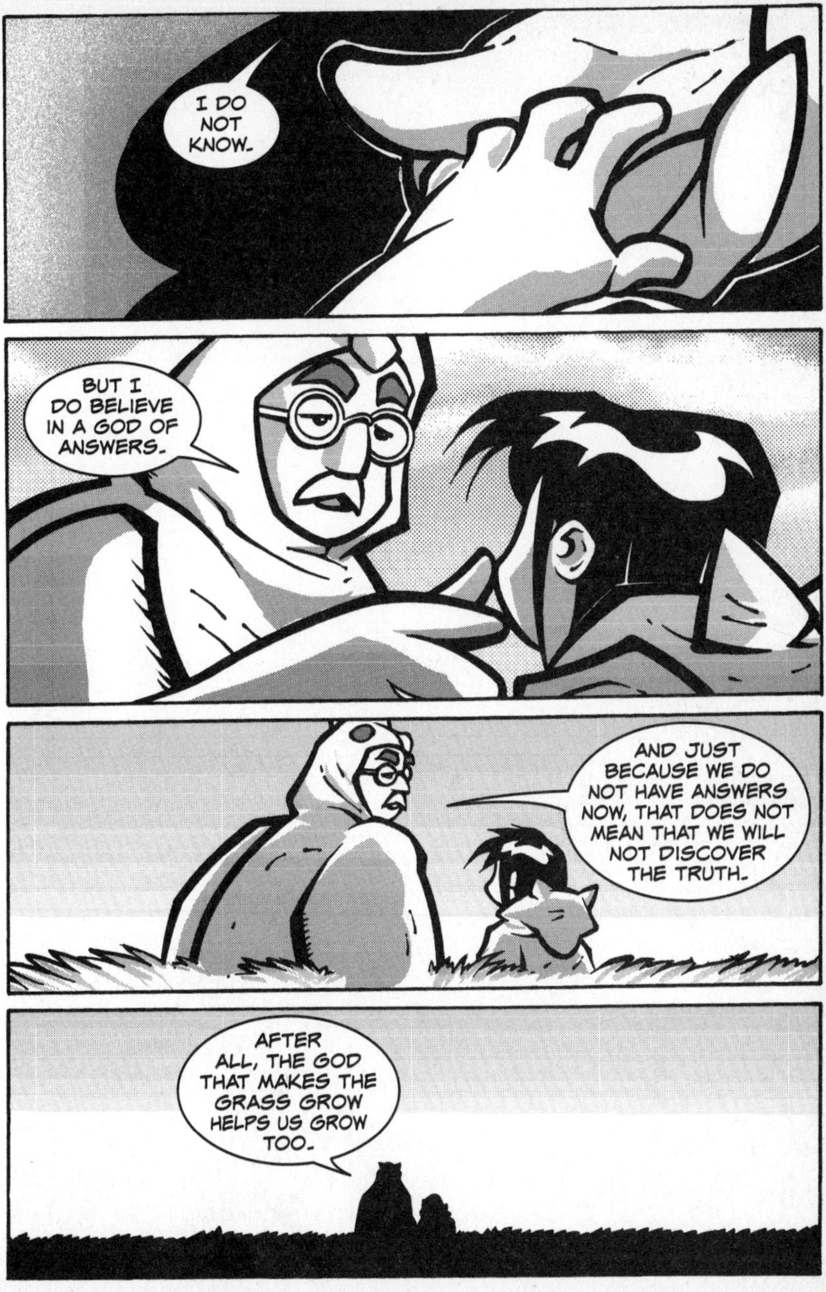
I DO NOT KNOW.
BUT I DO BELIEVE IN A GOD OF ANSWERS.
AND JUST BECAUSE WE DO NOT HAVE ANSWERS NOW, THAT DOES NOT MEAN THAT WE WILL NOT DISCOVER THE TRUTH.
AFTER ALL, THE GOD THAT MAKES THE GRASS GROW HELPS US GROW TOO.

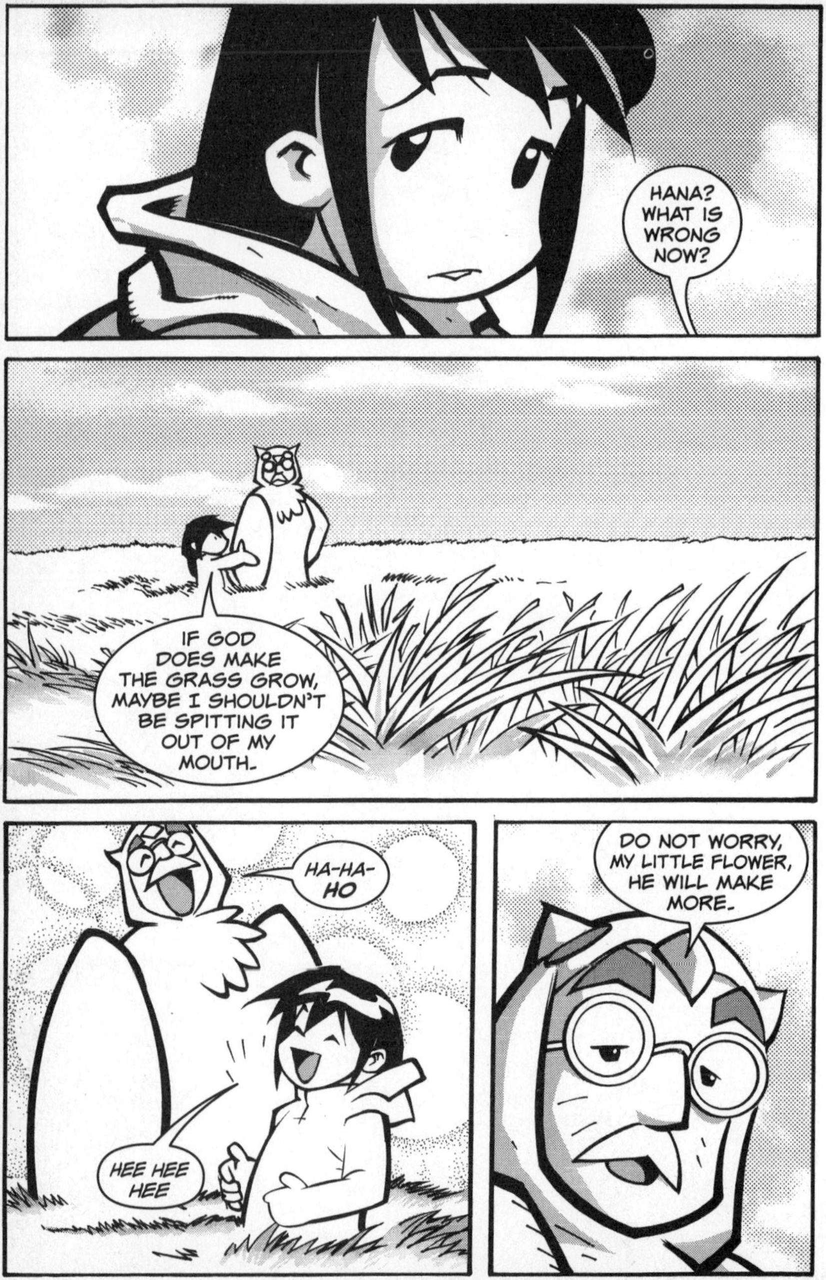
HANA? WHAT IS WRONG NOW?
IF GOD DOES MAKE THE GRASS GROW, MAYBE I SHOULDN'T BE SPITTING IT OUT OF MY MOUTH.
HA-HA-HO
HEE HEE HEE
DO NOT WORRY, MY LITTLE FLOWER, HE WILL MAKE MORE.

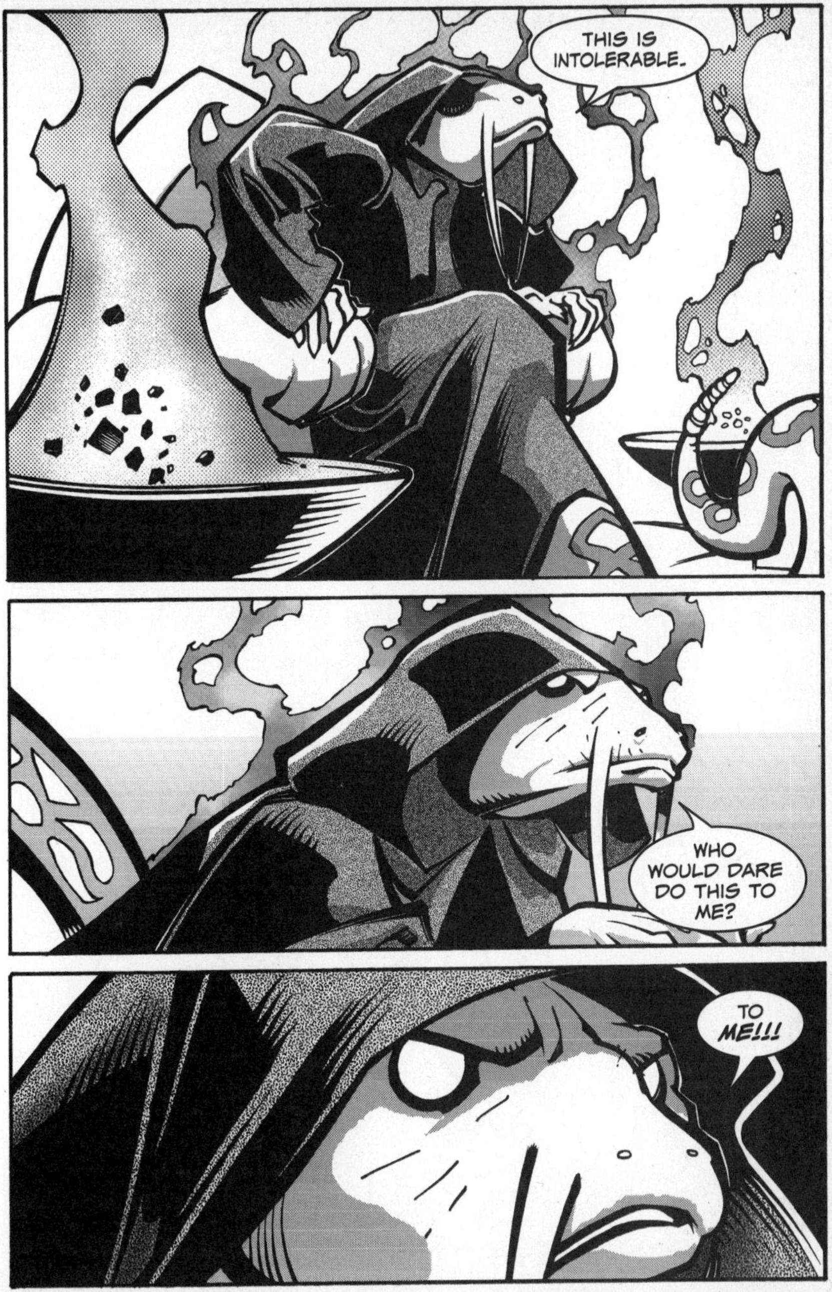
THIS IS INTOLERABLE.
WHO WOULD DARE DO THIS TO ME?
TO *ME!!!*

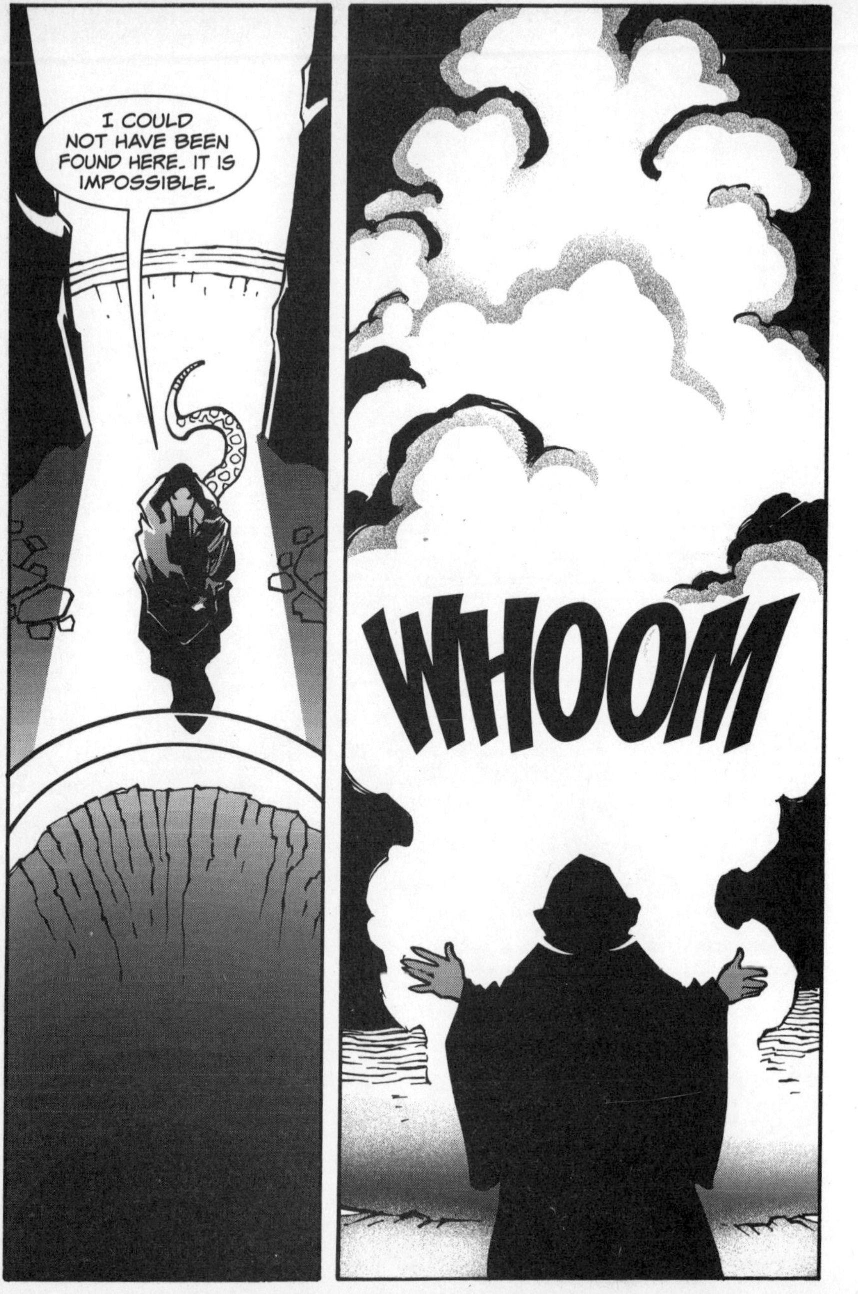
I COULD NOT HAVE BEEN FOUND HERE. IT IS IMPOSSIBLE.
WHOOM

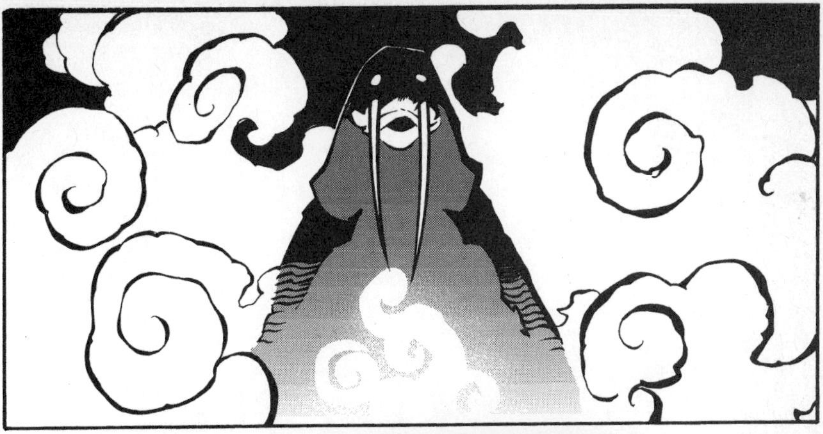

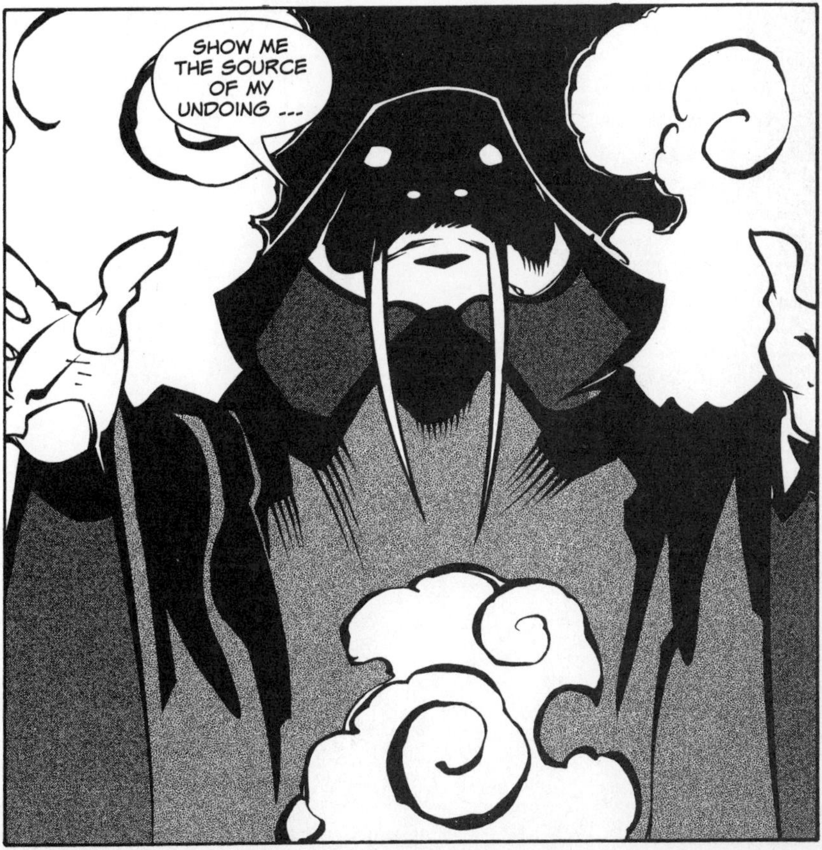
SHOW ME THE SOURCE OF MY UNDOING ---

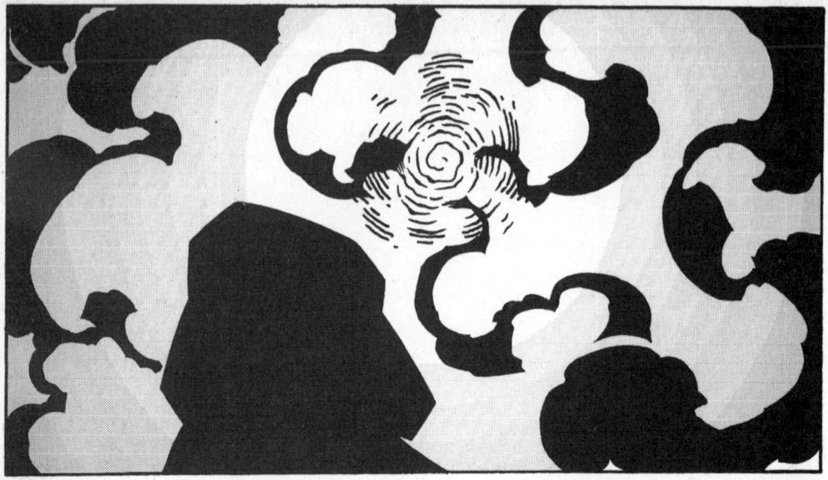

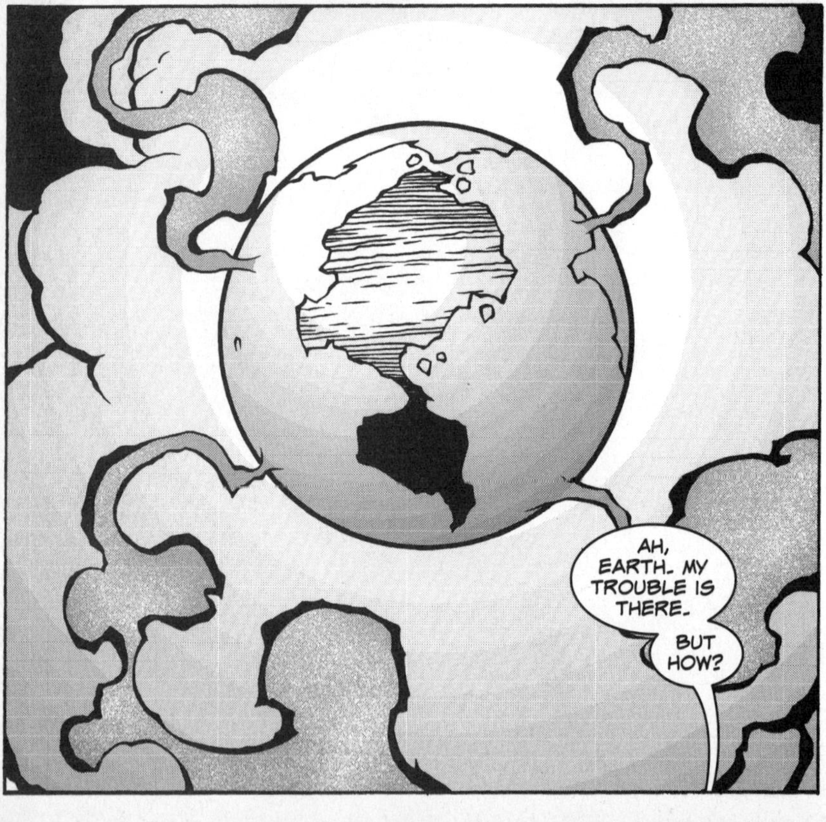
AH, EARTH. MY TROUBLE IS THERE.
BUT HOW?

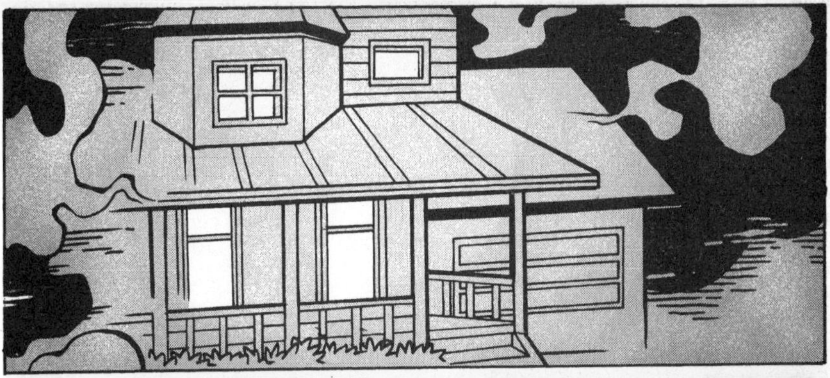

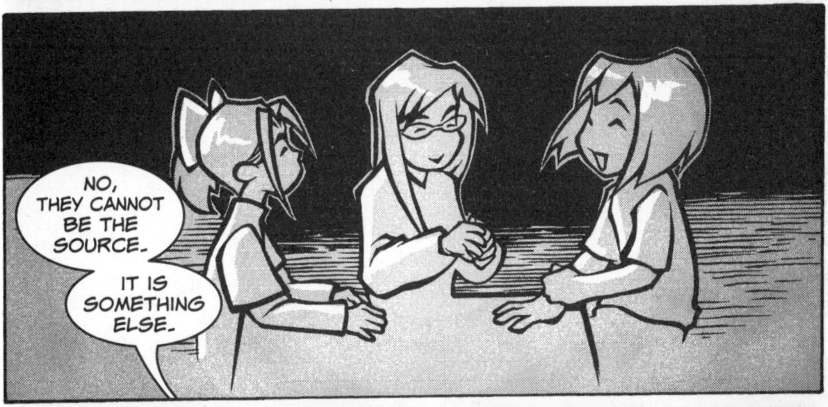
NO, THEY CANNOT BE THE SOURCE.
IT IS SOMETHING ELSE.

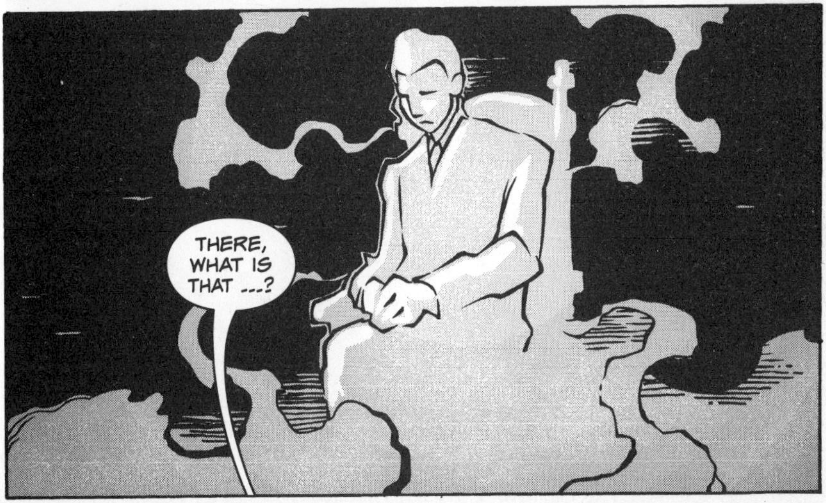
THERE, WHAT IS THAT ...?

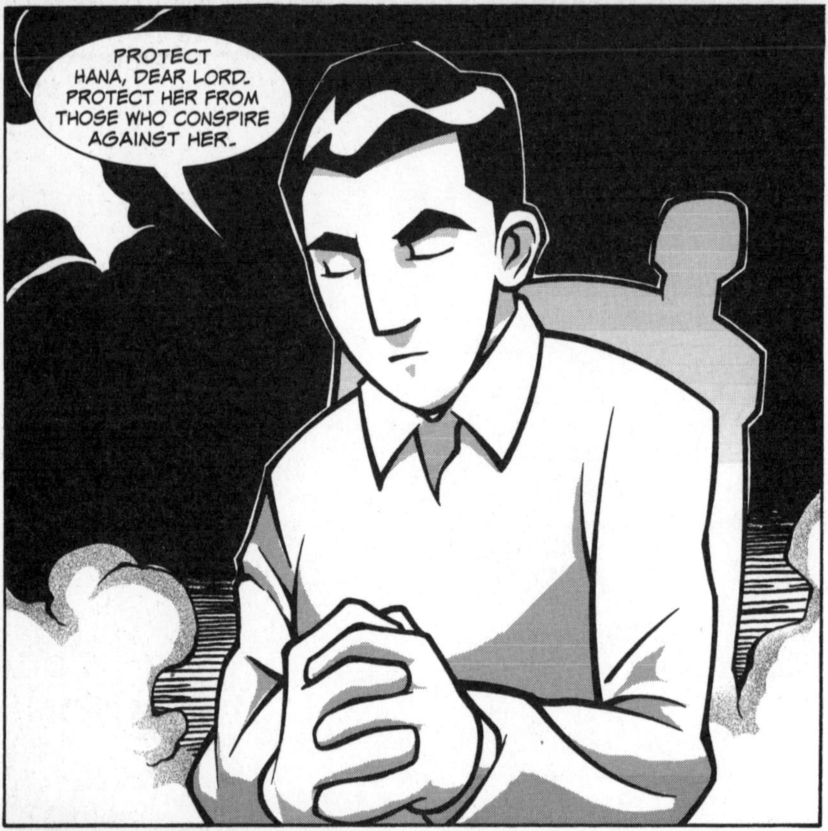
PROTECT HANA, DEAR LORD. PROTECT HER FROM THOSE WHO CONSPIRE AGAINST HER.

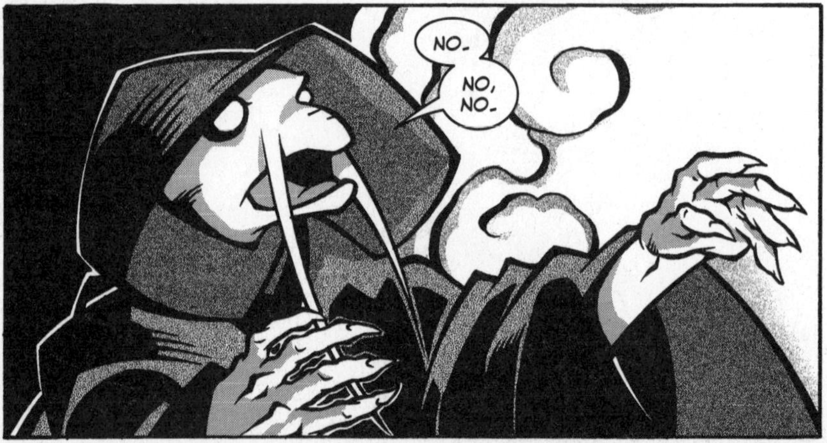
NO.
NO, NO.

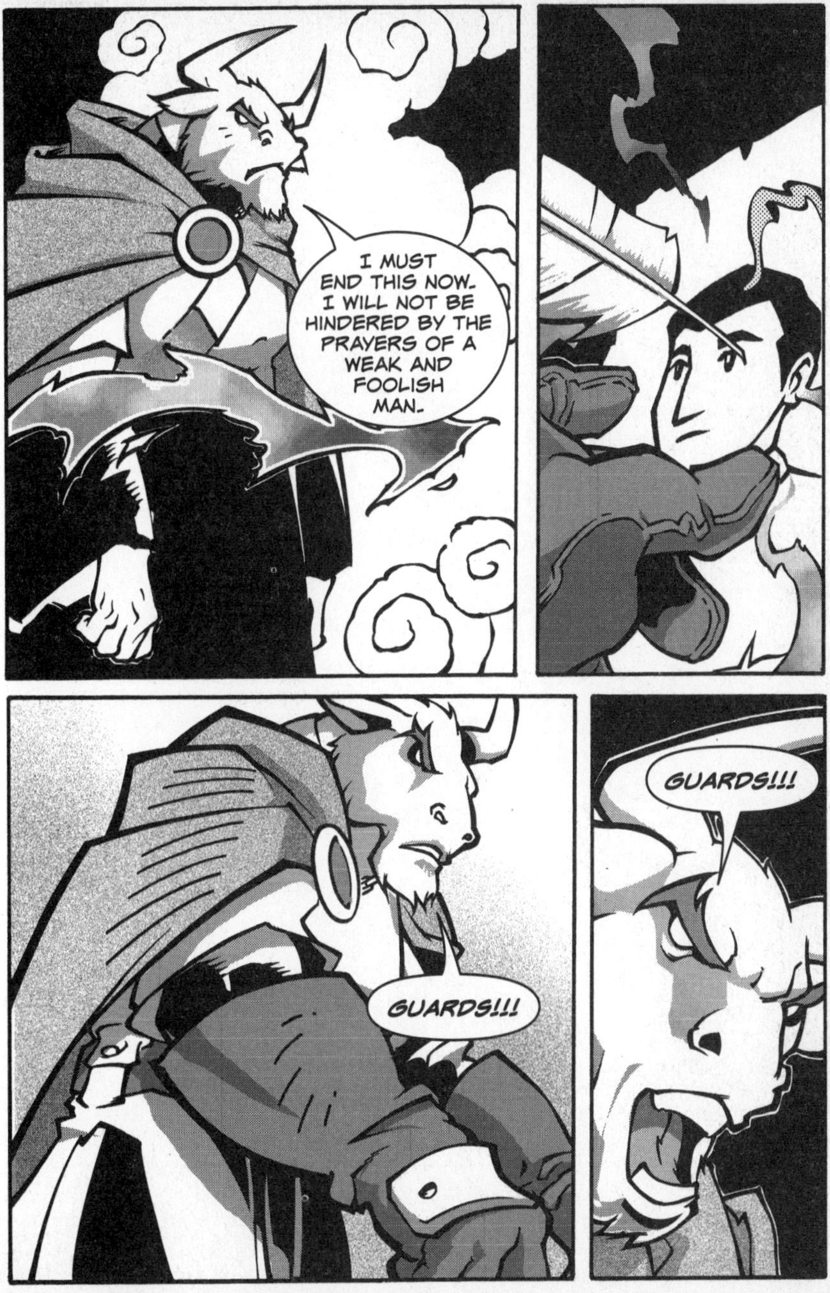
I MUST END THIS NOW. I WILL NOT BE HINDERED BY THE PRAYERS OF A WEAK AND FOOLISH MAN.
GUARDS!!!
GUARDS!!!

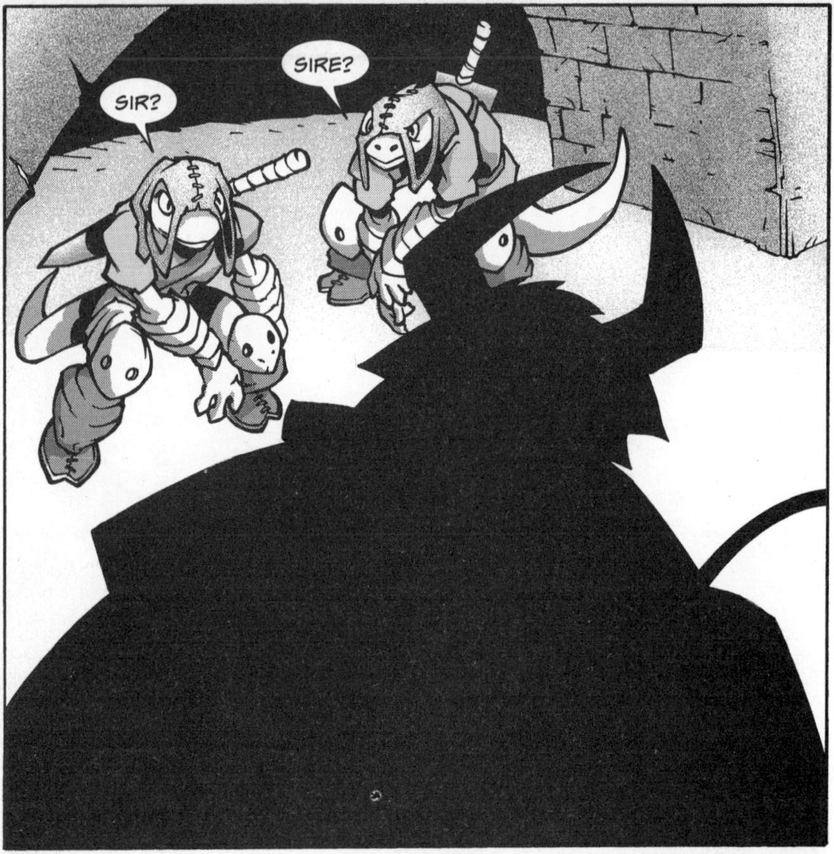
SIR?
SIRE?

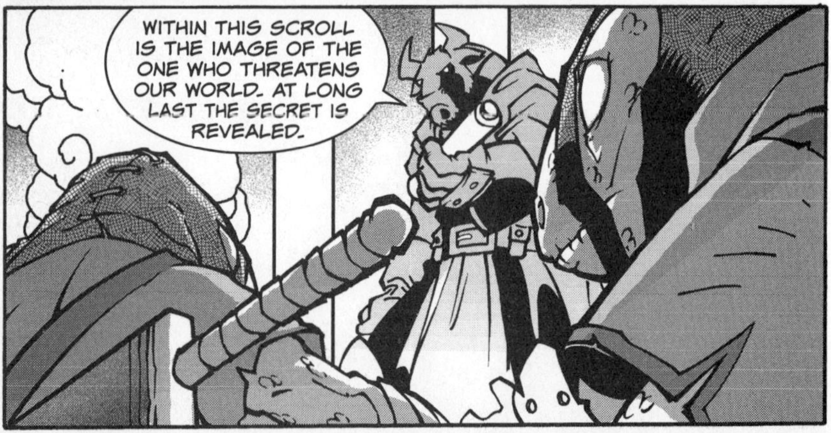
WITHIN THIS SCROLL IS THE IMAGE OF THE ONE WHO THREATENS OUR WORLD. AT LONG LAST THE SECRET IS REVEALED.

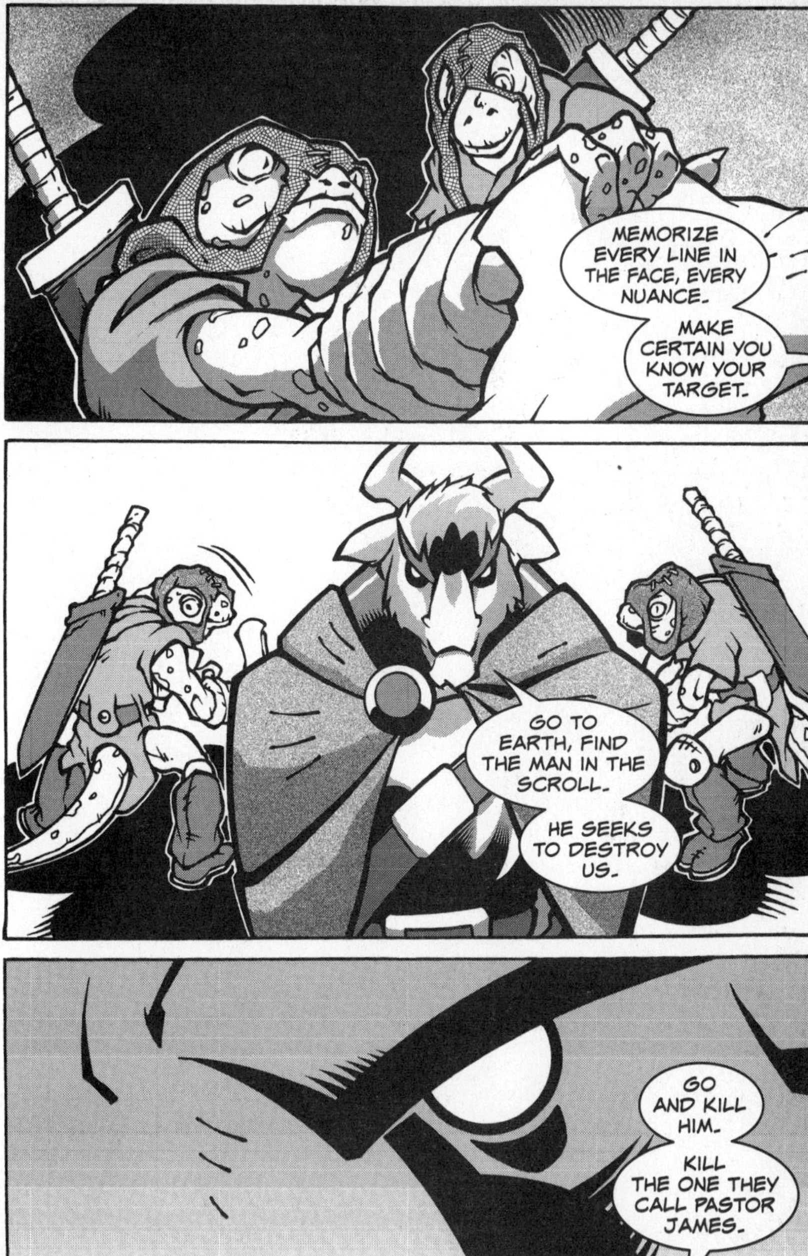
MEMORIZE EVERY LINE IN THE FACE, EVERY NUANCE.
MAKE CERTAIN YOU KNOW YOUR TARGET.
GO TO EARTH, FIND THE MAN IN THE SCROLL.
HE SEEKS TO DESTROY US.
GO AND KILL HIM.
KILL THE ONE THEY CALL PASTOR JAMES.

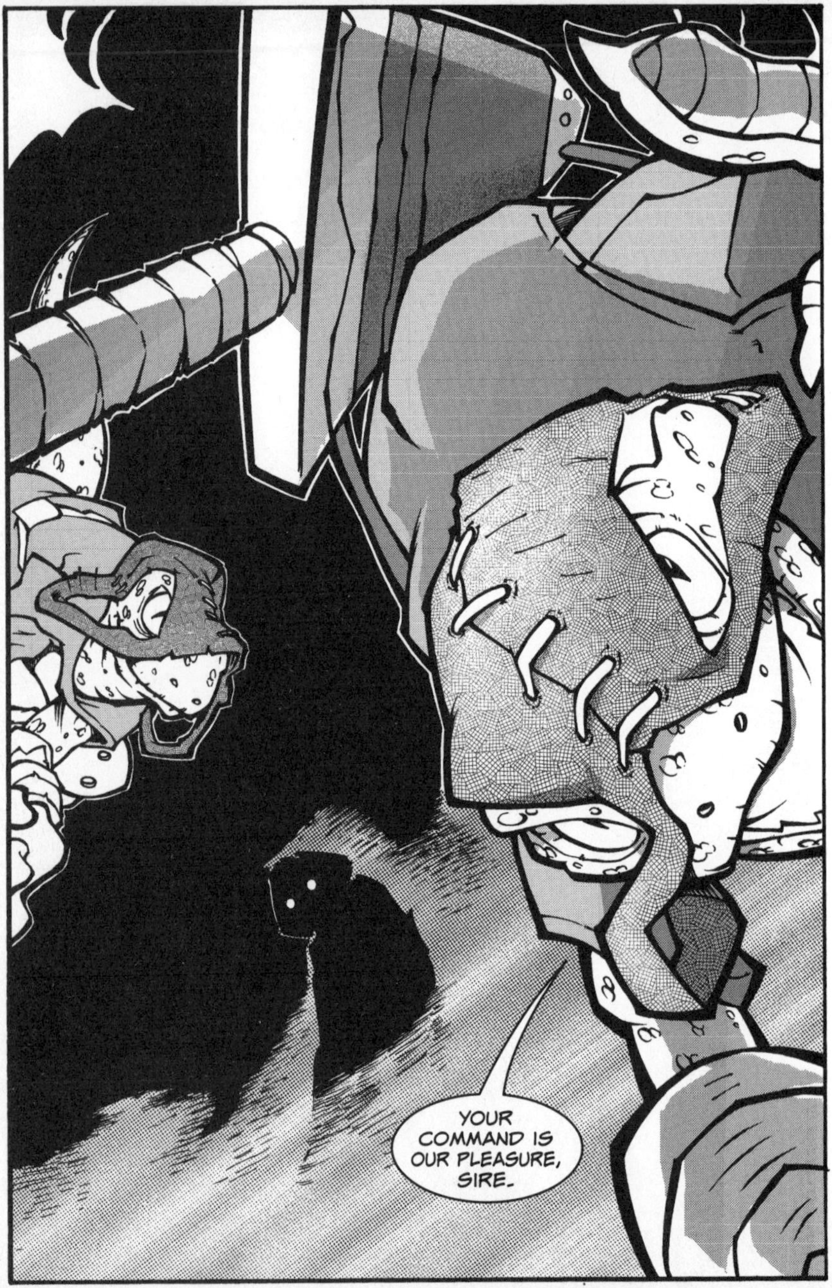
YOUR COMMAND IS OUR PLEASURE, SIRE.

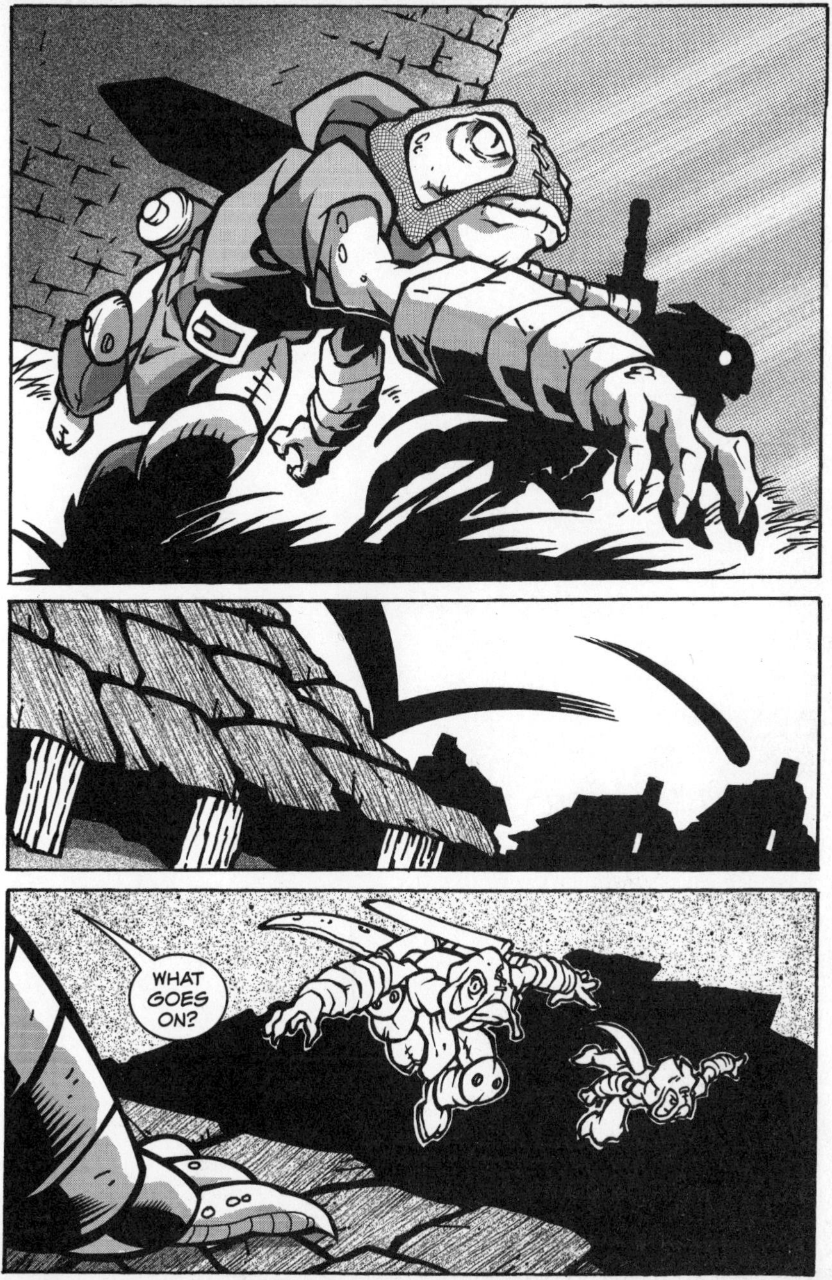
WHAT GOES ON?

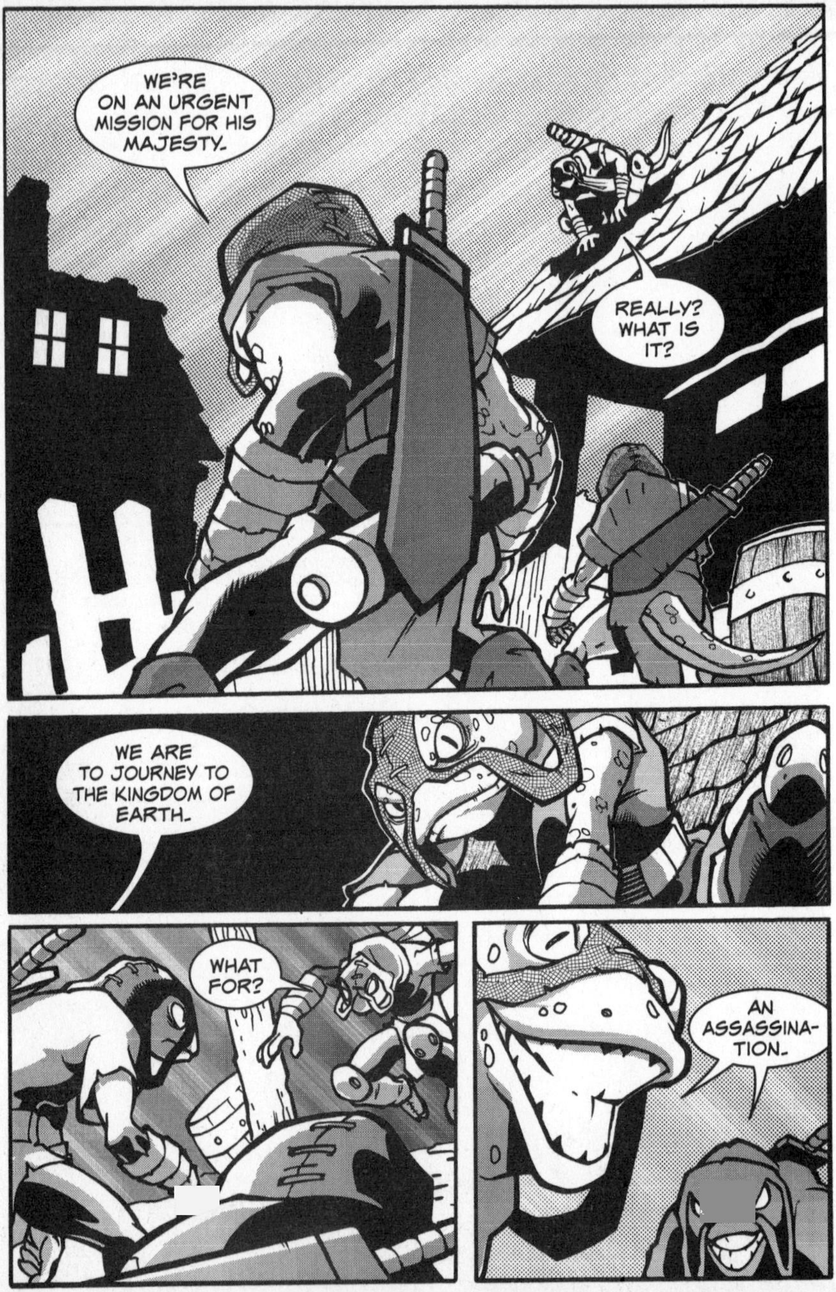
WE'RE ON AN URGENT MISSION FOR HIS MAJESTY.
REALLY? WHAT IS IT?
WE ARE TO JOURNEY TO THE KINGDOM OF EARTH.
WHAT FOR?
AN ASSASSINATION.

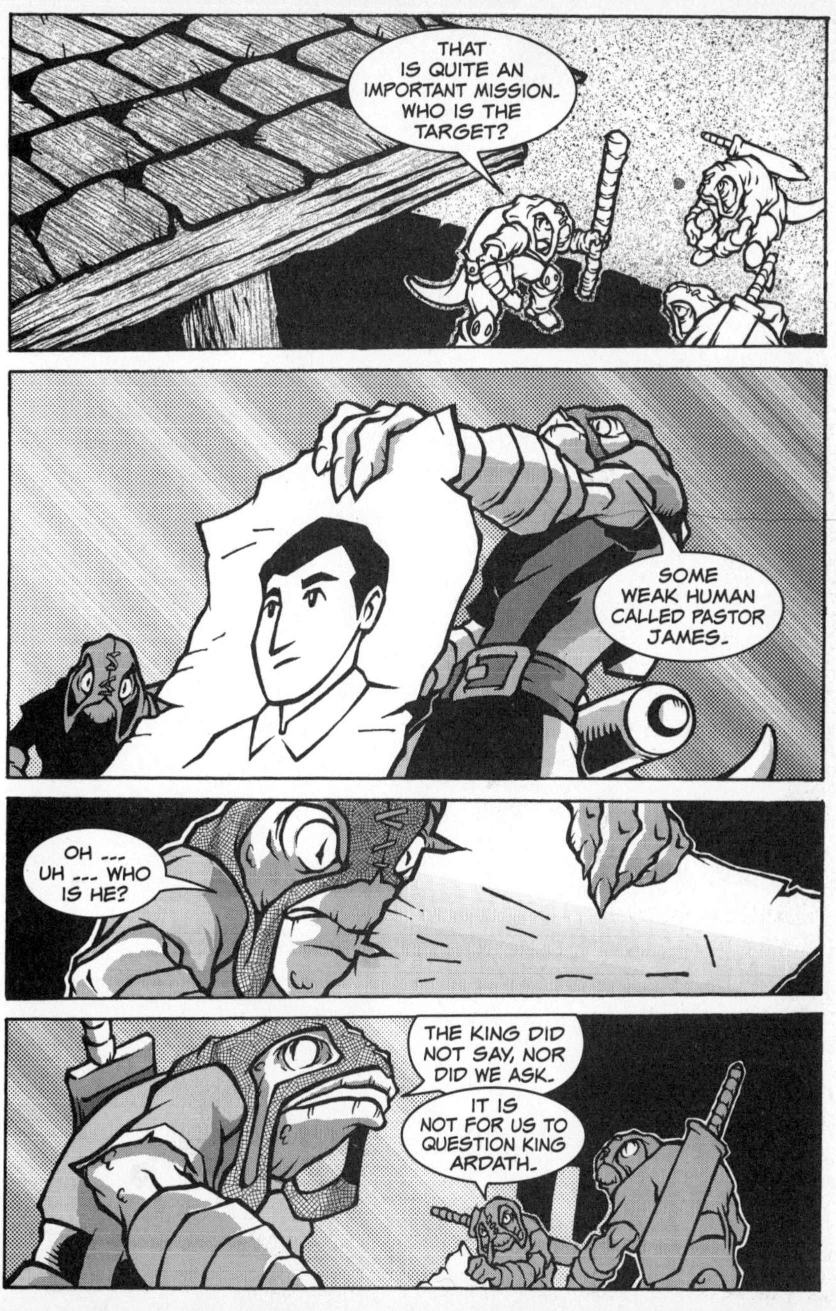

THAT IS QUITE AN IMPORTANT MISSION. WHO IS THE TARGET?
SOME WEAK HUMAN CALLED PASTOR JAMES.
OH ... UH ... WHO IS HE?
THE KING DID NOT SAY, NOR DID WE ASK.
IT IS NOT FOR US TO QUESTION KING ARDATH.

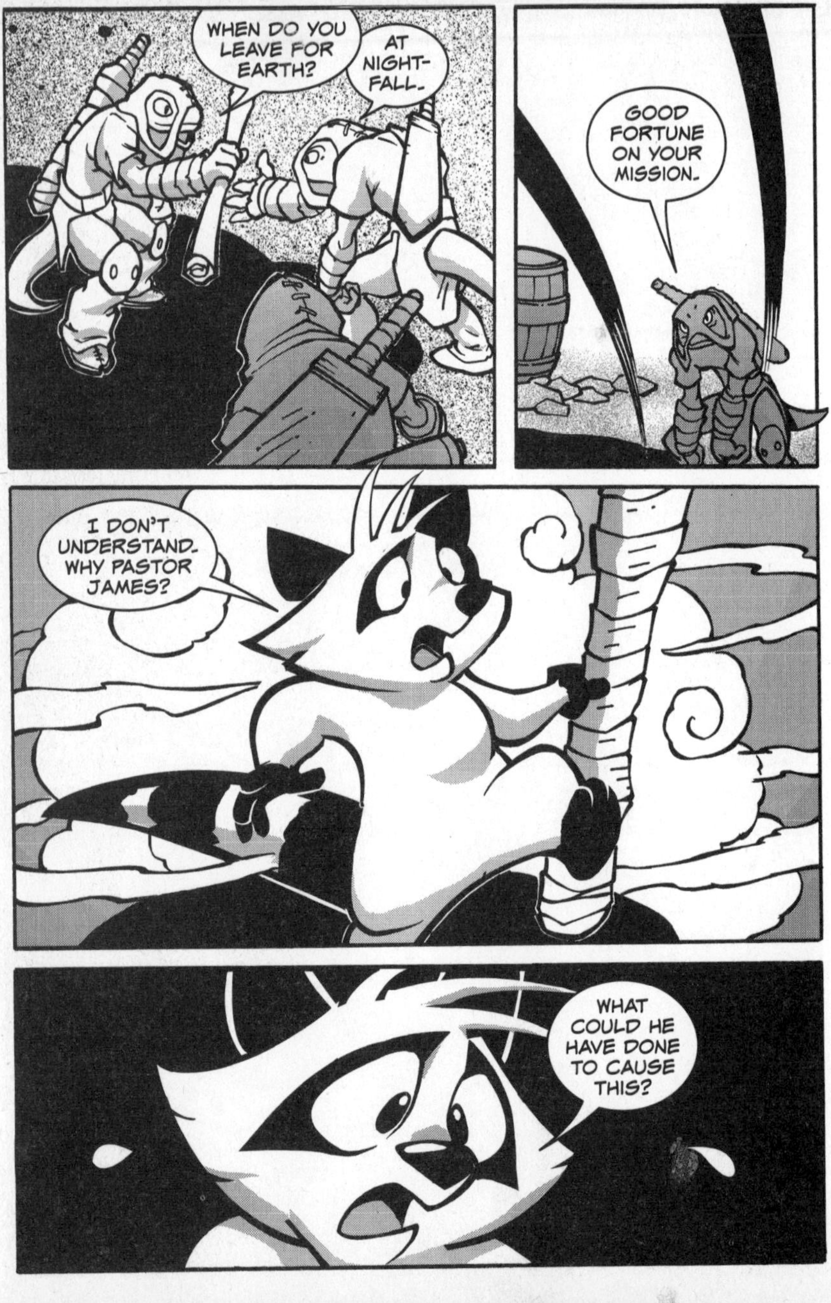
WHEN DO YOU LEAVE FOR EARTH?
AT NIGHT-FALL.
GOOD FORTUNE ON YOUR MISSION.
I DON'T UNDERSTAND. WHY PASTOR JAMES?
WHAT COULD HE HAVE DONE TO CAUSE THIS?

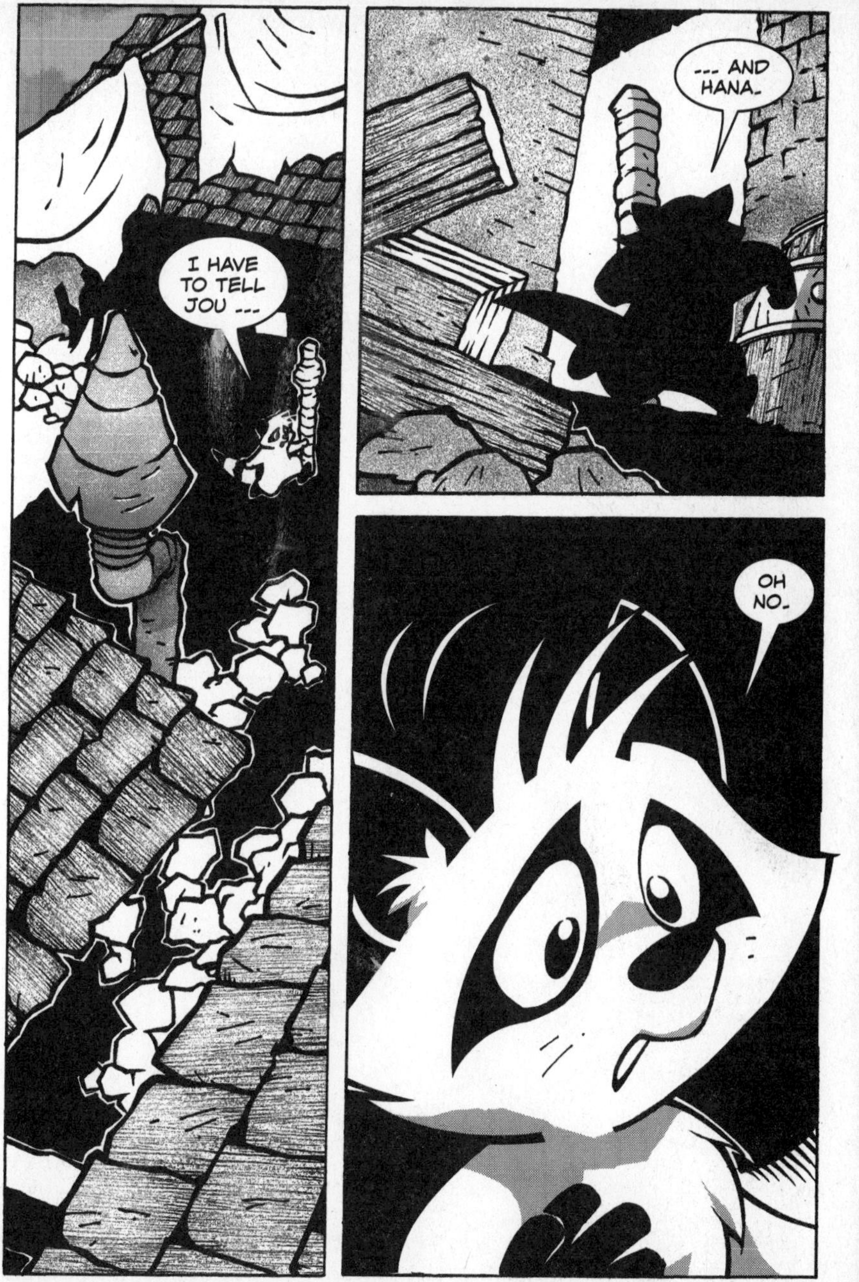
I HAVE TO TELL JOU ---
--- AND HANA-
OH NO-

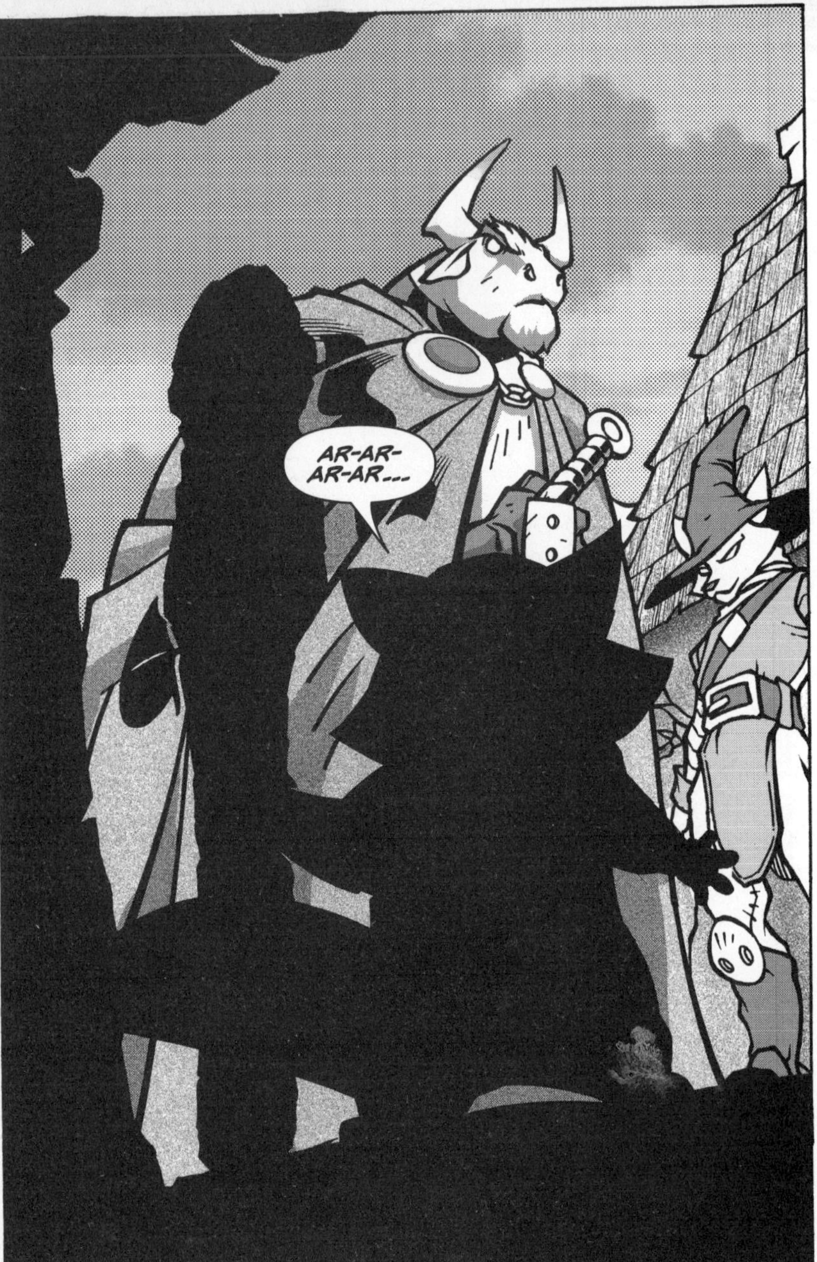
AR-AR-AR-AR...

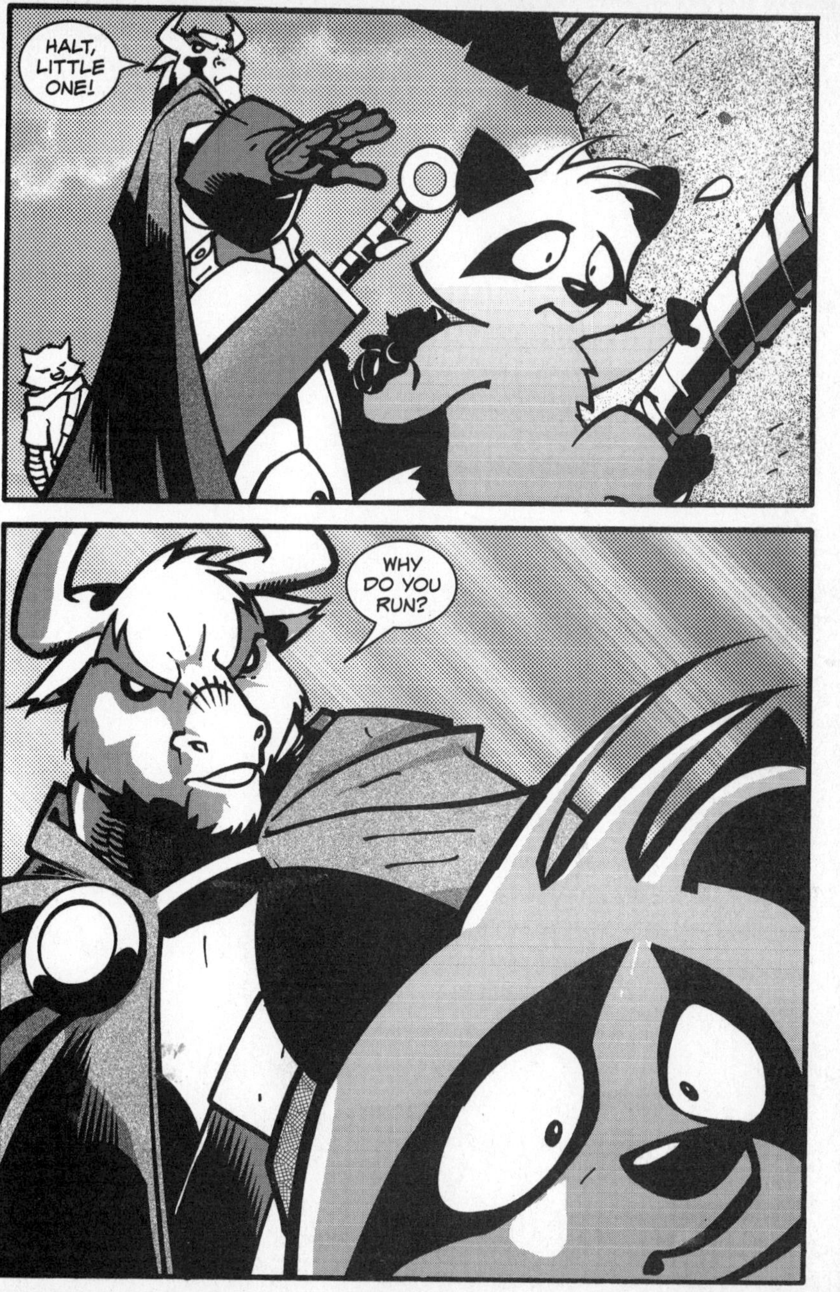
HALT, LITTLE ONE!
WHY DO YOU RUN?

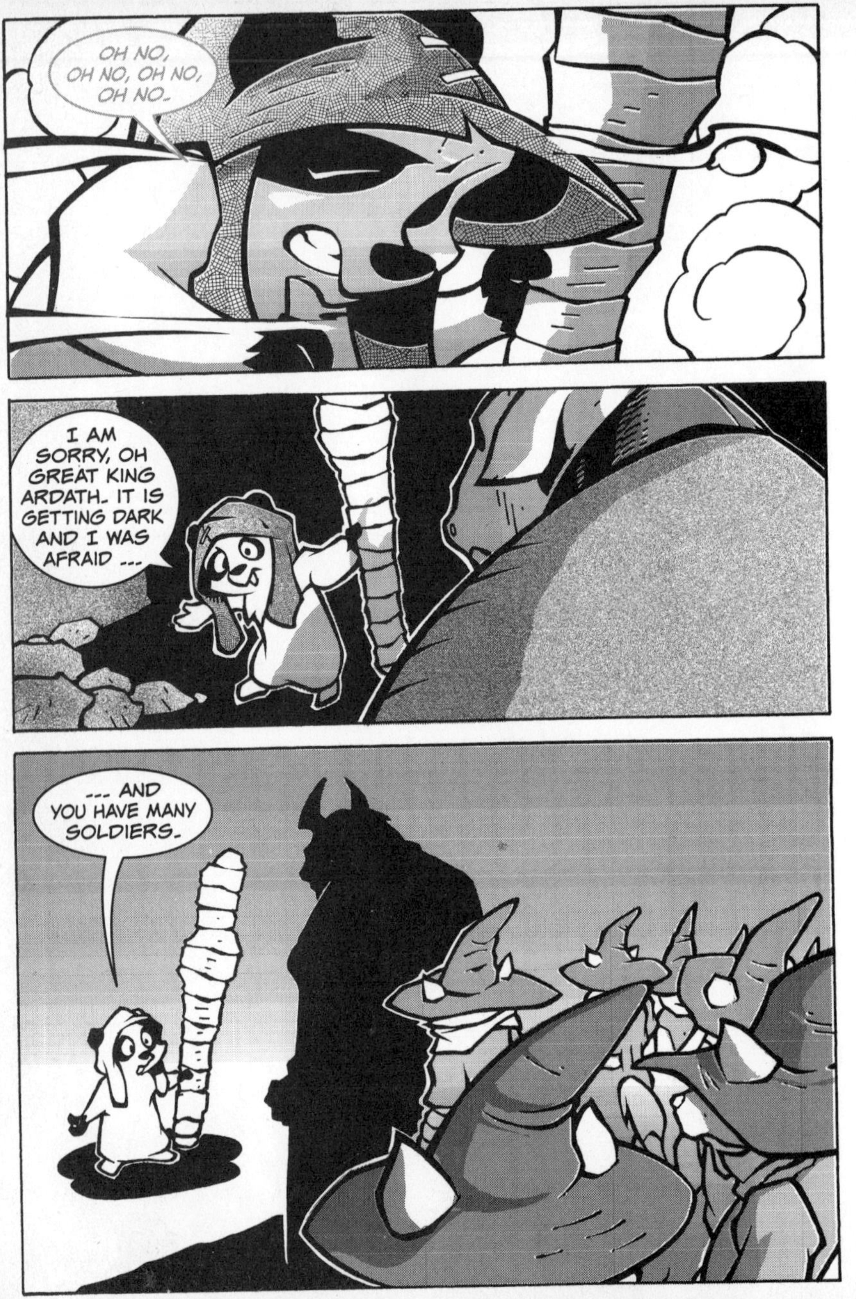
OH NO, OH NO, OH NO, OH NO.
I AM SORRY, OH GREAT KING ARDATH. IT IS GETTING DARK AND I WAS AFRAID ---
--- AND YOU HAVE MANY SOLDIERS.

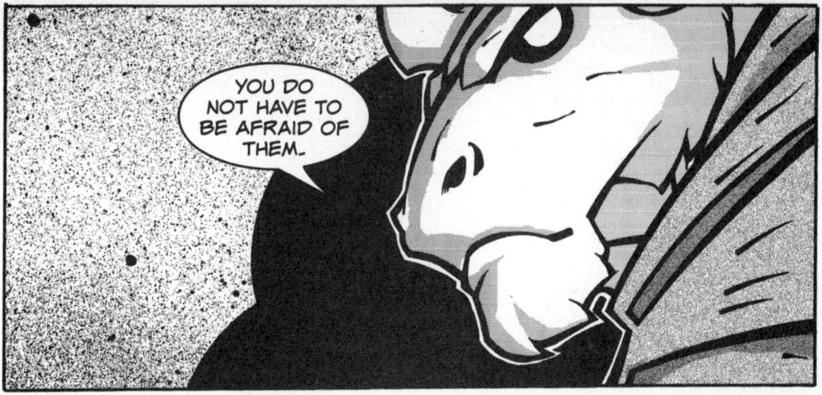
YOU DO NOT HAVE TO BE AFRAID OF THEM.
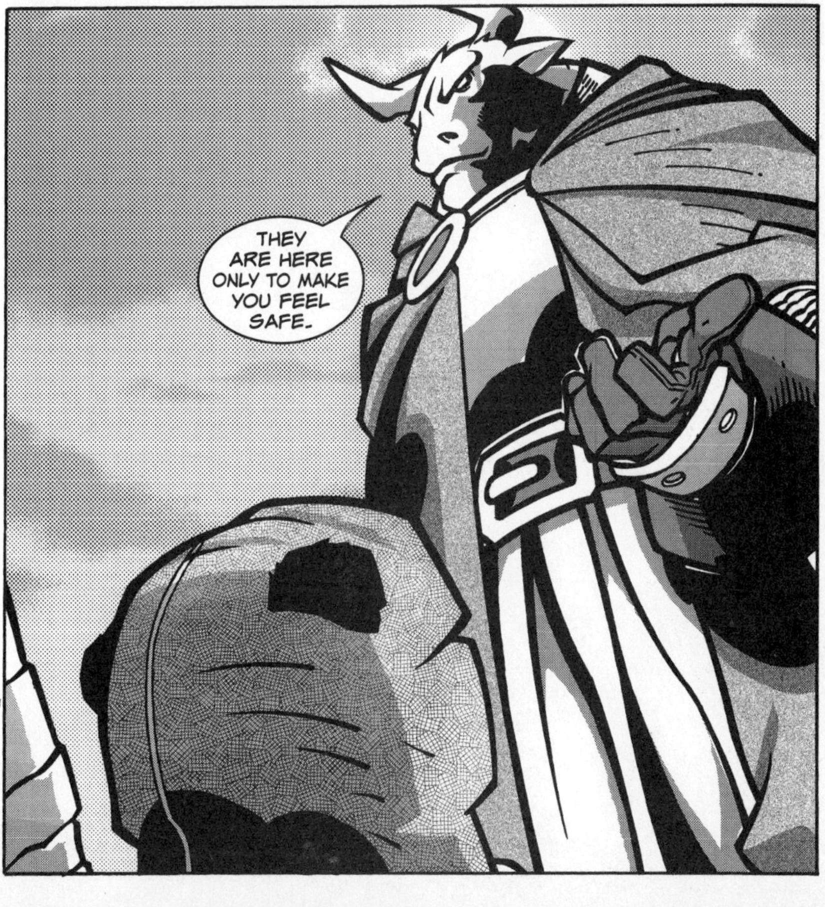
THEY ARE HERE ONLY TO MAKE YOU FEEL SAFE.

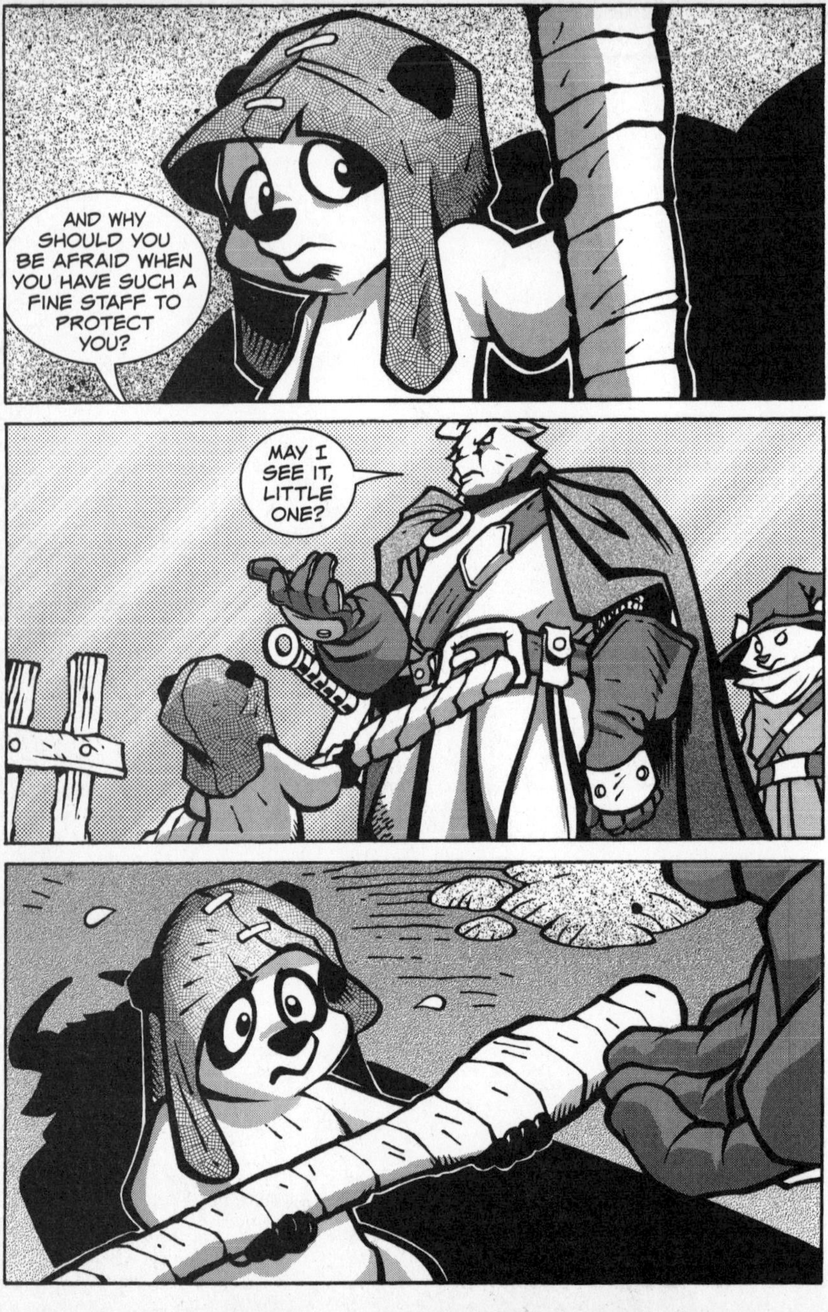
AND WHY SHOULD YOU BE AFRAID WHEN YOU HAVE SUCH A FINE STAFF TO PROTECT YOU?
MAY I SEE IT, LITTLE ONE?

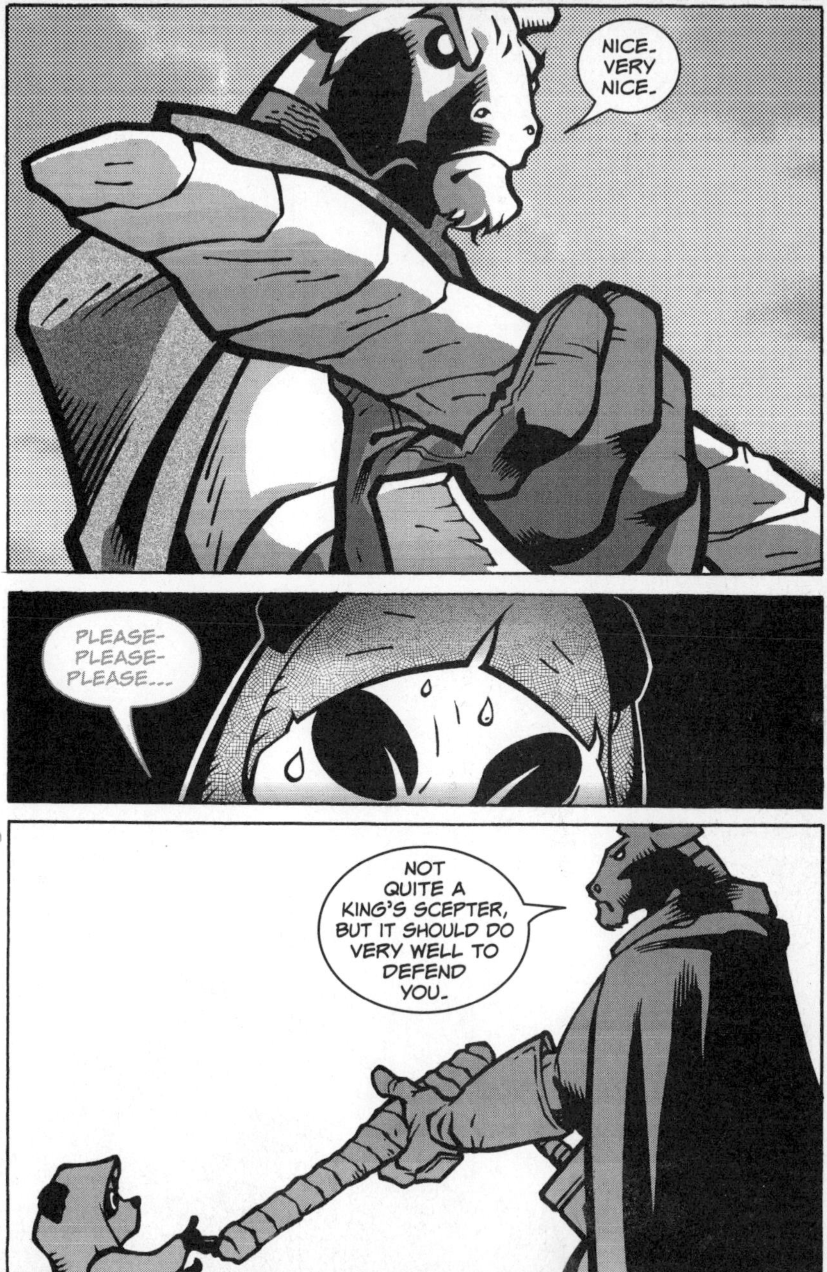
NICE. VERY NICE.
PLEASE- PLEASE- PLEASE...
NOT QUITE A KING'S SCEPTER, BUT IT SHOULD DO VERY WELL TO DEFEND YOU.

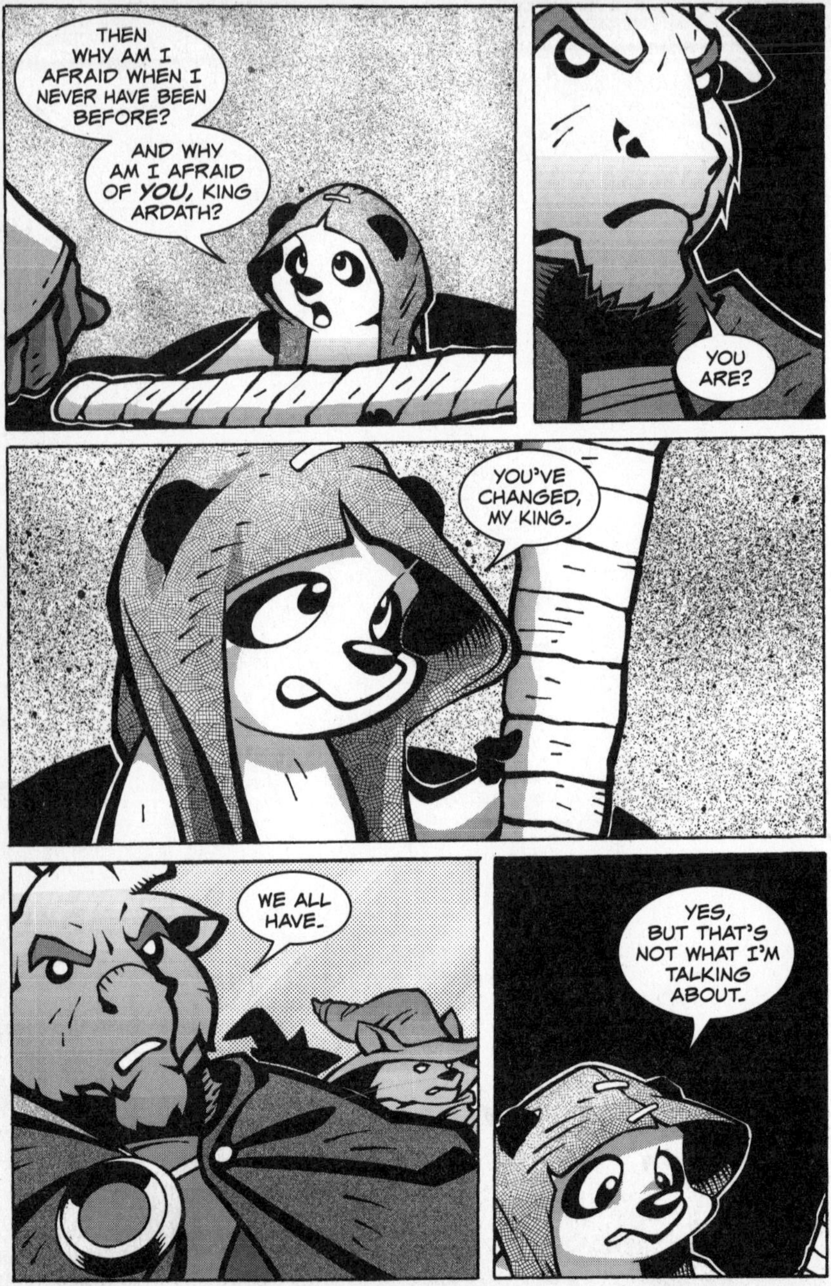
THEN WHY AM I AFRAID WHEN I NEVER HAVE BEEN BEFORE?
AND WHY AM I AFRAID OF YOU, KING ARDATH?
YOU ARE?
YOU'VE CHANGED, MY KING.
WE ALL HAVE.
YES, BUT THAT'S NOT WHAT I'M TALKING ABOUT.

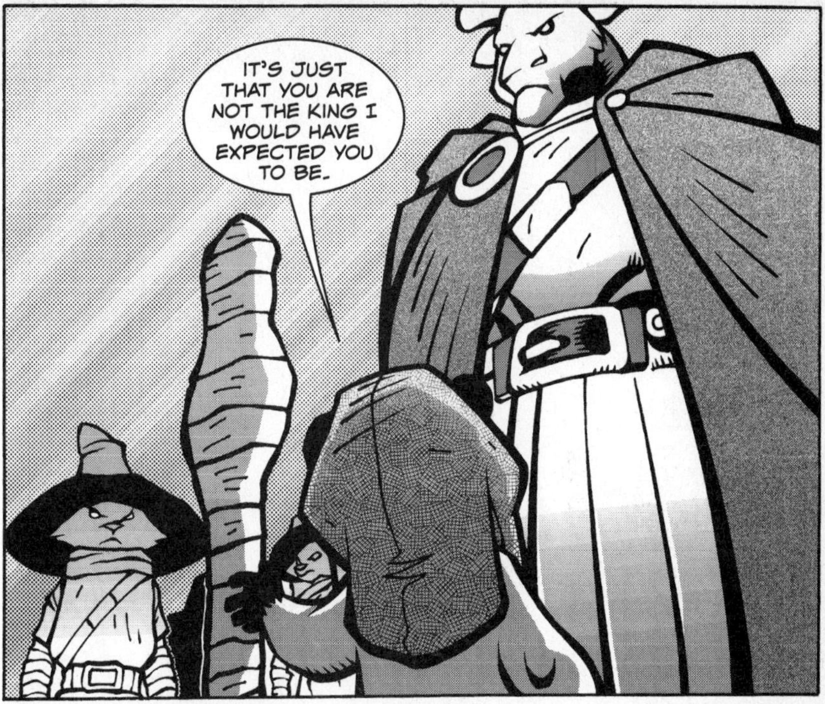
IT'S JUST THAT YOU ARE NOT THE KING I WOULD HAVE EXPECTED YOU TO BE.

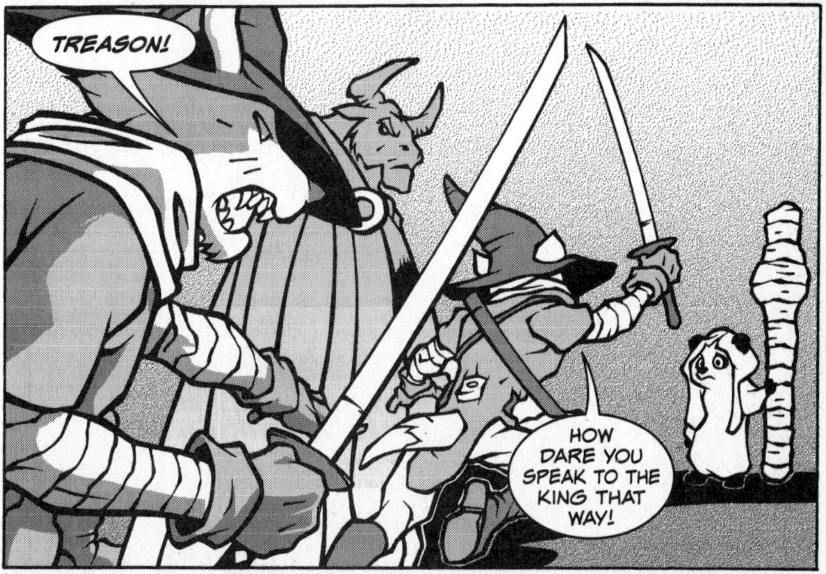
TREASON!
HOW DARE YOU SPEAK TO THE KING THAT WAY!

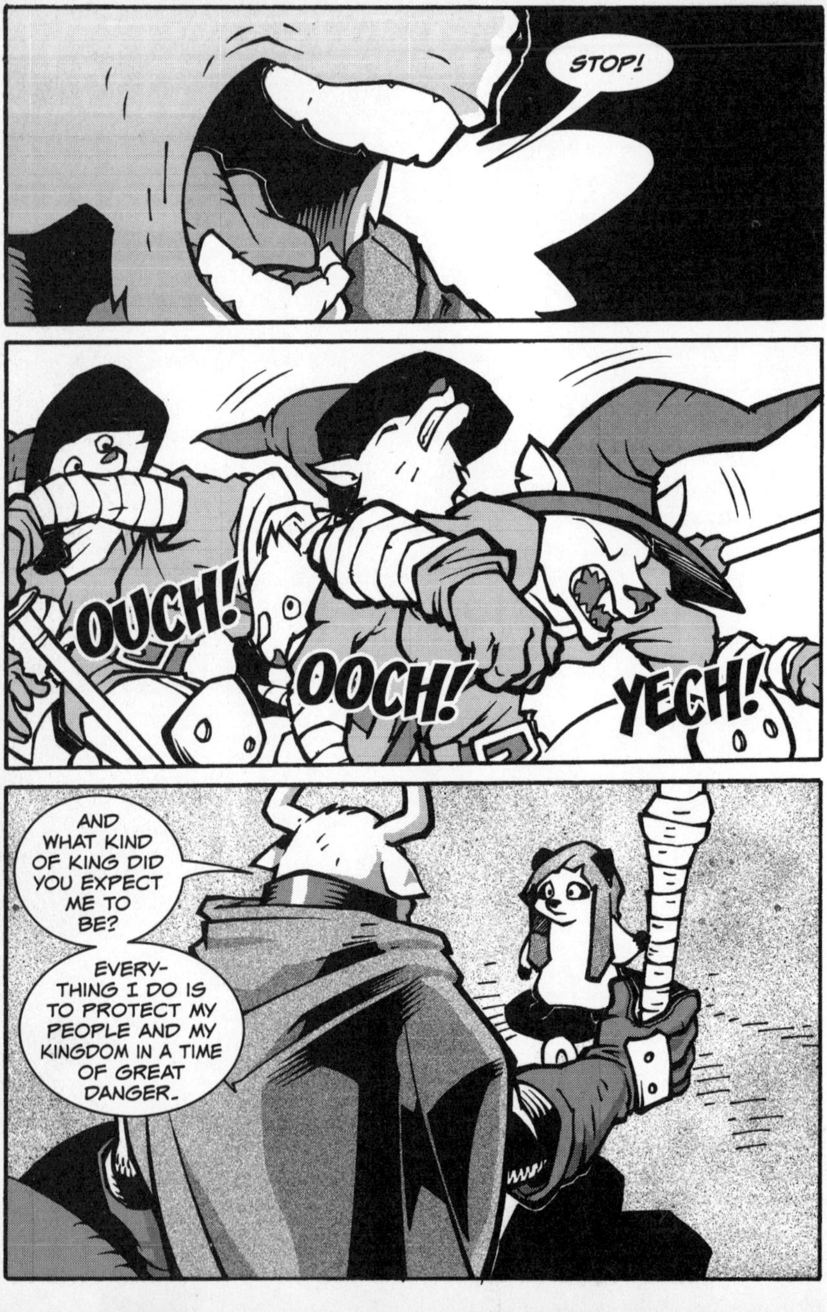
STOP!
OUCH!
OOCH!
YECH!
AND WHAT KIND OF KING DID YOU EXPECT ME TO BE?
EVERY-THING I DO IS TO PROTECT MY PEOPLE AND MY KINGDOM IN A TIME OF GREAT DANGER.

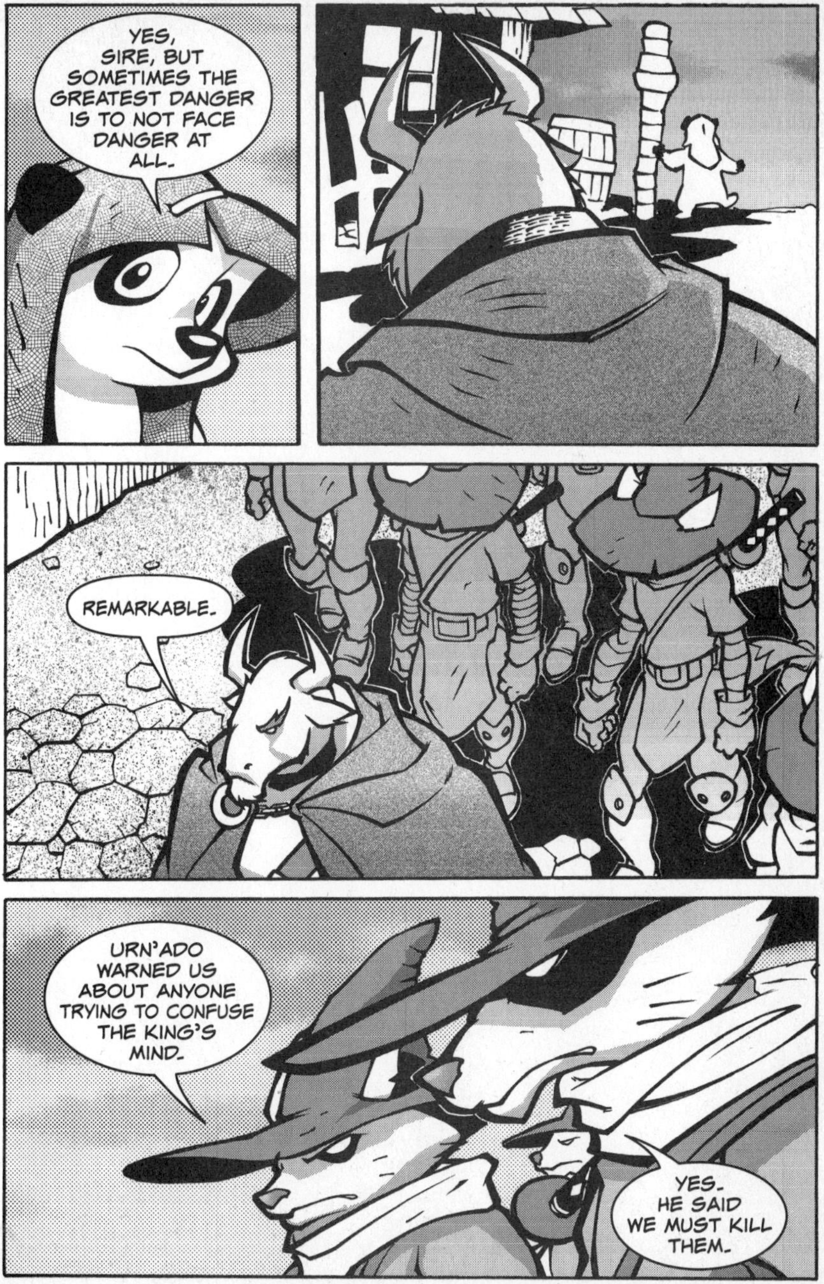
YES, SIRE, BUT SOMETIMES THE GREATEST DANGER IS TO NOT FACE DANGER AT ALL.
REMARKABLE.
URN'ADO WARNED US ABOUT ANYONE TRYING TO CONFUSE THE KING'S MIND.
YES. HE SAID WE MUST KILL THEM.

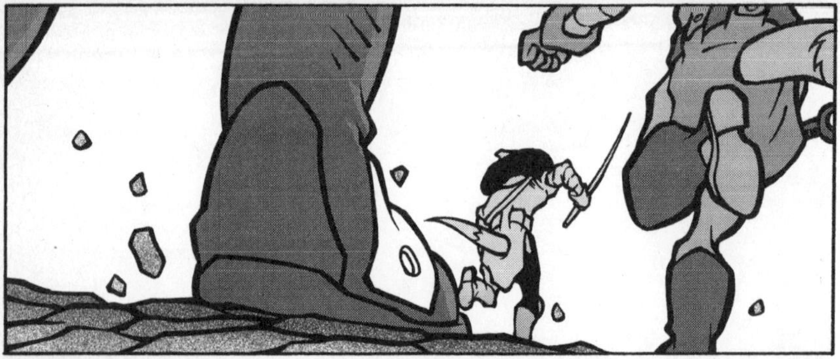

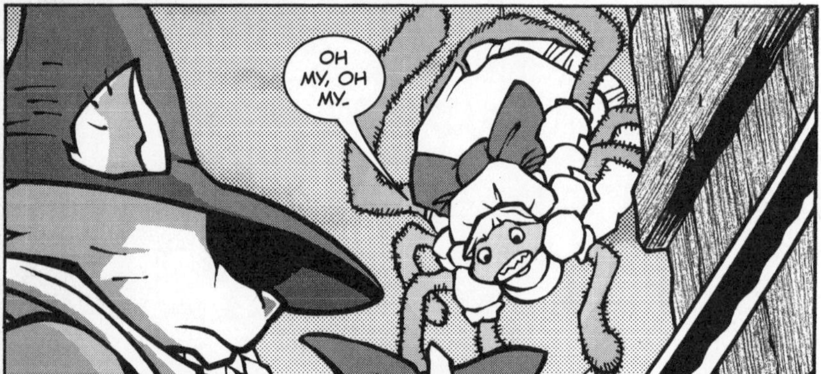
OH MY, OH MY...
OLD WOMAN, DID YOU SEE A SMALL BEAR COME THIS WAY?

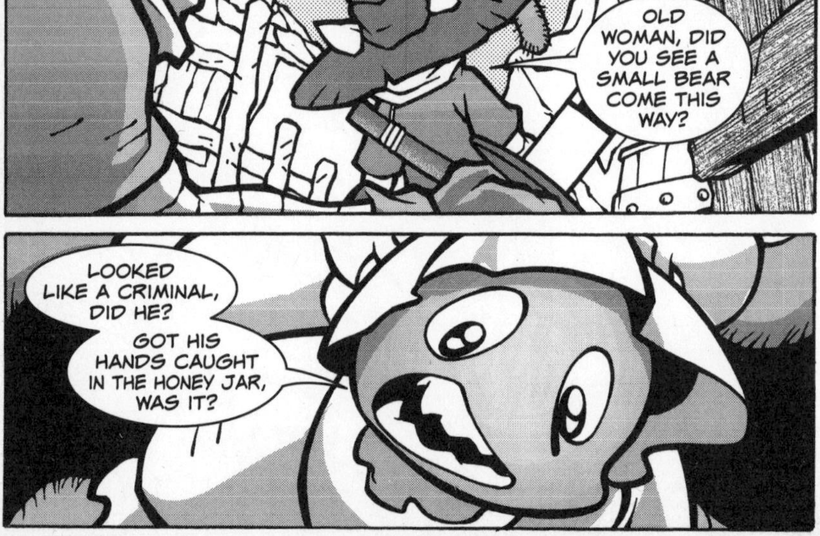
LOOKED LIKE A CRIMINAL, DID HE?
GOT HIS HANDS CAUGHT IN THE HONEY JAR, WAS IT?

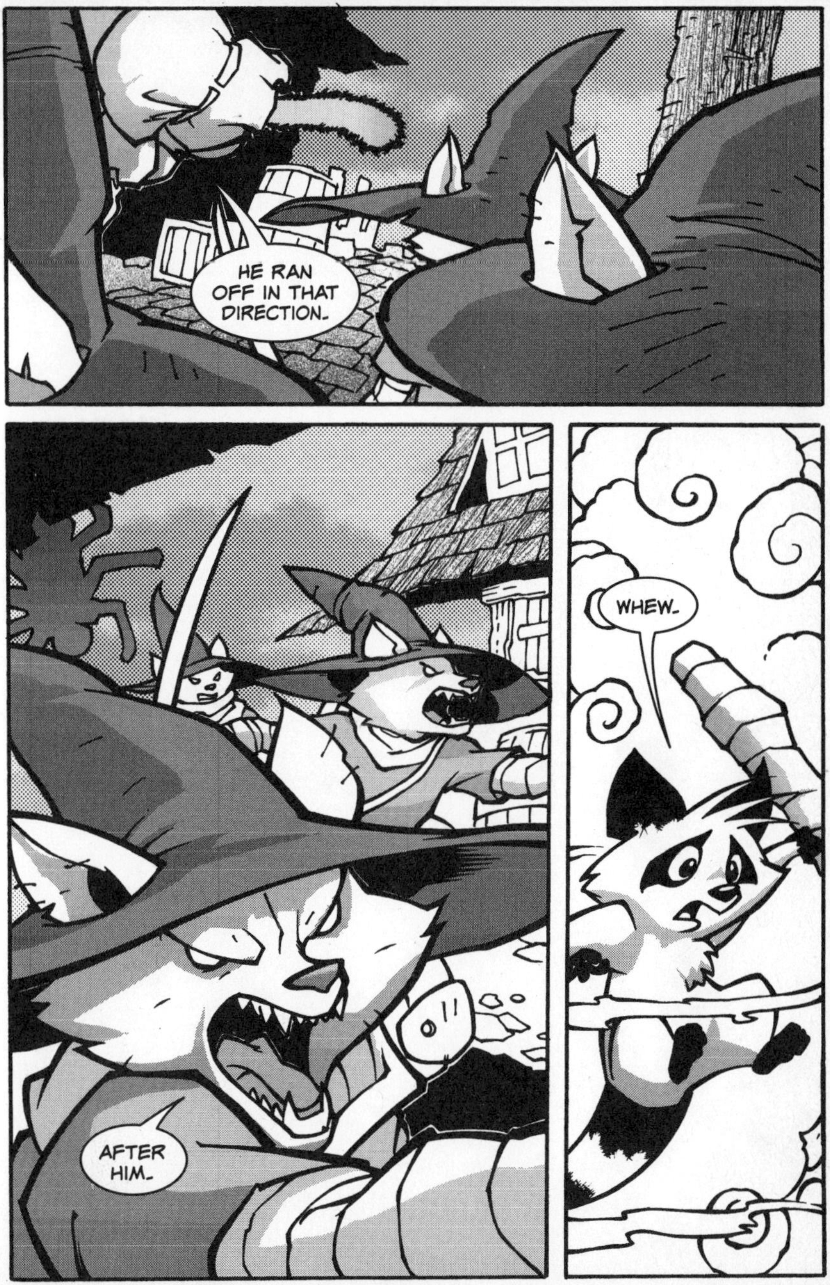
HE RAN OFF IN THAT DIRECTION.
AFTER HIM.
WHEW.

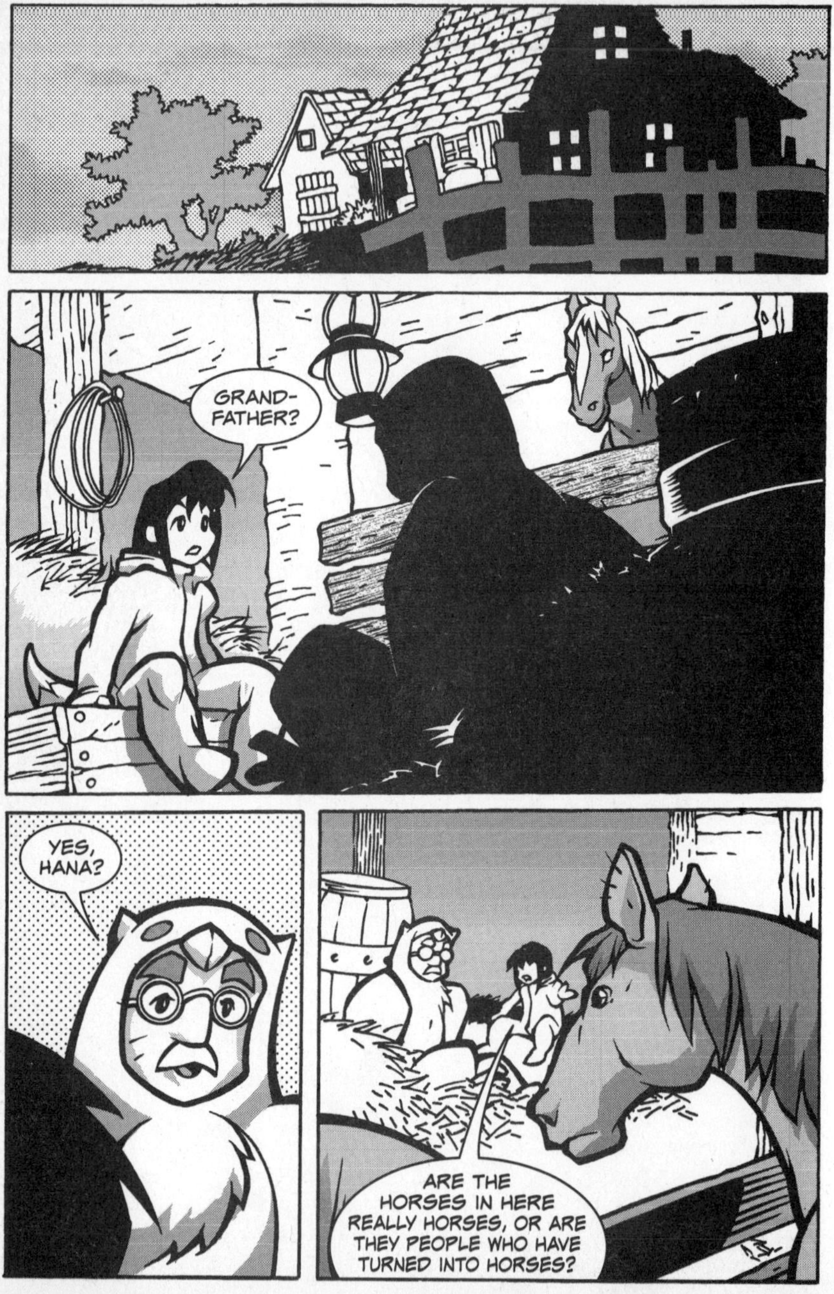
GRAND-
FATHER?
YES,
HANA?
ARE THE
HORSES IN HERE
REALLY HORSES, OR ARE
THEY PEOPLE WHO HAVE
TURNED INTO HORSES?

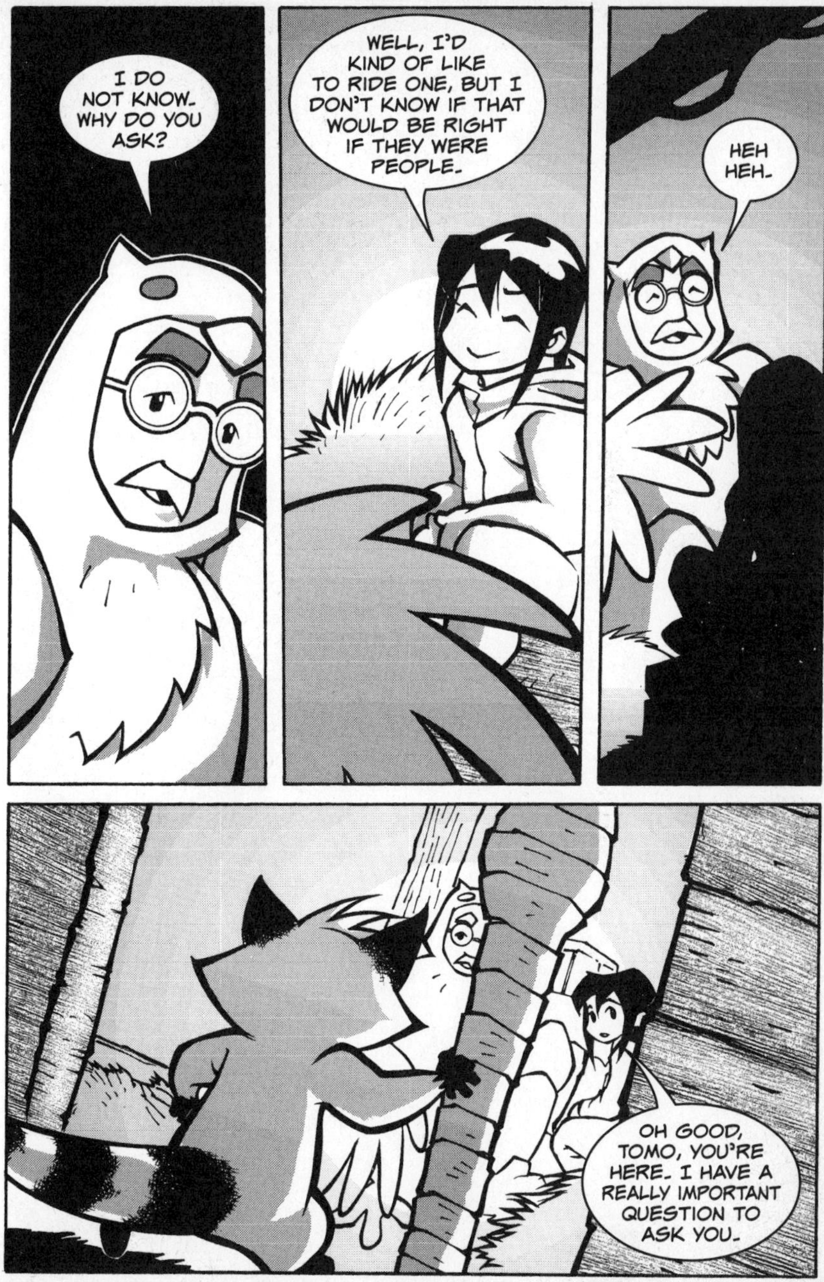
I DO NOT KNOW. WHY DO YOU ASK?
WELL, I'D KIND OF LIKE TO RIDE ONE, BUT I DON'T KNOW IF THAT WOULD BE RIGHT IF THEY WERE PEOPLE.
HEH HEH.
OH GOOD, TOMO, YOU'RE HERE. I HAVE A REALLY IMPORTANT QUESTION TO ASK YOU.

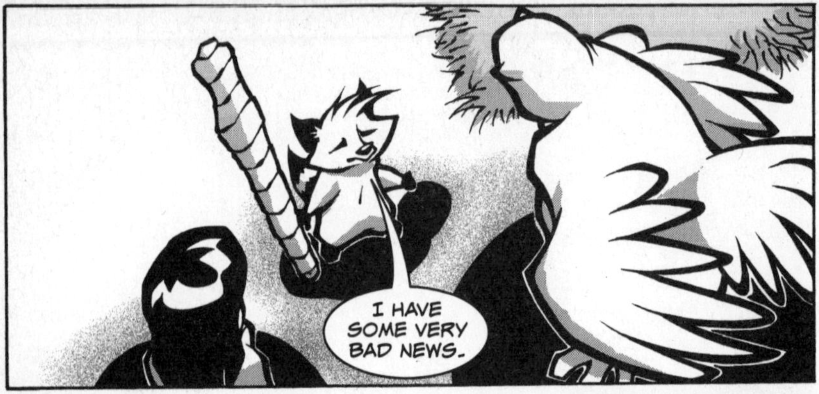
I HAVE SOME VERY BAD NEWS.
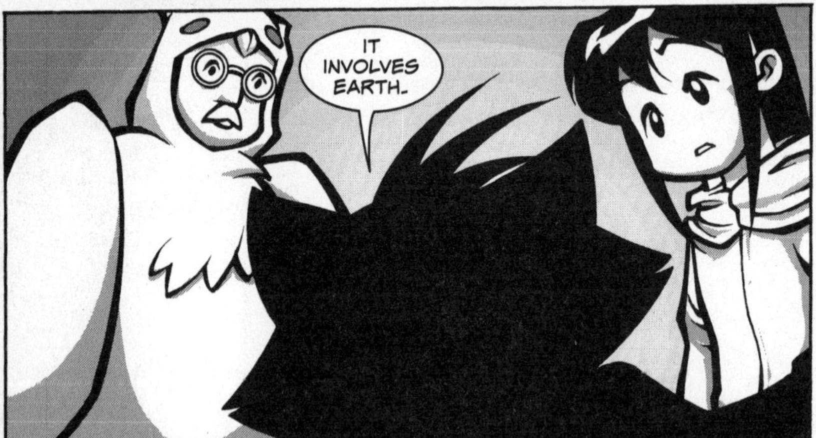
IT INVOLVES EARTH.
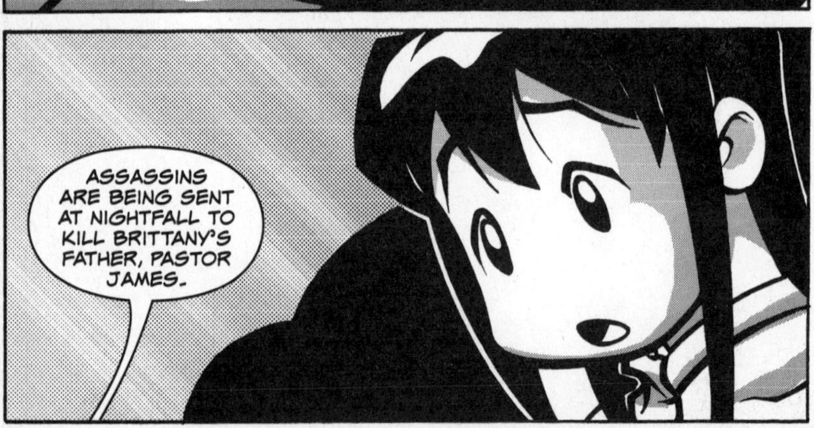
ASSASSINS ARE BEING SENT AT NIGHTFALL TO KILL BRITTANY'S FATHER, PASTOR JAMES.

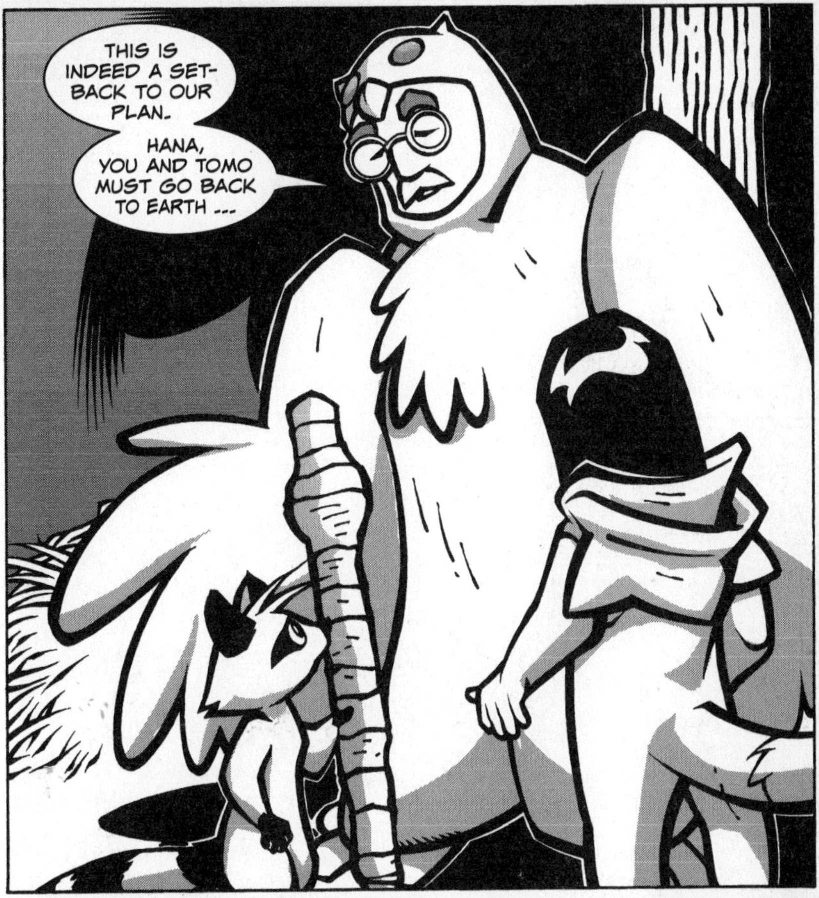
THIS IS INDEED A SET-BACK TO OUR PLAN.
HANA, YOU AND TOMO MUST GO BACK TO EARTH ...

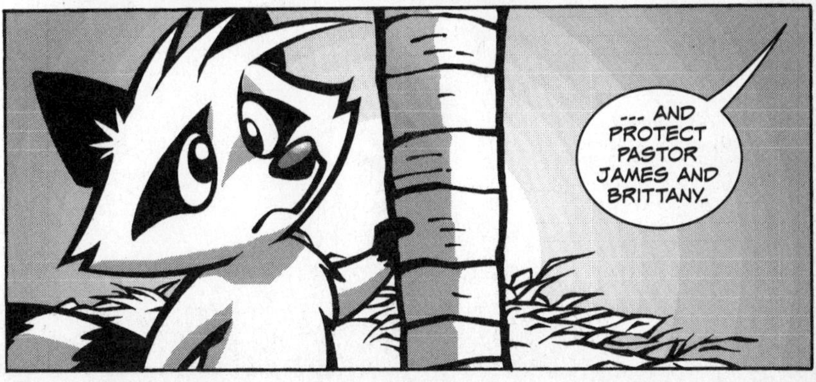
... AND PROTECT PASTOR JAMES AND BRITTANY.

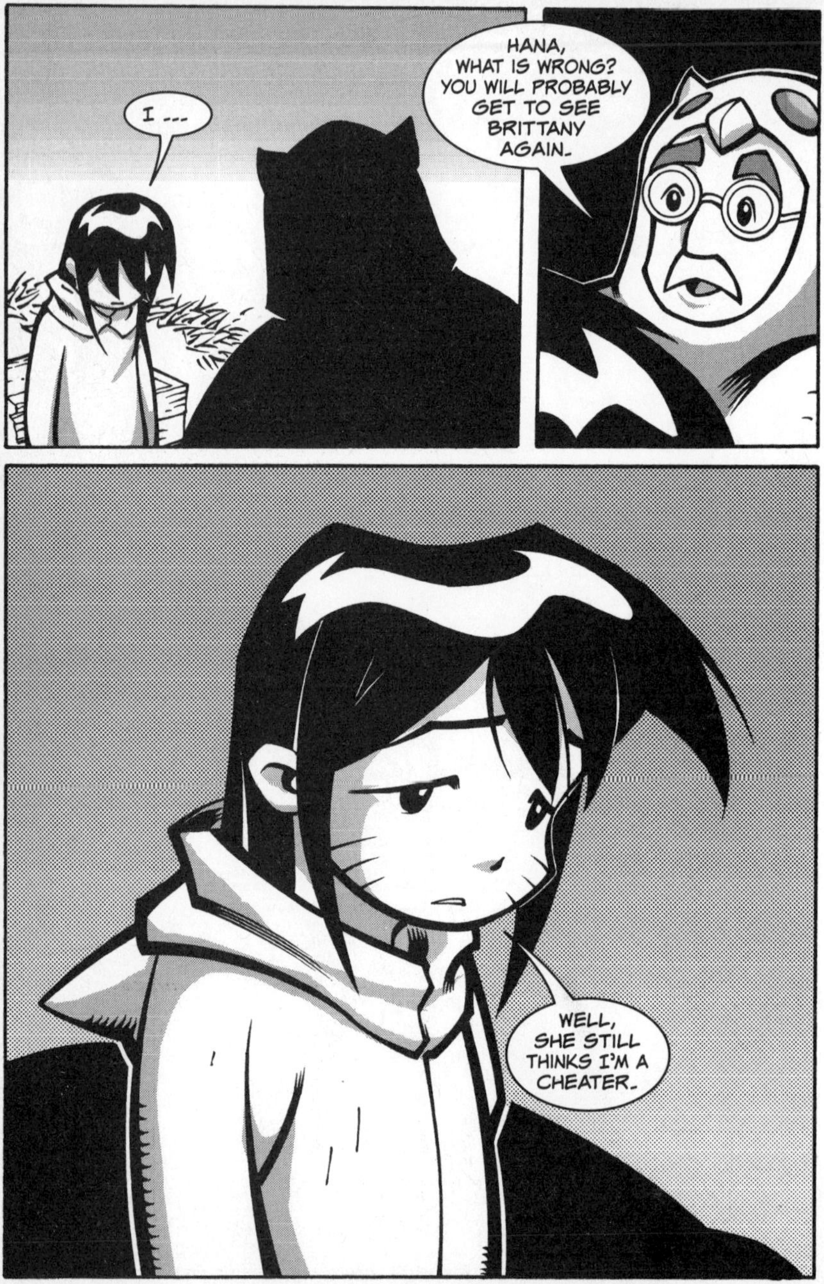
I ---
HANA, WHAT IS WRONG? YOU WILL PROBABLY GET TO SEE BRITTANY AGAIN.
WELL, SHE STILL THINKS I'M A CHEATER.

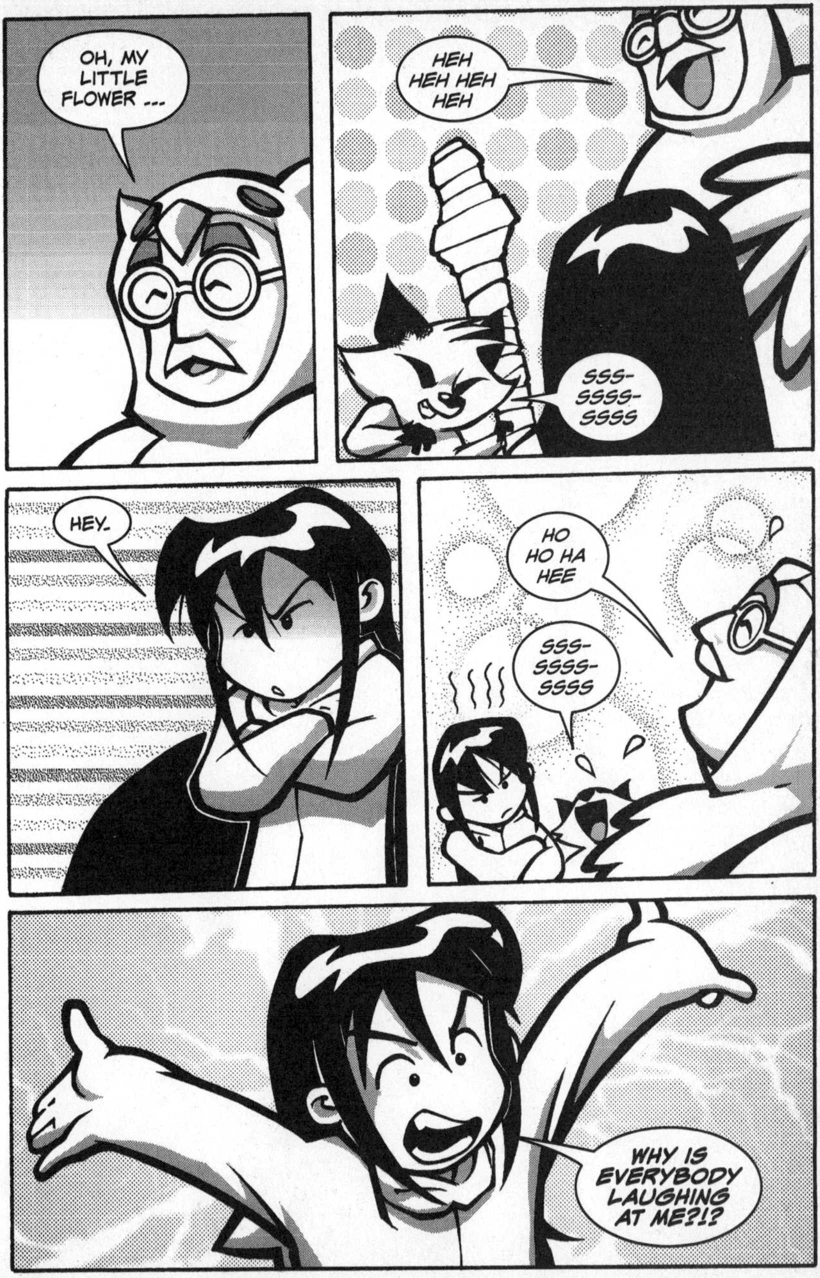
OH, MY LITTLE FLOWER ...
HEH HEH HEH HEH
SSS-SSSS-SSSS
HEY.
HO HO HA HEE
SSS-SSSS-SSSS
WHY IS EVERYBODY LAUGHING AT ME?!?

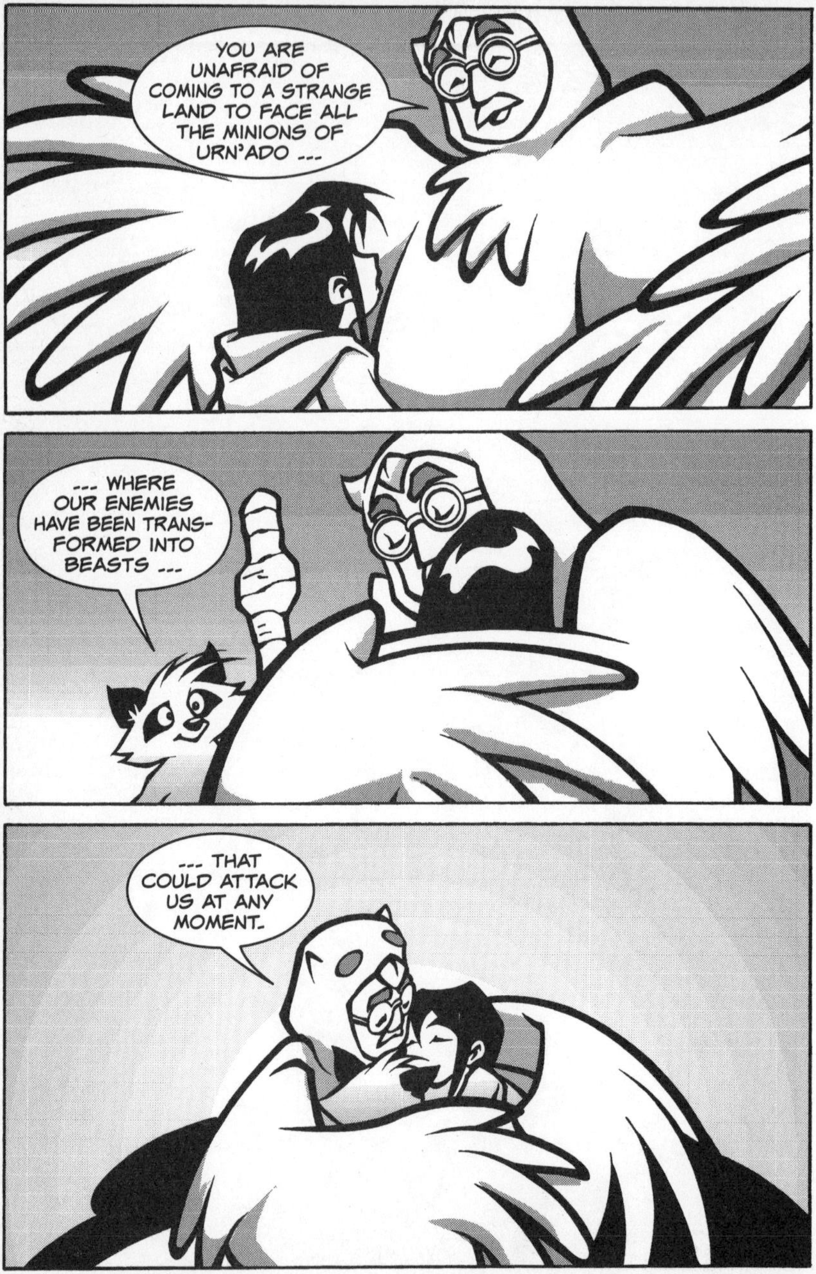
YOU ARE UNAFRAID OF COMING TO A STRANGE LAND TO FACE ALL THE MINIONS OF URN'ADO ---
--- WHERE OUR ENEMIES HAVE BEEN TRANS- FORMED INTO BEASTS ---
--- THAT COULD ATTACK US AT ANY MOMENT.

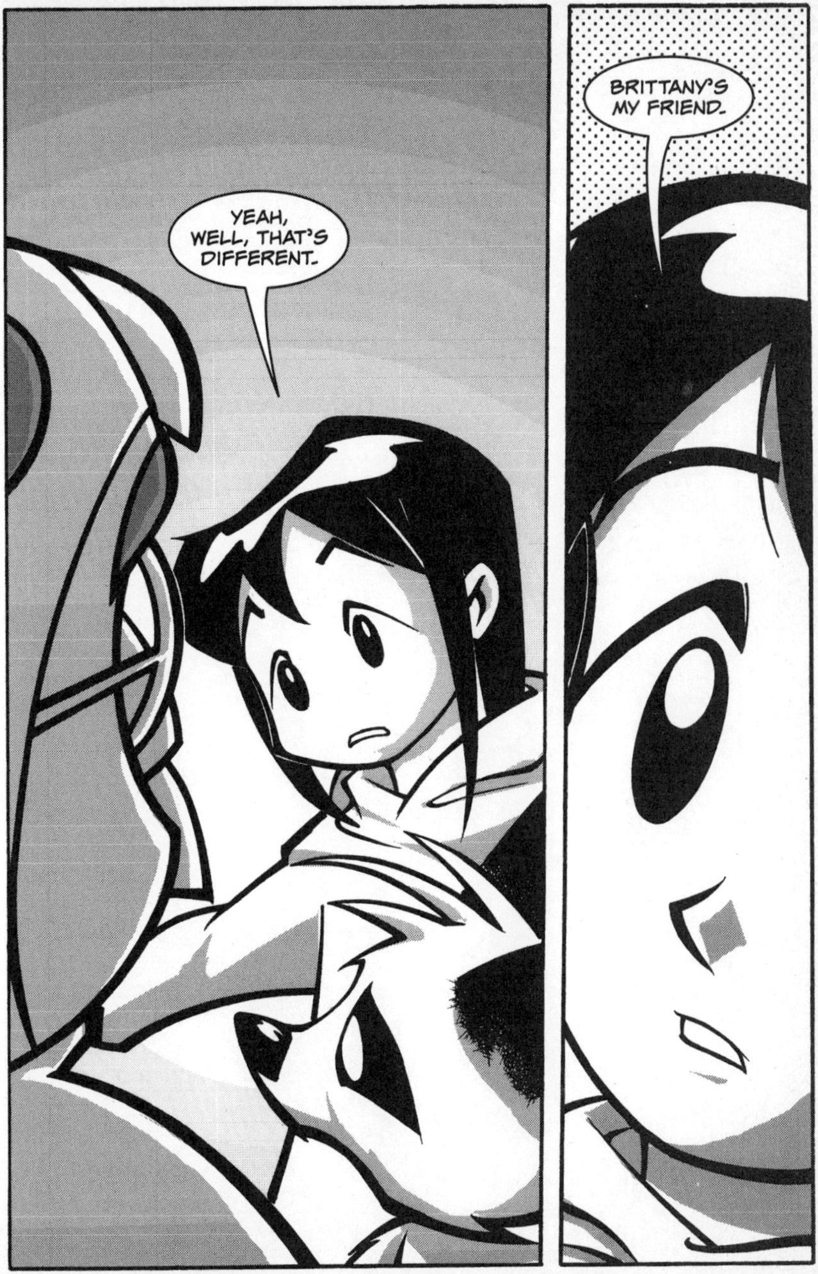
YEAH, WELL, THAT'S DIFFERENT...
BRITTANY'S MY FRIEND...

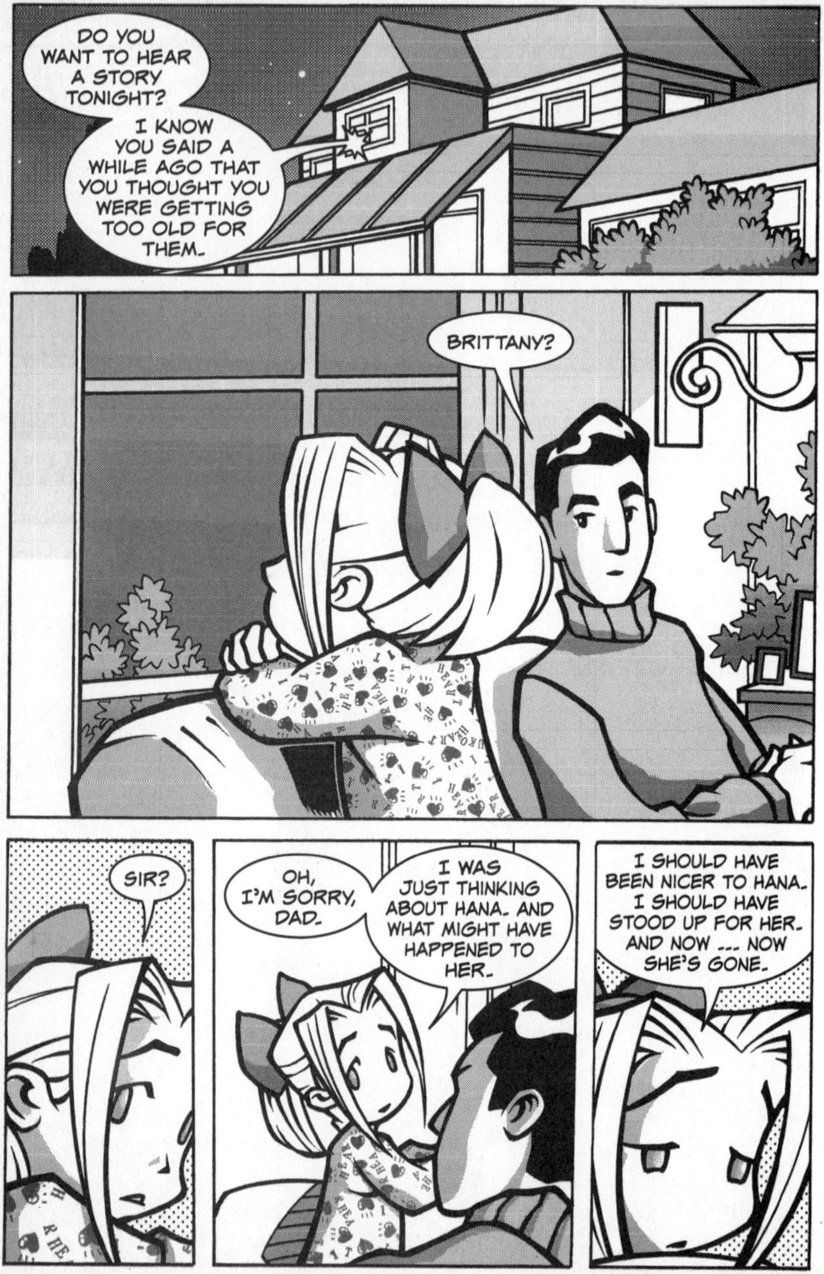
DO YOU WANT TO HEAR A STORY TONIGHT?
I KNOW YOU SAID A WHILE AGO THAT YOU THOUGHT YOU WERE GETTING TOO OLD FOR THEM.
BRITTANY?
SIR?
OH, I'M SORRY, DAD.
I WAS JUST THINKING ABOUT HANA. AND WHAT MIGHT HAVE HAPPENED TO HER.
I SHOULD HAVE BEEN NICER TO HANA. I SHOULD HAVE STOOD UP FOR HER. AND NOW ... NOW SHE'S GONE.

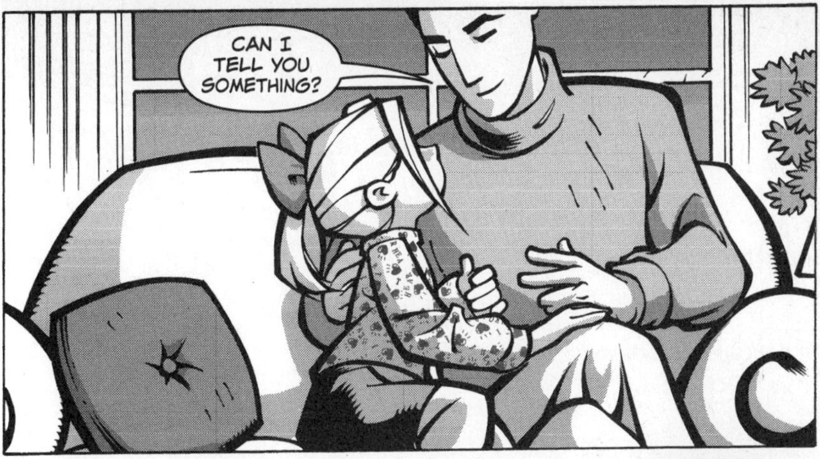
CAN I TELL YOU SOMETHING?
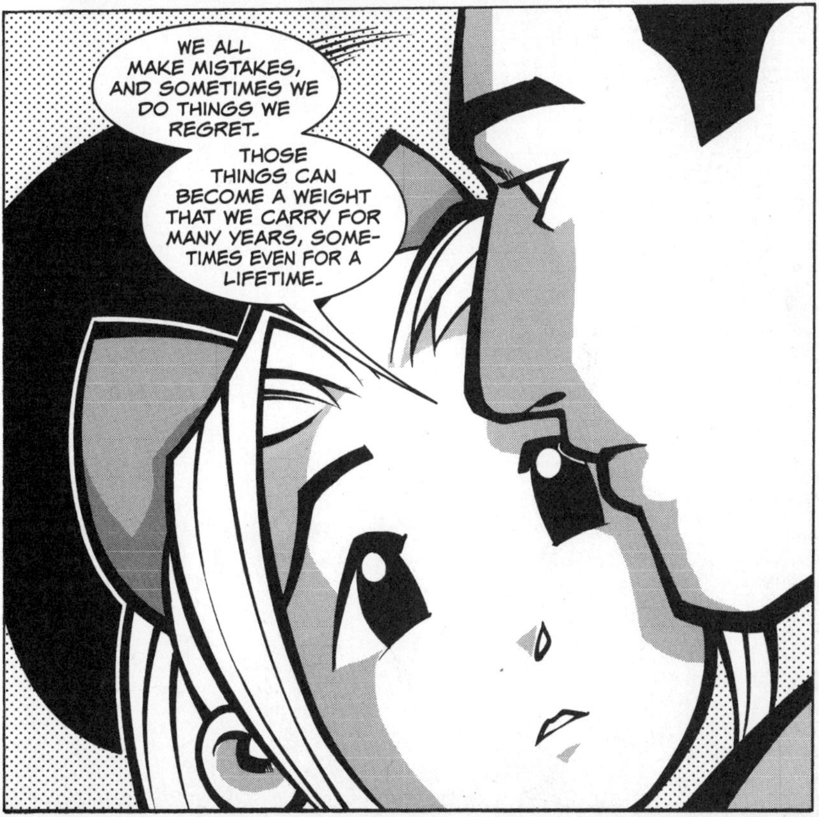
WE ALL MAKE MISTAKES, AND SOMETIMES WE DO THINGS WE REGRET.
THOSE THINGS CAN BECOME A WEIGHT THAT WE CARRY FOR MANY YEARS, SOMETIMES EVEN FOR A LIFETIME.

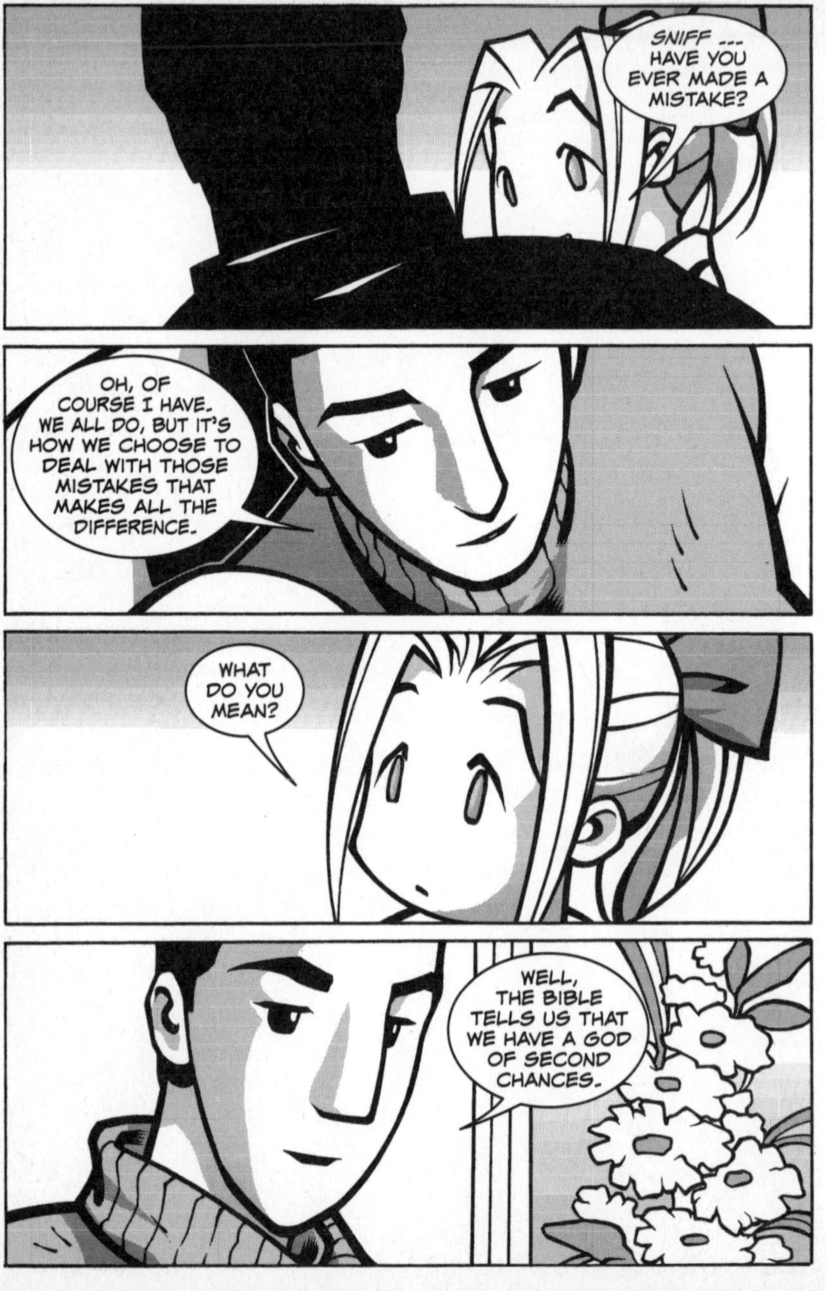
SNIFF ... HAVE YOU EVER MADE A MISTAKE?
OH, OF COURSE I HAVE. WE ALL DO, BUT IT'S HOW WE CHOOSE TO DEAL WITH THOSE MISTAKES THAT MAKES ALL THE DIFFERENCE.
WHAT DO YOU MEAN?
WELL, THE BIBLE TELLS US THAT WE HAVE A GOD OF SECOND CHANCES.

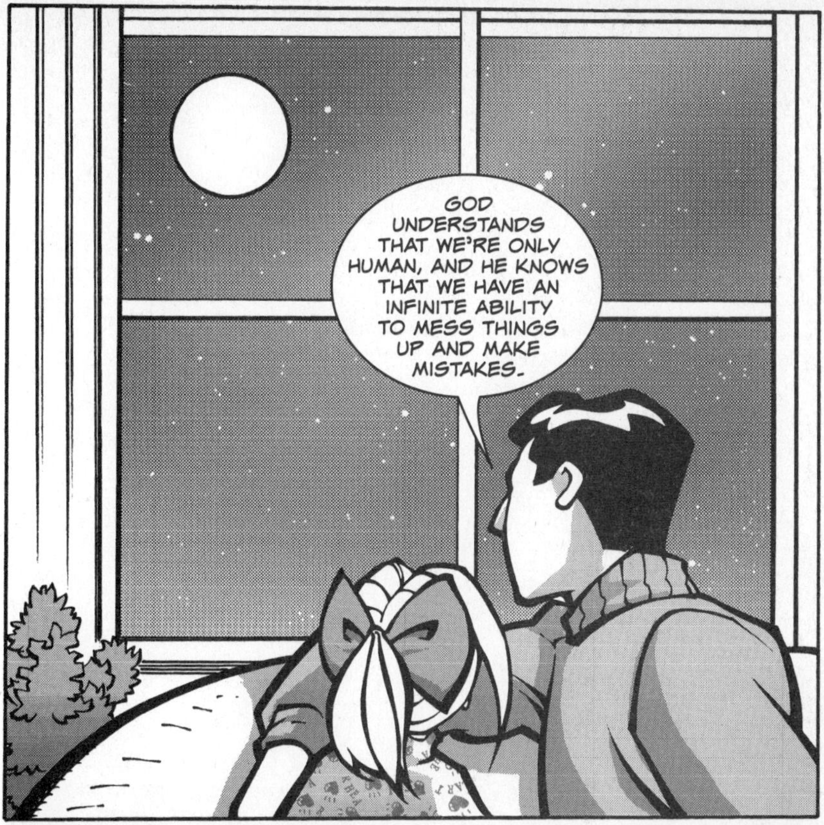
GOD UNDERSTANDS THAT WE'RE ONLY HUMAN, AND HE KNOWS THAT WE HAVE AN INFINITE ABILITY TO MESS THINGS UP AND MAKE MISTAKES.
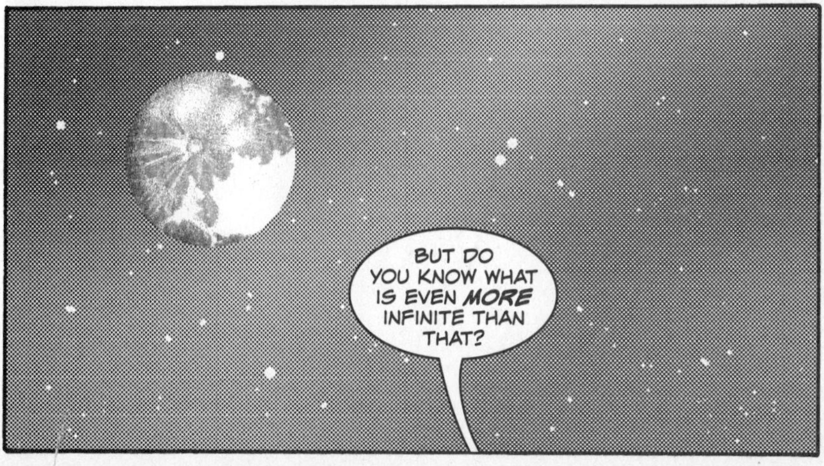
BUT DO YOU KNOW WHAT IS EVEN *MORE* INFINITE THAN THAT?

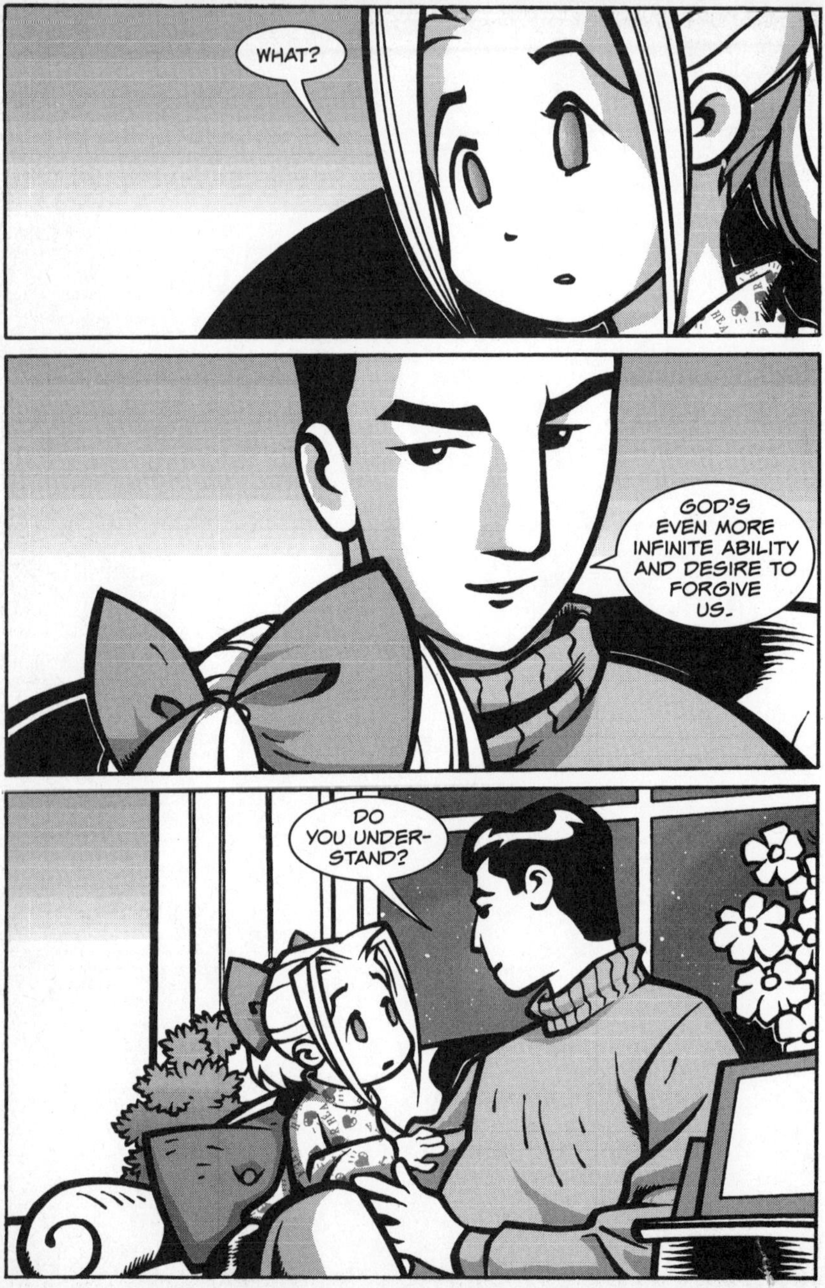
WHAT?
GOD'S EVEN MORE INFINITE ABILITY AND DESIRE TO FORGIVE US.
DO YOU UNDERSTAND?

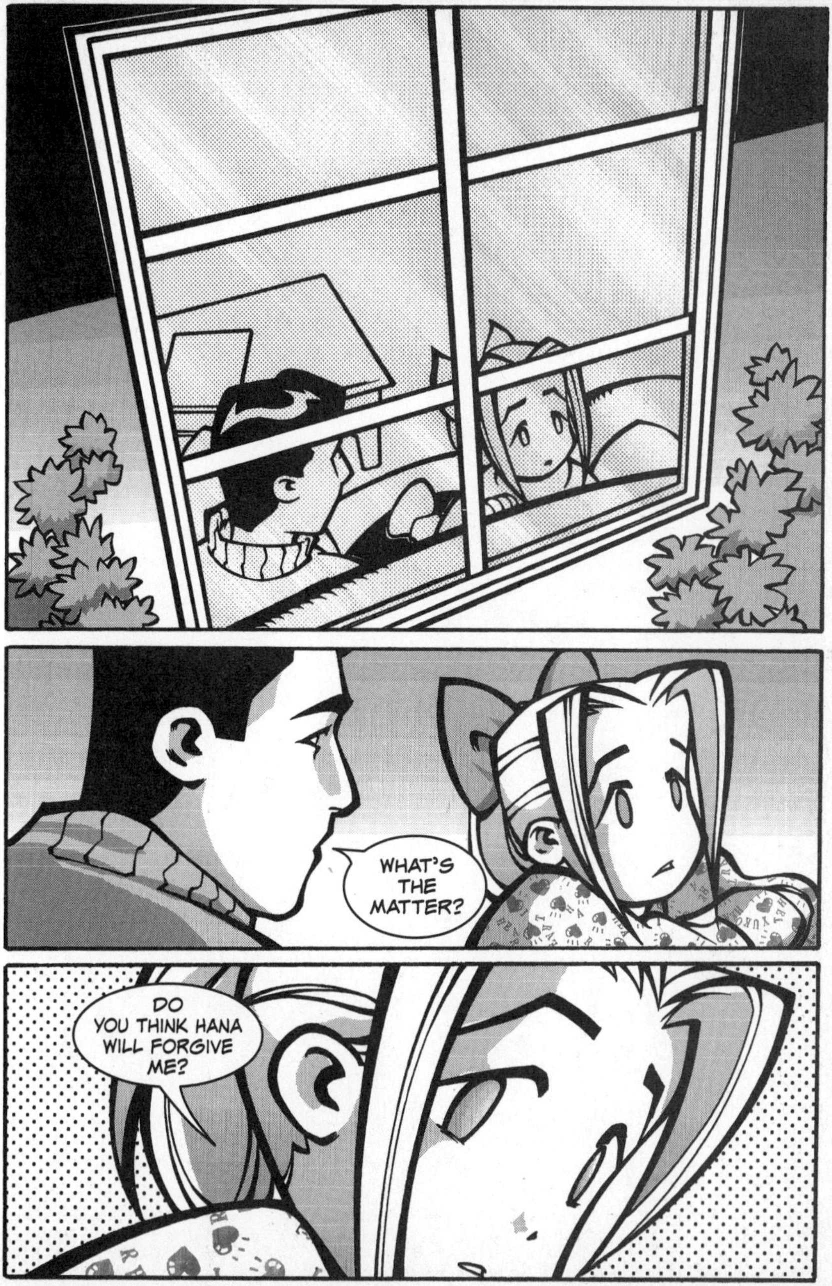
WHAT'S THE MATTER?
DO YOU THINK HANA WILL FORGIVE ME?

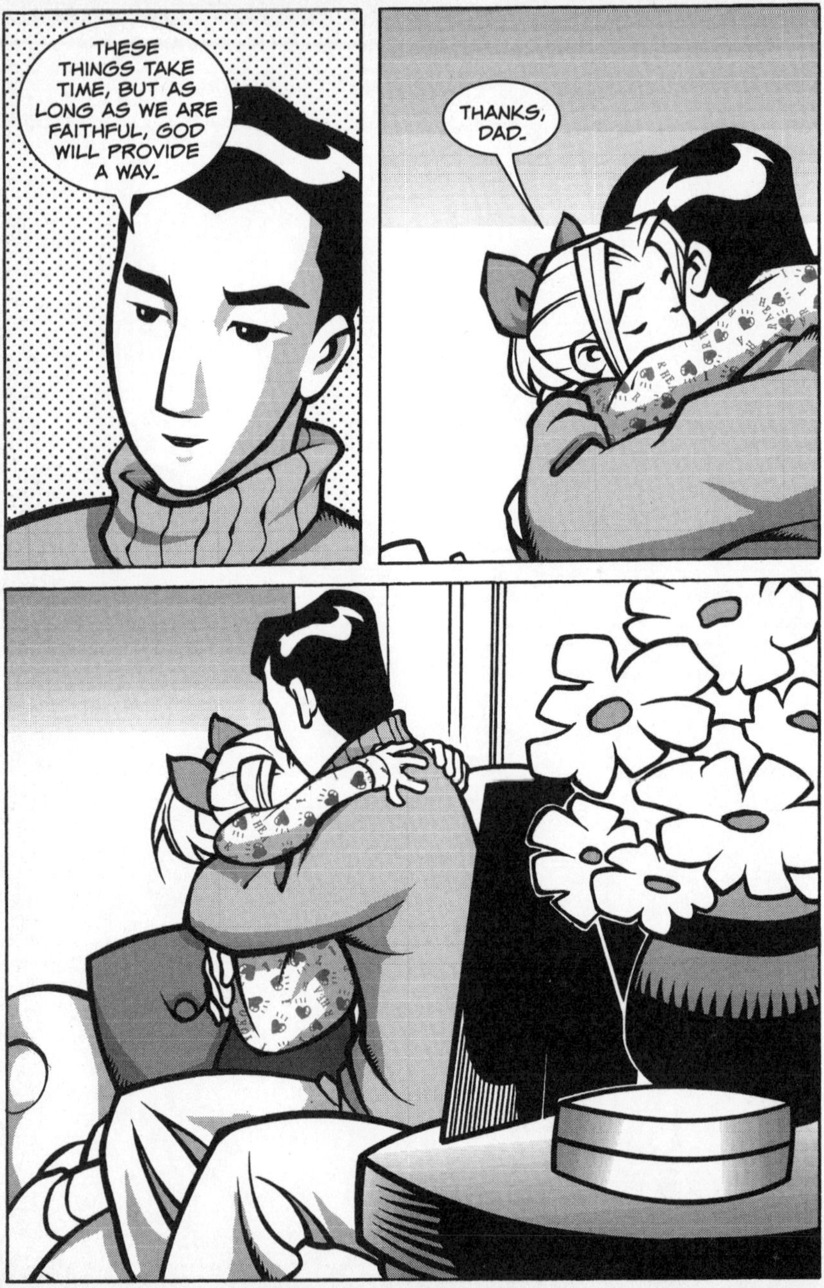
THESE THINGS TAKE TIME, BUT AS LONG AS WE ARE FAITHFUL, GOD WILL PROVIDE A WAY.
THANKS, DAD.

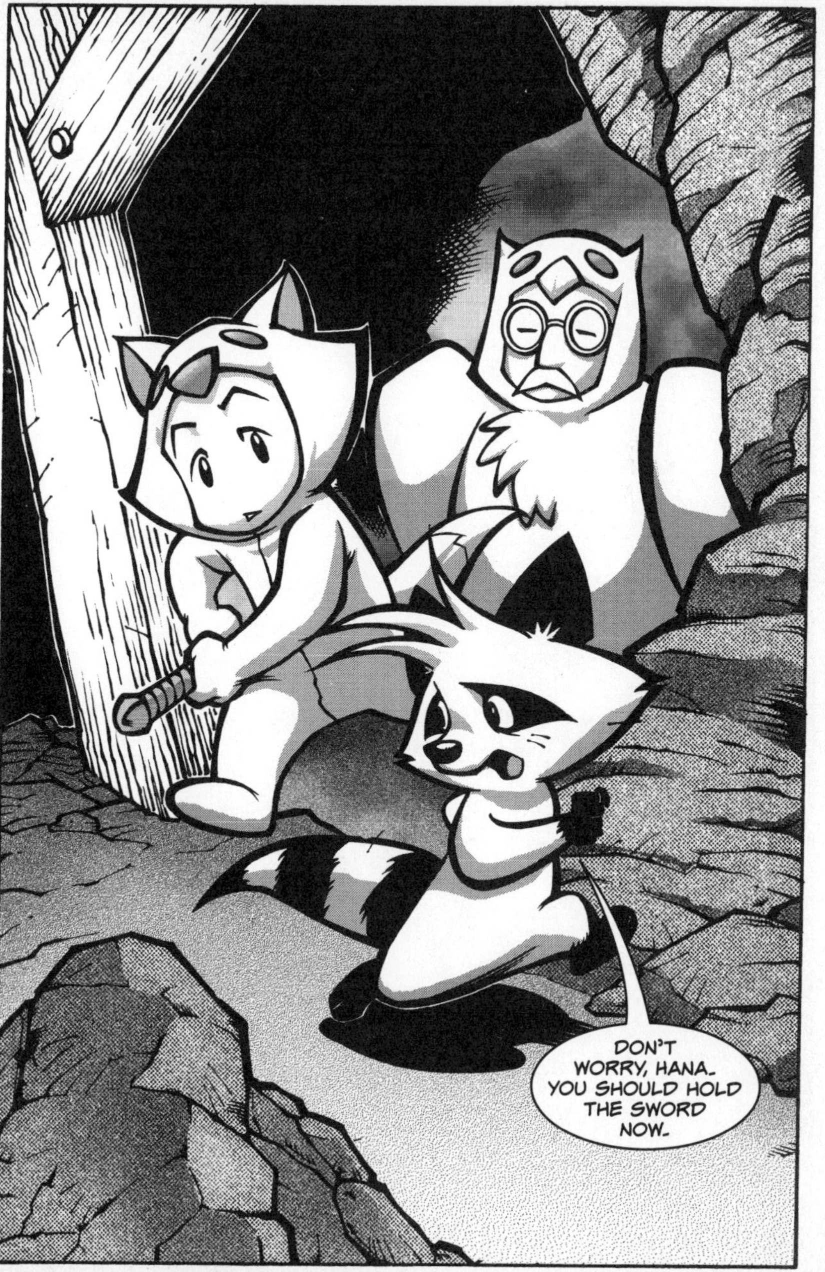
DON'T WORRY, HANA. YOU SHOULD HOLD THE SWORD NOW.

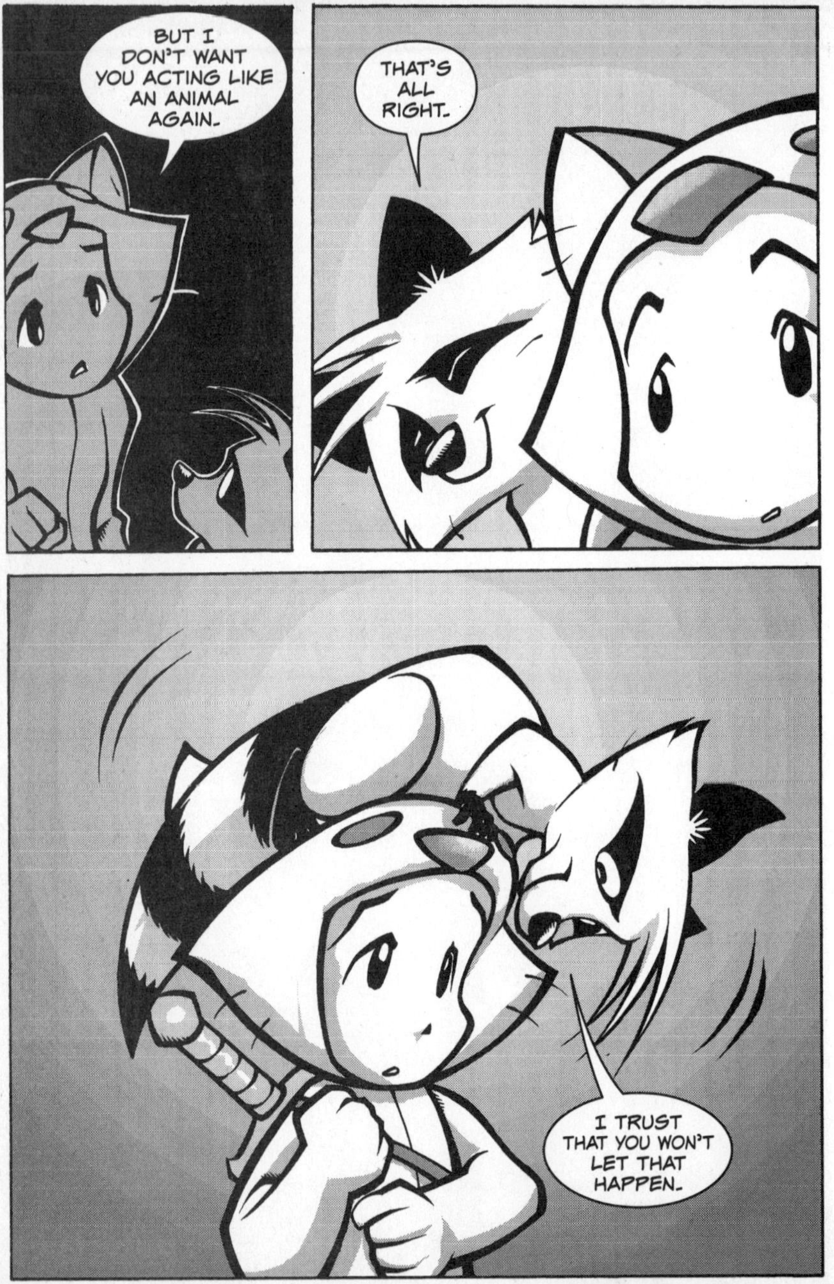
BUT I DON'T WANT YOU ACTING LIKE AN ANIMAL AGAIN.
THAT'S ALL RIGHT.
I TRUST THAT YOU WON'T LET THAT HAPPEN.

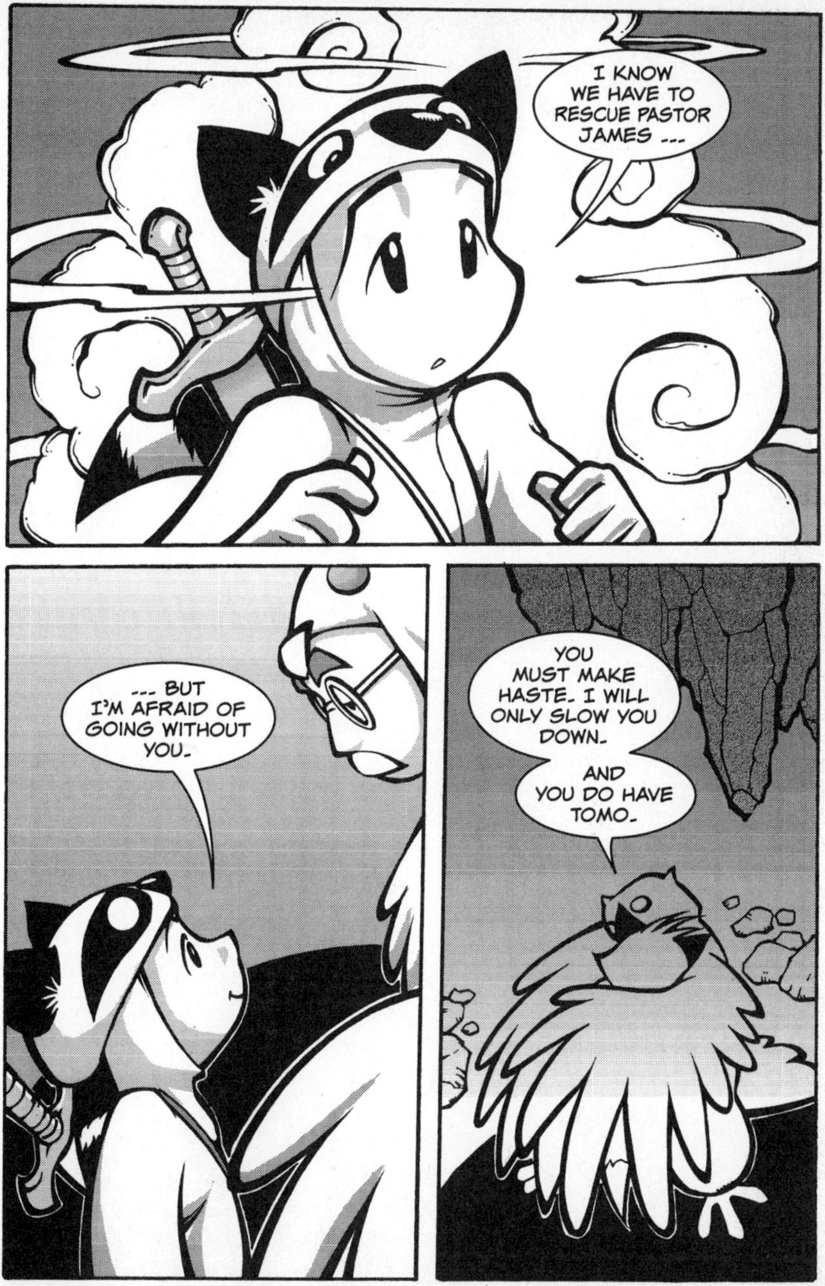
I KNOW WE HAVE TO RESCUE PASTOR JAMES ...
... BUT I'M AFRAID OF GOING WITHOUT YOU.
YOU MUST MAKE HASTE. I WILL ONLY SLOW YOU DOWN.
AND YOU DO HAVE TOMO.

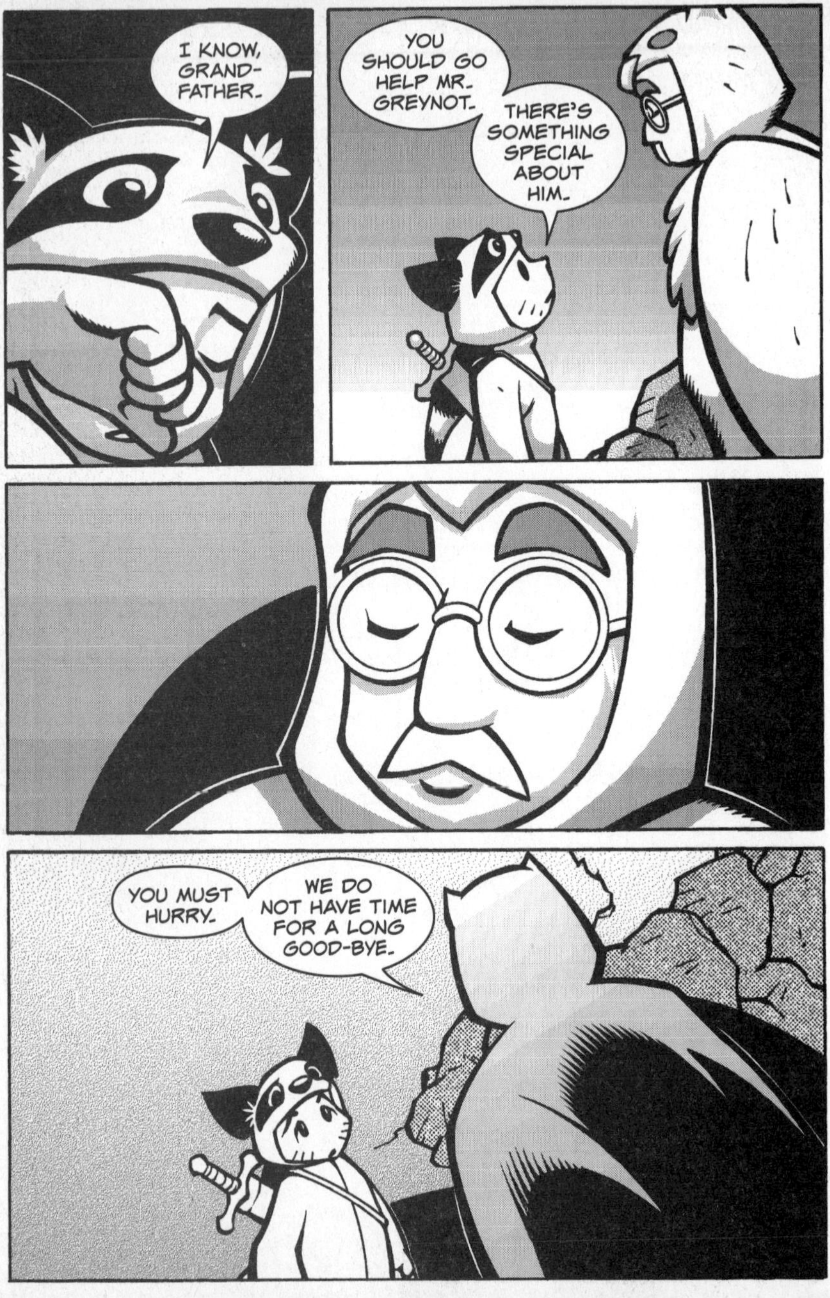
I KNOW, GRAND-FATHER.
YOU SHOULD GO HELP MR. GREYNOT.
THERE'S SOMETHING SPECIAL ABOUT HIM.
YOU MUST HURRY.
WE DO NOT HAVE TIME FOR A LONG GOOD-BYE.

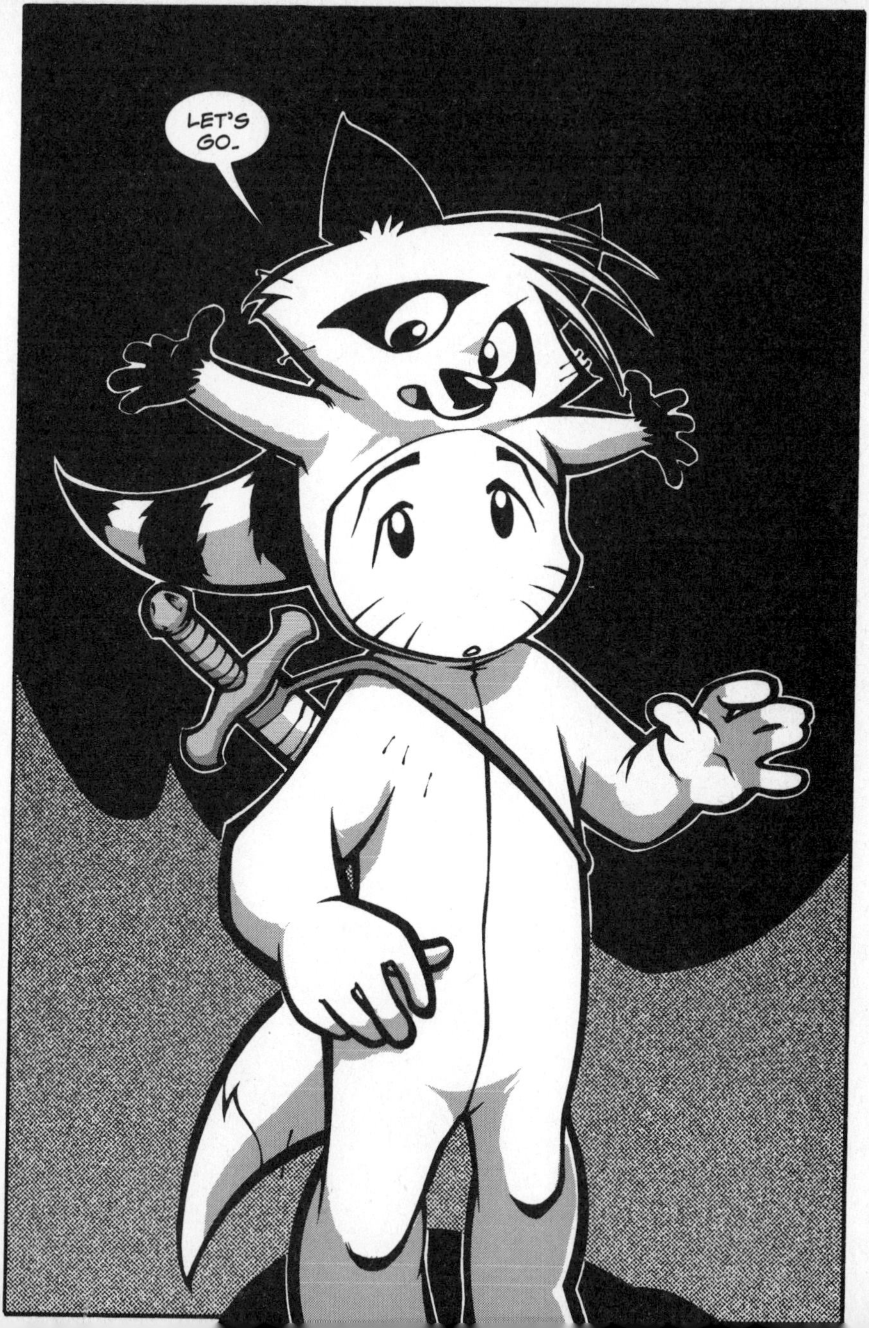
LET'S GO.

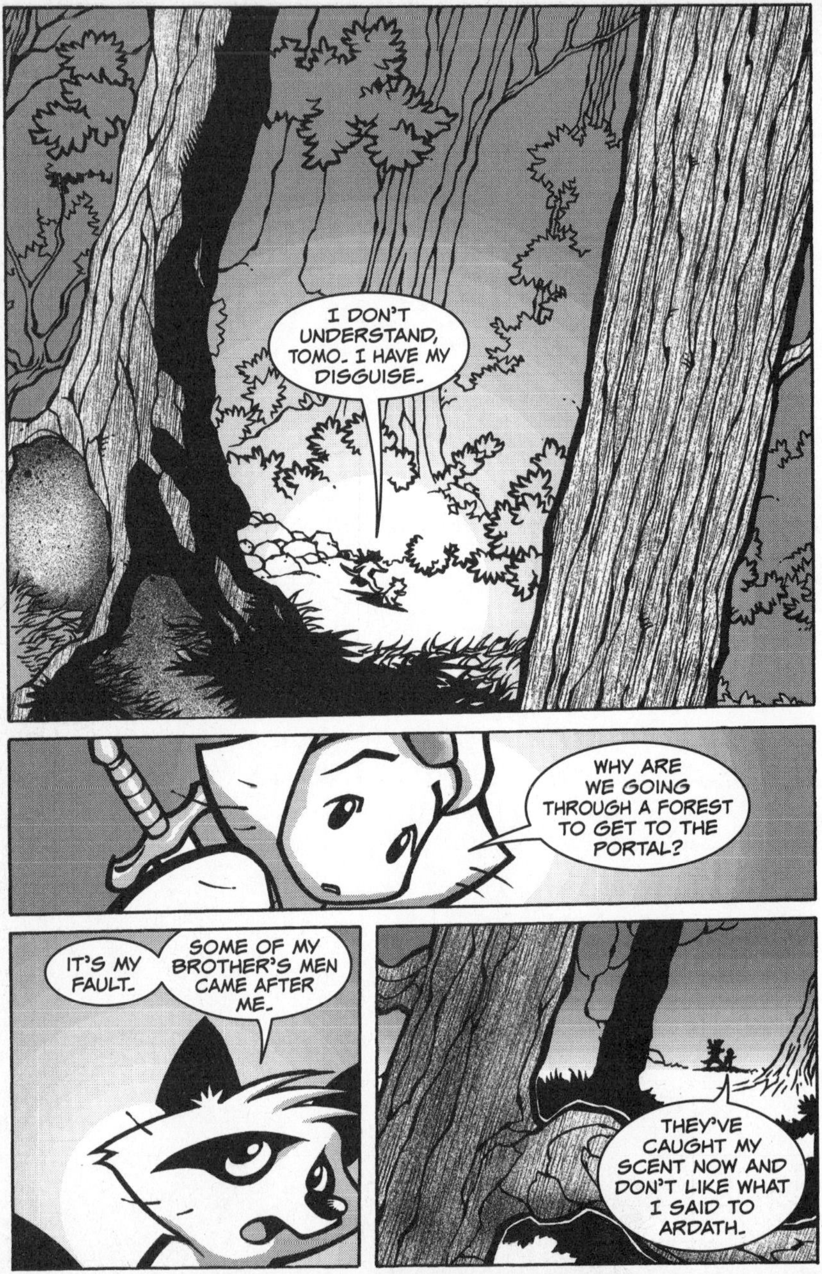
I DON'T UNDERSTAND, TOMO. I HAVE MY DISGUISE.
WHY ARE WE GOING THROUGH A FOREST TO GET TO THE PORTAL?
IT'S MY FAULT.
SOME OF MY BROTHER'S MEN CAME AFTER ME.
THEY'VE CAUGHT MY SCENT NOW AND DON'T LIKE WHAT I SAID TO ARDATH.

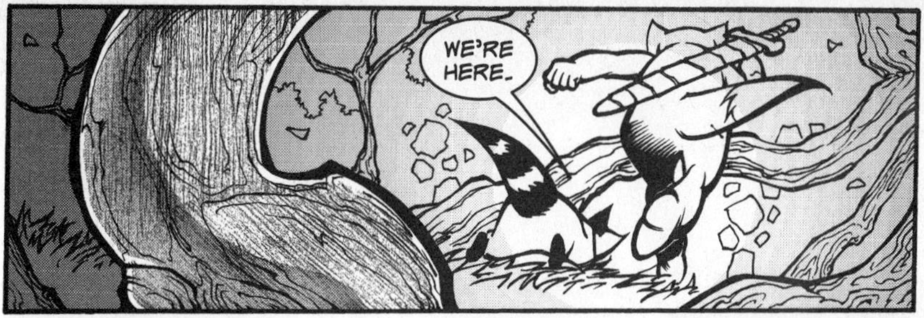
WE'RE HERE.

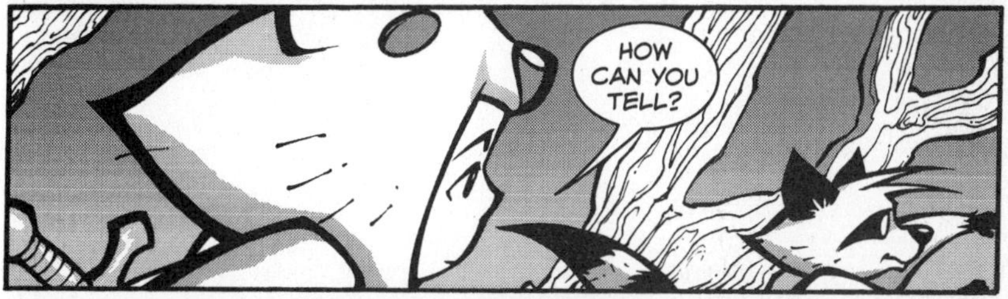
HOW CAN YOU TELL?

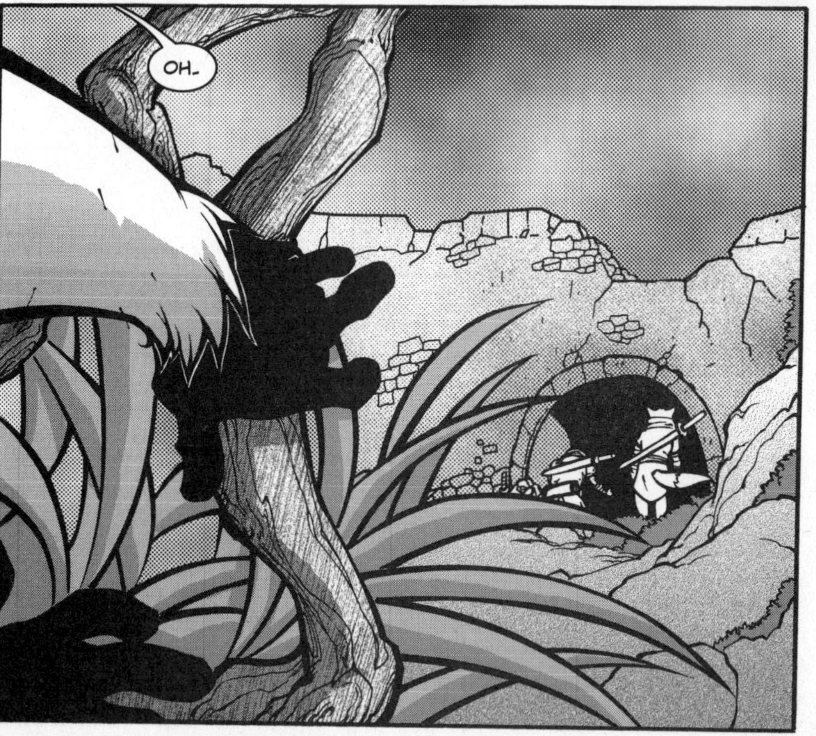
OH.

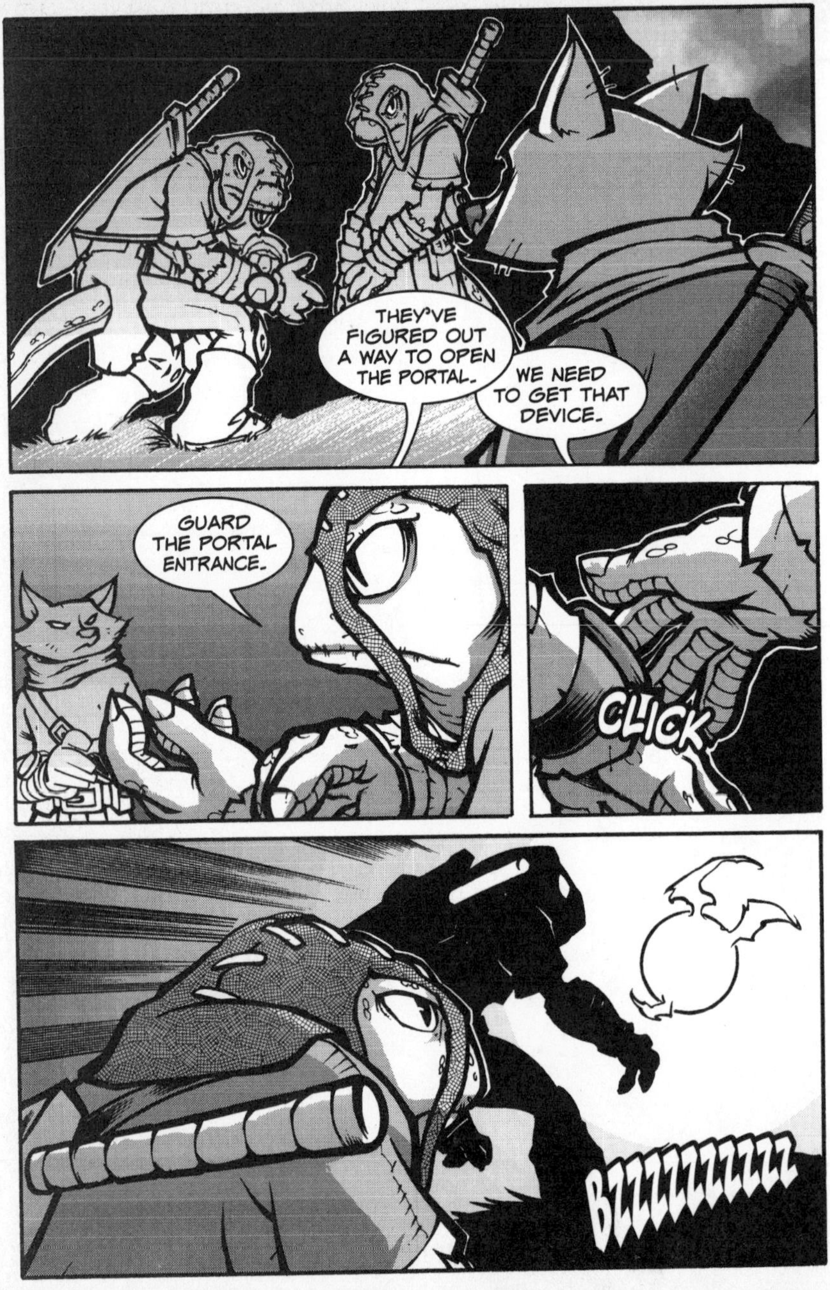

THEY'VE FIGURED OUT A WAY TO OPEN THE PORTAL.
WE NEED TO GET THAT DEVICE.
GUARD THE PORTAL ENTRANCE.
CLICK
BZZZZZZZZZZZ

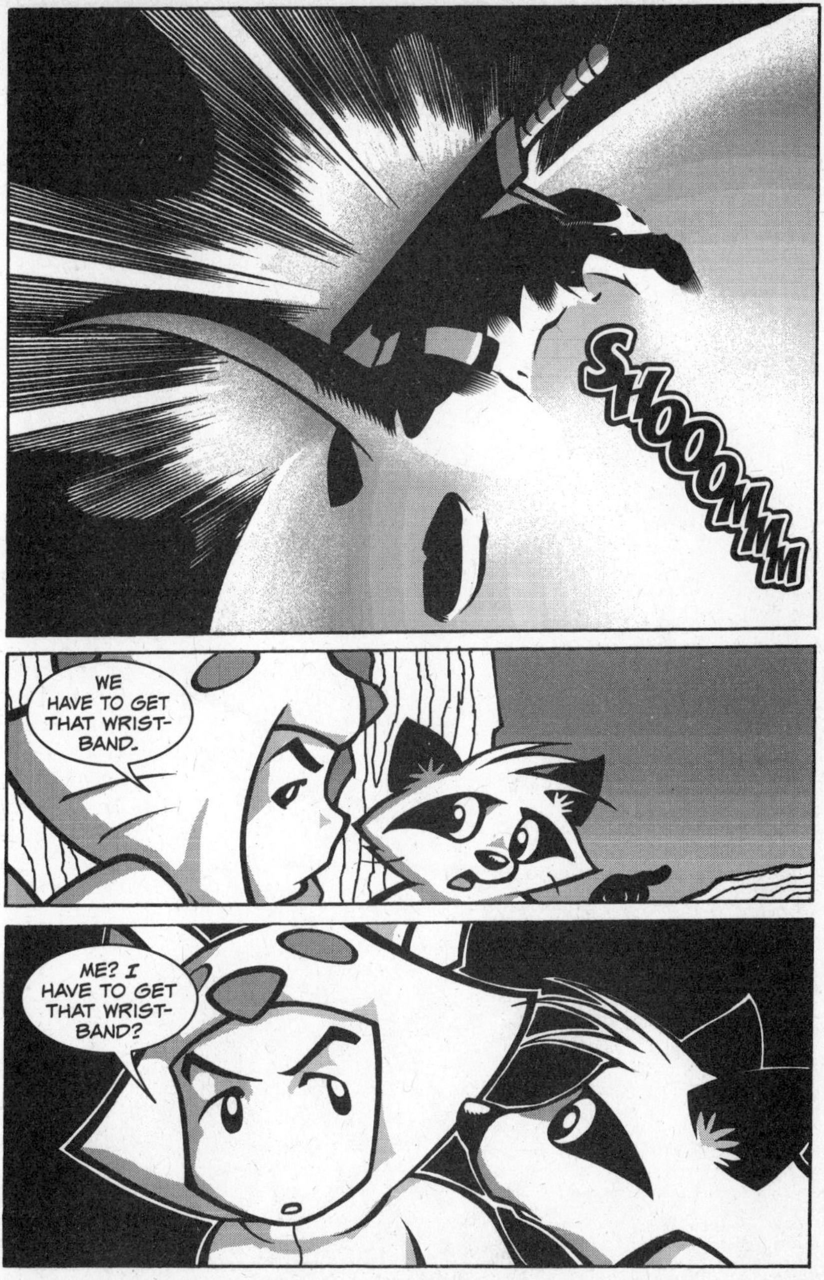
SHOOOMMM
WE HAVE TO GET THAT WRIST-BAND.
ME? I HAVE TO GET THAT WRIST-BAND?

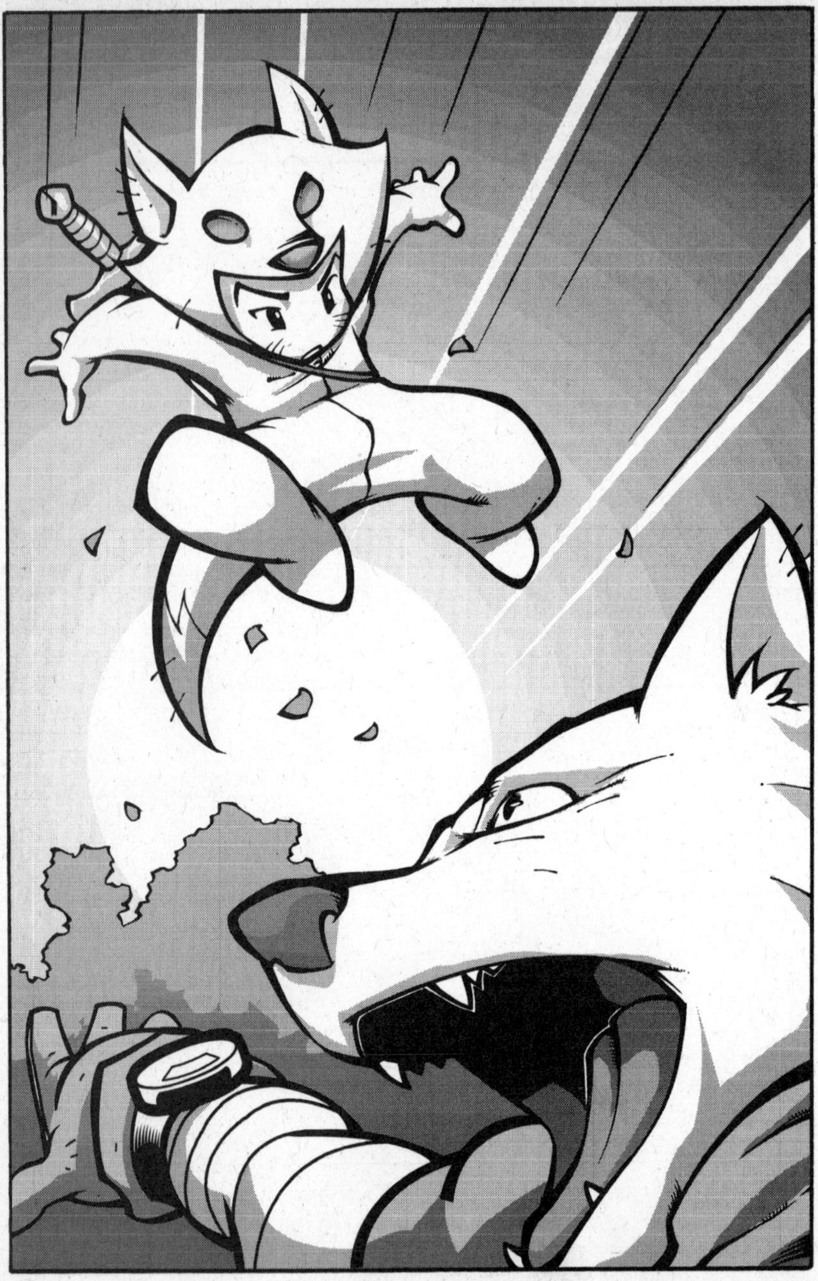

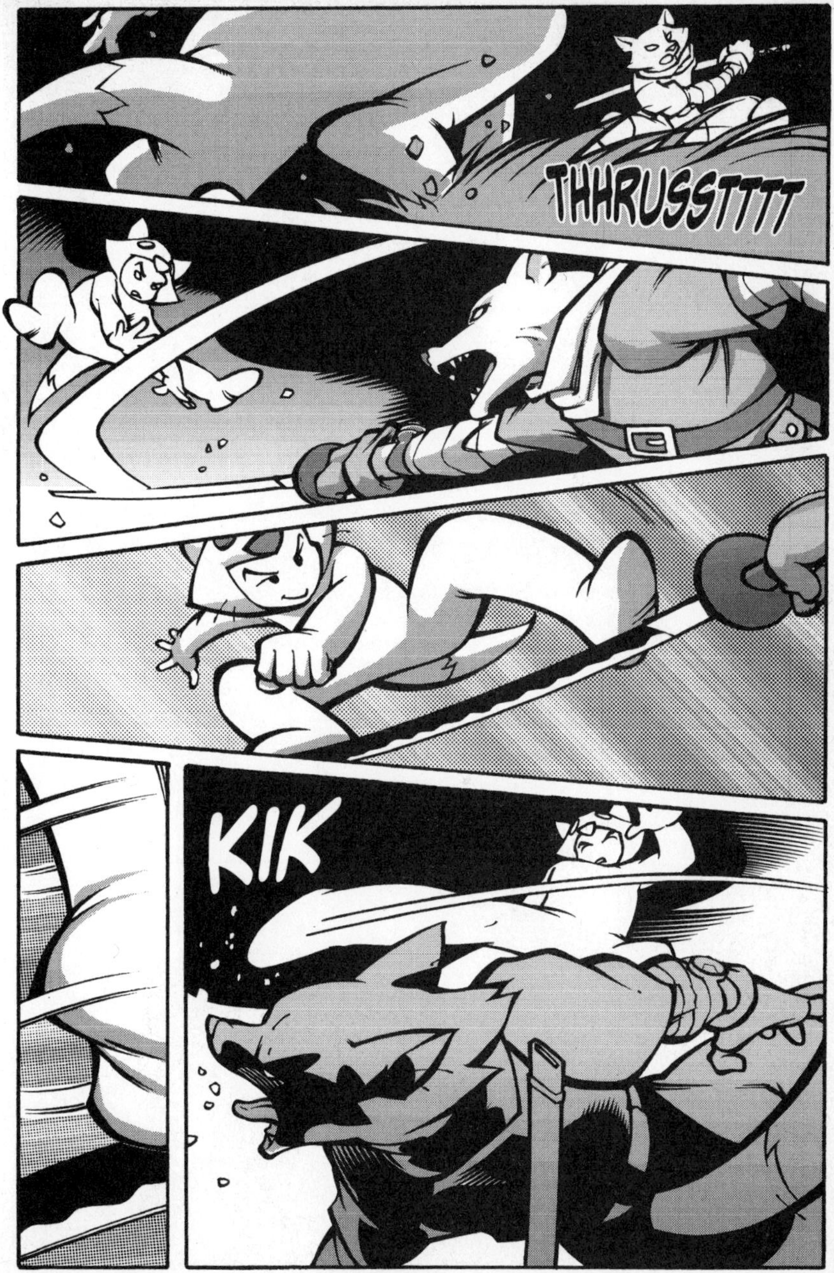
THHRUSSTTTT
KIK

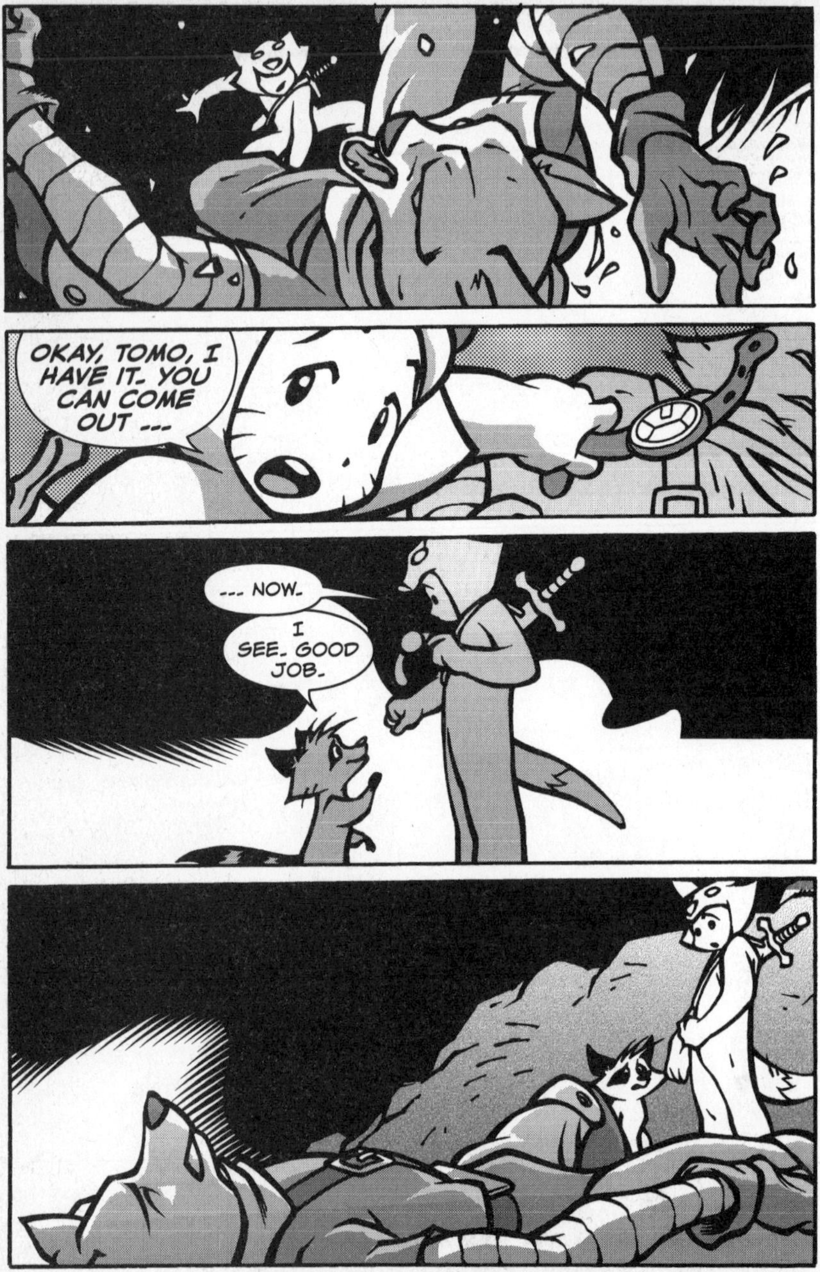
OKAY, TOMO, I HAVE IT. YOU CAN COME OUT ...
... NOW.
I SEE. GOOD JOB.

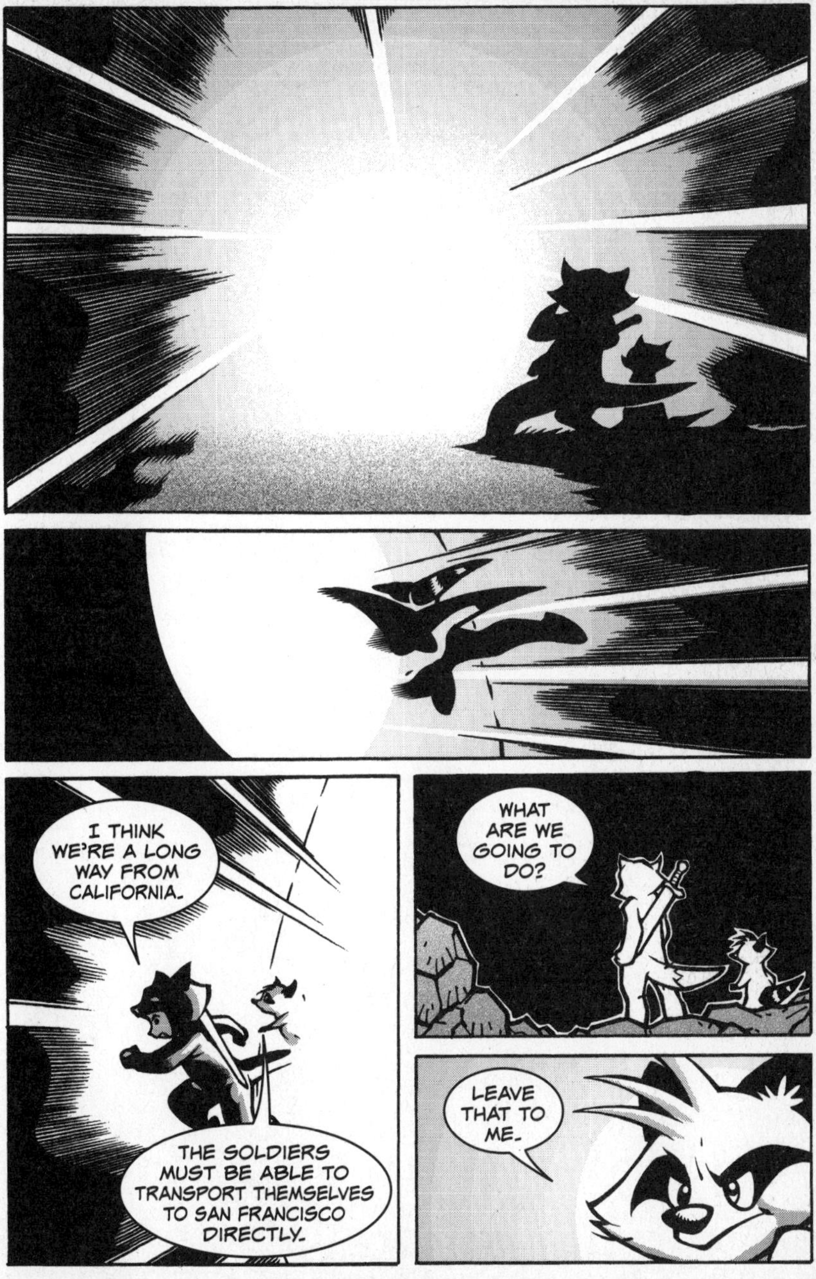
I THINK WE'RE A LONG WAY FROM CALIFORNIA.
THE SOLDIERS MUST BE ABLE TO TRANSPORT THEMSELVES TO SAN FRANCISCO DIRECTLY.
WHAT ARE WE GOING TO DO?
LEAVE THAT TO ME.

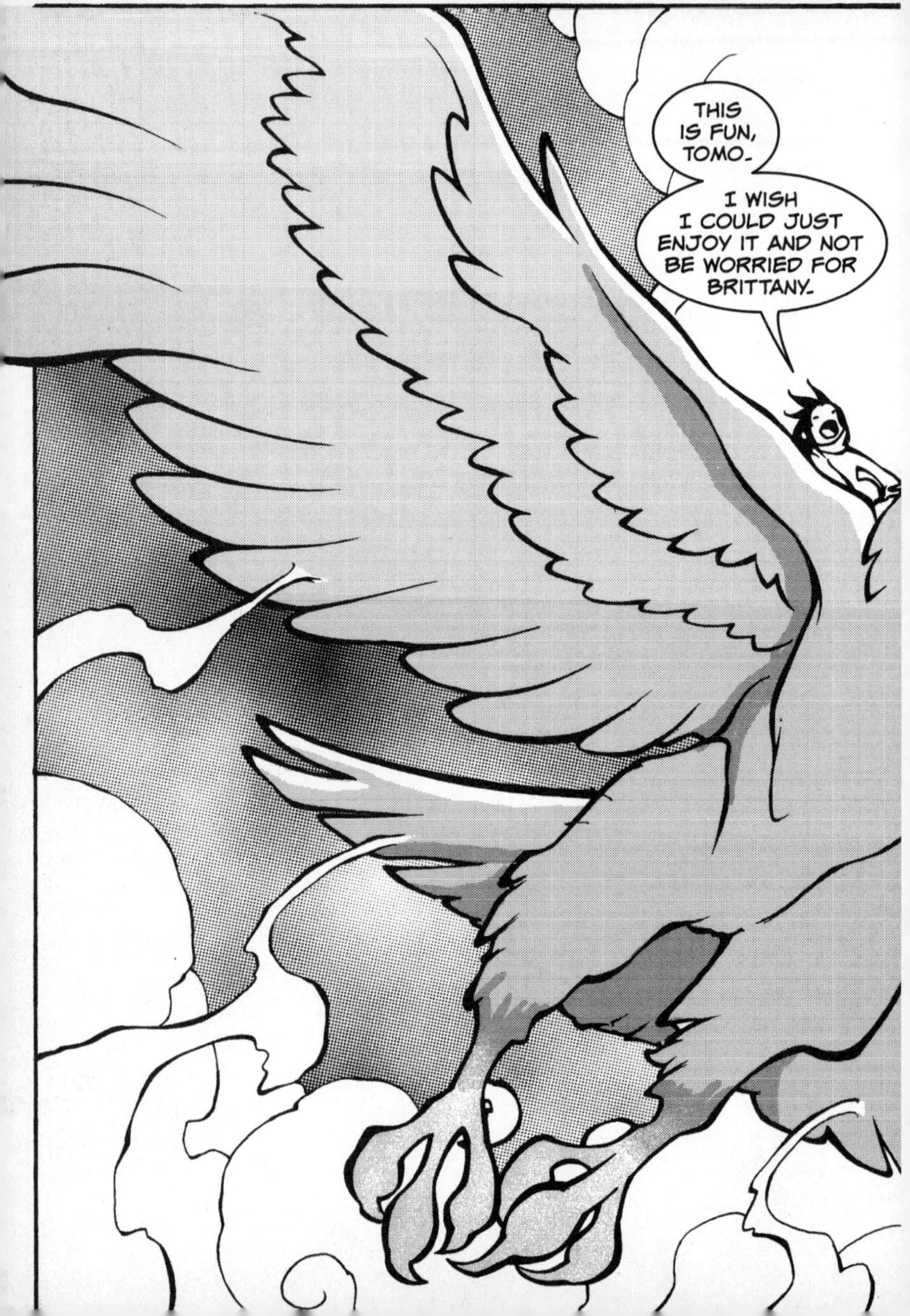
THIS IS FUN, TOMO.
I WISH I COULD JUST ENJOY IT AND NOT BE WORRIED FOR BRITTANY.

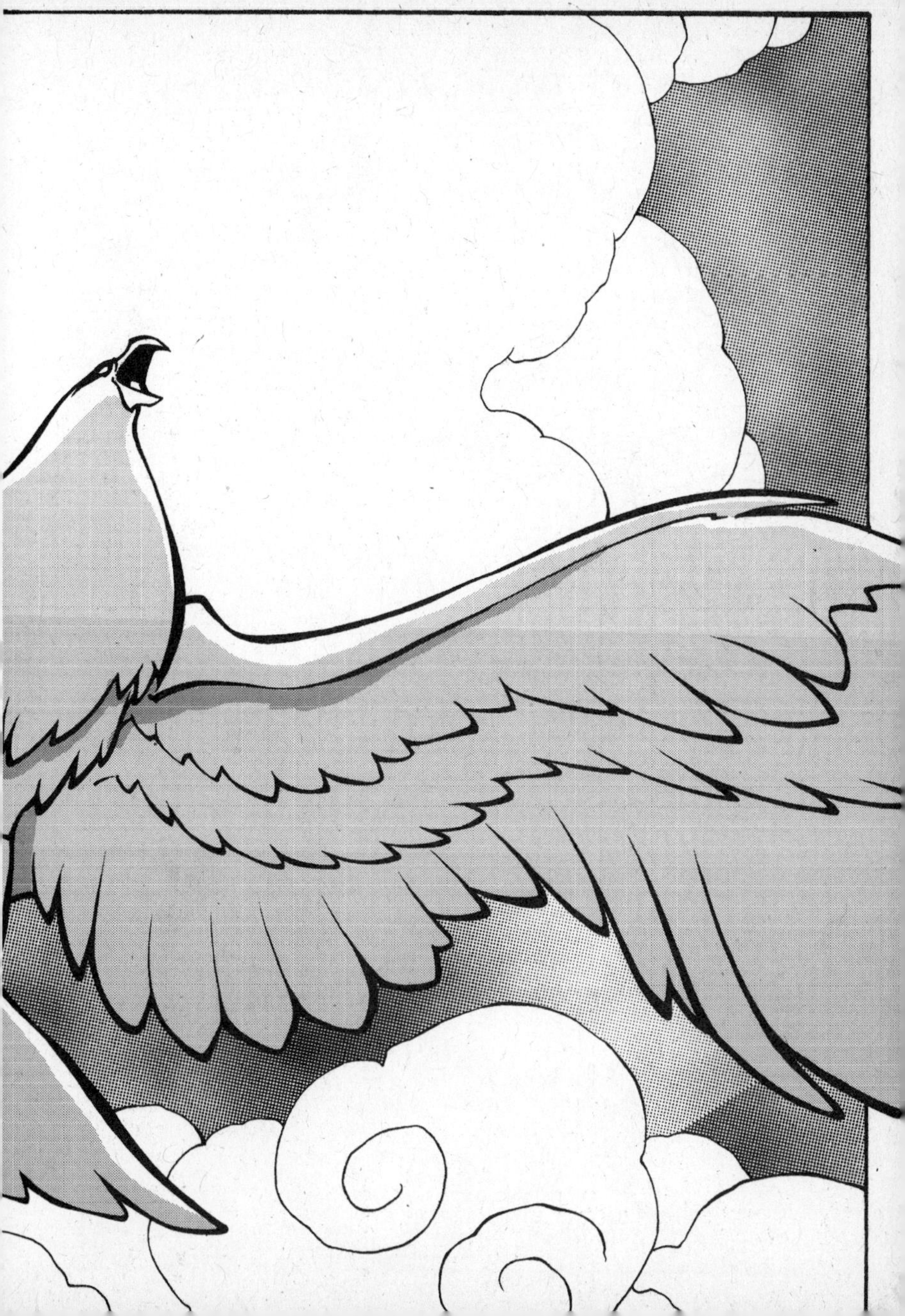

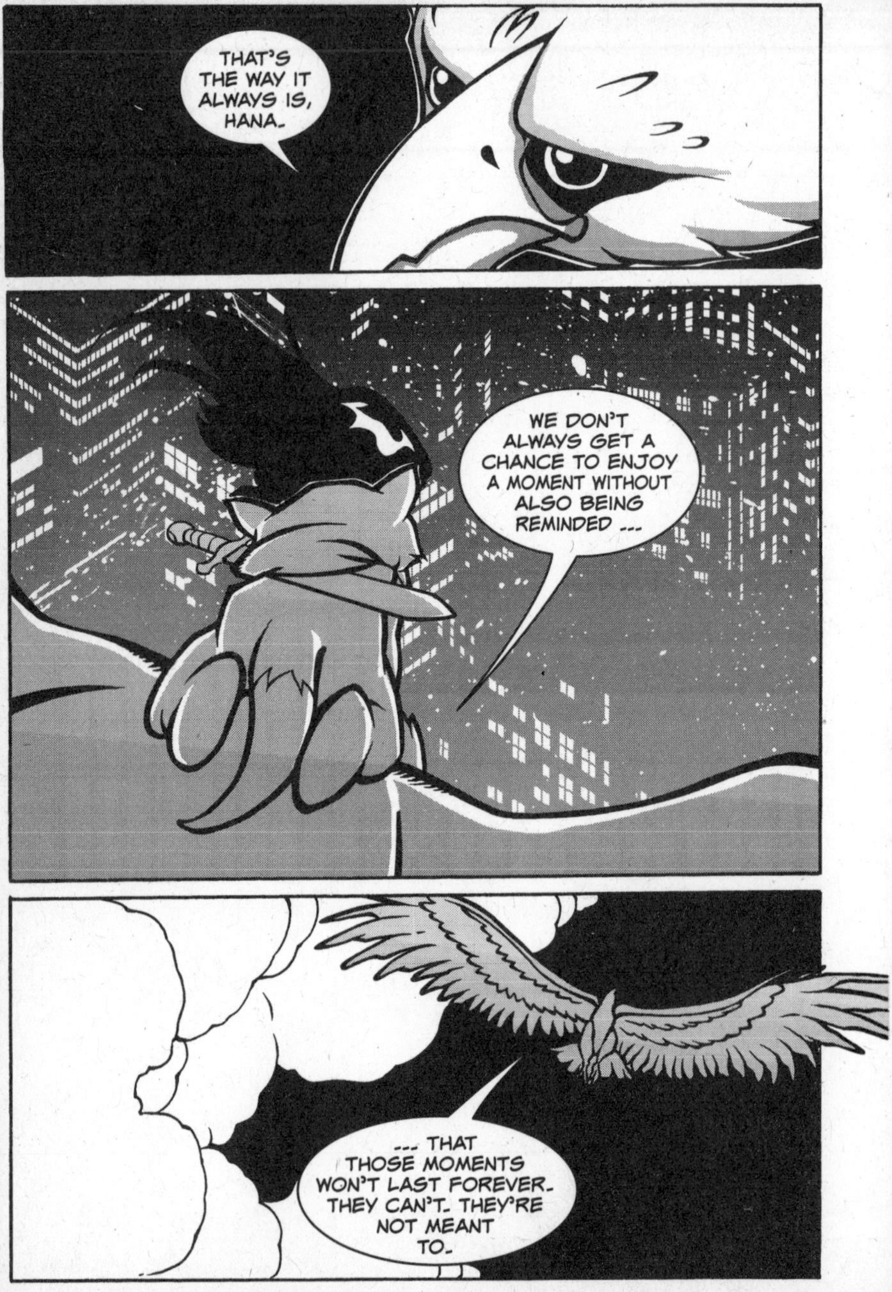
THAT'S THE WAY IT ALWAYS IS, HANA.
WE DON'T ALWAYS GET A CHANCE TO ENJOY A MOMENT WITHOUT ALSO BEING REMINDED ...
... THAT THOSE MOMENTS WON'T LAST FOREVER. THEY CAN'T. THEY'RE NOT MEANT TO.

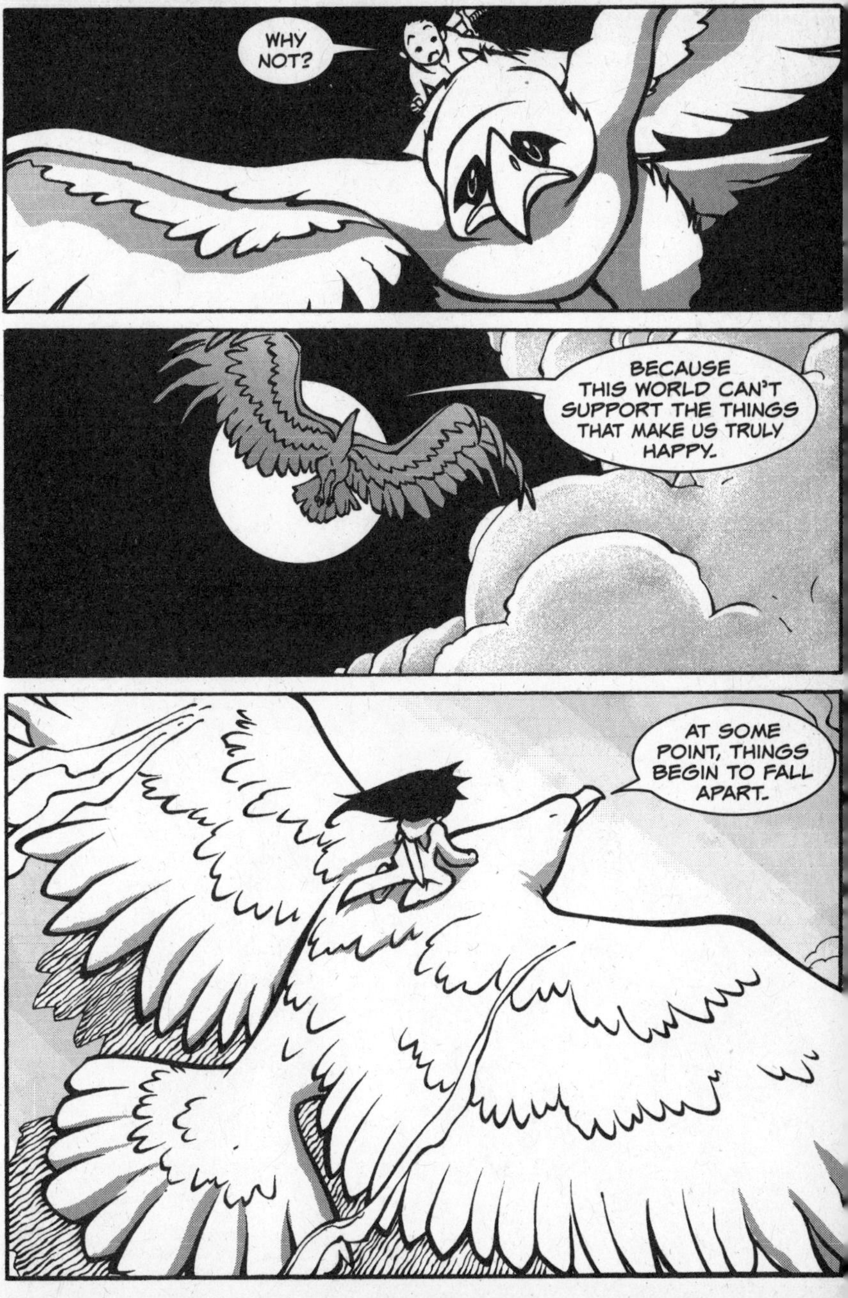
WHY NOT?
BECAUSE THIS WORLD CAN'T SUPPORT THE THINGS THAT MAKE US TRULY HAPPY.
AT SOME POINT, THINGS BEGIN TO FALL APART.

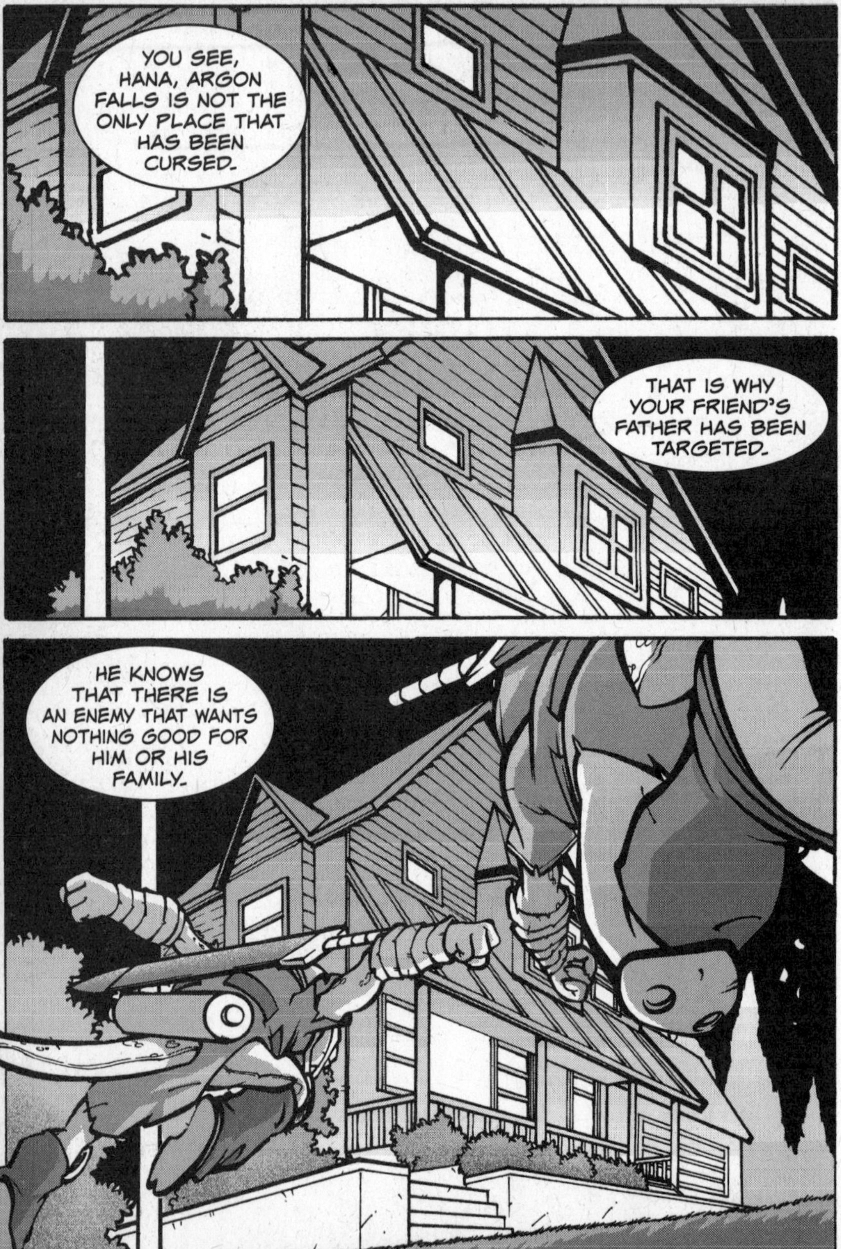
YOU SEE, HANA, ARGON FALLS IS NOT THE ONLY PLACE THAT HAS BEEN CURSED.
THAT IS WHY YOUR FRIEND'S FATHER HAS BEEN TARGETED.
HE KNOWS THAT THERE IS AN ENEMY THAT WANTS NOTHING GOOD FOR HIM OR HIS FAMILY.

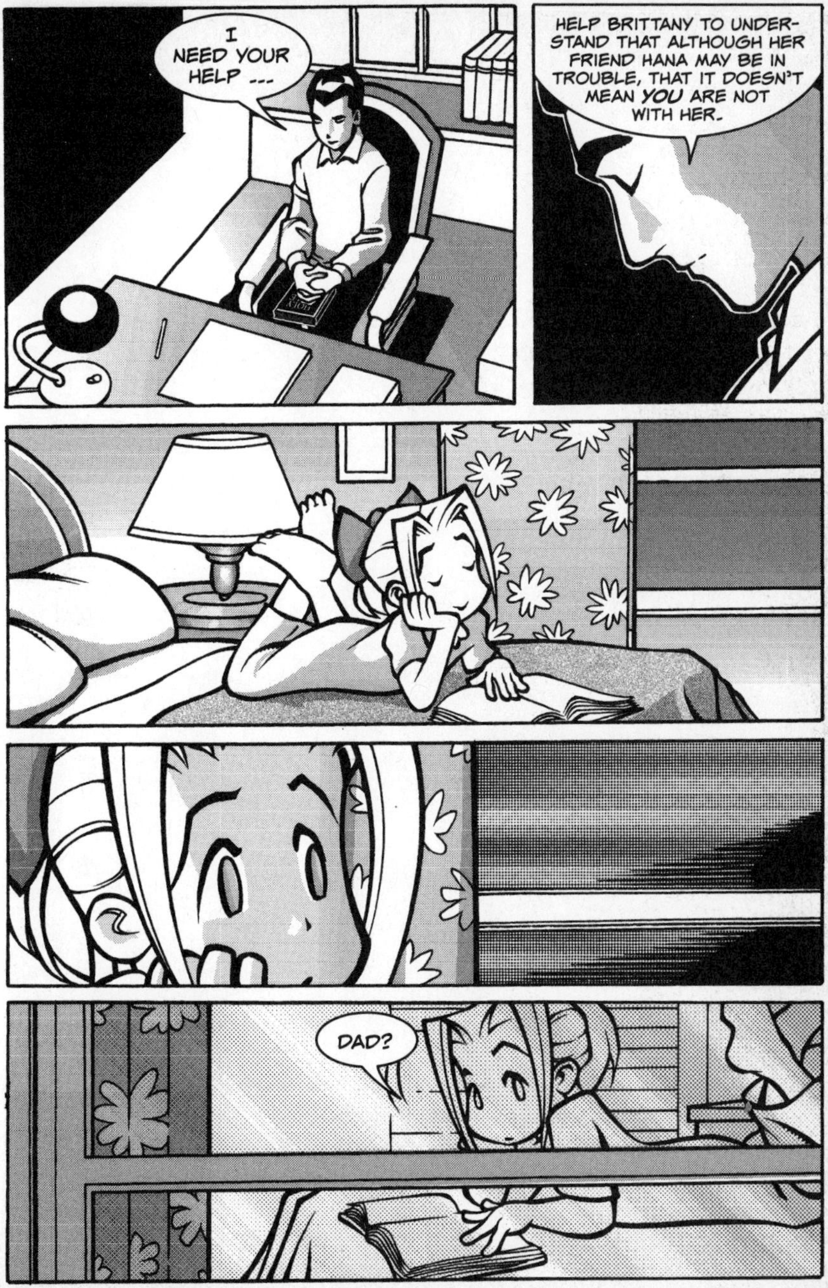
I NEED YOUR HELP ---
HELP BRITTANY TO UNDERSTAND THAT ALTHOUGH HER FRIEND HANA MAY BE IN TROUBLE, THAT IT DOESN'T MEAN *YOU* ARE NOT WITH HER.
DAD?

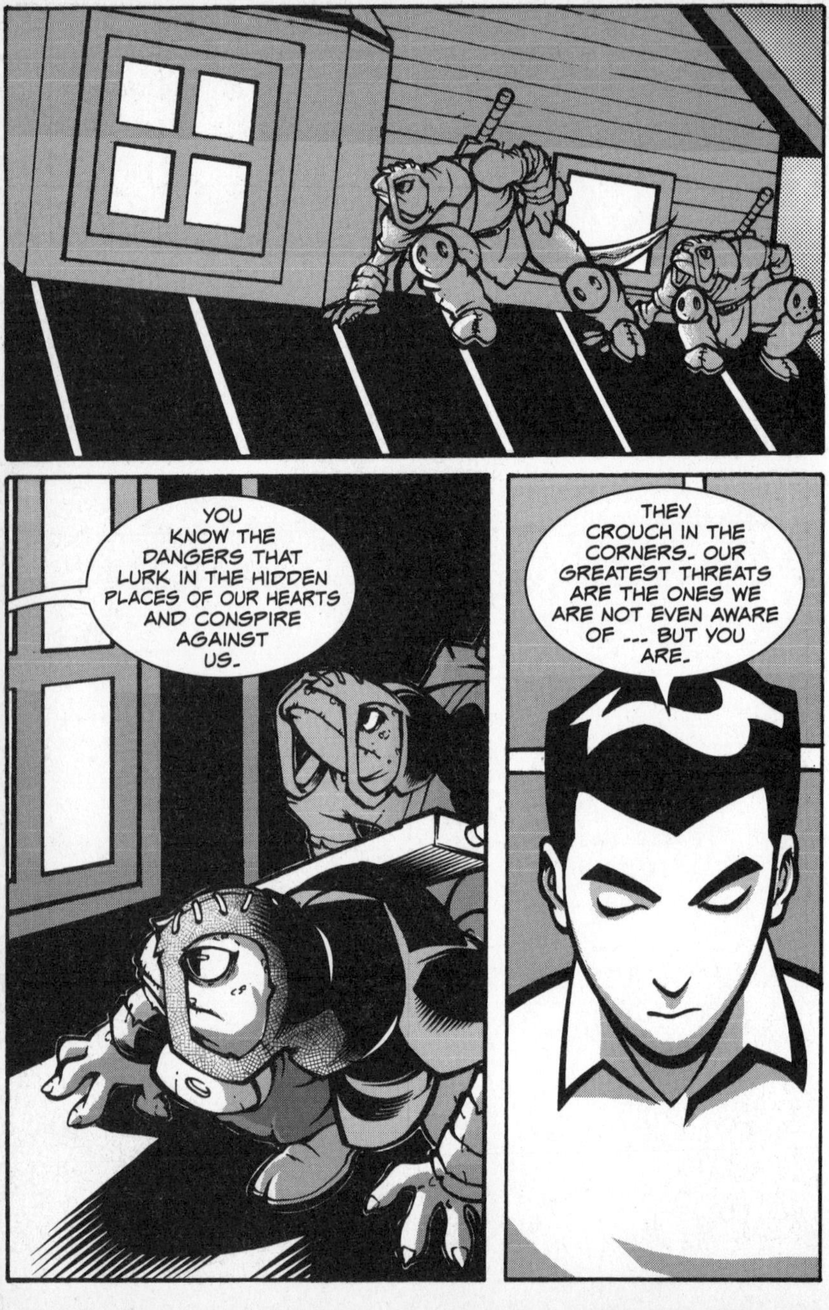
YOU KNOW THE DANGERS THAT LURK IN THE HIDDEN PLACES OF OUR HEARTS AND CONSPIRE AGAINST US.
THEY CROUCH IN THE CORNERS. OUR GREATEST THREATS ARE THE ONES WE ARE NOT EVEN AWARE OF ... BUT YOU ARE.

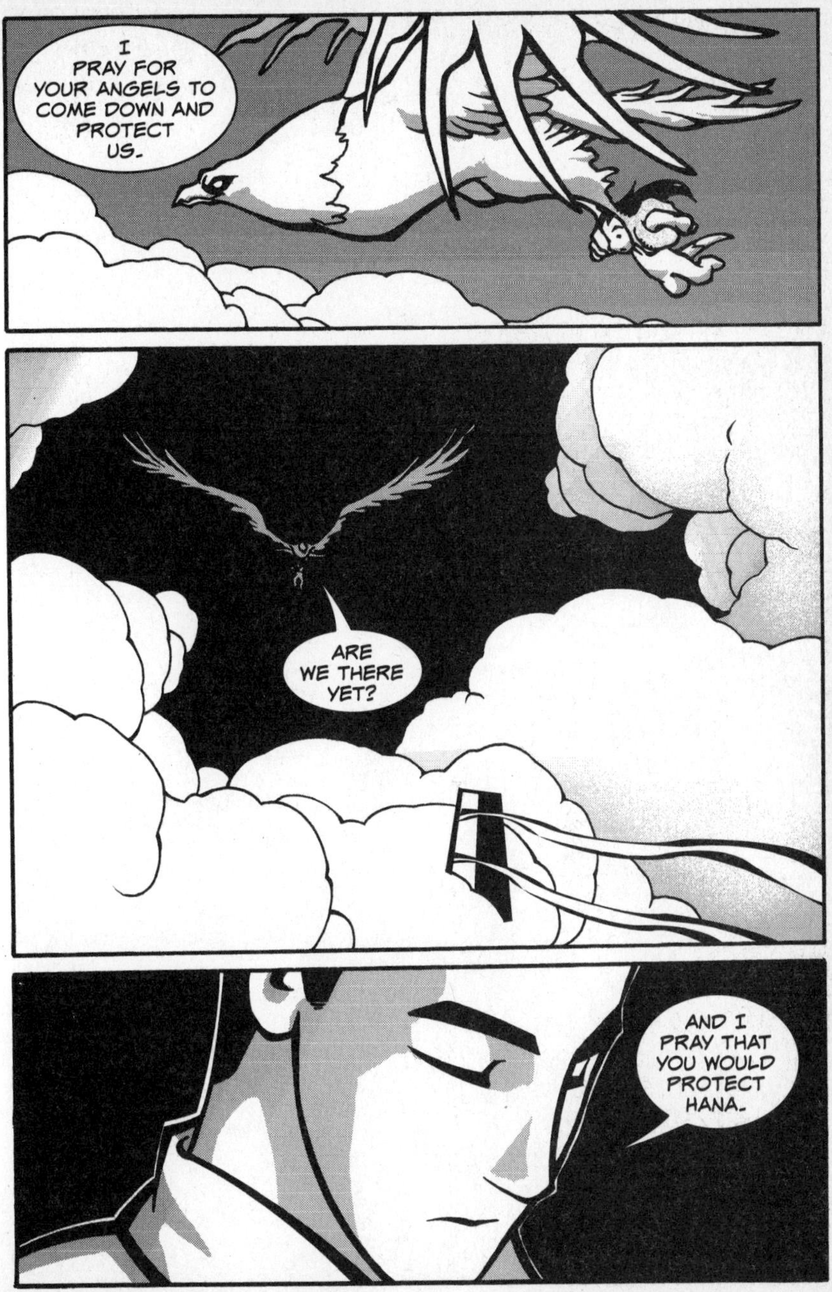
I PRAY FOR YOUR ANGELS TO COME DOWN AND PROTECT US.
ARE WE THERE YET?
AND I PRAY THAT YOU WOULD PROTECT HANA.

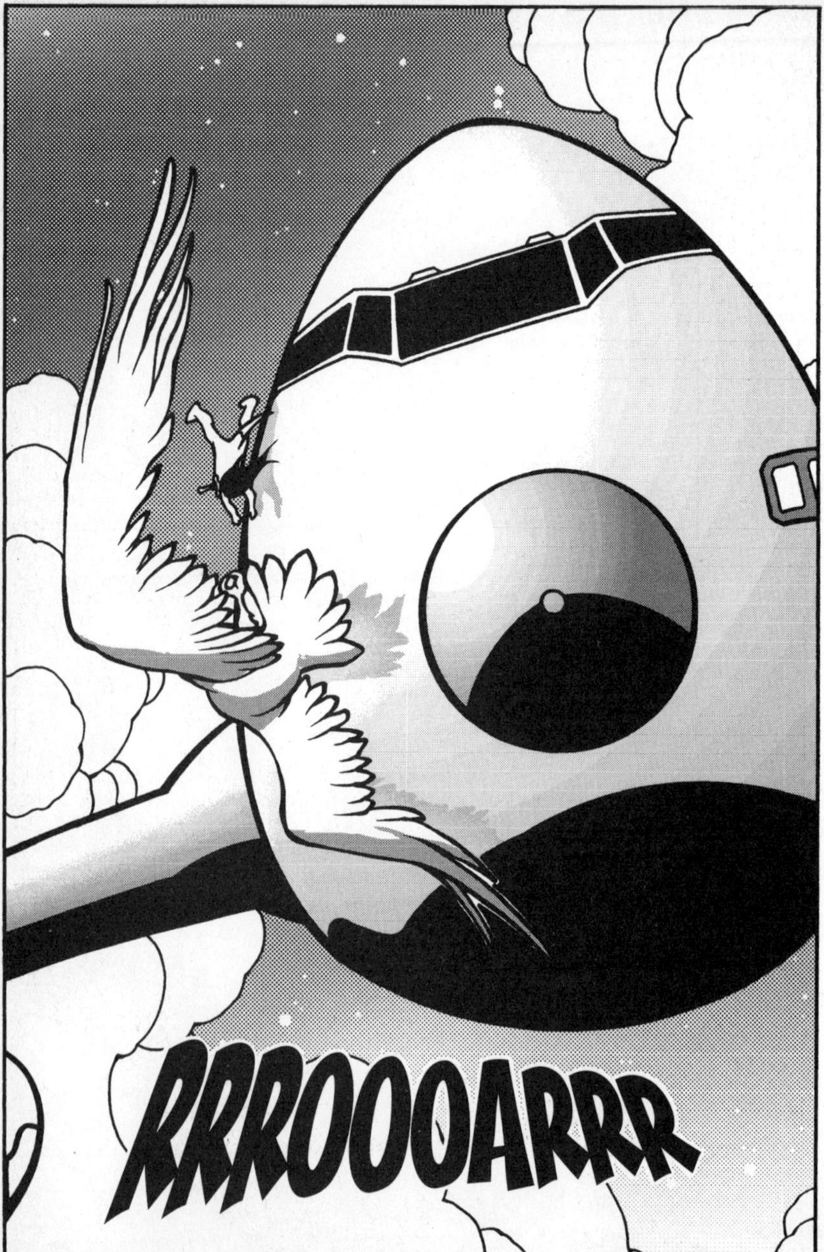
RRROOOARRR

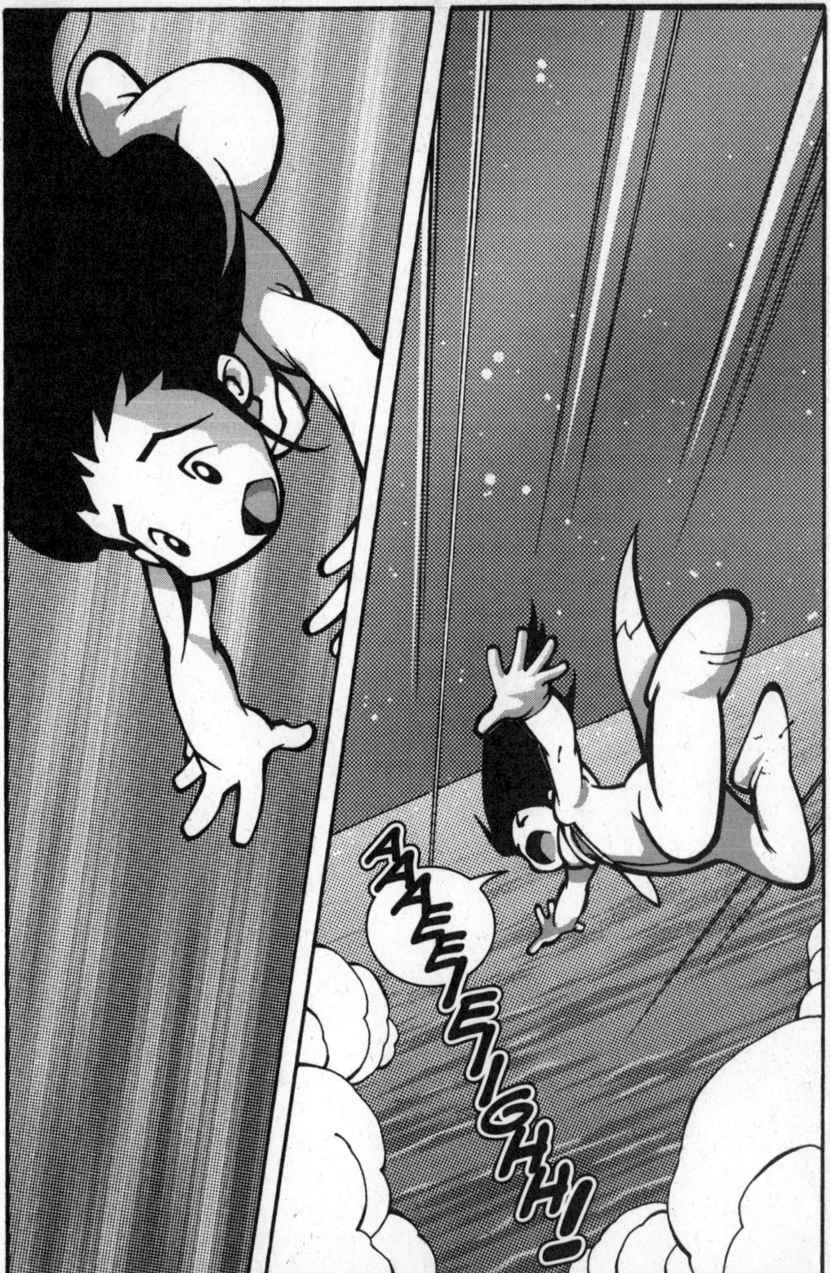
AAAEEEIIGHH!

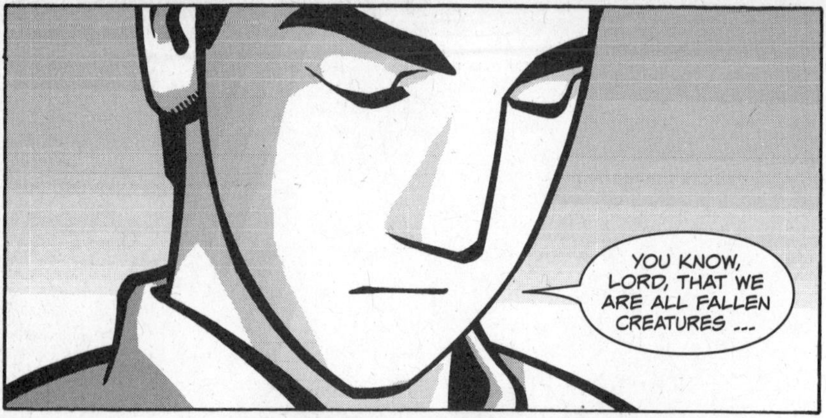
YOU KNOW, LORD, THAT WE ARE ALL FALLEN CREATURES ...
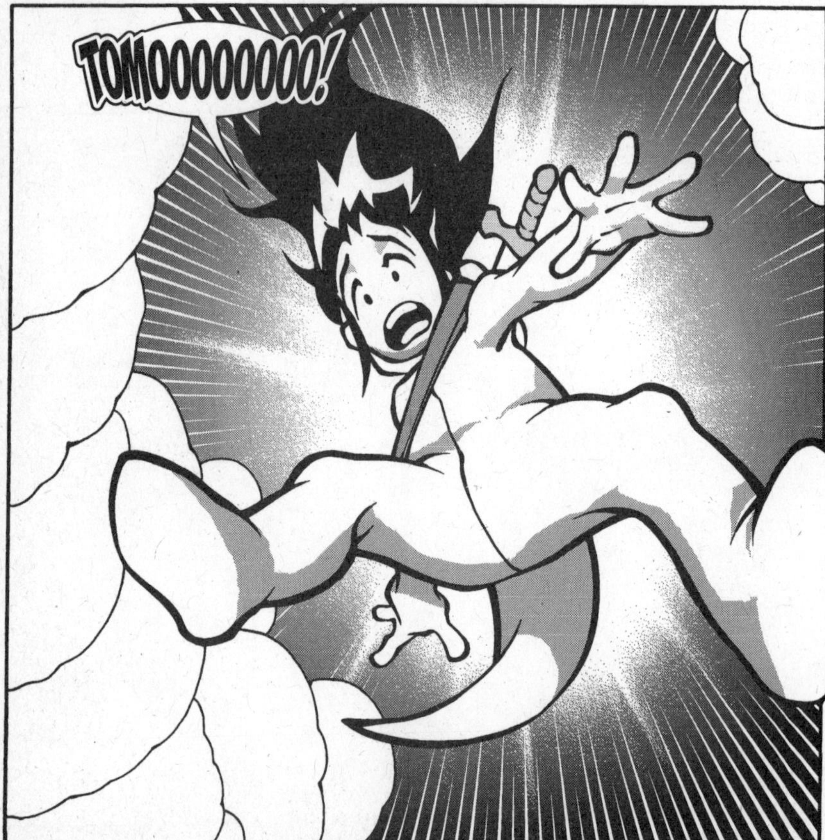
TOMOOOOOOOO!

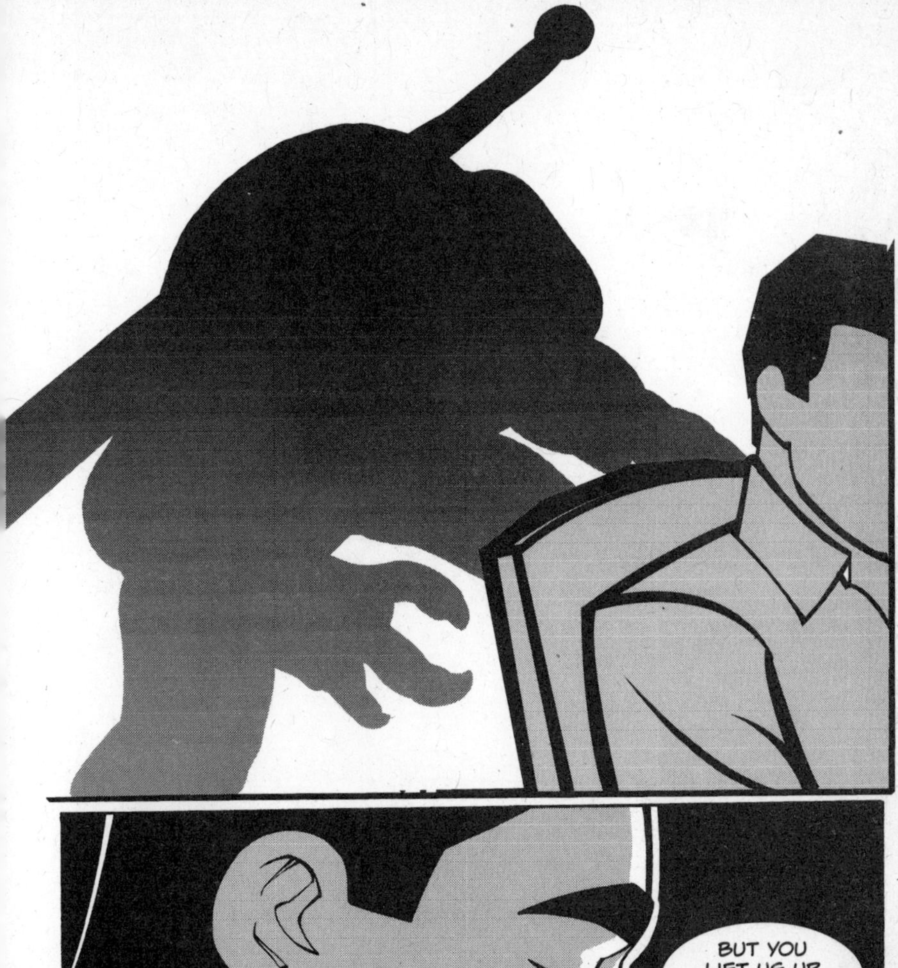

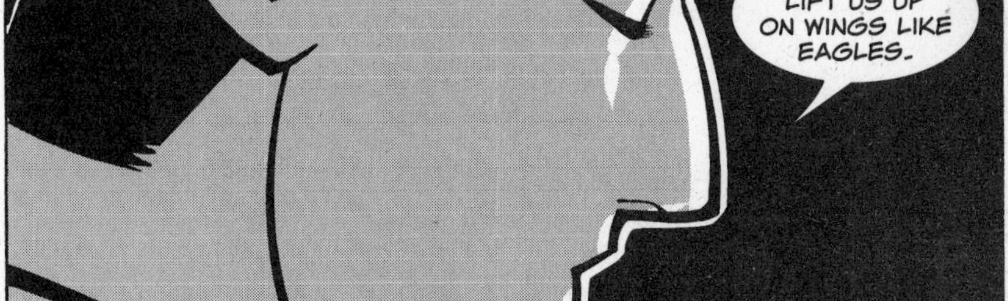
BUT YOU LIFT US UP ON WINGS LIKE EAGLES.

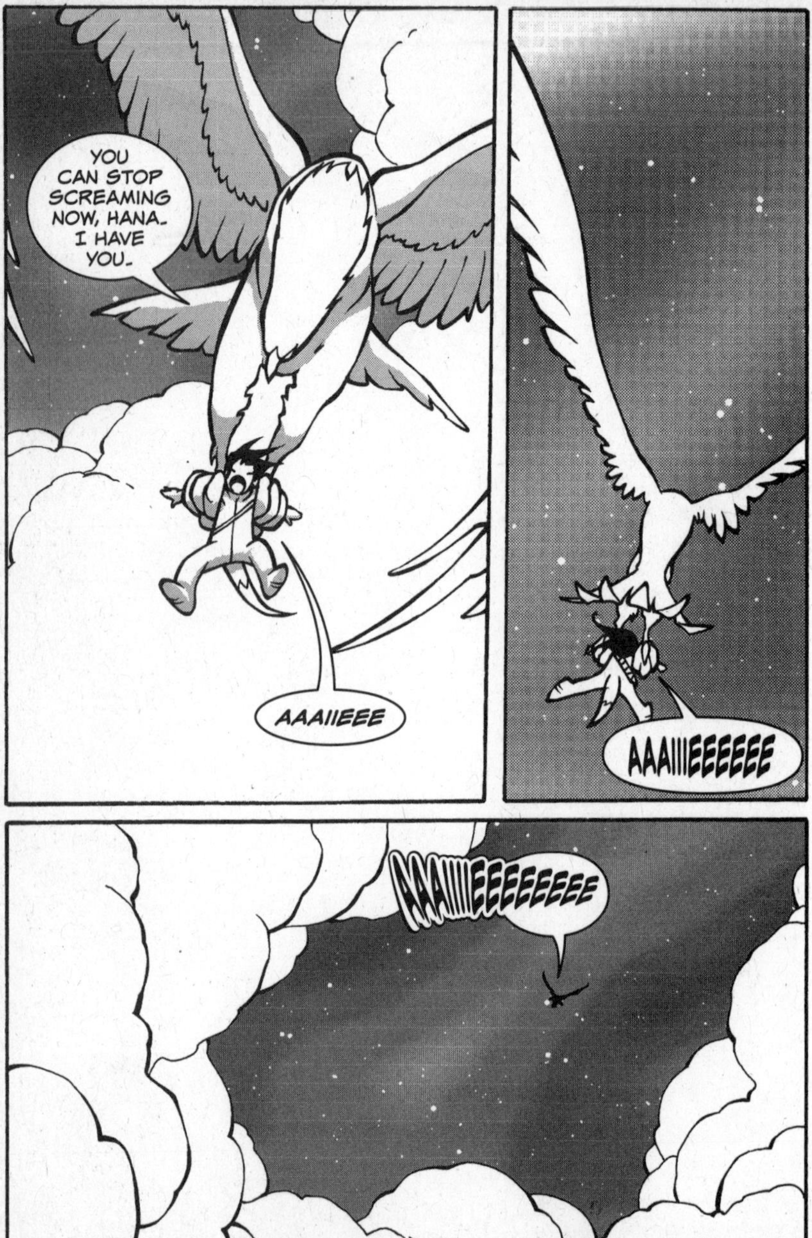
YOU CAN STOP SCREAMING NOW, HANA. I HAVE YOU.
AAAIIEEE
AAAIIIEEEEEE
AAAIIIIIEEEEEEEE

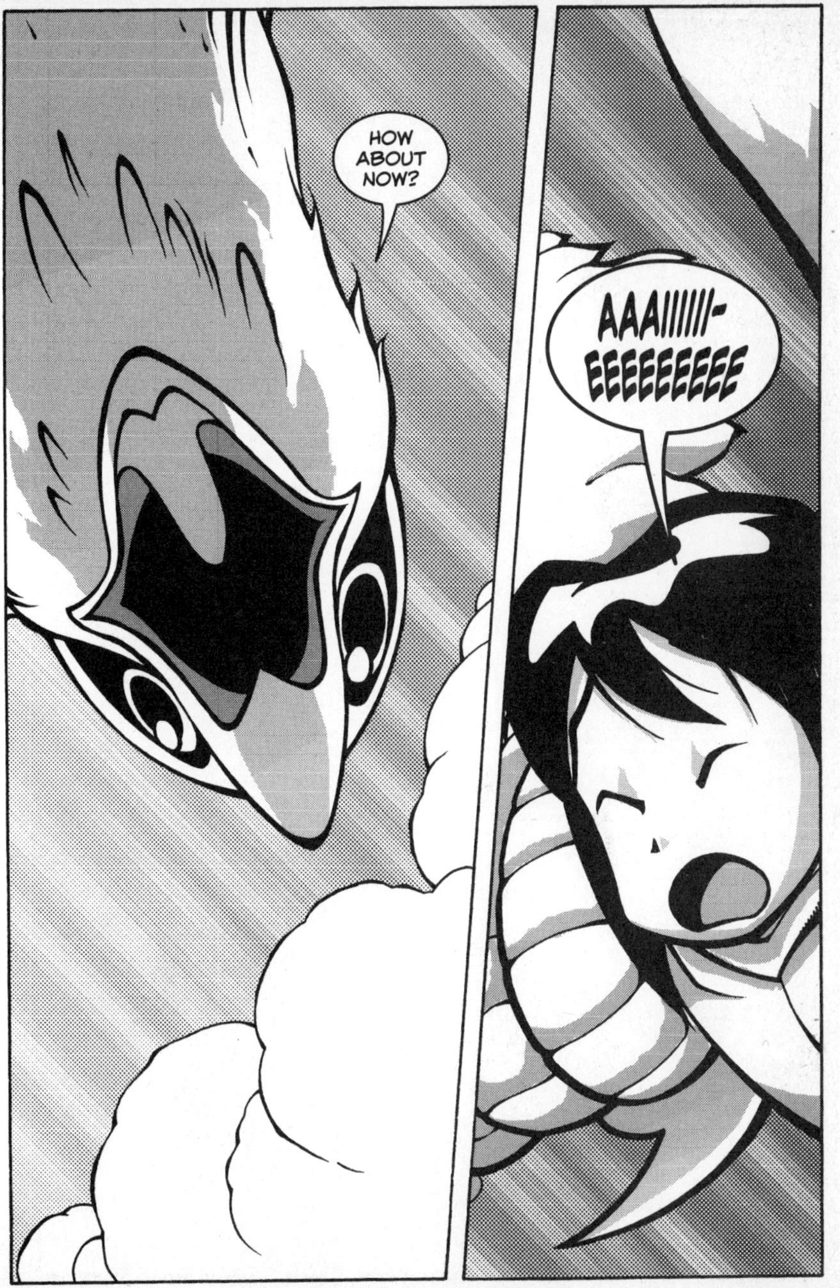
HOW ABOUT NOW?
AAAIIIIII-EEEEEEEEE

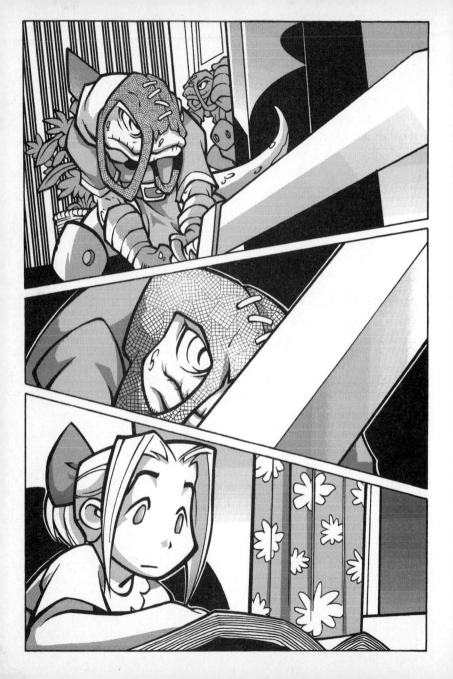

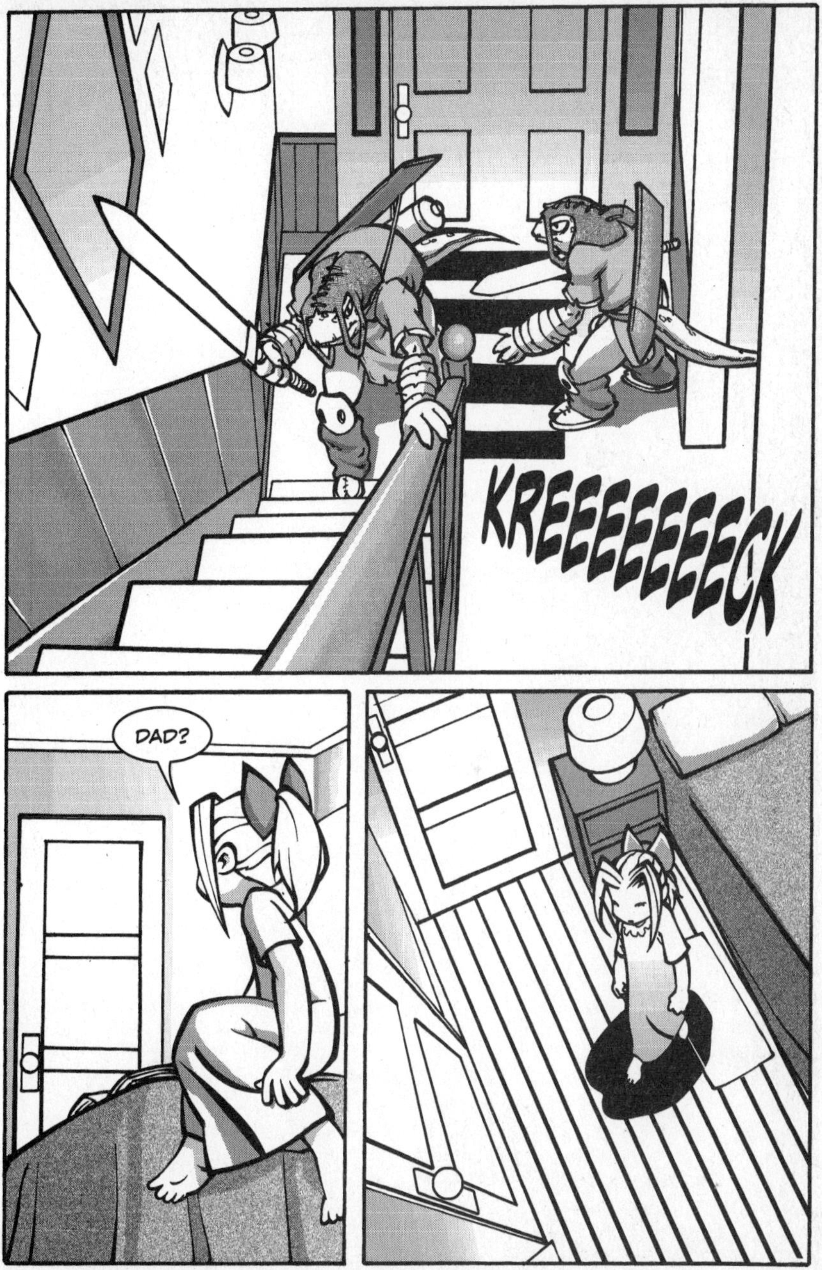
KREEEEEEEECK
DAD?

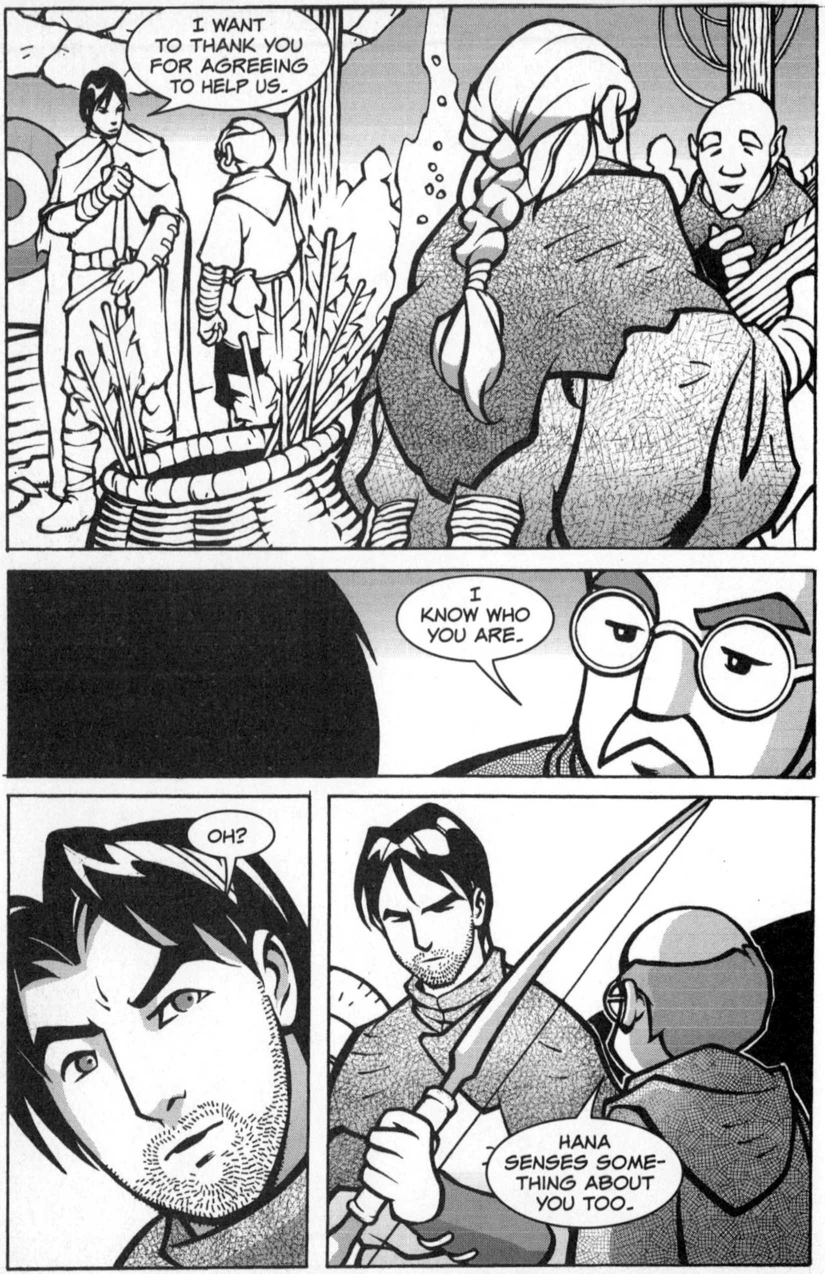
I WANT TO THANK YOU FOR AGREEING TO HELP US.
I KNOW WHO YOU ARE.
OH?
HANA SENSES SOME-THING ABOUT YOU TOO.

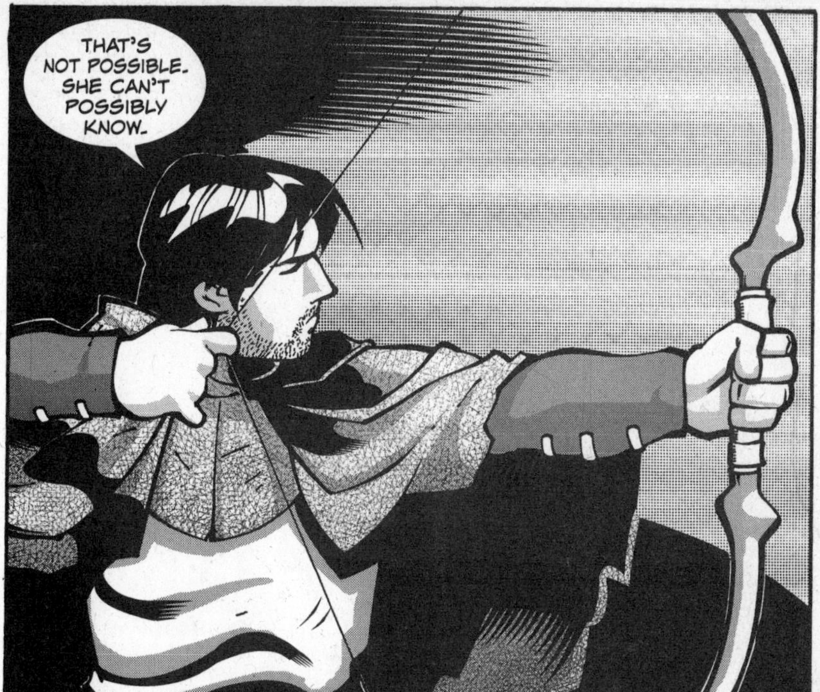
THAT'S NOT POSSIBLE. SHE CAN'T POSSIBLY KNOW.
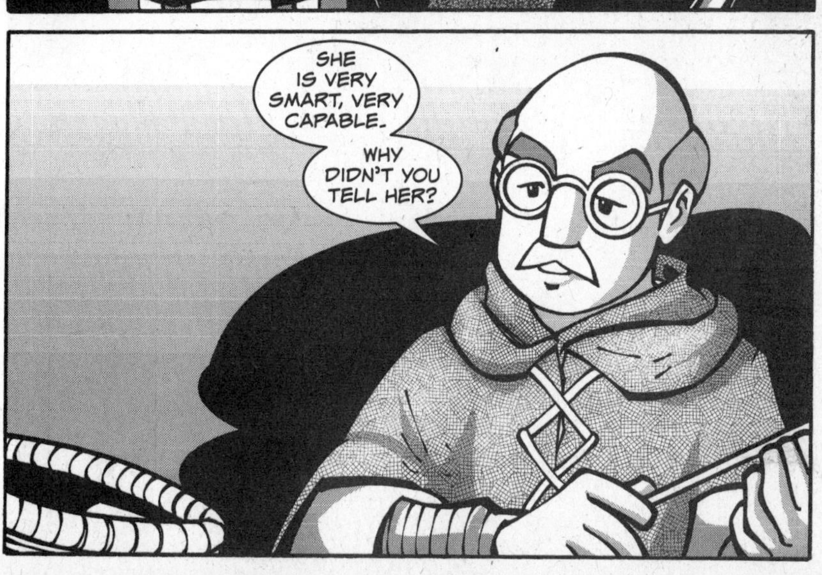
SHE IS VERY SMART, VERY CAPABLE.
WHY DIDN'T YOU TELL HER?

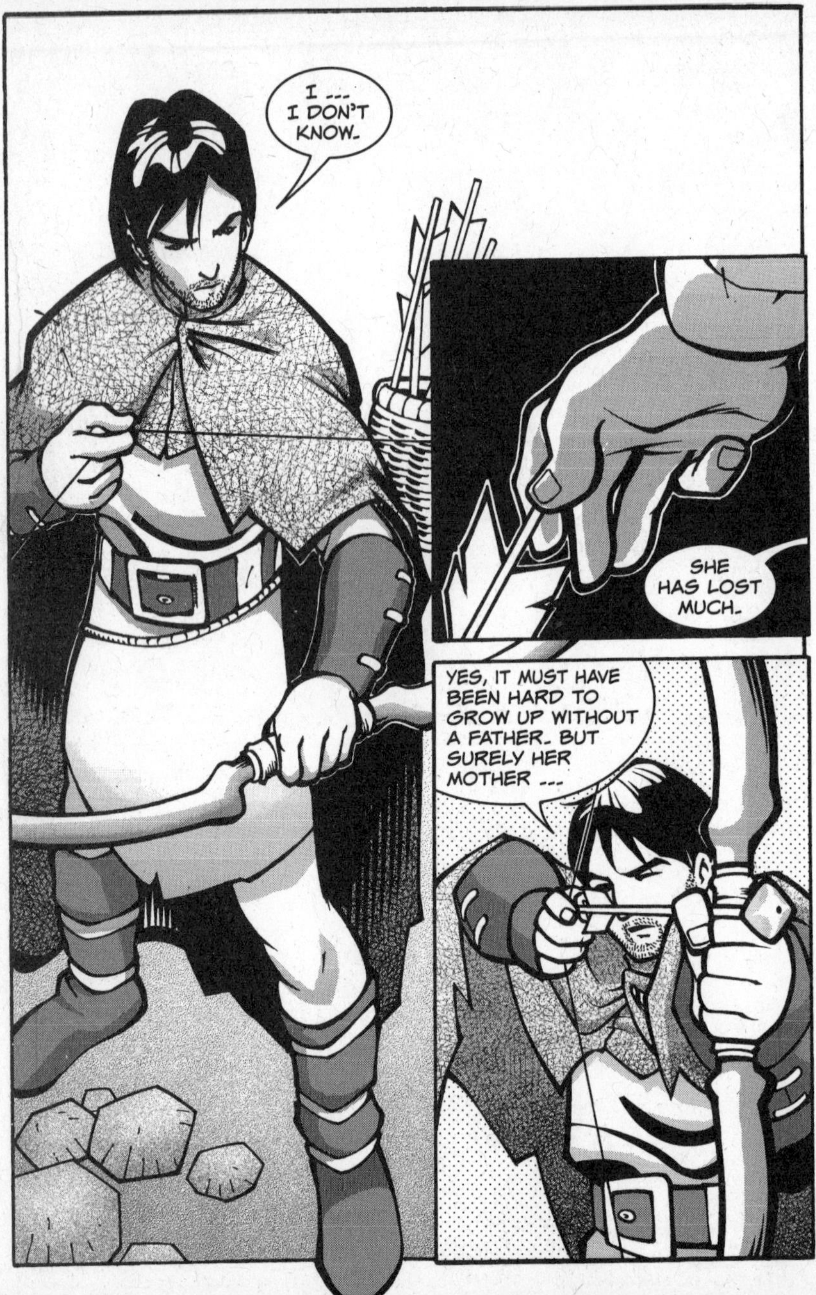
I ...
I DON'T
KNOW.
SHE
HAS LOST
MUCH.
YES, IT MUST HAVE
BEEN HARD TO
GROW UP WITHOUT
A FATHER. BUT
SURELY HER
MOTHER ...

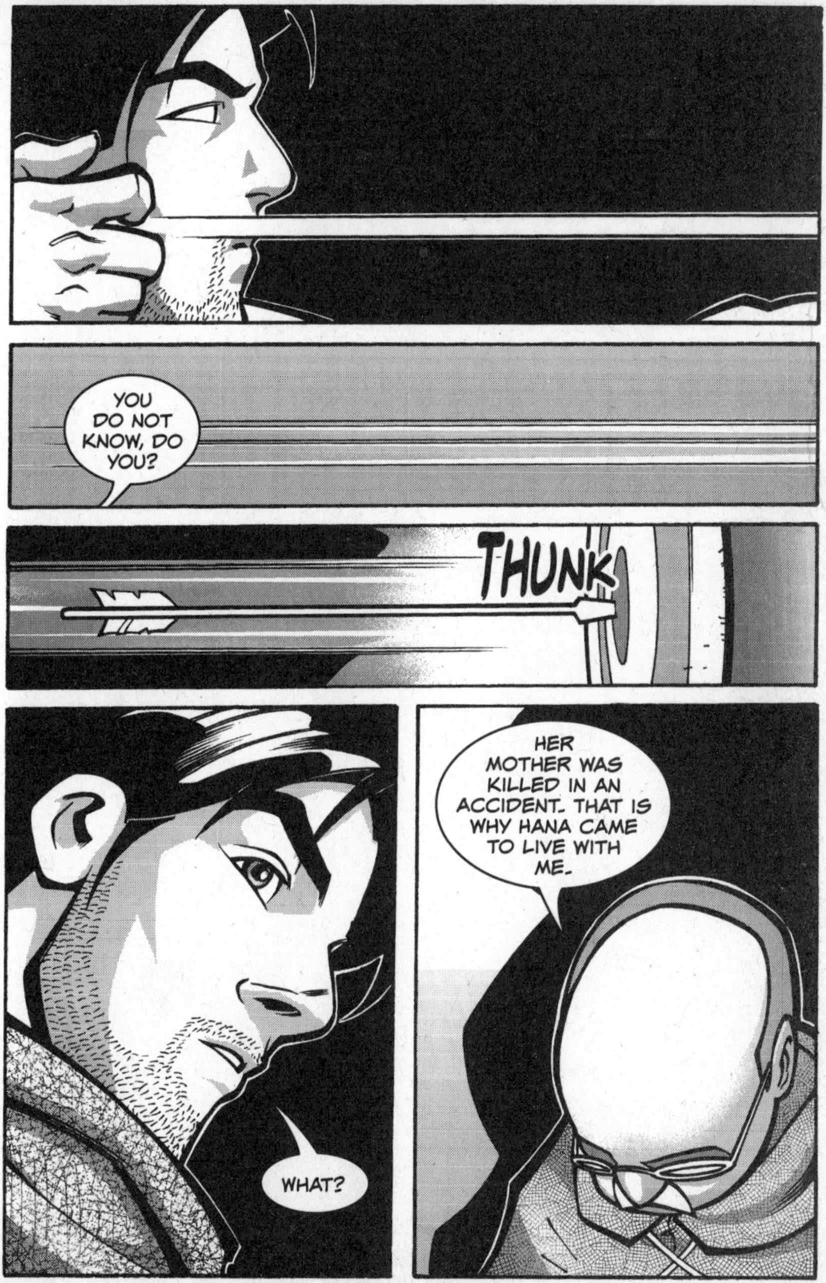
YOU DO NOT KNOW, DO YOU?
THUNK
WHAT?
HER MOTHER WAS KILLED IN AN ACCIDENT. THAT IS WHY HANA CAME TO LIVE WITH ME.

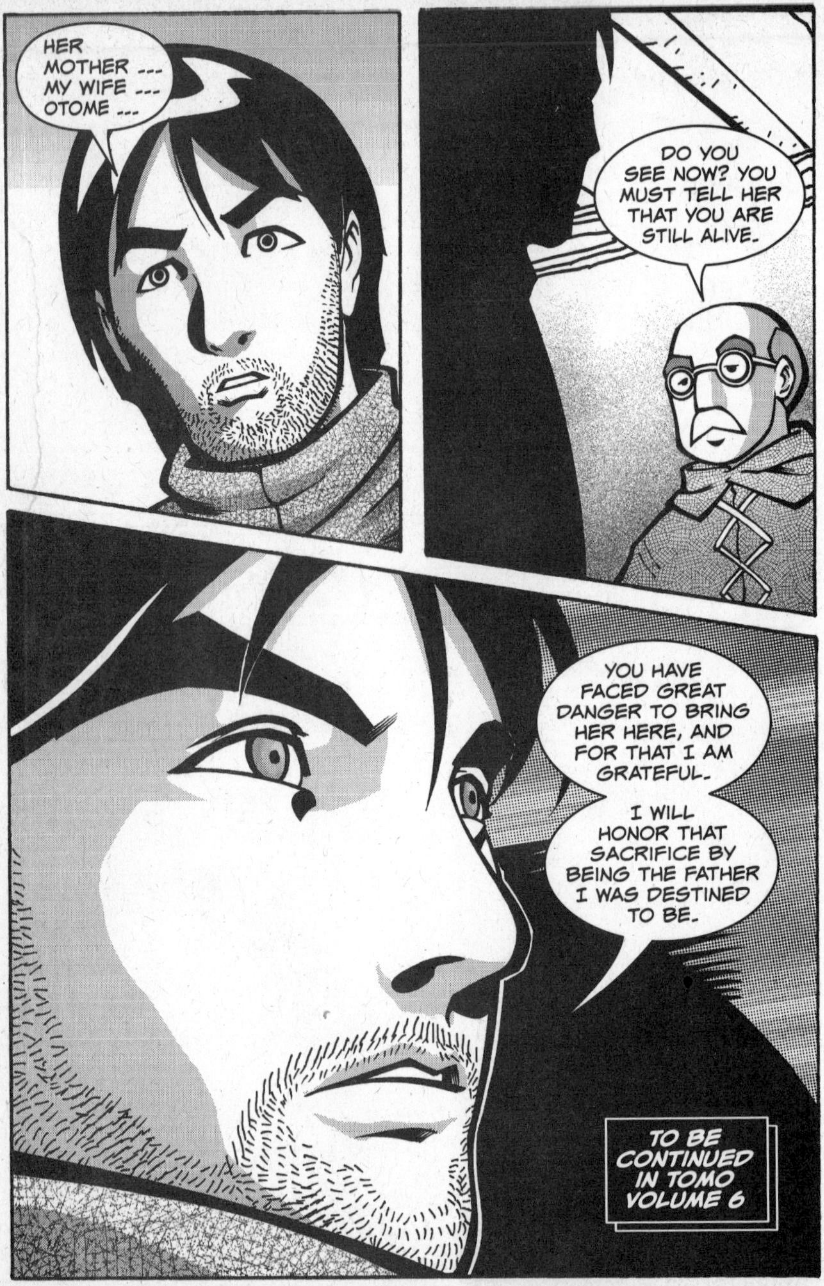
HER MOTHER --- MY WIFE --- OTOME ---
DO YOU SEE NOW? YOU MUST TELL HER THAT YOU ARE STILL ALIVE.
YOU HAVE FACED GREAT DANGER TO BRING HER HERE, AND FOR THAT I AM GRATEFUL.
I WILL HONOR THAT SACRIFICE BY BEING THE FATHER I WAS DESTINED TO BE.
TO BE CONTINUED IN TOMO VOLUME 6

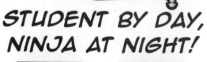